About the Author

...y **Parkes** survived a Convent education largely thanks
...ready supply of inappropriate novels and her passion for
...ng and languages.

...ie studied International Management in Bath and
...nany, before gaining experience with the BBC. She then set
...i independent Film Location Agency and spent many happy
...s organising shoots for film, television and advertising –
th...eby ensuring that she was never short of travel opportunities,
...ance writing projects or entertaining anecdotes.

...enny now lives in the Cotswolds with her husband, two
cl...dren and an excitable puppy with a fondness for Post-its.
...will often be found plotting epic train journeys through
...lps, baking gluten-free goodies or attempting to reach
...sive state of organisation.

...novel *Out of Practice*, the first book in the Larkford
... , won the RNA Romantic Comedy of the Year Award
in 2017. This is her third novel.

Follow Penny on Twitter and Instagram: @CotswoldPenny

ALSO BY PENNY PARKES

Out of Practice
Practice Makes Perfect

eBook only:
Swept Away (eBook short story)

Penny Parkes

Best Practice

SIMON &
SCHUSTER

London · New York · Sydney · Toronto · New Delhi

A CBS COMPANY

First published in Great Britain by Simon & Schuster UK Ltd, 2018
A CBS COMPANY

Copyright © Wibble Creative Ltd, 2018

3 5 7 9 10 8 6 4 2

Simon & Schuster UK Ltd
1st Floor
222 Gray's Inn Road
London WC1X 8HB

Simon & Schuster Australia, Sydney
Simon & Schuster India, New Delhi

www.simonandschuster.co.uk
www.simonandschuster.com.au
www.simonandschuster.co.in

A CIP catalogue record for this book is available from the British Library

Library Hardback ISBN: 978-1-4711-6399-9
eBook ISBN: 978-1-4711-6401-9
Paperback ISBN: 978-1-4711-6400-2
eAudio ISBN: 978-1-4711-7493-3

Typeset in the UK by M Rules
Printed and bound by CPI Group (UK) Ltd, Croydon, CR0 4YY

MIX
Paper from
responsible sources
FSC® C020471

for Sam . . .
Third time lucky!! xxx

Best Practice

'Of all possessions, a friend is the most precious'

HERODOTUS

Chapter 1

Dr Holly Graham bit her lip hard and tried not to laugh. It was all very well promising to help out at the Larkford Country Show, but she'd had no idea that everyone would be taking things quite so very seriously.

'I love you,' she said, in lieu of being able to formulate any other sentient response as she took in her fiancé's rakish attire.

Taffy Jones smoothed his hair back from his brow, his unruly curls attempting to escape the firm hold of whatever unguent he'd employed for the occasion. His quick change from Saturday-doctor-on-duty to debonair-gentleman-about-town had been achieved by the addition of not only a bow tie, but also a gaudily striped blazer and cane to boot. 'Too much?' he asked with a grin, pivoting to best effect in the doctors' lounge at The Practice, knowing full well that he looked a right plonker, but unwilling to concede a win to Dan on their annual bet.

Holly walked towards him, laughter now shaking her slender shoulders, as she spotted the beribboned boater hat in his other hand. 'You're quite, quite mad,' she said happily, leaning in to kiss him firmly on the lips. She didn't dare hope that a similar wager on his wedding day attire might yet be avoided, but she was damned if she was even going to mention it, for fear of planting the seed of an idea. 'Have you seen Dan yet? Does he realise what he's up against?' Holly asked, all thoughts of her stressfully rushed morning surgery forgotten.

'He's stuck on the phone with Shylock,' Taffy grimaced.

'Who?' Holly queried, despite their years together still bemused at times by Taffy's beloved shorthand references.

'Derek bloody Landers,' Taffy clarified. 'You know, because he's always after his pound of flesh. You'd think we'd have met all of our NHS commitments by now, but he's always there, clammy paws outstretched, determined to squeeze a little extra.'

It was true: their nomination as a Model NHS Surgery had certainly brought The Practice all sorts of praise, plaudits and pecuniary incentives, but it had also come at a cost. Derek Landers – or Walrus-features, or now apparently Shylock – could be relied upon to renege upon his promises at every opportunity unless handled very firmly. And poor Dan Carter was bearing the brunt of it as The Practice's nominated NHS liaison, alongside Grace Allen, their thankfully highly motivated Practice Manager.

'What more can he want though?' asked Holly. 'We've offered up our records, Grace and Dan have handled all the endless seminars and I've filled in enough compliance forms to give me RSI.'

Taffy took her hand in his and gently massaged her aching fingers, her engagement ring rotating easily, as the pressure of the last few months had been enough to put even Holly off her Danish pastry habit. 'Look, let's not worry about that today. Let's really try and switch off a bit and enjoy the show. I have to confess, I'm rather honoured that they're trusting me with the commentary,' Taffy said.

'Actually, I was robbed,' said Dan, striding into the room

in a pair of cream, blousy trousers held aloft by some striking red braces and looking like someone from a *Mary Poppins* montage. 'How did I get lumbered with the bloody judging and you get to hide behind the mic all afternoon?' He shook his head and held out his hands as he gave a slow twirl. 'But at least I'll have my prize to look forward to at the end of the day. I think we can all recognise a winning ensemble when we see one? I hope you've been practising your Abba solo, mate?'

Alice Walker ambled into the lounge behind him, rubbing her forehead as though to erase the last three hours of thoughtful and considerate counsel. Coco, the small chocolate-coloured spaniel who served as Alice's diabetes assistance dog, trotted happily at her heels in her little red jacket. Alice stopped dead and frowned. 'Oh God, did I miss something? Were we supposed to come in fancy dress?'

Taffy scowled. 'This isn't "fancy dress", you heathen. This is the appropriate attire for gentlemen doctors, such as ourselves, when attending a county event.' He'd abandoned his naturally melodic Welsh tones to make his point, sounding plummily English and rather comical, Holly noticed. Taffy was never one to do anything by halves.

Alice looked from Taffy to Dan and back again in confusion, before turning to Holly, as she often did, for a little clarification.

Holly shrugged cheerfully. 'Ignore them – it's just another one of their bonkers bets. The Major is adjudicating and the loser has to sing "I Have a Dream" in the Main Arena later. Attention seekers,' she accused them fondly, loving the fact that both their personal and professional relationships still had room for some stress-diffusing silliness.

Alice laughed. 'Can we at least put it on YouTube this

time? When Dan did his pirouettes in the Market Place at Christmas, we could have seriously raked in the Likes.' It was typical of Alice, Holly realised, to think of social media, when the rest of them were still coming to terms with the fact that they had a camera on their phone. What a difference a decade made to their approach to technology.

'Do you fancy swinging by Elsie's on the way to the show?' Holly asked, as Dan and Taffy wandered off to the men's room to perfect their bow ties, bickering like brothers as they went. 'I've traded childcare with Lizzie today, so I can't be too late. She's had the twins all morning and I've got hers all afternoon.' She shook her head in amusement. 'God knows what I was thinking – five kids, Elsie and Eric at the Country Show. What could possibly go wrong? But I have plenty of money for ice-creams and cake, so I'm thinking I'm on to a winner.'

'I can help if you like,' said Alice easily. 'Jamie's not coming along until later.'

Holly smiled, still quietly holding out hope that Alice and Coco's trainer, Jamie, might yet make an adorable couple, no matter how much Alice denied even the possibility.

'That would be lovely,' Holly said. 'I'm rather aware how much I've been calling on Lizzie for help with the boys lately, so I figured a child-free afternoon with Will might be just what she needs. The very least I could do.' Holly shrugged, feeling a little helpless as always when it came to supporting Lizzie and her ongoing anxiety issues, but nevertheless determined to be on hand when her best friend needed her.

'Well, I for one can't wait to see what Larkford has in store. Every time there's one of these bonkers events, I get a little more insight into how this town works,' Alice said, a gentle rosiness colouring her cheeks. 'You all really look out for each other, don't you?'

Holly twisted her hair into an impromptu bun and stuck a pencil through it to hold it firmly in place, before ferreting around in her handbag for some lip gloss. 'We do,' she replied simply. 'And that includes you, Miss Walker. If you'll ever let us.' She gave Alice a cheeky grin as she teased her, Alice's determined self-sufficiency having already become a standing joke at The Practice. 'So if you decide you want me to march down to the training centre and give that bossy Judith a talking-to, you have only to ask. It's really not right to put you on the spot like this.'

Holly felt rather strongly about this particular issue, as it happened. Obviously it was wonderful that they'd been able to explore Coco's inherent talent for sniffing out not only blood sugar fluctuations, but also rogue cancer cells over the last year. God knows, the whole team owed that little dog a vote of thanks, and Alice's friendship with Jamie had certainly deepened as a result, but Holly didn't envy them the decisions that were on their horizons. It was one thing for Coco to have acquired this amazing skill naturally and organically, it was something else for Alice to find a way to harness it, without making some enormous concessions with regard to her own health in the process. And Judith Lane, the head trainer at the Canine Oncology Department, wasn't one to compromise willingly.

'Actually,' said Holly, 'I could take Elsie with me. We're quite the formidable good–cop–bad–cop team these days. You should have seen us the other day when those builders were flytipping in the parkland. Batman and Robin eat your heart out.' She grinned and wrapped a soft cotton scarf around her neck and considered herself ready; there was very little point getting all dressed up for the show only to be covered in ice-creamy handprints and face paints within minutes.

Alice smoothed down her immaculate linen jacket and sighed. 'I think we could all use a little Elsie Townsend on tap, don't you? I bet Judith wouldn't try any of her emotional blackmail on Elsie, now would she?'

'She wouldn't dare,' Holly agreed. 'Just say the word. Seriously.'

There was something very special about her relationship with Alice, Holly had recently decided. It wasn't so much having another female doctor on staff, as having a like-minded soul who shared her beliefs and priorities, even if only in medicine and patient care. Socially, Alice remained a bit of an enigma, no matter what Holly tried. It didn't mean she was ready to give up just yet though.

'Right, let's get Elsie and then it's show-time!' Holly waggled her hands in the air, having overindulged on the espressos that morning at merely the thought of the child-count this afternoon. Adding Elsie into the mix was often just enough to turn a picnic into a party, guaranteeing a seemingly endless supply of scandalous anecdotes about their neighbours and Larkford in years gone by. If Alice was on board as well, then they might even have a hope of staying in control! It certainly promised to be interesting.

Holly picked up her jacket and held open the door, Coco needing no invitation to head out into the summer sunshine and Alice seemingly revitalised by the prospect of Elsie's legendary presence.

Elsie Townsend was Larkford's resident celebrity. A star of stage and screen in her youth, she was now in her eighties and no less outspoken for it. Her sage and insightful advice, coupled with her fuck-it attitude and incorrigible sense of fun, meant that she was one of Holly's favourite people in the whole world. Without Elsie, indeed, there was every chance that Holly would still be saddled with her narcissistic first hus-band, rather than embarking on a new life with Taffy Jones.

She left The Practice door on the latch; who knew how long Taffy and Dan would spend fannying around getting ready? Sometimes it was just easier to leave them to their own devices. A waft of warm honeysuckle filled the gentle breeze as fronds of acid-green foliage lifted and danced around the window frames. The Practice was a funny little building, built of Cotswold stone with small red-brick 'eyebrows' arch-ing above each window. It was only the recently built glass atrium that lent light and space to their workplace, giving their patients a bright and airy waiting room and bringing this ancient building into the twenty-first century.

And indeed, much as Taffy and Dan's outfits had given Holly a sense of stepping back in time, there was little in Larkford's Market Place to jar the senses. The pastel-coloured Georgian buildings lined one side of the square, Elsie's house bossily taking centre stage with its newly painted hot pink front door that had ruffled so many feathers on the local planning committee.

Even the golden stone of the shop-fronts on the other side of the Market Place bore wrought-iron signs hanging above their doorways, in keeping with the vintage-style lamp-posts that had been Larkford's contribution to the Millennium. On a warm summer's day like today, nestled in their lush green valley, there was nowhere else on earth that Holly would rather be. Or indeed, anyone she would rather spend her time with than the ramshackle group of friends and colleagues that had become her family.

She knocked smartly on Elsie's front door, the brass jester doorknocker leering at her as always and giving her a frisson of discomfort. She wasn't quite sure if she was imagining it,

but Elsie seemed to be growing more and more troublesome
with each passing month, taking an impish delight in dis-
rupting the status quo. As if to reinforce that opinion, Elsie
pulled open the door abruptly and posed in the doorway to
her parquet hall.

'Ta-da!' she cried joyfully, one hand on her hip, the other
resting on a lace parasol. The parasol was in fact the least
bizarre thing about her outfit, which Holly vaguely recognised from the Audrey Hepburn movie *My Fair Lady*. Indeed,
for a second, Holly found herself oddly moved to shout out
to poor Dover-the-racehorse that he should, indeed, move
his bloomin' arse . . .

'Well, don't you look fabulous!' she said, smiling, after the
merest hesitation, leaning forward to kiss Elsie fondly on each
powdered cheek.

'Hi,' offered Alice, hanging back, unusually reticent in the
face of such lavish and oddly incongruous glamour.

'You are such angels for coming to collect me, but you're
cutting it a little fine if you're going home to get changed,'
Elsie said, attempting tact, but missing her mark as she eyed
them both up and down.

Holly held out one arm for Elsie to take, as she pulled the
hot pink door closed behind her. 'Don't worry, we'll be fine
as we are.'

Elsie squeezed her hand affectionately, clocking immediately the porridge that smeared Holly's engagement ring,
causing her perfect eyebrows to shoot up in alarm. Since
the antique, square-cut diamond had previously been one of
Elsie's prized possessions, donated in the spirit of optimism
and affection following her matchmaking between Holly and
Taffy, they were both a little amazed by Elsie's restraint in
not commenting.

She merely leaned in and gave Holly an affectionate kiss. 'You do well with your juggling, my darling,' she said. 'And I honestly don't mind waiting if you want to get changed. I know it's hardly Ladies' Day at Ascot, but there will be photographs. And lovely young men to talk to. Did I mention my new physio is utterly divine? Sicilian, you know. Felice.' She gave a little shiver. 'So appropriately named! He's popping along later.'

Alice caught Holly's eye, and by tacit agreement they too said nothing. Elsie's penchant for a glimpse of firm manly thigh meant that her physiotherapists had to be thoroughly vetted in advance, not to mention persuaded that Elsie was all talk and no trousers, before any more unfortunate misunderstandings could occur.

'Well,' said Alice, after a moment's awkward silence, 'I think it's just wonderful that you're joining in on Dan and Taffy's bet. They don't stand a chance against your fabulous outfit. You've definitely nailed it.'

Elsie looked at her in confusion. 'What *are* you talking about?' She glanced down at her ensemble and then turned to Holly, as Alice flushed. 'I don't know anything about a bet, darling, do you? Have I missed something?'

Chapter 2

Entering the showground on the banks of the River Lark, Holly pushed her hair back from her face and surveyed the chaos around her. She stepped smartly to one side as a Shetland pony barged past, head down, eyes on the prize of the apple-bobbing stall behind her. The young girl on board clearly had very little control and her freckled grin made it clear that she didn't really care. After all, in the water meadows of the Larkford Valley, and with most of the population gathered together on this sunniest of Saturdays, there were more pairs of hands to help than was probably necessary.

Holly caught hold of the twins as they each attempted to pull in separate directions, Tom heading for the cake stall as per usual and Ben entranced by the Barn Owl Rescue Charity. Lizzie's three children looped around her legs like excitable puppies, their little faces painted like tigers, already slightly smudged, and their energy certainly not in short supply. No wonder Lizzie had been so keen to hand them all over and take to the Main Arena for her moment in the spotlight.

'We've got all afternoon,' Holly protested. 'We can do cakes and barn owls later. We need to get to the Main Arena or we'll miss Eric and Lizzie in their competition.'

Alice fell happily into stride beside them. 'I can't believe how fantastic this is! It's a proper country show. Elsie's already ensconced in the VIP tent and I just walked past Cassie and Marion having a real to-do about the correct jam-to-cream ratio in a Victoria sponge.' The rivalries in Larkford over the best cake/marrow/flower display had been building for weeks in anticipation of this very day and Alice was clearly enjoying every spat.

Holly noticed that Coco pressed herself tightly against her owner's ankles, evidently not enjoying the spectacle quite so much. It took quite a lot to throw Coco off her game, but the general noise and hubbub of the Larkford Country Show seemed to be properly testing her bombproof credentials. The little spaniel flinched slightly as the loudhailer crackled into life and Taffy's voice, returned to its more usual Welsh cadence, could be heard echoing across the meadows.

'Could all the entrants for "Dog that looks most like owner" please come to the Main Arena. And to be clear, folks, we do actually need the dog *and* the owner to be there in person.'

Holly grinned. She knew exactly why this announcement had been necessary. Mrs Greene – undefeated champion for the last three years – had been threatening to enter by Skype this year, as the show happened to coincide with her family holiday to Ireland. The ruckus in The Kingsley Arms at the very suggestion had been quite the eye-opener as to how high the passions ran in this country market town when there were prizes and bragging rights up for grabs.

Alice bent down to scoop Coco out of the path of a vast four-wheel-drive pram, and stroked her silky chocolate-coloured ears. 'It's quite something, all this ... I'm even slightly tempted to join in next year.'

Holly tried not to look surprised. Alice had been in Larkford for a year now, but although she had clearly softened to their way of life, there was still a certain reserve. She hadn't leapt into Larkford with both feet the way Holly had, but then maybe, she thought, Alice had less to prove?

'For the record,' said Holly, 'I think you're quite mad to wait. You and Coco would steal the title now, if only we could persuade you to enter.' Holly reached across and lifted a strand of Alice's mahogany bob to prove her point. 'I can't tell where your hair ends and Coco's ears begin. Definitely lookalike champions in the making.'

Alice blushed slightly, uncomfortable with the scrutiny. 'I think Coco and I might lack the competitive edge,' she said, as Major Waverly walked past, he and his terrier, Grover, sporting matching bow ties. To be fair, their salt and pepper whiskers and twinkling eyes made them dead ringers for one another, but it did bemuse Holly that a well-respected septu-agenarian might set such store by a lookalike contest.

Holly leaned in, her twins hanging off each hand. 'Do you know, I wouldn't be Dan today for all the money in the world. Whoever he chooses to win, there'll be consequences. When he chose your aunt's brownies over Cassie Holland's last year, she didn't speak to him for a month!'

The two women both smiled, secretly thinking that a month without Cassie Holland in your ear actually sounded more like a perk of the job than a downside. 'Speak of the devil,' said Alice quietly.

Even Coco and all the children tensed slightly as Cassie hove into view, her clipboard pressed officiously to her hessian-clad chest. 'Don't dither around, ladies – if you've time on your hands then there's plenty to do. We're not just here to have fun, you know.' She thrust a printed sheet towards Holly and waggled it annoyingly when Holly refused to take the bait.

It was one thing spending hours last night printing out blank certificates and twisting coloured ribbons onto safety pins for the prize-winners, but Holly had really hoped that she was now off duty and would be able to properly relax and enjoy the Larkford Country Show. If there was one thing she'd learned with Cassie Holland, if you gave her an inch she would take a mile. 'I've done my bit, Cassie. I'm here with the children now,' she said pleasantly, but firmly.

'What about you then, Dr Walker?' pressed Cassie with an edge to her voice. 'Spit-spot. Don't just dither on the edges in your designer togs. I do hope you're not afraid to get your hands a little dirty?'

'Oh Cassie, leave the poor girl alone,' interrupted Holly, taking umbrage on Alice's behalf. It was hardly as though Alice was teetering in four-inch Chanel heels; apparently merely looking smart, on-trend and un-muddied was the equivalent though, in Cassie's beady little eyes.

Alice herself just shrugged. Seemingly unfazed.

Holly truly felt for her – they all knew that the locals enjoyed discussing Alice's wardrobe, commenting without filter on her figure and her looks. As the newest young, single doctor in town, it was probably to be expected, and Alice seemed to accept a certain amount of scrutiny without question. But then, as Holly knew only too well, that didn't mean she necessarily appreciated it. In fact, the more time she spent with Alice, the more she realised how carefully Alice guarded her privacy. A year in, and Alice's hidden depths were no closer to revealing themselves. Holly was beginning to feel almost protective of her – not in a maternal way, more of a sisterly solidarity in the making.

The tannoy crackled into life again. 'Would Cassie Holland please come to the cake tent. That's Cassie Holland to the cake tent. Your son is, er, waiting for you.' There was an ear-splitting squeal of feedback and Taffy carried on talking, clearly under the illusion that his conversation was no longer being broadcast. 'And causing chaos. Little sod. I can't believe he ate the Best In Show! What that boy needs is a— Ah, thanks, Lucy.' With an abrupt click, the transmission ended.

Holly deliberately avoided catching Alice's eye, the two of them frozen by some unspoken agreement to avoid the overwhelming urge to laugh. Cassie paused, the form she had been waggling in Alice's face now hanging limply from her hand. She opened her mouth as though to speak and closed it again, before wordlessly turning on her heel and barrelling towards the cake tent.

If only there were a bollocking on little Tarquin's horizon, thought Holly, there might still be time for him to become a decent member of their community. As it was, with his liberal and free-range upbringing veering towards the negligent – all in the name of child-centred parenting – he was actually becoming a mini-tyrant. Poor Marion had been forced to ban him from the Spar shop for pilfering the Pick-And-Mix, and many a resident automatically moved their beloved dog out of range as he ran by, for fear of a kick or a poke from his omnipresent stick.

'Oh poor Taffy,' said Holly in consternation, knowing only too well what it felt like to be on the receiving end of a Cassie-tirade.

Alice shook her head. 'It really does take all sorts, doesn't it? How does she get away with being so opinionated and so utterly wrong, without fuelling an angry mob?'

Holly nodded, still quietly fuming on Alice's behalf about Cassie's ignorant assertions the previous week. For God's sake, as a doctor and a Type One diabetic, Alice knew perfectly well that diabetes was not a self-inflicted illness, but by the time Cassie had said her piece, the poor girl had looked shattered. Holly could only hope that Alice wasn't allowing those vile comments to stick in her head and torment her.

'She's all talk though, isn't she?' Holly said reassuringly. 'I just try to remind myself that every little dig and jibe is another window into her own insecurities. And that, actually, we should be feeling sorry for her.' She paused and wrinkled her nose cheerfully. 'Well, sometimes that works. Sometimes I have to physically restrain myself from clobbering her.'

Alice nodded, seemingly comforted that she was not alone in that temptation at least.

Holly turned her head to the sunshine, drinking in the laughter and conversation around her. The Larkford Country Show really did have to be seen to be believed – a slice of Middle England on parade. The Major's cronies were demonstrating the best way to cast with fly-fishing rods over the River Lark; one of the farmers had rigged up a whack-a-mole (thankfully not with a real mole this year); the ladies of the Larkford WI were keeping the cake and produce competitions running and under control (no mean feat actually when the competitive edge around here was so acute) and there was a bouncy castle to exhaust toddlers and offer parental reprieve. Holly couldn't help thinking that the Pimm's stand would do a roaring trade if it had been adjacent to Kiddie Korner, but she wasn't prepared to weather the looks of judgement should she dare to suggest it.

At least she could relax in the knowledge that Lucy, their ponytailed yet formidable receptionist, was on hand to keep Taffy on track in the commentary box today. Whoever had thought it was a good idea to give her garrulous fiancé free rein with a microphone clearly didn't know him very well!

'Oh, how lovely!' exclaimed Alice. 'Would you look at that?' All heads turned as a parade of ponies trotted through the showground, all dressed up to the nines. The children on board sported immaculate white jodhpurs and fitted tweed jackets and their ponies' highly groomed coats shone in the sunlight. It was a remarkable and beautiful sight to behold, if only because the riders themselves were so diminutive and yet so accomplished. This was no ordinary Pony Club, this was the Larkford Equine Association. There were Arabellas, Imogens and Clementines galore in this subset of their community and most of these children radiated the glowing health of privilege. In fact, Holly realised, she had rarely seen any of them in her consulting rooms – perhaps they had a private GP on the Pony Club payroll?

Their parents strolled casually through the parkland, their gilets and shades cutting quite the stylish dash through the quilted waistcoats and Tattersall check shirts of Larkford. Holly quietly bit her tongue, realising that young Alice may not be quite so quick to join in with the jokes about their voguish pack-mentality as Lizzie always was. It was tough out there on the streets of Larkford if you failed to measure up to the yummy-mummy standard; indeed Holly had long since given up trying and was all the happier for it.

As Charlotte Lansing strode into view, her lips pursed against a hunting horn, Holly tried hard not to laugh. Charlotte's corduroy trousers and leather boots had a soundtrack all of their own as she marched past. 'Ride halt!' she bellowed, and every single pony stopped on a dime and turned into line – a noticeable improvement in obedience on the previous class of puppies and dogs leaping about excitedly.

Dan Carter strolled up beside them. 'Well, I'm glad I'm not judging *this* class as well.' He looked almost shell-shocked, covered in muddy paw prints and with an alarmingly vivid lipstick imprint on his cheek. 'I'm not sure it was a good idea to put Lizzie and Eric in first place. Even if they were the best match by a mile. I can't throw a brick around here without cries of nepotism!'

Holly laughed, delighted that Eric, the 'time-share puppy' she owned with Lizzie, had picked up a prize, even if her best friend's lipstick on Dan's face had obviously ruffled a few feathers. 'What did they win?'

'A year's supply of doggie treats,' Dan answered, 'so it's not as if I'm in for a cut of the swag, now is it? Even if she is my cousin.'

The tannoy above their heads squealed its introduction and Taffy's increasingly tense, increasingly Welsh tones echoed around the valley. 'Could the person with the Mercedes reg B16 DIX please move your vehicle – you are blocking the exit from the car park.' There was a clunk of a button being depressed. 'And you clearly need to get a life, I mean really, who are they kidding, Big Di— Oh, thanks, Lucy.' Another squeal and the tannoy fell silent.

'Somebody seriously needs to teach your fiancé how to use an off-switch,' said Dan, laughing so hard it was only a silent exhalation.

'In so many ways,' Holly agreed. 'He's like a whirlwind of energy. All the time.' She shook her head, still laughing. 'It's like living with the Duracell Bunny.' And she loved it, she thought to herself; her house was filled with laughter and fun and chaos. So what if she occasionally needed a long, long shower just to get some peace? Living with Taffy Jones had changed her life and Holly treasured every moment.

As a small bunch of boys hurtled through their group, swinging around legs and tent poles in their haste to catch one another, Coco shied away and Alice bent down to pick her up again. Holly knew it wasn't training protocol to do so in a busy area, but as the number of visitors multiplied and the number of events going on simultaneously grew, Holly was aware of a faint peripheral nervousness that she couldn't quite place. Perhaps Alice had the right idea? She held on tightly to the children's hands, gathering them around her, and looked about, trying to place the source of her unease.

Major Waverly marching up to Dan in indignation didn't exactly help. 'I'm very disappointed in you, young Daniel. Grover and I were clearly a shoe-in for that award. I have to confess I feel rather let down – and after I'd organised such a lovely surprise for you all as well.'

'A surprise?' asked Dan, looking around, refusing to be drawn into the debate.

The Major looked at his watch and then up at the sky. 'Any moment now, in fact. Supposed to be my glory parade. Too late to cancel,' he harrumphed.

A smattering of applause from the Main Arena announced that the 'Under-Ten Ridden Show Pony' class had clearly reached some kind of denouement and Holly wondered whether the entrants there would take the result as personally as the Major clearly had.

Coco suddenly scrabbled in Alice's arms. It was so unlikely, so unusual, that Alice nearly dropped her. This trembling bundle of chocolate-coloured fur pressing tightly into Alice's neck and whimpering took all of them by surprise.

Only moments later, it all made sense. A growling from the skies grew to apocalyptic proportions and a vintage biplane buzzed overhead. Holly barely had the chance to register that there were two small figures standing on the wings, before it turned into an ambitious loop-the-loop.

There was a second's delay on the ground but that was all, before absolute chaos broke loose.

Chapter 3

Holly watched in sheer disbelief as the bucolic scene around her dissolved, as though hit by a tsunami of sound. Only those who actually had the presence of mind to look upwards could identify the source of the flattening roar – babies and small children simply burst into wails of confusion and distress. Lizzie's children and the twins clapped their hands over their ears in mute astonishment at the scene in the sky above them, pressing themselves instinctively against Holly's legs, mouths open in matching O's. Coco whimpered pathetically, craving security and comfort.

But it was the intensity of the screams from the Main Arena that grabbed everyone's attention, as beautifully polished ponies scattered in every direction, their riders clinging on for dear life or indeed bailing out onto the soft sawdust of the arena. Even Charlotte Lansing's commands to her 'gals' were drowned out by the chaos.

As quickly as the biplane had arrived, it swooped up into the heavens again, leaving a trail of vapour and an aftermath of pandemonium. Holly instinctively looked around, assessing their immediate environment for casualties and breathing an enormous sigh of relief that everyone was still standing.

Everyone except the Major.

Dan was already guiding him towards a chair and loosening that ridiculous bow tie, as the Major's face turned puce and he struggled for air. 'He's fine,' Dan called over his shoulder to Marion, reaching for the Major's nitro spray. 'Just his angina acting up.'

'That was close,' Holly said to Alice. 'That could have been so much worse. What was he even *thinking*—' It was only then that the rhythmic hammering of hooves, punctuated by a gasping cry, caught her attention.

A small bay-coloured pony, its mane and tail exquisitely plaited and shining with health and vigour, was bolting towards them. Charlotte Lansing was in pursuit, but the wide-eyed fear on little Jessica Hearst's face was clear to everyone watching as she clung on desperately. Out of control, the pony was picking up speed, the prized rosette for Best Turned-Out flapping on his bridle only serving to escalate his panic.

Mothers grabbed their children, dogs were pulled abruptly to heel on their leads, nobody wanting to be caught in Jessica's path as she gamely tried to slow their flight. Perhaps she would have succeeded, her petite frame was certainly stronger than it looked, as she managed to regain her balance and sit deep, anchoring her feet into the stirrups to give herself leverage on the reins. Perhaps, thought Holly for a split second, everything really would be okay.

And then the world seemed to blur and refract around them, as a stray string of bunting caught in the light summer breeze and snaked out into the air, a twirling multicoloured rope of flags tipping the balance out of Jessica's favour. That one second felt never-ending, as the distracted pony's front hoof folded into a divot in the grass, his whole body crumpling in on itself as it hurtled towards the ground, with Jessica propelled forward by sheer momentum.

The impact of their bodies hitting the ground in tandem was nothing compared to the sickening thud as a flailing hoof caught Jessica's helmet.

Hollow fear followed a heartbeat later, as the terrified pony staggered back to its feet and Jessica remained, motionless, on the ground.

Her twins and Lizzie's brood were all truly sobbing now and Holly froze, utterly conflicted as to where her attention should be focused. But Alice didn't even hesitate in taking the lead, thrusting Coco's harness into Holly's hand and dashing over to Jessica's side, as others tried to catch the distraught and flailing pony before any more damage could be done. Gently, so gently, Alice reached for Jessica's wrist, looking to find a pulse.

'Don't move her,' called Holly unnecessarily, torn between trying to soothe the children and keep an eye on Alice at the same time.

The crack in the little girl's helmet was like a fissure through the resin, as though an axe had struck her, and Holly looked around her for support. Marion Waverly swooped in, gathering all five young children into her ample bosom and allowing Holly to run over towards the poor girl still lying prone and unresponsive.

Teddy Kingsley was on his mobile only a few feet away, calling for an ambulance and trying to convey the severity of their situation. 'Teddy!' Holly called in an urgent whisper, trying not to alarm the people around them, who were already panicking. 'Tell them there's a GP on site, an obvious head injury, loss of consciousness and we need a direct transfer to Frenchay Hospital. Tell them we need the Air Ambulance.' She paused, 'Tell them it's critical, Teddy.'

She crouched down beside Alice, who was checking

Jessica's vitals again, keen to ensure that she wasn't missing anything in the stress of the moment – it had been a long time since her trauma rotation as a medical student, but Holly was impressed to see that Alice's composure was absolute. 'You're doing fine,' Holly encouraged her. 'You've got this.' Thank God.

Alice nodded, muttering, 'ABC,' over and over under her breath. She looked to Holly for reassurance. 'Airway's clear now. I did a modified jaw thrust because of the likelihood of spinal injury?' It wasn't really a question, it was a statement of fact, still it was obvious Alice needed Holly's confirmation that she was doing the right thing. 'She's breathing on her own and there's decent capillary refill.' Alice pressed the fingernail bed on Jessica's tiny hand again and counted until the colour suffused the tissue again. 'And her heart rate's pretty steady at sixty-five, but she's still unresponsive. Pupils reactive though,' she added, ever hopeful.

Holly placed a supportive hand on Alice's arm. 'You're doing great, Alice. Keep an eye on her, tell me the minute anything changes, okay? I'll talk to dispatch to get an ETA and make sure the team at Frenchay know she's coming.' Holly stood up and held out her hand for Teddy's mobile.

Holly noticed in her peripheral vision that Cassie Holland was trying, in vain, to corral people away from the scene. Charlotte Lansing had managed to catch the pony, now tiredly lashing out in fear, and Holly could only hope that this gloriously rustic afternoon was not going to end in tragedy for anyone.

She looked up, utterly appalled that the thought hadn't occurred to her sooner. 'The parents? Where are Jessica's parents?'

'I'm on it,' said Teddy, gratefully thrusting his phone into Holly's hand, relieved of his post as ambulance liaison. He jogged away across the showground, heading straight for the VIP hospitality suite. There was no way that Jessica's family would have been roughing it with the hoi polloi in the beer tent, but surely it wasn't possible that the carnage outside their silk-lined cocoon had eluded them, thought Holly crossly.

The vulnerable figure of their only daughter lying on the grass in such an awkward position would be horrifying either way, Holly realised, shrugging off her jacket and laying it over Jessica despite the warmth of the day. Even though she wasn't conscious, her slight body would be experiencing all manner of shock reactions.

There was a flurry of conversation behind them, as Holly methodically updated the trauma unit in Bristol as to what they might expect and Alice diligently checked Jessica's vitals again – whispering, shouting, tears and a wailing sob that could only have been Lavinia Hearst. Quite why she was yelling at Teddy and the Major rather than rushing to her daughter's side was not for her to say, thought Holly, but seriously? There would be plenty of opportunities for blaming and shaming later; herself included, for that awful moment of frozen indecision between her role as parent or doctor.

With no helpful information about the Air Ambulance ETA forthcoming on the phone, time seemed to expand and contract around her. Holly felt swamped. Somebody needed to talk to the parents and Jessica required absolute focus – there was no margin for error here. The slightest slip could mean paralysis or, with a traumatic injury to the head like this, there were any number of complications that Holly didn't even want to contemplate.

But she simply didn't know whether Alice was up to the job of coping with an hysterical Lavinia Hearst, and Jessica had to be their priority.

The discussions around her grew more strident as Lavinia ranted.

'Lavinia? Hi, I'm Dr Graham. Jessica's vitals are stable at the moment but there's help on the way to take her to Frenchay. She's had rather a nasty bash on her head. Can you take a deep breath for me, because Jessica needs you to be calm right now. We need to focus on Jessica. Okay?' Holly said with gentle but non-negotiable firmness, unwilling to leave Alice unsupported in such a challenging situation for too long, but aware that Lavinia was two ticks away from spiralling into a panic attack.

Dan arrived, slightly out of breath from his exertions with the Major, and knelt down in the grass beside them; it was obvious from his whole demeanour that he didn't come bearing good news. 'You're doing a great job, guys,' he said softly, 'but now I want you to listen to me and then we're going to work together, okay? I've just spoken to dispatch. There's no Air Ambulance available today. It's not coming. This is going to be a longer journey for Jessica than I'd like.'

The commotion of voices and moving equipment broke over them like another wave, jolting Holly out of her focus, as the ambulance pulled up beside them and the doors were flung open. Discussions about the bumpiness of the track across the showground began throwing open a whole new set of problems.

Holly and Alice were both swept aside as Dan took over, conferring with the paramedics and taking control.

Holly gave Alice a hug. 'You did such a brilliant job, Alice. But it's time to let Dan step in. He really is the best person for this job now; the things he learned in the Army . . . '

Alice nodded, her eyes never once leaving the tiny figure now being transferred to a backboard and swamped by the neck brace that the paramedics and Dan had prioritised before anything else. 'It's the right thing to do,' Alice said awkwardly.

From this point though, as Holly remembered only too well from her years in A&E, 'time was brain' – it was a race now to stop any secondary swelling causing yet more irreversible damage.

They might not see too many traumatic brain injuries at The Practice, but they all knew that Dan was no stranger to life-changing injuries, and his experience patching together survivors of roadside bombs gave him the obvious advantage.

Holly turned her attention back to Lavinia Hearst, outlining in simple terms what would happen next and gently explaining the reality of the situation for her – a filthy concussion was actually a best-case scenario for Jessica right now, as she still remained unconscious. Not that Lavinia appeared to be listening – whether from shock or sheer bloody stupidity, she swung from yelling at the Major to trying to reach her daughter 'just to hold her'.

Watching the paramedics gently transferring Jessica to a backboard was a lesson in caution all of its own; any benefit from rushing negated by the obvious risks of paralysis. Allowing Lavinia into the mix while she was so overwrought and unpredictable could have devastating consequences.

Holly glanced up and saw that Alice's face was now sheet-white and her eyes were wide, as the shock of the whole accident began to catch up with her. 'You okay?' Holly said gently, grateful that Mr Hearst had finally turned up in time to comfort his wife in her transition from anger to terrified disbelief.

'He was right to bench me,' said Alice quietly, if a little begrudgingly. 'I'm out of my depth.' She waved a hand towards Dan, where he was intently discussing and implementing the optimum oxygenation rate for Jessica. It was all a question of balance to avoid the twin extremes of hypoxia and hypocapnea. 'In all honesty,' Alice confessed to Holly, 'I'm not sure I would have remembered that, would I?'

Holly said nothing for a moment – it was a common rookie mistake: when it came to oxygen, the instinctive assumption was that more would be better. It was also much better that Alice had come to this realisation on her own. 'Don't over-think this, Alice,' Holly said quietly. 'This is why we have paramedics. Obviously we need to know the basics of trauma management, but we're GPs, not A&E consultants. I can see you beating yourself up about this already, but we can't all be everything. Or we'd end up being jacks of all trades and masters of none.'

Alice nodded, watching as Dan leapt into the back of the ambulance and the doors swung slowly shut. 'You're right, of course, but shouldn't we have the best emergency train-ing possible?'

Her plaintive question gave Holly the perfect opportunity to bring her back into the moment; whilst Jessica's injuries were obviously life-threatening, there were still plenty of Larkford's residents around them that needed their help. From cuts and bruises, to a shock-induced asthma attack, to the Major, who now seemed to be having some sort of nervous breakdown, aghast that his celebratory surprise might yet have such catastrophic consequences.

Holly took a deep breath. 'That's certainly a conversation we should have. Another day. Right now, our patients need us. You take the Major and I'll pop Geoffrey Larch on the portable nebuliser,' Holly said, surveying the damage.

Taffy had already established a triage system in the Main Arena and now had all the riders dismounted and under control. To Holly's immense surprise it was Cassie Holland who was in her element. She was walking amongst them with her clipboard and a mobile phone, contacting relatives, handing out hot sweet tea to those in shock. She looked poised and in control – clearly someone who rose to a challenge.

Alice nodded and walked over to the Major, Holly watching her closely. It was clear that Alice had always considered herself to be one of those people too. And, as with all high-achievers, she could only focus on her weaknesses, rather than her achievements. Holly was quite convinced that Alice couldn't see the amazing courage that had propelled her forward to Jessica in those first few minutes; she would, in all likelihood, be focusing instead on the ambulance driving away without her on board. Replaceable, replaced and out of her depth. Alice Walker was a fabulous doctor, no doubt, but she was also her own harshest critic.

Holly sighed deeply, hoping that Alice's confidence wouldn't be yet another tragedy of this afternoon's events.

Chapter 4

It was only natural, Alice supposed, that she might experience a shock reaction to what she had seen – strike that, what she had been involved in, earlier that day. She still shuddered slightly at the idea that her own arrogance in pushing forward to help might ultimately have had a negative impact on Jessica's recovery. She couldn't put her finger on why she'd done it though, and with Holly standing right there beside her! And once she'd begun to take care of Jessica, she couldn't deny that she'd felt personally invested in that little girl's recovery and utterly piqued when Dan had swept in and taken over.

She shivered under the blanket that her aunt Pru had wrapped around her shoulders, tucking her feet up under herself on the sofa and sipping at her cup of tea – tea being the balm for all ills, in her aunt's opinion. With Coco fast asleep beside her, Alice tried to relax.

But it wasn't that easy.

'Honestly,' she said to her aunt, who was fussing around her sitting room, 'do leave it. I'll get everything sorted when I get a weekend off.' It took all of Alice's restraint not to leap up and prise the books and photographs out of her aunt's well-meaning hands, as she continued to 'give the place a little tidy'.

Catching the edge in her niece's voice, Pru sat down reluctantly – one of those women for whom sitting idle was anathema. After all, she would reason, time spent chatting could also be time spent cleaning, cooking, gardening.

'Alice, love,' she began tentatively, casting her eye around the sitting room, 'I really think you need to take some time to unpack properly. You've been in this house for months now and you've storage boxes everywhere. How long would it take for the two of us to really knuckle down and get you properly settled?' She waved a hand at the large wall behind the sofa. 'A nice bookshelf from that Swedish Eekoo place would do just the job.'

Alice couldn't help but smile at her aunt's earnest expression. 'Do you mean Ikea, Aunty Pru?' she offered, without judgement. She was well used to her aunt's propensity for muddling up words – indeed this habit had often been the only highlight of family get-togethers when Alice had been small and the only child in the family, not a cousin in sight.

'I think I'll wait until I've time to do it properly,' she said, taking a sip of tea and trying not to let the panic show on her face. The very idea of somebody else unpacking her boxes or decorating her sitting room made the skin on her neck prickle. She attempted to soften her abrupt tone as soon as she saw the hurt expression on Pru's face. 'It is my very first home of my own, after all. Even if it is just a rental. I want it to be fun and take my time with it – get it just the way I want it. Maybe head into Bath for the Antiques Market and sniff out a bargain?'

'Of course,' her aunt nodded, mollified at least that Alice had a plan in place. 'You're quite right.' As Pru stood up yet again to go and fiddle in the kitchen, a running narrative floated through the archway that divided the ground floor of this terraced cottage in two, with Alice only picking up half the monologue. The other half of her attention was focused on ways to keep her aunt downstairs; if she thought this looked bad, there was no way Alice was going to allow her to see the bedrooms upstairs.

'You know, I'm so grateful for you bringing me home,' Alice began, pushing off the blanket and wandering through to the kitchen, 'but I think a good night's sleep is probably just what the doctor ordered.' She didn't specifically ask her aunt to leave, couldn't bring herself to be that blunt, but the message was clear, as she let the sentiment dangle.

Pru wiped her hands on a tea towel and cast one more glance around the newly sparkling kitchen. 'Well, at least I don't have to worry about you starving,' she said, with an attempt at humour. She waved a hand at Alice's over-stocked larder. 'In fact, with all that food in there, you're probably covered through to Christmas.' She leaned in and kissed Alice on the cheek, brushing away the stray frond of hair that always tumbled forward into her eyes. 'I'll give you a ring tomorrow, love, okay? Just to make sure there's no ill-effects from your heroics?'

As the front door slammed shut behind her, there was a moment of suspended silence, before Alice's anguished sobs could be restrained no longer. She slid down against the cabinets in the kitchen, her bizarre bunny slippers sticking out in front of her, as the roiling anxiety in her stomach was allowed free rein. Holding it together in front of her aunt had only served to exacerbate the angst – not just about poor little Jessica Hearst or the unexpected trauma of the afternoon, but all of it compounded by the stress of having someone, anyone really, rootling through her things.

She knew it wasn't a proportionate reaction, just as she

knew it was a sentiment best kept to herself. She simply couldn't stand to share her space and incur judgement. And judgement was inevitable really, if anybody looked too closely.

Coco's sniffing attentions brought her back into the moment, as they always did. There was only ever unconditional love and acceptance from her little spaniel – and for Alice, this was one of the greatest gifts of all.

Hours later, as Coco lay diagonally across Alice's bed, the only light in the bedroom came from the flickering glow of Alice's laptop. An early night may have seemed like the best recovery plan, but her body refused to comply. With her blood sugar fluctuating more than usual, Alice felt the ever-present nervousness about submitting to sleep. She knew that Coco was there to alert her to any problems in the night, but that wasn't always enough to take away the fear. Especially after a day like today.

She missed Tilly, her best friend, confidante and social conscience. Tilly brought focus and perspective to Alice's life, even though their friendship these days was mainly conducted via Skype and Facebook, while Tilly was busy travelling around the world, taking her medical skills to wherever needed her most. She was in South America right now and, to Alice, had never felt further away. She clicked onto Skype in hope more than expectation of finding a little green tick next to her name. No such luck.

So instead, Alice trawled the internet as she always did, erratically clicking from one designer website to another, with no particular goal in mind. The very action of hunting out a bargain soothing in itself.

As she compared prices on a particularly lovely MaxMara bracelet she categorically did not need, Alice's focus was so absolute that she finally felt that 'give' – the release she'd been hoping for. It was hard to know when this habit had become a ritual, but Alice tried not to think about it. All she cared about was that it worked.

She clicked through the checkout, her card details already saved, but barely missing a beat when the font changed to red and her transaction was declined. She reached across a slumbering Coco for her wallet on the bedside table, ignoring the little dog's groans of protest at being disturbed. Without hesitation, Alice picked a different credit card at random and typed the numbers in by the light of the screen. As her order confirmation number flashed up and the bracelet became rightfully hers, she sighed. Maybe this time, her pick-me-up purchase would actually do its job when it arrived.

The phone beside her trilled into the darkness, jolting Coco awake, startling them both – who could be phoning at this time of night, Alice cursed. 'Hello?' she answered curtly, before noticing the digits on the clock beside her – it was only ten o'clock.

'Alice? It's Jamie. Everything okay?'

Typical of him to notice every nuance of her tone, she thought as she hurriedly tried to regroup. 'Fine, honestly fine,' she said. 'I just grabbed an early night, that's all.'

'And I woke you up? Shit. And here was me trying to be helpful and supportive!' When Alice didn't reply he blundered on. 'I just saw the local news, that's all. I wanted to see if you were alright?' The openness and ease in his voice was something Alice envied – his motivations always transparent. If he said he was phoning to see how she was, that was actually what he was doing – this was no late-night booty call.

If only, Alice sighed, before sharply reining in her thoughts. Jamie Yardley was categorically *not* the answer to her problems. But he was her friend, one of her best friends really, and she appreciated their relationship more than he would probably ever know. 'That's very sweet,' she replied, her tone softening. 'And you only woke up Coco, so she'll be expecting restitution when she sees you next.'

Jamie's laugh rumbled down the phone line. 'She can have some extra bacon, how's that? I imagine she's earned it today—' The humour barely disguised the concern in his voice. After all, as Coco's dog trainer, he was utterly au fait with the nightly balancing act that Coco and Alice endured, knowing only too well how much stress and adrenalin could throw a Type One diabetic off balance. There were certainly very few other people in her life who realised, truly realised, what she went through every day just to appear normal and functional. 'How are you two *really* doing?'

Jamie was never one to be fobbed off lightly and Alice struggled with that – some days it was exactly what she needed, longed for even, but others? Well, it was only a small click over to intrusive.

'We're okay, Jamie,' Alice replied, after a pause, where she had weighed up the options of bullshitting him. 'It might be a long night though.'

She could almost hear him nod down the line, his phone wedged under his chin as always, another chronic multitasker. 'The news said Jessica's making a good recovery,' Jamie said gently, 'so you can relax now. Your part is over and, by all accounts, Walker, you did good.'

Alice took a breath, about to interrupt, about to tell him that she'd had no business stepping forward to help that girl in the first place, but something stopped her. She didn't want him to see *all* her insecurities after all. 'I might watch a movie,' she proffered.

'Do you want me to stay on the line and watch the same one, Harry-met-Sally style?' he suggested teasingly, knowing exactly what kind of movie Alice always reached for. He'd tried to widen her horizons, offering DVDs of epic spy movies, Marvel superheroes or even *Star Wars* trilogies, but Alice was firmly wedded to the Happy-Ever-Afters – anything by Working Title, or starring Hugh Grant, and Alice was happy. It was the only area of her life where she was content to be a cliché.

'Night, Jamie,' she said instead, unable to disguise the smile in her voice at his suggestion. 'Thank you though.'

'You're very welcome,' he said, registering the change and seemingly content that all was now well. 'Phone me if you get bored of Julia Roberts.' He hung up with a click and Alice stared at the receiver in her hand, the dialling tone loud in the darkness.

She sighed. There was something about Jamie Yardley that made her smile every time; he seemed to know without prompting exactly what she needed. Just like every best friend should.

She scrunched up her eyes tightly in the darkness, as though by doing so she could ignore the room around her, the chaos around her.

And therein lay the solitary problem with Jamie – he was altogether too local. And if Alice's dating life had one parameter, it was distance. Not so much the old adage that absence made the heart grow fonder, more that the likelihood of somebody sharing her personal space was dramatically reduced.

She opened her eyes, ignoring the shapes looming in the darker recesses of her bedroom, and stared intently at her laptop screen, clicking on the windows until her Match.com profile appeared and she could access her messages. Her heart did a small flip-flop as she saw that Ollie was already online.

Hey – she typed – how was the surf this morning?

They had nothing in common.

They would, in all likelihood, never meet.

But chatting with Ollie Turner online was the closest that Alice got to dating these days.

And, of course, it helped that Sydney, Australia was just far enough away to discourage any thoughts of sleepovers or spontaneous visits.

Chapter 5

Holly shook her head as Dan continued to rage on Monday morning, pacing up and down her consulting room at The Practice, being forced to make a turn every four strides. It wasn't just that she didn't agree with him; she simply couldn't understand the scale of this reaction. She'd tried, without success, to interrupt him and explain the reality of the situation, but obviously Dan was so worked up that he wasn't going to let something as boring as the facts get in the way of a good argument.

'I mean, they have every right to be fucking furious, don't they? The partners were all there – on the scene, literally as it happened – but we let Alice, our junior, take the lead?' He rubbed his eyes tiredly and, whilst Holly could understand how spending the whole of Saturday night at the hospital with Jessica's distraught (and litigious) parents might have taken its toll, she still owed him the truth.

'Look,' she reminded him gently, 'it wasn't as though Jessica was the only casualty. And I was there beside Alice until you took over her care. In many ways,' she ventured, 'we should be proud that Alice had the wherewithal to clear Jess's airway so promptly and cautiously, or we could be looking at an entirely different outcome.'

They'd been going round in circles for ages, their coffees grown cold on the desk and their Monday morning anything but a fresh start. 'Lavinia's on the warpath, Holly. How this has become the fault of the people who saved her daughter, rather than that idiot pilot, or the Major for booking the bloody plane in the first place, I do not know.' He sat down abruptly, as though somebody had cut his strings. 'That poor kid,' he said.

Holly nodded. There was no avoiding the fact that Jess had a long road to recovery ahead of her. The Traumatic Brain Injury team would be assessing her in the next few days, once the swelling had subsided. They could only be grateful at this point that there was no spinal injury or brain bleed. Only time would tell what young Jess Hearst was actually dealing with.

There was a gentle tap at the door and Grace, their Practice Manager and all-round saviour, poked her head into the room. 'I've brought fresh coffee and a heads-up.' She deftly placed two steaming mugs on Holly's desk. 'You two are giving the patients in the waiting room *quite* the show.'

Holly flushed instantly at the idea of their patients hearing their heated debate, as time had obviously run away with them, but Dan looked unperturbed.

'Perhaps it's a good thing they know they shouldn't rely on the Air Ambulance around here,' he said. 'Do you know what the ground crew said, when I followed up? Budget cuts! Can you believe it? They only have one operational bird at the moment, because the other one's in the workshop, awaiting funds for repair. Do you ever wonder how many other patients are missing out?' He looked up bleakly. 'It's a vast area they cover too.' Picking up his drink, he nodded his thanks to Grace and wandered dejectedly out of the room.

'He's taking this pretty hard,' Holly said to Grace unnecessarily.

'He's taking it pretty personally too, from what I can see,' Grace replied, tucking her bobbed hair neatly behind one ear to reveal a silver twisted-vine cuff that merely hinted at Grace's Ayurvedic tendencies. She might be the one to keep the ship firmly afloat at work, but her personal life was altogether more Zen. She stretched out her shoulders and sighed. 'I gather the Hearsts really laid into him yesterday too. I know they were probably frightened out of their wits, but it sounded as though they were pretty brutal.' She shrugged, 'I guess the same rules don't apply to everyone.'

They both looked automatically towards one of the new posters that were now dotted throughout The Practice – 'We don't tolerate abuse' – a zero-tolerance approach, allowing the staff to refuse treatment when confronted with angry, hostile or violent behaviour. It was such a shame they felt the need to display these, in Holly's opinion, but it had become a necessity of late as the number of incidents had escalated. Normally drink- or drug-related cases, to be fair, but there was always the odd hothead that one couldn't predict. They had drawn the line at a Perspex screen in Reception thankfully – none of them had any desire to work in a self-imposed prison.

'He'll be okay,' Holly reassured her. 'It's probably a good thing you two are off-site today. Give him a little space and perspective rather than stomping around here like a bear with a sore head. Have you got supplies?'

It was widely known amongst the staff at The Practice that both Dan and Taffy were much nicer human beings when regularly fed. Indeed, Dan's outburst this morning was most likely the direct result of skipping breakfast in his haste to get to work.

Grace nodded. 'We'll pick up some bacon sandwiches from The Deli before we leave. I'm not letting a h-angry Dan loose on a roomful of regional delegates!'

Holly nodded, pushing the door closed with her foot. 'Hang on a sec, we can raid my emergency stash, if you like?' She pulled a file box down off the shelf, flipping it open to reveal bags of Jelly Babies, Fruit Pastilles and mini Mars Bars.

Grace couldn't help but look shocked.

Holly shrugged. 'When you live with Taffy, it always pays to be prepared. Between him and the twins, ninety per cent of my handbag is snacks these days!'

Grace laughed. 'Well, how Dan and Taffy eat that much crap and still look so great is beyond me, but I'm all for an easy life and it's quite the drive to Bristol.' She reached forward and picked out the family-sized bag of Jelly Babies. 'Wish me luck then. One more day to get through and then that's it! Last seminar done and dusted.' The relief on her face at the prospect was plain to see and Holly didn't dare mention that Derek Landers had already been pushing for more.

She pressed a couple of mini Mars Bars into Grace's hand – just as a precaution. 'Knock 'em dead,' she said with a smile.

After a few hours of her regular Monday clinic, Holly could have been forgiven for thinking that all would be back to normal in no time. It was only when her last patient of the morning walked into the room that she realised she'd been kidding herself.

'I'm so sorry to take up your time, Dr Graham, but I think I might need a little help with this.' Charlotte Lansing slipped out of her quilted jacket and Holly tried hard not to look shocked. It was all very well that the Lansings prioritised their horses above all else, but never had she expected this. As she peeled back the veterinary dressing on Charlotte's arm, the true extent of the wound became clear.

'Oh, Charlotte,' Holly exhaled, compassion laced into every syllable.

'I know, I know,' Charlotte said with a sigh, 'but there was so much going on after the show and some of the ponies had been injured too. It just seemed easier.'

Easier in the short term maybe, thought Holly, as she examined the horseshoe-shaped gash in Charlotte's forearm. She gently palpated the area around the open wound, checking the extent of the thickening and swelling. The angry redness of the wound itself told its own story. Simply packing a sterile dressing on a dirty cut was some kind of madness, but Holly tried not to judge her patients, aiming to guide them towards better choices if she possibly could. She couldn't however completely hide her own stunned reaction to how appalling this wound was looking.

'You can say it, you know,' said Charlotte. 'It's infected, isn't it?' She shook her head. 'You'd think I'd know better.'

Holly looked up, unable to offer a different perspective. 'Did this happen at the show?' she asked, trying to confirm a timeline that made sense.

Charlotte nodded. 'Can you believe I didn't even notice until later though? I was trying to help one of our novices after the plane went over and the pony just panicked. It looked pretty clean at the time.'

'It's still a hoof, though,' said Holly gently. She didn't like to draw the parallels with a filthy hiking boot, but nevertheless, who knew what bacteria were currently festering in this cut? 'Charlotte, there's no way around this, you're going to need stitches. And this cut is pretty deep and angry, so they'll want to irrigate thoroughly at the hospital, maybe take some swabs for the lab.' She paused, before deciding that forewarned was forearmed. 'A targeted IV antibiotic wouldn't be the worst idea.' She let the idea sink in.

Charlotte just shook her head though. 'But that would mean staying in, wouldn't it? I can't do that – the horses—'

Holly interrupted smoothly, 'There's a time to prioritise them, and a time to prioritise yourself, Charlotte. It's boring but true that a stitch in time saves nine. An infection like this can be quite virulent and it's already had quite a head start.'

Charlotte nodded and Holly breathed a sigh of relief that she was now taking her own health seriously without Holly having to employ scare tactics. 'I'll just pop back to the farm and muck out and I'll drive straight on to Bath, how's that?'

Holly closed her eyes for a moment. Just because she was tired, it didn't excuse the unfamiliar wave of frustration with her patient washing over her. She typed the referral into the computerised system to take a moment to compose herself. 'Charlotte,' she said gently, as she turned back to face her recalcitrant patient, 'this has to be your priority now. I don't know what kind of infection this is yet, but it is not good. Seriously, not good. And you need to get straight to the hospital. In fact, I've half a mind to—' She paused, not wanting to make a fuss, but unable to ignore the persistent alarm bells at the back of her mind.

'What?' asked Charlotte abruptly, actually looking bothered for the first time, as it dawned on her that she wasn't being sent home with a tube of industrial-strength Savlon.

'I think we need to get you there as promptly as we can,' said Holly apologetically, picking up the phone and typing in a number by heart. 'Hi, this is Dr Holly Graham in Larkford. I need a Priority Two transfer to the RUH – an infected wound, five inches, deep, small possibility of NF from initial observation, but the wound was sustained yesterday and not treated, so—'

Holly looked up and could tell from the shocked expression on Charlotte Lansing's face that she could hear the tone of the response at the other end of the line. 'Is there someone you'd like to call to meet you there, Charlotte?' Holly asked. 'I think some company would be good, don't you?'

Charlotte shook her head. 'Henry will need to take care of things at home.' She visibly bit back tears. 'Dr Graham, what's NF?'

Holly wanted to be evasive, to let the consultant at the hospital explore this possibility with her, but from what Holly had just seen, the likelihood of necrotising fasciitis – or flesh-eating bacteria as the media liked to call it – wasn't out of the realms of possibility, especially in a filthy wound like this one.

Holly took Charlotte's hand as the clock ticked round and they waited for the paramedic team to transfer her to Bath. One of the first things she'd learned as a med student was that, if you hear hooves, think horses not zebras – the most common illnesses being by definition the most likely. But sometimes, thought Holly, you still had to be prepared for a bloody great zebra to gallop through your surgery and be open-minded enough to see it.

Either that, or they were all on such high alert for drama after the weekend's events that she was just looking for trouble. 'It's just a possibility, though, Charlotte. Better to be safe than sorry with this,' she said reassuringly, as Charlotte's grip tightened.

'So you've scared me senseless for nothing?' Charlotte said, her usually charming demeanour swamped by fear. 'This is appalling, Dr Graham. You must see that?'

Holly held her ground. 'If I didn't mention the possibility

to you, Charlotte, you'd have every right to say that you hadn't been kept informed about your treatment.' Sometimes bureaucracy was a bitch that would trip you up whichever way you turned, Holly had long since decided. Her best parameter, since the very moment she became a GP, had been to treat her patients as she would her friends, even if some of their prickly behaviour made that incredibly challenging at times.

Charlotte glowered, no longer apologetic for her part in the exacerbation of her infection.

Taffy's timing could not have been more impeccable, thought Holly, as he tapped on the door and strode into the room. 'Hello, hello. Are we getting a bulk discount on ambulance transfers this week?' he asked, his entire demeanour at odds with the tension in the room. He smiled at Charlotte and offered his arm chivalrously to help her to her feet. The expression on his face as he caught sight of the offending wound was like a caricature of shocked disgust – after all, even doctors were allowed to be squeamish. 'So I gather we're going to pop on a sterile dressing for transport and the team in Bath know you're coming?'

He looked meaningfully at Holly, clearly trying to transmit his own diagnosis without saying a word.

'It's alright, Dr Jones. You don't need to bother with tact around here. Dr Graham has already given me a dressing-down for not taking care of it properly. The way she's talking, I'll be lucky to keep the arm!' She glared at Holly, as though the whole conversation had been cleverly designed to chastise her for her flippant approach to her own health. The potential severity of her condition apparently still eluded her.

Taffy, however, was not in the loop of their conversation. 'Better to cross that bridge with the consultant, Mrs Lansing.

We'll have a much clearer picture of the degree of infection once your labs come back. It's possible a simple surgery can—'

'Surgery?' screeched Charlotte, wheeling round to glare at Holly. 'You never said anything about surgery!'

Holly had never been so grateful to see the paramedics in the hallway. Never so grateful to pass the medical baton to somebody else. It was some measure of her own anxiety this morning that she could no longer see the whole picture here. Following her instincts was one thing, alienating her patients by overreacting was something else entirely.

She genuinely had no idea in that moment whether she had just royally pissed off one of her favourite patients, or actually saved her life. The only thing she could be sure of, after Saturday's fiasco, was that she would rather be safe and unpopular, than sorry and potentially negligent.

As the ambulance pulled away, Holly leaned her head against Taffy's chest. 'I think Charlotte Lansing's pretty furious with me right now.'

He leaned down and kissed the top of her head. 'Yup. Until she talks to the consultant. Then I'm guessing she might just change her mind.'

Chapter 6

Dan clicked to the final slide of the presentation with relief. This was the very last of the fortnightly seminars and he had to confess that his enthusiasm had waned rather. With each repetition, the emotive and persuasive evidence that he and Grace put forward to their medical cohort had begun to sound somewhat pedestrian and uninspired. In light of the weekend's drama, both of them appeared to be running on empty and he was a little embarrassed that today's seminar would hardly count as his best work.

'Was that okay, do you think?' he asked Grace under his breath.

'I think I may have zoned out actually,' she replied sheepishly. 'Sorry, but this is the twenty-fifth time we've done this now.'

'Well done, you two,' said Harry Grant, bustling over to congratulate them and completely missing their rather despondent mood. 'That went extremely well, don't you think?'

Harry, their bespectacled and unlikely champion, was their like-minded mole inside the Primary Care Trust. It had been his idea to nominate The Practice as a Model Surgery the year before and, despite his senior rank, he had chosen to continue co-ordinating the programme himself. His main role these days, however, appeared to be providing a buffer between the team at The Practice and the ever-escalating demands of his own superior, in the shape of Derek Landers. Harry was what Grace liked to refer to as 'a good egg'.

'I've been getting some really fabulous feedback, you know,' Harry said happily. 'That last diagram you added to the hand-outs? The one with the statistics about staff integration in the decision-making process? Well apparently it's hopping its way around the internet, because someone from Harvard left me a voicemail last night. So you must be doing something right!'

He laughed at his own joke, such as it was, and clapped Dan on the shoulder, dropping his voice so the departing delegates wouldn't hear him. 'Now, be honest, how glad are you that this is all nearly over?'

Dan allowed him a small smile that spoke volumes. 'What on earth makes you say that, Harry? Anything to help the PCT.' He threw one arm around Harry's shoulders and gave them a relieved squeeze.

Harry grinned. 'I'd be careful what you say around here, or they'll have you volunteering for all sorts before you can blink.'

'Hmm,' said Grace with a chuckle, 'now why does *that* sound familiar?'

Harry had the decency to blush. After all, The Practice's involvement in this Model Surgery programme hadn't exactly been voluntary. 'Right then, on that note, let's get you packed up. There'll be a few loose ends to tie up, but I think we can call the educational boxes ticked, don't you?'

He followed them outside to Dan's Land Rover, chival-rously offering to carry Grace's files. She politely demurred, as Dan watched on with amusement – it was hardly an arduous load to carry two lever arch binders after all.

'I'll be in touch,' promised Harry, as they drove away.

'I'm sure he means to give us feedback, yes? Not to ask any more favours?' Grace said, as Dan deftly manoeuvred into Bristol traffic.

'I wouldn't hold your breath there, Gracie. I reckon this nomination is the gift that keeps on giving, don't you?' There was an edge to his voice, behind the smile.

Grace reached into her bag and passed him a mini Mars Bar.

They drove in comfortable silence for a mile or two, as three lanes of traffic merged into one, and they could honestly have walked faster. Abruptly, Dan signalled and pulled down a side road, swung in a three-sixty arc and joined the free-flowing traffic in the other direction.

'Worth it though,' Dan said, as though their conversation had never paused. 'Having Alice and the extra nursing clinics has been a godsend.'

'It has,' Grace agreed. 'And whether we want to admit it or not, having one less partner has put the books in a healthy position for the first time in a long time. We're even in danger of running a surplus this quarter.'

It wasn't often that they spoke of Julia Channing. Occasionally, her name would crop up in the doctors' lounge, so accustomed had they all become to her disparaging commentary on their dietary habits that nobody could eat a frosted doughnut without expecting to hear her voice. And of course, they would see her on television or in magazines from time to time, Unicef making full use of her media savvy to communicate their agenda on immunisation.

Dan nodded. 'We manage okay with three though, don't we? I mean, I even forget Alice isn't a partner at times. She's so switched-on, that girl. I just—' He hesitated. 'I just worry that she hasn't really settled in to Larkford.'

Grace nodded. 'I know what you mean, but I think some-one like Alice is a slow-grower. Once she decides to settle, she'll stick like glue, you'll see.'

'Hmm,' replied Dan. 'You might be right, but until then, I reckon she's a bit of a flight risk.'

'Not everyone is desperate to leave Larkford,' Grace said gently, knowing all too well that Dan's history with Julia was probably playing a part in his concern.

He nodded, sweeping around a roundabout and taking the exit sign for the motorway.

'Er, Dan, I'm all for avoiding the traffic, but this short cut of yours seems to be taking us in the opposite direction,' Grace said tactfully.

'Ah, about that ... ' said Dan, avoiding her inquisitive gaze and pretending to concentrate on the road with delib-erate nonchalance, 'I hope you don't mind, but I thought we deserved a little rendezvous after all our hard work.'

He glanced sideways to see the flush of unexpected pleasure on Grace's face. 'How very lovely.'

Her newly pink cheeks and the twinkle in her eye gave Dan a momentary start. The last thing he had ever intended to do was to give Grace the wrong idea, even if actually, normally, it would have been exactly the right idea, if he wasn't so focused on—

His thoughts tumbled over one another quickly, making no real sense by the time he needed to open his mouth and actually say something.

'The Air Ambulance HQ is just up here,' he began and saw her expression change almost imperceptibly. 'So, I thought we'd just pop in and have a look around. Talk to the troops, as it were – if I'm going to get involved I want to see for myself what they're dealing with, you know?'

'Of course,' said Grace with studied ease, turning to look out of the passenger window at the countryside flying by as they left the city.

'A pub lunch afterwards would be nice though, wouldn't it?' Dan offered belatedly.

'Let's just play it by ear,' said Grace, not angry, just quiet and a little withdrawn. He could sense the disappointment in her voice that his Big Idea wasn't quite what he'd seemed to be suggesting. Who the hell referred to a work meeting as a rendezvous, he thought crossly – no wonder they were talking at cross purposes.

It was only as they pulled up in the car park, the enormous aircraft hangars dwarfing them on both sides, that he realised something. Surely Grace would only be reacting this way if she had actually quite fancied the idea of skiving off work with him. He slipped out of the Land Rover with a secret smile and walked round to hold open Grace's door. 'After you,' he said.

No matter how old you were, there was still a sense of wonderment that came from peeking behind the scenes, thought Dan, as he took in the equipment and vehicles around him. The distinctive neon body of one of the helicopters caught his eye immediately, sitting silently on the tarmac, just waiting for the call.

'Can I help?' called a voice from over by the line of immaculate four-wheel-drive vehicles, and Dan turned to wave. The chap may have been decked out in the fluoro jacket of the Air Ambulance Team, but right now he seemed to be wielding a bucket and sponge rather than an oxygen mask. He strode towards them, only managing to get taller and more imposing as he approached.

'I called ahead,' Dan said, holding out a hand. 'I'm Dan Carter, from The Practice in Larkford. This is our Practice Manager, Grace Allen.'

'Chris. Chris Virtue.'

Chris's handshake was so firm that Dan began to wonder whether this man was actually cut out for the delicate procedures a paramedic needed to perform. That is, until he saw the gentleness with which he shook Grace's hand.

Ah, thought Dan instinctively, so it's like that, is it? And then he gave himself a shake; he really needed to get his head in the game.

'Come on up,' said Chris easily. 'Meet the team.' He turned as they approached the staircase up to the offices. 'We were so sorry not to be able to help on Saturday. Poor kid. Was she okay?'

'She's over at Frenchay now,' Dan replied. 'You know how it is with these head injuries. Bit of a waiting game.'

He caught Grace looking at him strangely and realised that he'd automatically slipped back into his abbreviated Army style of conversation the moment he'd met Chris. There was something about the man's demeanour that screamed ex-military and the subconscious part of Dan's brain had obviously responded.

'How long have you been with the team, Chris?' Dan asked casually.

'Just over two years, I guess. Makes a bit of a change to jinking about with the Taliban,' he said, 'but honestly, I think this job has turned out to be more harrowing.' He stopped on the stairs and turned to look at them both. 'We get more calls every day than we can possibly respond to, and we're still pulling in two thousand sorties a year.'

Pilot then, not paramedic, Dan realised.

'Cup of tea?' Chris said, switching gears without missing a beat and welcoming them into the Control Room. 'I'll get the kettle on and you can meet the team.'

It was obvious that, here, it was all hands on deck, and Chris clearly thought nothing of doing the tea run. No room for ego. Dan felt instantly at home and, if it wasn't for the fact that Grace seemed so entranced by their guide, he conceded he might even be enjoying himself.

They were certainly made to feel welcome. Pilots, paramedics, telephone operators and admin staff alike all took a moment to greet them, as Chris gave them the guided tour. He took a sip of his tea from an enormous mug bearing the ambiguous message 'In Thrust We Trust'.

'Listen, I know you spoke to one of the girls on the phone about the cutbacks, but it seems to me as though we're all being told something slightly different,' said Chris. 'The maternity unit in Rosemore just had an unscheduled audit, apparently. We've had our maintenance budget slashed. There's trouble ahead, if you ask me, even if nobody's telling *us* the full story yet.'

He looked around his team with an expression of proud concern; it was obvious that he was deeply committed to his role here and anything that jeopardised that had best beware. There was a steady hum of activity in the atmosphere, even if the crew were currently taking a moment to relax, albeit poised for action.

Dan was about to comment as such, when Chris cut him off. 'Don't say it. Preferably, don't even *think* it.' He laughed nervously. 'We're all a bit predisposed to the jinx around here.'

Even as he finished speaking, a different telephone trilled loudly into their midst and the whole team slipped into action like a well-oiled machine. It seemed like mere moments before the blades on the helicopter outside were rotating and three people in high-vis vests were running across the tarmac to jump in.

Dan and Grace stayed out of the way, watching the whole situation develop, crackling radios conveying the details of the disaster unfolding on the M5 even as the bird took flight.

'You do realise we were on that exact stretch of road half an hour ago,' whispered Grace to Dan, her eyes wide with the possibilities of what-might-have-been, as yet more details of the horrific pile-up came in by radio and telephone over the next few minutes.

A young girl with a clipboard materialised beside them. 'Chris sends his apologies, but he asked me to give you this.' She held out an information packet for fundraisers.

'Where is Chris?' asked Grace, looking around, obviously impressed by the calm and well-ordered protocols that were clicking into action without drama or panic.

The girl just pointed out of the panoramic window, at the neon bird disappearing out of sight.

'Wow,' said Grace, with more feeling than Dan thought was actually necessary.

He reached out and took the fundraising pack. 'Can I ask?' he said. 'The second helicopter? Any news on the repairs?'

The girl shook her head. 'It's been months now. And with crashes like this, with multiple casualties . . . Or at the weekend, when there was a race meeting in Bath and the Larkford Show running at the same time . . . We can only be in one place at a time.' She shrugged. 'Saying it would be useful to have it back in action is a bit of an understatement.'

Message received and understood, thought Dan, his mind already relishing the possibilities of what he might be able to achieve for this undoubtedly vital cause. Even if that meant inviting Chris Virtue into Grace's orbit. Sometimes, you had to step back from your personal desires, to look at the bigger picture.

Chapter 7

The Practice always felt strangely adrift on the days that Dan and Grace were away at HQ, sharing their pearls of wisdom. Harry Grant from their Primary Care Trust had been true to his word and the clock on these time-consuming seminars was winding down, their commitments as a Model Surgery almost fulfilled. It seemed to Holly as though Grace in particular would actually miss these sessions when they were over, much as they all liked to moan about their inconvenience. She certainly seemed to make an effort to look her best when 'on parade'.

At least with Alice on board, they still had a full complement of doctors on duty when Grace and Dan had their 'away days', even if occasionally that meant Holly got lumbered with one of Dan's somewhat misogynistic frequent fliers.

She bumped into Taffy outside the waiting room. 'Fancy taking my three o'clock?' She pulled a face. 'Rock, paper, scissors? I've got Gordon Lightly.'

Taffy laughed. 'No chance.' Gordon's reputation for being a pain in the proverbial preceded him.

'Go on,' Holly said, switching on the charm. 'There have to be some perks from sleeping with one of the partners.' She grinned. 'I'll even cook supper—'

Taffy shook his head in defeat and held out his hand, reliably a pushover whenever it came to his girlfriend. 'On the count of three then—'

Holly stared at their hands in disbelief. 'Best of three?' she offered.

Taffy leaned forward and kissed her with a smile. 'He's all yours, baby,' he said as he retrieved his own patient and left her dithering in the doorway.

Gordon Lightly scowled at her as he unwillingly followed her from Reception to her consulting room. Holly really wanted to say that, since he'd arrived for his appointment with only seconds to spare, perhaps going on the immediate offensive wasn't his brightest idea.

'Perhaps it's just better if I come back another day? Like I said, I do usually see Dr Carter and I think a man's perspective on this might be better. No offence, miss, I'm sure you're a lovely doctor, but . . . ' His voice petered out, unable to articulate his reasons.

Holly could empathise, she really could. It wasn't always easy discussing intimate issues with a doctor of the opposite sex, but they were already overbooked for the next few days, so it was her job to put him at ease, not turn him away.

She gestured to the seat beside her desk and sat down. 'Well, why don't we have a brief chat and you can outline the problem for me. And if you need any tests run, I can get those sorted and you can discuss the results with Dr Carter another day.' She was already making a mental assessment of her patient, playing the probabilities of what he had come to discuss.

Fifty or so, clearly overweight, balding.

His forehead had a sheen of perspiration, whether from

nerves or the effort of walking from the car park she couldn't tell.

Sallow skin, heavy jowls, broken spider veins on his cheeks.

This was not a man in perfect health; equally, this was not a man to whom health was a priority. The nicotine stains on his teeth were a dead giveaway that he had not, in fact, quit smoking as his file suggested.

Gordon looked so uncomfortable, though, that Holly could only surmise that they were looking at a problem in the trouser department. She'd put money on erectile dysfunction or trouble peeing, she decided.

Gordon fidgeted. 'Well, I suppose you *are* a doctor ... ' He sighed. 'Look, it's not me I've come about, it's my wife. She refuses to come, you see. She says there's nothing wrong and I should stop going on about it, but I worry, Dr Graham. She's just not herself.'

Holly had to quickly recalibrate her perceptions. Far from being the misogynist she'd pegged him as, might he in fact be a loving husband, a concerned husband at that? 'Okay,' she said. 'Well, first of all, I can't tell you anything about your wife's health without her consent, but I am only too happy to have a chat about what's concerning you and maybe a bit more information might encourage her to seek advice herself?'

Gordon grunted his approval. 'Dr Carter's known me for years. And my wife. So he'd know what I'm saying is true.'

'I'm not doubting you, Mr Lightly, but then you haven't really told me anything yet. Let's start with what's worrying you the most.'

Gordon's neck immediately flushed scarlet. 'Well, you see, I don't know how to put this but ... ' He coughed awkwardly. 'She's lost all interest in the bedroom. No sex drive at all.

Almost flinches at the very idea.' Having blurted this news out in staccato sentences, Gordon was now on a roll. 'And she doesn't want to cook, doesn't even care if the house is a mess. I think she's depressed, Dr Graham. She keeps taking long walks and watching those endless bloody box-sets in the evening. It's been like living with a different person these last few months.'

'And her health?' prompted Holly, trying to steer this consultation in a useful direction. 'Has she lost her appetite? Is she having trouble sleeping? Is she down all the time – teary, perhaps?'

He concentrated for a moment. 'She's been making lots of those vegetable smoothie things. And she's always up before I'm awake.' He frowned. 'But she's not crying all the time, Dr Graham, it's more a distracted thing – as though she's not really there.'

Holly clicked through a few screens on her computer and pulled up poor Mrs Lightly's file, angling the screen slightly so it was for her eyes only. Amanda Lightly was one of their rare patients without repeat prescriptions, ongoing health issues or indeed the odd appointment for coughs and sniffles. In terms of considering depression, though, it told her precisely nothing.

She looked at Gordon, frankly considering him a much more likely candidate. 'And how are you feeling about all this?' she asked. 'It must be difficult?'

'It *is* difficult,' he said, the surprise evident in his voice that she might appreciate that. 'Since I've taken early retirement, I'm at home all the time, you see.'

For Holly, the picture he was painting wasn't necessarily one of medical causality; in fact it seemed perfectly possible to her that poor Amanda Lightly was utterly resenting her husband's omnipresent retirement and doing her very best to look after herself in light of all the stress.

'Have you and your wife been arguing a lot, Mr Lightly?' Holly asked tentatively.

'Too right we have. She just doesn't want to see things from my point of view. When I rearranged the kitchen so it was more efficient, she told me I could, well, I'm quoting directly here, Dr Graham – told me I could cook my own fucking dinner myself then.'

'And it was about that time that she lost interest in cooking, was it?' Holly ventured.

'Are you saying that her depression is my fault?' Gordon accused. 'All these years of going out to work every day, and the minute I get some time at home, she's out that front door every chance she gets.'

Holly said nothing, hoping against hope that the penny might finally drop without her having to spell it out. This wasn't, after all, such an unusual situation. And, as Gordon dabbed at his sweaty upper lip and the rings of dark fabric under his armpits grew, she could actually empathise with the departure of Amanda's libido as well.

'I see from my screen that your wife is actually due her Well Woman check next year. Why don't I bring that forward a little and invite her in for a chat? It might help put both of your minds at rest,' she said obliquely. 'And in the meantime, while you're here—'

She had to swallow a smile at that one. Mostly it was her patients trying to cram several ailments into one tiny appointment. But the chance was just too good to miss.

'Let's get you in tip-top shape so you can enjoy your retirement – get you out on the golf course, or maybe a spot of fishing?' She plugged in the blood pressure monitor and by the time she'd finished, poor Gordon had a lot more to think about than whether Mrs Lightly was fulfilling her wifely duties.

The process of becoming a wife again herself was something Holly chose not to think about too much. In all honesty, the engagement ring on her finger was all the commitment to Taffy that she actually needed. Perhaps they could just skip the whole wedding fandango and concentrate on what was important, Holly wondered – and not for the first time – as she waited for Elsie to answer the door later that day. Holly and Taffy had a future together and that was what mattered. Certainly not whether the napkins at their wedding breakfast were oyster or ecru, which in either case just looked cream to her own, undiscerning eye.

But try telling Elsie that.

On the one hand, Holly was beyond touched at Elsie's almost maternal interest in her wedding and all its minor details; on the other, the whole thing was in danger of getting a little out of control. As evidenced by this latest get-together with The Wedding Folder.

Elsie pulled open the front door with gusto. 'There you are!' Her hot pink velour tracksuit and flushed complexion were a sure sign that her physio session had not long finished. But there was something else too; a skittish excitement that immediately had Holly on her toes.

Following Elsie through to her gorgeous kitchen, Holly noticed that the beautifully decorated binder, which had kept Elsie busy for weeks, if not months now, was open on the kitchen island, fluttering with Post-its and magazine clippings. Planning Holly and Taffy's wedding had captured Elsie's imagination and forced her to adhere to all the health advice she'd been given to try and avoid another stroke. With the launch of her book being constantly postponed, Holly couldn't help be concerned that this binder represented the only thing keeping Elsie occupied and sane of late.

'So,' Elsie began, before Holly could even say anything, clapping her hands together excitedly, 'I have news! Fabulous news! I've pulled in a few favours with Vivienne and they can squeeze you in for a fitting, if you're happy to have ready-to-wear tailored to fit. I know you don't want anything fancy – as you keep reminding me, it *is* your wedding, not mine – but short of going couture, this will be utterly wonderful. You, my darling, will look utterly wonderful.'

'About that, actually—' Holly attempted to rein Elsie in before she got even more carried away.

'And I've just gone ahead and given some thoughts to the printer. If we waited any longer, then they couldn't do the leitmotif on the invitations to match your theme.'

'We have a theme?' clarified Holly in surprise.

'Dear gods,' said Elsie, shaking her head with benevolent affection. 'I do wonder how you manage to run a household, let alone putting people's lives in your hands!' Elsie had never been one to understand the way Holly prioritised her time, and the wedding planning – or lack of it – had rather brought that into focus.

Holly flicked through the endless pages of The Wedding Folder that Elsie had compiled, insisting it was essential. As always, she was blown away by the thought, care and attention that had been invested in it.

'Let's just get on and make some decisions, *any* decisions!' Elsie chivvied her, thrown a little by Holly's lack of enthusiasm.

'Oh Elsie, you're right of course, and thank you,' said Holly, pulling her attention back to the list at the front of the folder, beautifully written in Elsie's swirling calligraphy. 'It all looks beautiful and incredibly stylish . . . You've put in so much effort to make this a day to remember, but maybe we could simplify everything a little bit, just to get the ball rolling? Think about the dress later? Yes?' Sometimes when dealing with Elsie, subtlety was not an option. It was, in fact, an over-application of tact that had led them to where they were now, with Elsie pulling in favours from British fashion designers, cinematographers and who knew what else?

Holly picked up a pen and skimmed her eyes down the extensive and highly detailed list. She deftly drew a line through doves, choir and croquembouche, only acknowledging Elsie's increasingly loud *tsk*s of disapproval with a humorously raised eyebrow. 'I thought we agreed we were going for small and intimate?' Holly queried, as she noted the seven-course tasting menu tucked underneath as a suggestion.

'Well, you could always go all Kate Winslet and have bangers'n'mash at The Kingsley Arms, but I think that would be rather a shame. For Taffy,' Elsie added pointedly, sipping at her post-workout power shake.

And this was where they hit the sticking point every time. For Holly, this was her second trip down the aisle and the big white wedding had done absolutely nothing to secure the future of *that* union. It was only Taffy's feelings on the matter that kept her moving forward, rather than booking four tickets to Florence and eloping with the twins for a simple *lo voglio*, followed by pasta and Chianti.

Elsie was nothing if not astute and immediately backed off at the expression on Holly's face, as though she were a young horse that might startle if she moved too quickly on this. It was a shame that Alice had recently introduced Elsie to Julia

Roberts' films; she'd been sleeping particularly badly since watching *Runaway Bride*.

'So,' Elsie said gently, changing tack. 'What did you two decide on your weekend away? You and Taffy must have come up with a *few* certainties on your little treehouse escapade that we can go ahead and put into action?'

'Ah,' said Holly. 'About that—' She couldn't help the adolescent smile that lit up her face, just remembering the unadulterated luxury of her night away with Taffy in that treehouse. Gorgeous bed linen and one of those claw-foot baths, not to mention their own little wood burner – she'd been gutted to leave actually. 'We got a little distracted, I'm afraid.'

Distracted barely covered it, remembered Holly contentedly. And what's more, she honestly didn't give a fig that they hadn't finalised the cars, or the flowers, or the wedding registry as instructed. The precious hours they'd spent hopping from bed to sofa, in front of the wood-burning stove, had done more for her well-being than ticking items off any arbitrary list ever could.

'I'll bet you did,' said Elsie, shaking her head with a filthy laugh, unable to remain annoyed for long. Even she could appreciate that it was probably more important for the future bride and groom to be in love than to have a personalised choral accompaniment to their vows.

'But the thing is, if you don't commit to the venue today, then they do have another couple waiting, so . . .' Elsie paused, waiting for a reaction – any reaction – to show that Holly would be devastated to learn that the swish country house hotel they had chosen was about to slip through their fingers. 'Holly,' Elsie said quietly, 'you need to confirm the booking, or there won't be a wedding. You need to tell me if you're having second thoughts.'

Holly shook her head, swallowing the wave of queasiness that followed. Was that what this was, she wondered? It was easy to assume that the stress of these last few days had provoked this reaction, but what if it was actually cold feet? What if she didn't want this wedding after all?

She blinked hard, relieved beyond measure that her subconscious was finally all but screaming in her head, tipped over the edge at the prospect of free-range doves. It wasn't the marriage she didn't want; it was this wedding. All her procrastination about flowers and menus and goblets and venues boiled down to one thing. She just didn't *want* a big fancy wedding.

'I want to marry Taffy,' Holly said simply, taking Elsie's hand affectionately. 'But this, all this grandeur, it isn't me. I'm so sorry, Elsie, but I need to talk to Taffy before we do anything else. I know this wedding is important to him, I do. And, before you say anything, I know that marriage is all about compromise. But last time around, I was the only one compromising and it made me miserable. And I'm not doing it that way again. Even for you.' She offered Elsie an apologetic smile, half expecting her to be furious after all her hard work and research.

Instead, Elsie looked proud beyond measure. She reached forward and took the hotel's booking form from Holly's fingers and tore it decisively into quarters. 'Well, okay then. Let's go back to the drawing board.' She gave a wicked smile. 'But this time, we're going to need gin.'

Holly gripped Elsie's hand tightly across the table. 'Thank you,' she said with feeling, oddly emotional with the relief. 'I really want to get it right this time – from the very beginning.'

'Well, Holly, far be it from me to give marital advice,' Elsie pulled a face, her own divorces testament to the fact that she was still learning too, 'but I firmly believe that, if you only do one thing in this new marriage of yours, then choose to be true to yourself. And look – you've already started. Without me! I honestly couldn't be more proud. Well, a little annoyed that you don't want a fancy frock, but if we gloss over that for a moment . . . And we can still make it an occasion to remember, just a little more boho-rustic-chic, yes? A little more *you*?'

Holly smiled, basking in Elsie's praise, whilst secretly noting away today's *mots justes* to add to the beautiful leather notebook beside her bed. Practice Makes Perfect: the gift from Elsie was one of her most treasured possessions and Holly delighted in keeping it 'up to date'. Its very pages were well thumbed and the entries all but memorised, Elsie's beautiful lessons in living remaining Holly's go-to bedtime reading any time she felt uncertain or in need of inspiration.

Elsie frowned for a moment. 'Leave it with me. Either way, I shall still enjoy having a little project on the go. Now everyone half-decent I know has moved into Sarandon Hall, I find myself rather adrift.'

She had a point.

Holly was actually a little annoyed at how the advent of Sarandon Hall had changed the dynamic in Larkford as a whole. The converted Grade II residence on the outskirts of Larkford had been cleverly divided into beautiful, eye-wateringly expensive apartments and was now The Place To Be for the landed gentry passing on their homes early to try and dodge inheritance tax. It wasn't enough that a particular cross-section of their own community had decamped, it was the number of ageing aristos and nouveau riche that had followed the promise of a little grandeur and delight for their retirement. The volume of red trousers and caviar being sold in Larkford had certainly doubled, just as the number of decent events and activities for their senior citizens had declined. It was one thing to be discerning and exclusive; it was quite another to be so discriminating as to cause waves of discontent.

'What's going on at Sarandon Hall that's so very fabulous then?' Holly asked, abandoning all talk of weddings and deciding to face the issue head on. It was obviously not going anywhere on its own, as Elsie had been griping about it for weeks now. First the bridge club had decamped, then the t'ai chi class. Holly couldn't help but wonder what had happened now.

'They've got a rosta of visiting professors coming in each week to talk to them about psychology, ecology, politics – there's even rumours that Sir David Attenborough is going to pop by and do a slide show!'

'Well,' said Holly, 'surely they could invite you along, if you're feeling left out?'

'I am *not* feeling left out,' Elsie protested in direct contradiction of herself. 'I just think it's rather small-minded that they haven't actually invited me along. That Cécile de Martin,' she spat in a flawless French accent. 'We all know she was plain old Sylvia Martin back in the day. A windfall inheritance and a few elocutions lessons don't make her queen, you know.'

'Elsie?' Holly asked, unable to resist a handful of the salted almonds beside her. 'Is it possible that Cécile is just stepping on your toes a little? I mean, before Sarandon Hall opened, you were rather the social centrifuge around here. But just because you haven't upped sticks and thrown in your lot over there, doesn't mean they should exclude you. Go along and join in. Be true to yourself,' she offered back with a smile.

Elsie paused for a moment. 'You are clever, Holly. I knew I should talk to you. I think I shall go and pay them all a visit. Invite myself along. Why wait? Let's find out what all the fuss is about.'

Chapter 8

The next morning, Holly was forced to stow her iPhone in her desk drawer as message after message from Elsie came in, flooding her inbox with boho-chic wedding suggestions that still stretched the definition of 'small and intimate' to its very limits but were altogether more 'Holly'. Even turned to silent though, the constant buzzing was distracting in the extreme.

'I'm so sorry, Molly, what were you saying?' Holly flushed in embarrassment, as she realised that not only had she missed whatever Molly Giles had said, but also how difficult it was for Molly to formulate her thoughts in the first place.

Molly tried to smile, to show it was no problem at all – she was a naturally sweet and caring person – but the Parkinson's made it so difficult to convey emotion. At only forty-two, Molly had been in a steady decline for the last four years and Holly could feel nothing but sympathy for this lovely lady with so much heartache on her horizon.

'I was hoping you could sign me off work for a week,' Molly said softly. She didn't elucidate her reasons and Holly waited for a moment before asking.

'Are you feeling worse, Molly? We might need to work with your consultant on this if you are.' Holly didn't like to say, didn't need to say, that with early-onset Parkinson's they could only slow the progression of the disease, but once the horse had bolted there was no getting it back in the stable.

To her surprise Molly shook her head. 'No, Dr Graham, it's not that.' She looked uncomfortable for a moment as she shifted in her seat, her face staying strangely immobile in the mask that had become her reality. 'It's my boss. He's making it so hard for me at work, I just need a little time to consider my options and he's refusing me annual leave at the moment.'

'Can he do that?' Holly asked, unclear of the motivations at play.

Molly made an attempt at a shrug, which seemed to set off a cascade of tremors along her arms and into her fingers. 'He's pushing me to resign. He knows he can't fire me, but he's been making my life hell for months now.'

Holly nodded, only too familiar with some of the more hateful ways in which Molly's boss had basically been tormenting her: from moving the staff bathroom privileges to a different floor, to embarrassing her in meetings by commenting on her tics and occasional slurring, to mocking her increasingly small and cramped handwriting by buying her a 'How To Do Joined-Up Writing' textbook as her Secret Santa gift. In Holly's opinion he sounded like an utter shit.

'Is a week actually long enough?' Holly asked, feeling rather helpless. There was so little in her medical arsenal that she could actually do to help the Molly Gileses of this world that a little fuck-it attitude often crept into her approach.

Molly laughed, or rather gurgled in a way that Holly had come to recognise as her laugh, as her symptoms had become increasingly obvious over the last year. 'Well, if you're offering, a fortnight would be nice. I need to stop pretending this is temporary and work out what to do next. It's lovely having Matthew home, but we both know that's no long-term solution. He should be off at university, not home again with me.'

'How did you get on applying for your disability?' Holly asked, wondering why Molly was still putting herself through the torture of a working week, even part-time, when it was obviously so challenging.

Molly shook her head. 'They said it wasn't so much how ill I was, but how it affected me and my daily activities. Not enough, apparently. Still, give it time.'

There was a bitter edge to her voice, and Holly could understand why. All those forms and assessments to get financial support were wildly skewed towards the obvious cases. Her patients that suffered with invisible disabilities always had a hard time proving their need. The very fact that they were able to walk into the assessment unaided meant that their very real struggles were often ignored and it made Holly's blood boil. Even Mr Peverill with his colostomy bag, and an obvious need for easy access to the disabled loo, was given constant flak by members of the public, as they assumed he was simply skipping the queue for the gents'.

As Holly filled out and signed the official sick note, she paused. 'Molly, is there *any* real support for you around here? A group? A local adviser?'

'There is, but it tends to focus on the elderly end of the scale. And to be honest, Dr Graham, I'd still rather meet my friends at the pub than go to a coffee morning at the care home.'

Holly nodded; she could understand why. After all, who would want a glimpse of their future so forcibly illustrated? 'Why don't you enjoy your thinking time then, and come back in for a chat in maybe ten days? Book a double appointment, Molly, and in the meantime, let me see what I can find by way of support. Something constructive, at least. For you and Matthew. I know Dan's already on the case, but many hands and all that. How does that sound?'

Molly dashed a small tear away from her eyelashes, unwittingly allowing her eyes to well up still further. 'Well,' she managed, 'at least I can still have a little cry when someone's kind to me. I suppose I ought to make the most of it.'

As Molly left the consulting room, her sick note clutched firmly in her hand, making slow progress as the dyskinesia threw her off balance, Holly wasn't entirely sure whether she meant the ability to produce tears, which would surely be one of the next things to go, or being shown patience and kindness, which apparently were in short supply in Molly Giles's challenging world.

She turned to her desk and made a note to research whatever support she could find for Molly and her family, doodling the words *Invisible Disability* across the page. Molly wasn't alone in Larkford and Holly was determined to make sure that she knew that. Tea and sympathy only went so far; empathy and a shared experience might make all the difference to her state of mind.

By the time Holly had updated Molly's file and seen her next five patients, she was beginning to feel the after-effects of a late night with Elsie, followed swiftly by an unconscionably early start with the twins. She looked longingly at her treatment bed for a moment, craving just a few minutes' uninterrupted slumber, before rallying herself and heading for the waiting room. 'Jemima Hallow?' she said, smothering a yawn and looking around for the local vet's petite, elfin wife.

As Jemima struggled to her feet, it was easy to see how Holly might not have recognised her. Gone were the neat

tailored trousers and the four-inch heels, to be replaced by
Birkenstocks and a soft cotton kaftan, which still strained
around her bump at the seams. 'Oh Mims,' Holly said with a
smile, holding out a hand to guide her through to some privacy in her rooms, 'you might need to give in and buy some
maternity clothes, you know.'

Mims just shook her head. 'Nope. I've told this little one
that, bearing in mind the exit strategy, he's not allowed to get
any bigger.' She sat down in the chair beside Holly's desk with
an obvious sigh of relief. Hot weather and pregnancy were
not really an ideal combination. 'Which is what I wanted to
talk about, actually—'

'Well, let's check your blood pressure before we start talking about exit strategies, shall we?' interrupted Holly lightly,
having made this rookie mistake one too many times before.
Once all the readings and measuring and dippings were done,
she swivelled her chair to face Jemima. 'Okay. All on track.
All looking good. But I have to tell you, there's plenty more
growing to come in the next couple of months. Do yourself
a favour and buy some stretchy clothes.'

Mims frowned. 'I can't believe I can actually get any
bigger.' She stroked her bump tenderly. 'This baby is going
to be the biggest chunky-monkey, isn't he?'

Even behind the affection in her words, Holly could see
her concern, although surely this was something that Mims
must have foreseen when, at barely five foot four, she had
married all six foot three of Rupert-the-vet. 'Have you given
any more thought to your birth plan?' Holly asked, easing in
gently to give Mims the opportunity to share whatever might
be uppermost in her mind.

'That's what I need to talk to you about,' Mims said,
fidgeting in her chair. Holly said nothing, waiting for the

not-uncommon request for an elective C-section, as the realities of birth suddenly began to loom large and unavoidable. Mims however continued to take her by surprise. 'Rupert and I have been dead-set on a water birth from the very beginning. I don't want that whole cycle of intervention you get in hospital and my midwife was really supportive about booking us into the centre at Rosemore. It's all midwife-led and there's just a lovely atmosphere. It's where I want to have our baby.' She stopped and placed a hand on her chest, obviously trying somewhat unsuccessfully to remain calm. After a moment she reached into her pocket and pulled out a crumpled letter and passed it across to Holly without a word. Not necessarily because she had nothing to say – the unspoken emotions in the room had certainly charged their conversation with a new and slightly uncomfortable tension – but probably because the letter spoke for itself.

The paper was already softened from repeated reading and folding, but the NHS logo was clear in the top corner. 'Thank you for your interest in Rosemore Maternity for your birth, but unfortunately—' Holly scanned the letter, before Mims began reciting it word for word.

'—due to a change in financial circumstances, the Maternity Unit at Rosemore will be closing with immediate effect and your designated centre is now Bath!' Mims made a strangled sound of restrained frustration. 'That's a good half an hour away and consultant-led: there's no guarantee of a water birth, no breast-feeding counsellor, no one-to-one midwife! What happened to my choice? And it looks like it's a foregone conclusion! Please tell me this is a mistake?' Mims asked plaintively.

Holly felt utterly blindsided. Of course there had been murmurs, rumours of audits, but nothing concrete. Perhaps they should have viewed the problems with the Air Ambulance funding as merely an opening salvo? She wondered whether Dan had gleaned anything more after his impromptu visit there. Pausing before continuing to read, she pulled open her desk drawer and sacrificed her elevenses mini-muffins to the cause, knowing only too well how hard it was to think on an empty stomach when pregnant.

Holly slowly read Mims' letter from start to finish, as Mims demolished two mini-muffins in close succession, watching Holly's expression wordlessly. 'Well, this is a joke,' Holly said in the end, tossing the letter onto the desk with the disdain it deserved. The rest of the letter went on to explain that many other birthing options in the county might not be available to them now, since they were 'late to apply'.

Jemima's face was etched with concern and helplessness and Holly floundered for a moment as to what she could actually, realistically, do. She had honestly thought that her days of political protesting were behind her. But this? She felt a wave of nausea and impotent fury wash over her.

Decisions being made with zero regard for their rural way of life, for their individual choices? She couldn't help the prescient shiver that this was not going to end well for some of her patients, but there was no point expressing this position with her patient still in the room. She took a breath to calm her own immediate feelings about the indecent speed of the closure, not to mention the secrecy – steaming rage was a fairly close approximation, but she had no intention of fanning the flames.

'You know,' said Holly calmly, 'even if Rosemore is closing, you don't need to have all the drugs and whatnot just because you're in hospital. You can still have the low-intervention birth you want, Mims. We can make sure of it.

Let me have a word with your midwife and find out what's really going on and then we can talk again. But please,' she said, her words filled with affection and concern, 'don't go worrying yourself over this – you've still got to grow that chunky-monkey in there for a bit longer, remember.'

Mims gulped down another mouthful of muffin. 'It's a cycle of intervention though, isn't it, once you're in the hospital? I heard all about it at my NCT class!'

Holly silently cursed the bloody NCT for their birth propaganda – no drugs, no formula, breast-is-best or you're failing your baby. Sure, the principles were sound, but the emotional fallout amongst the mothers for whom nature didn't oblige was terrifying to witness. She wasn't prepared to let Jemima's birth become another casualty of that idealism.

She took a gulp of her coffee and grimaced. Cold and disgusting. She glared at her mug for a moment, feeling unaccountably let down – after all, without coffee to fuel the rest of her day, that notion of a power nap was becoming less of a fantasy and more like a necessity.

Mims got to her feet. 'Let me know what you find out, won't you? Until then, I suppose I should keep looking on the bright side. After all, who knew that one night away for our anniversary would succeed where all that fertility treatment failed?' She attempted a wobbly smile. 'You want to be careful having Elsie's fertility icon on your bookshelf there, Holly. He certainly worked his magic for me and Katie House. Borneo witch-doctor two: IVF zero, isn't it now?' Holly laughed and shook her head as she saw Jemima out of the room, before sitting back down in her chair feeling utterly drained and yawning widely.

She reached for her coffee on autopilot and gagged a little at the smell, tiny pieces of her mental jigsaw rearranging themselves in her head as she did so.

Chapter 9

'Porridge, Dr Walker?' said Taffy, as he walked into the doctors' lounge for his morning break. 'Do you have to be such a cliché?'

Alice grinned as she deliberately sprinkled salt rather than sugar onto her breakfast. 'I do try,' she said, ramping up her usual soft Scottish burr to roguish proportions.

'Are you also secretly pining for a fjord?' he asked with interest.

'A loch, possibly,' Alice replied, without missing a beat at his dodgy Monty Python impression. 'And cold tap water that feels as though it's run straight from the ben. You don't get that here,' she said wistfully.

Taffy nodded. 'I know what you mean. It's the same at home.'

'Surely not,' Alice protested. 'I mean, you've some lovely *hills* in Wales, but they're no match for Ben Nevis.'

'What's the odd three hundred metres between friends anyway?' Taffy said defensively. 'Have you ever actually climbed Snowdon? Well I have, and it's not for the faint-hearted.'

Alice shook her head. 'I haven't actually, but I'll take your word for it. I'd just started Munro-bagging with my dad when he died.' A flicker of pain passed across her face at saying those words aloud. Words that she normally preferred to allude to with euphemisms. She wasn't sure what it was about Taffy's sincerity that made such evasiveness seem unnecessary, aloof even.

Taffy, to his credit, didn't push the point. 'I didn't know you knew your way around a crampon. We could do the Three Peaks Challenge, you know? Ben Nevis for you, Snowdon for me and Scafell Pike for The Practice.'

Alice paused for a moment, their easy banter suddenly changing pace. 'That's not such an entirely crazy idea, you know,' she said slowly.

'It's a little bit crazy,' Taffy countered happily. 'But entirely doable – if you think you're fit enough.'

He laid down the gauntlet with a grin and waited for her to respond.

Alice knew that he was testing her, waiting for her to bow out, but she really didn't feel like giving him the satisfaction, although chances were they were just mucking about. Even taking into account the trouble that her overconfidence might have caused of late, it was a difficult habit to break. Could she imagine keeping pace with Taffy Jones? No, not really. Was she prepared to say sod it and give it a try? Absolutely.

'I'm in if you are,' Alice said. 'And if you're up for getting sponsors, I know the charity that's helping train Coco would be only too delighted with a big fat cheque.' Alice chose not to say that the big fat cheques might buy her a little more time, before deciding on Coco's commitment to the cause, but it certainly factored in her own enthusiasm for the challenge.

Taffy rubbed at the back of his neck, his shirt collar fraying slightly and his hair tousled from an early start. Alice wondered how he found the energy some days. He was forever on the move: with the twins, or training with Dan, or hustling through the corridors at work like a mini-tornado. Watching him mainline an entire packet of Penguins gave her some idea of the sugar rush behind the scenes and a moment of jealousy assailed her.

What she would give to view food as pleasure, rather than fuel to be calibrated. What she would give to pick up a menu and order whatever the hell she liked, without totting up how much exercise she'd already done that day and compensating accordingly.

Over the last year, Taffy had become like the big brother she'd never had, teasing her, calling her out on dodgy outfits or experimental hairdos. The only thing he never mentioned was her diabetes. It was almost as though he had decided that it was a taboo subject, a step too far in their fledgling friendship. But for Alice, it was such an integral part of her life that it felt wrong to dance around the topic. She ought to have 'Love me, love my diabetes' stencilled on a mug.

In the calm before the storm of the next influx of patients, not to mention caffeine-seeking doctors, Alice tried to pluck up the nerve to ask the question that had been haunting her for days. Who better really to give her a straight answer than Taffy?

'Did I mess up? At the show on Saturday, with Jessica Hearst?' she asked, seemingly out of nowhere and rather blindsiding him, judging by his shocked reaction.

He shook his head. 'I don't think so. You did everything by the book, Alice. And I know there's been some argy-bargy with the parents—'

'That's one word for it,' Alice interrupted.

'But,' continued Taffy with a hard look, 'that doesn't mean

you did anything wrong. It's more an issue of hierarchy, I suppose.'

Alice nodded. 'With Holly and Dan on site, it should have been them, I know. But with all the chaos and the panicking . . . ' She shrugged. 'I guess I just didn't stop to think.'

'Have you been stressing about this?' Taffy looked concerned.

'A little bit. Okay, maybe a lot. But if I did anything that has consequences for Jessica . . . '

'Listen,' said Taffy, balling up his Penguin wrappers and lobbing them expertly into the bin, 'you wouldn't be a half-decent doctor if you didn't play the what-if game after an incident. Did I choose the right drug? Did I give the right advice? Was clearing the airway a priority, considering the risk of paralysis?'

'Well, that's awfully specific,' said Alice quietly.

'And a question without an answer. We all make mistakes, Alice, and at some point you will make the wrong call. The only thing we can do, as doctors, is respond to the best of our ability in that moment. And for the record, I think you did. I think it shows serious mettle, that you didn't even hesitate to put yourself forward while that pony was still going berserk.'

Alice frowned. 'What do you mean? The pony was long gone.'

Taffy paused in his pursuit of further snackage. 'The pony was freaking out all around you, Alice. That's why everyone else held back. Did you honestly not even notice it?'

'Not even a little bit,' she said, the confusion evident on her face as she mentally replayed her version of events. 'The Pony Club lady caught the pony though, yes?'

Taffy nodded. 'Charlotte Lansing? Yeah – in the end.'

'What do they say about stupid people being full of confidence, and intelligent ones full of doubts?' Alice said wryly.

Taffy laughed. 'Oh, we are both so screwed if that's true. But seriously, stop tying yourself in knots. What's done is done – learn from it and move on. Our lesson is to remember that, all evidence to the contrary, you aren't one of the partners here. Yet. It's so easy to forget and we'd be letting you down if we did. It's all this calm conviction that throws us off, you know.' He grinned and left the room, snaffling a jumbo packet of crisps from the worktop that clearly had 'Jason' written on it in permanent marker and leaving her feeling just a little bit brighter.

In the car with Jamie that evening, after yet another session at the training centre, that feeling was long gone and Alice wondered what Taffy would make of her supposed 'calm conviction' now. It was only really the presence of Jamie beside her that was keeping the tears at bay.

'For what it's worth,' said Jamie, 'I think Judith had a bloody nerve putting you on the spot in front of everyone like that. She may be the head of acquisitions over there, but that doesn't give her the right to talk to you like that. And I'm happy to tell her so.'

Alice shook her head. It was very sweet of Jamie to be so incredibly supportive, but she knew that this was her decision to make, possibly her battle to fight. At least she had this time now, as they barrelled along the motorway together, Coco at her feet in the passenger footwell and Jamie at the wheel. This time without any other calls on her focus or attention.

'I need a little longer to decide,' she said quietly, as the realisation dawned.

He glanced at her briefly, before returning his concentration to the road. The summer outbreak of caravans in the South West was only just beginning, but nevertheless slowing them down. 'We can try that, of course, but I gather they feel they've been pretty patient already. And all you're really doing is delaying the inevitable.'

It was true, thought Alice, as she wove her fingers through the long fur on Coco's head. But this was an impossible decision. A Sophie's Choice. Whatever she decided was sure to break her heart a little.

It had been months of toing and froing. Coco's visits to the medical detection training facility only serving to prove what they already knew: she was a remarkable little dog. Her skill in detecting cancer cells just from the volatiles of one tiny urine sample, hidden amongst eight on the carousel, was almost one hundred per cent accurate. But now the time was looming where Alice had to choose: did she keep Coco as her own personal diabetes assistance dog, or did she release her into the cancer detection programme so that she could help hundreds, possibly even thousands of other people?

It was no small wonder that Alice wasn't sleeping properly. If she held on to her beloved dog, she felt she was being selfish; if she let her go, she would be lost. And not just emotionally. She had come to rely on Coco to help her manage her diabetes to such a degree that she had no idea how she would cope without her. There had been a small part of Alice hoping that, at each stage of selection, Coco would fail the criteria required.

No such luck, she thought.

Coco pressed her nose into Alice's hand, her hot breath almost a kiss, and the affection clear in her deep brown eyes.

'Do you think Coco gets bored, being with me every day?' Alice asked, as Jamie signalled to overtake a carful of students with music blaring, carefree in the sunshine. 'Do you think she'd find it more fulfilling doing the detection job?'

Jamie frowned. 'Stop giving that dog human emotions. She doesn't know she's sniffing for cancer – she can't evaluate the consequences. And she has an amazing life with you.' He fell silent, manoeuvring through the traffic as he quickly changed course and pulled into the motorway services, stopping abruptly before they even reached the cluster of shops.

He unclipped his seat belt and swivelled in his seat. 'That's better. I can't have a conversation like this without seeing your face. You're a genius at hiding your emotions, Alice Walker, but I like to think I'm learning the signals.'

Alice flushed. She wasn't entirely sure that made her feel comfortable.

'Look, I can't deny that you're in a spot here. And, to be honest, part of me wishes we'd never even pursued this. But I get it, Alice. I truly do. How anyone can expect you two to part ways is beyond me. And I genuinely feel that you need to think of yourself in all this. And, if that's not enough, then your livelihood. Can you be your best self at work, if you're constantly on edge about hypos?' He shrugged. 'It's probably not for me to say, but please don't get swept up in the guilt. There's a lot of pressure on you to decide, to commit, to sacrifice for the greater good and God knows, Judith is a professional at laying it on with a shovel. But I don't see it that way. Okay?' He reached over and squeezed her hand, Coco instantly leaning in to lick him. 'I've got your back,' he said firmly.

Alice could only nod, his empathy so genuine and insightful. If only it really were that easy. How many patients had she seen at The Practice this week alone, whose lives would have been fundamentally altered by early detection?

'Thank you,' she said simply. Their friendship allowed a certain shorthand these days, the hours spent together seemingly bringing them closer together, even as Alice's decision time loomed inexorably on the horizon.

Alice sank back into her seat as Jamie rejoined the steady flow of traffic and his beloved Eighties soundtrack filled the silence. Maybe Bucks Fizz had a point, she realised, as the lyrics of their song filtered into her subconscious – the time really had come for making her mind up. One way or the other.

She closed her eyes and allowed her thoughts to drift. Maybe if she climbed the Three Peaks with Taffy, they could raise enough to train another dog, a different dog? And that was when Alice realised the extent of her problem – she didn't want just any dog, she wanted Coco. And she wasn't entirely sure that money could buy the skill in detecting cancer that Coco had so spontaneously acquired. So, even with funding on the table, somebody somewhere was going to be short-changed.

As she swallowed hard and pretended to be asleep, Coco's head heavy on her knees, she didn't see the look of concern on Jamie's face; his emotional investment in their project so obviously running far beyond the professional.

It was probably just as well.

Chapter 10

Holly glanced at her watch impatiently, hoping that today would find Lizzie in a forgiving mood for her tardiness. She'd been hovering outside Taffy's consulting room every chance she got all morning, trying to find a moment to talk, but their schedules seemed destined not to coincide. He'd come home so late last night that she'd been out for the count.

'Dan!' she called, as he strode purposefully from the front office like a caffeine-seeking missile. 'Did you get my message about Rosemore?' She jogged over to him, mentally changing gear as she did so – so many balls in the air at the moment, so little time.

He frowned. 'I can't quite believe they moved so quickly on this. I checked with Chris Virtue, and a few days ago it was just vague rumours of an audit, apparently. That letter though—' He shook his head. 'It's hardly patient-centred care, is it?'

'Thank God we'd only got a handful of people booked in there. Emily Arden's my biggest concern; she's due any day now and talking about a home birth instead. I'm seeing her later to get the lie of the land.'

'Okay,' said Dan. 'I'll do a little more reconnaissance and

we'll compare notes later.' He sighed. 'I keep waiting for someone to shout April Fool,' he confessed. 'I'm so over the politics of medicine when the people making decisions have no idea what's actually happening on the front line.'

Holly nodded. 'Information first, okay, *then* we'll panic.'

'Deal,' Dan replied, walking away and immediately tapping into his iPhone, the very figure of despondency.

Holly hovered a moment longer, but from the wisps of conversation on the other side of Taffy's door, he wasn't finishing up any time soon. She checked her watch again, as her own phone rang out loudly in the echoing hallway. She'd been waiting on tenterhooks all morning to hear the outcome of Charlotte Lansing's surgery, and her priorities shifted once again.

'Dr Graham?' came the harried voice at the end of the phone. 'Cally Lomax, the ward sister, here, returning your call. I've good news and bad news, I'm afraid. The good news is that we've got her on a targeted IV antibiotic and we've managed to halt the spread of the infection. The bad news unfortunately is the amount of tissue damage in her arm, especially the muscle. The consultant is coming back in later to assess whether we managed to achieve a clear margin with the excision of the damaged tissue or, well, whether we need to look at more dramatic intervention.'

There was an awkward pause, as both women considered what that might mean. Holly couldn't begin to imagine how the energetic horsewoman might react to even the possibility of an amputation.

'Shall I come in?' Holly offered, genuinely floored by the implications for Charlotte's way of life. 'Offer some support when you break the news? A familiar face at least?'

Cally's voice softened as she clearly recognised in Holly a

caring soul and kindred spirit. The detachment in her voice disappeared and Holly half-wondered whether the ward sister had been expecting a bollocking for not having pulled off a medical miracle.

'It might be a good idea, if it does come to that,' Cally said. 'She's really awfully traumatised. She keeps muttering about it just being a little scratch.'

Necrotising fasciitis was no joking matter and Holly had been hoping against hope that she had actually been wrong in her initial assessment. Sometimes there was just no way around it. When it was time to hit Code Red and rush a transfer to hospital, it had to be done, even if Holly knew it was traumatic for the patient. Coming here, to The Practice, sometimes lulled patients into a false sense of security about the severity of their condition.

With promises to keep each other in the loop, Holly got off the phone and checked her watch; it was becoming a nervous tic. There was little point phoning Frenchay Hospital yet again for an update on Jessica Hearst. One might say that no news was good news – after all, the consultant had promised to phone immediately there was any change, but still . . . Holly sighed – she was counting the days since the accident and couldn't pretend she hadn't been hoping for a more positive update.

She tucked her phone into her pocket and headed out to meet Lizzie, immediately reversing and taking the side exit when she saw old Mr Jarley in Reception. She wasn't sure what it was about that man, but on some subliminal level he just gave her the creeps. Although to be fair, on a logical level, it might also be that he was a pervert of the first order and had been known to flash the local joggers when he got bored. Well, that and his ever-sweaty hands, his hugely dilated pupils and his not-so-very-secret history of dallying with pharmaceuticals.

Lizzie was waiting in the Market Place in true Lizzie fashion, impatiently stylish: hip tilted, sunglasses in hair, face in the sun. She really had spent too much time working on glossy magazines, thought Holly fondly. It was only as she got closer that she realised the entire pose was a case of style over substance.

Knowing Lizzie so well was a mixed blessing at this point – with anybody else she would have just dived in and asked them how they were feeling, but Lizzie was skittish. Throughout all her issues with anxiety last year, when she'd abruptly quit her job and started to look for a career with more purpose and more flexible hours, she'd kept Holly at arm's length. It was only recently, following a lengthy course of CBT, that Lizzie had begun to open up a little, and even then, it was mainly to joke about whatever latest fad she was following to try and find her balance again.

'Sorry I'm so late. Let's grab a coffee and then we can find somewhere sunny to set up camp, shall we?' Holly held up a logoed hessian bag containing an earlier drive-by sweep of the counter at The Deli. Lizzie picked up a cardboard tray of takeout coffees from the wall behind her. 'One step ahead of you. But do we have to have our lunch in a bag advertising thrush medication?'

Holly looked down, so readily bombarded with promotional bits and bobs as to have become oblivious to their messages. 'Could be worse,' she said with a grin. 'I was given one the other day with a floppy willy looking sad on the side. Now *that* would have been a downer over lunch!'

They walked in easy silence for a moment, navigating

their way around a swathe of yummy mummies and their practically platinum-plated pushchairs. Holly knew that she often harboured uncharitable thoughts about these women who seemed to have nothing but time and cold hard cash on their hands, but the reality was that some of them were really nice people who just happened to have won life's lottery, or worked for it, or both.

As Davina Davis ran over her foot without so much as an apology, Holly mentally corrected that statement: some of them also happened to be absolute bitches and, when she became aware of the appraising looks they were shooting at Lizzie, not to mention the whispered comments that followed, Holly was about to lose her rag.

Except that Lizzie – always on parade, never knowingly underdressed – didn't seem to have noticed a thing. 'Do I smell like roast chicken?' she asked instead, apropos of nothing, as they settled on a sunlit bench in the park.

Holly leaned in and lifted the soft cashmere of her silver-grey wrap to tentatively sniff. 'Maybe not chicken per se, but—' She closed her eyes and inhaled. 'Roast potatoes?'

Lizzie shook her head. 'Well that's another idea down the pan. My masseuse reckons burning sage in the house will give me clarity and calm. But I think it's now in the very fibre of my clothes.'

'But did it work?' asked Holly, walking the line as an intrigued cynic.

'Kind of, but now I'm just anxious about smelling like a Sunday roast instead,' Lizzie replied in an easy-come-easy-go spacey fashion that suggested she hadn't quite given up on her traditional prescriptions either.

'Although,' she leaned in and gave an impish smile as she pressed a business card into Holly's hand as though it were contraband, 'you *have* to see my reflexology guy. I'm telling you, the things he can do with his fingers . . .'

Holly blinked, thrown a little by Lizzie's heartfelt endorsement. 'To your feet?' she clarified, unwrapping a packet of salami for grazing.

Lizzie's face lit up as she laughed and Holly couldn't help feeling a small swell of relief – obviously she wanted to hear Lizzie's news, but she also needed a little friendship herself today and, increasingly of late, that was only really on offer if Lizzie happened to be on good form.

Lizzie took a swig of her coffee and looked from side to side as though imparting state secrets. 'I have to tell you that it hasn't helped with the panic attacks one tiny little bit, but I have discovered a new erogenous zone that I never knew existed. Seriously – I'm forty-one and I just found out that feet are sexy!' She wiggled her beautifully pedicured toes in their fancy new sandals delightedly.

'Is that?' Holly bent down to look closer. 'Lizzie, do you have Kermit the Frog tattooed on your ankle?'

Lizzie looked smug. 'I do. He reminds me to moisturise. If I forget, he starts looking a little bit, well, toady. And nobody wants that.'

'Indeed,' replied Holly drily. 'I actually wanted to ask you something—'

'Is it about Eric?' Lizzie interrupted. 'Because I have to tell you, he's developed rather a fondness for joining in my yoga practice.'

'Please tell me there are photos,' Holly said, laughing at the expression on her face and the mental picture of their exuberant labradoodle striking a pose.

Lizzie gave her a sideways look. 'He *has* to have the snip, Holls, no matter how much Taffy defends his honour. The merest prospect of Downward-Facing Dog gets him all unnecessary.' She grinned. 'It took Elsie's poor physio-chap quite unawares the other day when we had a joint session.'

'Oh my God!' exclaimed Holly, knowing only too well that they had both stuck their heads in the sand about Eric's increasingly hormonal behaviour. 'I'll call Rupert and book him in. And maybe you and Elsie need a small chat about boundaries with your health professionals while we're at it?'

She reached for a slice of Brie, before hesitating with her hand in mid-air. 'Actually, it wasn't so much Eric's fertility I wanted to talk to you about,' Holly said tentatively after a moment.

Lizzie looked up instantly. 'Are you thinking of trying for a baby?'

Holly shook her head, unable to disguise her excitement and apprehension a moment longer. 'I think there's a tiny chance that ship may have sailed.' She held her breath slightly; Lizzie's reaction to even the possibility was unpredictable at best and she wanted – no, strike that, she *needed* – her best friend to be on board before she even felt brave enough to pee on a stick.

'Bloody hell!' Lizzie cried, pulling Holly into a smothering hug. 'Are you excited? Are you throwing up? What does Taffy think? Argh! You're going to get SO fat.' She stopped dead as the thought occurred to her, 'Oh Holly, what if it's twins again?' She fell about laughing, apologising even as she did so, but seemingly unable to stop. When she eventually caught her breath, she clasped Holly's hand tightly. 'Well that would certainly put my issues into perspective!'

Holly shook her head, relieved, if not a little startled, by Lizzie's overdramatic reaction. 'Nah, not this time. This time feels ... Different.' She laid her hand on the gentle swell of her stomach that she had previously ascribed to stress-eating Hobnobs, until the thought had leapt into her mind fully formed, in a moment of perfect serendipity the day before: the smell of coffee no longer alluring but nauseating; their spontaneous night in the treehouse; not to mention the little fat Bornean icon sitting on her bookshelf ... 'Besides,' she clarified, 'lightning doesn't strike twice and I'm using a different recipe these days.'

Lizzie shook her head. 'I can't believe it. Seriously, what did Taffy say?'

'Well, I haven't told him yet,' Holly confessed guiltily. 'I thought we should take the test together and I was already asleep when he got in late last night and I keep missing him this morning ...'

'You mean you haven't even taken the test yet?' Lizzie said, her whole demeanour dropping like a pebble. 'You're basing this solely on the fact that coffee tastes a bit funny at the moment?'

'Pretty much,' admitted Holly with a nervous laugh. 'Mad, isn't it?'

'Er, yes.'

'No, you daft muppet, I mean – once you know, you know, right?' She stuck her shoulders back to illustrate her point. 'Once you *see*—'

'Oh my God,' said Lizzie, 'your boobs are enormous. Hobnobs can't do *that*,' she said firmly, as though that settled the matter once and for all, and peeing on a stick was now simply a formality.

Holly grinned. 'I wanted to tell you first,' she said quietly, 'just in case it's a false alarm. Boys don't really understand.'

Lizzie nodded, only too familiar with the exhilarating rollercoaster of excitements and disappointments that had accompanied the conception and birth of her own three children.

'Ah, but then Taffy Jones is not your regular "boy", now is he?' She reached out for yet another hug. 'Whatever the outcome, I'm so thrilled for you. Even if you're not pregnant right now, I only need to look at your face to see that it's something you really want. And I'm not convinced you knew that before.'

Holly wiped away a little tear; Lizzie on a good day always knew exactly what to say. 'I can't put my finger on why this feels so different to last time.'

'Oh that's easy,' Lizzie said flippantly. '*This* time you're happy. *This* time, the father of your baby will be Taffy Jones. If not today, then one day, yes?' She swallowed for a moment, as a flurry of emotion flitted across her face. 'You two are going to have properly beautiful babies, one at a time, the way God intended, and I intend to spoil them rotten.' She reached across and pinched the last of the Brie. 'And by the way, you have no idea how much it means that you told me first.' She discreetly wiped away a rogue tear. 'Even if it was just-in-case.'

Chapter 11

Holly sat at the kitchen table, savouring a moment of silence and sipping peppermint tea. It was amazing how much Holly was prepared to let slide when she felt quite so excitable and distracted herself and the twins had finally worn themselves out after a particularly passionate pillow fight. All she wanted now was Taffy home. The need to share her suspicions was almost overwhelming and she'd had to bite her tongue not to blurt anything out at work all afternoon. The magnitude of her secret knowledge bubbled away inside her and she fidgeted impatiently.

She looked up as Taffy came in, quietly for once, having spotted that all the lights were off upstairs. It had taken him a while to get used to the shadow hour, where the difference between a peaceful evening with Holly and an unruly chaos with the twins might be as simple as slamming the front door just as they were drifting off to sleep. She smiled. 'Hello, stranger. Don't jinx it, but I think they're asleep.'

He dumped his bag on a kitchen chair and wrapped his arms around Holly's shoulders, his chin resting on her head. 'God, I've missed you. There just hasn't been a moment, has there?' He reached forward and leafed through the diary in front of Holly on the kitchen table. 'Are you still trying to squeeze in a quick elopement, before Elsie hires the London Symphony?' He pulled up a chair beside her and grinned. 'I do love that woman, but she doesn't make things easy, does she?'

Holly didn't reply, the wedding so much in the periphery of her thoughts as to be almost irrelevant at that moment. She leaned forward and kissed Taffy lightly on the lips, savouring the feel of him and his breath against her cheek as he pulled her into his arms. 'Taffs,' she murmured, 'you know our little treehouse escape?'

'I still think we should have just stayed there and never come home,' he replied with a slow, soft smile that meant his thoughts were heading in only one direction.

'The thing is—' Holly paused, suddenly, genuinely, with no idea how best to float the idea. 'Well—' She slid the diary across the table towards him. 'I think I might be pregnant.'

'Are you serious?' breathed Taffy, his face wreathed in smiles and leaping to his feet in a burst of excitable energy. 'You little beauty!' He crouched down beside her and clasped both her hands in his, his eyes flickering over her face to check that they were both on the same song sheet. 'And are you okay with this?'

Holly nodded, suddenly choked up by his emotional reaction. 'I haven't taken the test yet, but I feel—'

'When you know, you know, right?' he interrupted.

'That's exactly what I said!' Holly exclaimed.

Taffy, to his credit, didn't even blink. 'To Lizzie?' he clarified, well used to the other Significant Other in his fiancée's life. 'I'm surprised she didn't make you take the test there and then!'

'Well, we were in the park—'

'Enough jibber-jabber, woman; go pee on that stick. Don't leave me in suspenders. I might be about to become a daddy.'

She grinned. 'You do know I have to cook it for a bit longer, yes?' she said happily. 'I believe nine months is traditional.' She stood up and opened her bag, pulling out a generic stick she'd snaffled from work.

Taffy frowned. 'Shouldn't I go and buy some of those fancy ones they advertise on the telly?'

'Only the best for your baby?' Holly teased gently. 'Look, in all honesty, this is fairly black and white – pregnant or not – it's not really a question of degree, is it?'

He followed her to the downstairs loo, bouncing on the balls of his feet with sheer enthusiasm, and would probably have followed her inside but for the stern look she gave him as she pushed the door closed. Taffy started doing calculations on his fingers. 'So, if we were at the treehouse five weeks ago . . . You would be due . . .'

'Stop it,' echoed Holly's voice through the wooden door. 'I can't pee and do maths at the same time.'

Taffy snorted with laughter. 'Do you need me to whistle? Apparently it makes horses pee, if you whistle.'

'Are you calling me a horse?' Holly protested. 'Now shut up, I need to concentrate.' Holly was discovering that it actually took quite a lot of concentration to pee when she didn't need to, especially on a stick that might have such transformative powers.

There was a gentle thud as Taffy sat down outside, his back against the door. 'Holly?' he whispered. 'Even if you're not pregnant today, I think that's something we should work on, don't you?' His voice was muffled and the occasional sniff gave him away, ever the softie that he was.

She emerged from the room a few moments later, flustered

and excitable. 'It might still be nothing.' She wasn't sure whom she was soothing with that sentiment – it was obvious that both of them were hoping for the same result.

Taffy nodded supportively, but unable to conceal the light that was dancing in his eyes. 'It might indeed. You're right. Early days and all that.' He paused, unable to resist. 'But then again, you have had that little bronze fertility icon in your office for a bit and Rupert Hallow says that—' He held up his hand and stopped himself as they both stared at the little white stick.

Holly's gasp when the little blue cross appeared was still one of absolute surprise. 'How?' she managed.

Taffy grinned, his eyes welling up. 'Well, when a man and a woman love each other very much …' She walloped him on the arm and gave a nervous laugh.

Holly clasped his hands and looked at him, her face a picture of tenderness. 'We're going to have a baby, Taffs.'

'Together, from the very beginning,' said Taffy. 'This is the most amazing news I have ever—' He sniffed. 'I love you, Holly Graham. You do know that, don't you?'

She kissed him and allowed herself to be swept up in his embrace, even as he held her a little more tenderly than normal, even as she could feel his heart racing against her chest. 'I love you too,' she murmured into his hair as he turned his attention to the side of her neck.

He paused for a moment and pulled away. 'And you feel okay? Not sick or tired or anything?' He looked guilty for a moment. 'Sorry, should probably have asked that sooner.'

Holly shook her head. 'I'm fine. I mean, I've been really queasy but I thought it was the stress at work—'

'And the Hobnobs,' Taffy countered. 'You have been eating an awful lot of Hobnobs.'

Holly shook her head. 'You rotter. That was to replace the coffee – you know, instant energy.'

Taffy looked worried for a moment. 'I've never met caffeine-free Holly before. Should I be afraid?' He leaned in and kissed her again, seemingly unable to resist. 'We're having a baby, Holls,' he echoed her words. 'I can't believe I get to do this with you.'

Holly grinned. 'I can't believe I didn't notice straight away. We're doctors! You'd think one of us might have realised.'

Taffy shrugged. 'I wouldn't have it any other way. Sitting outside that door just now, all I could think was how perfect this would be—' He pulled her into his arms and kissed her thoroughly once again, dropping his voice intimately. 'You know, although we have worked out what caused this, we should probably re-enact things, just to be sure.' He kissed the sensitive side of Holly's neck once more and she shivered with delight.

The knock at the door startled both of them and they froze like randy teenagers caught in the act.

Holly clapped her hand over her mouth as a thought occurred to her. 'Oh God, Elsie! The wedding!'

Taffy stilled. 'More to the point, who's going to tell her?'

They stood on the doorstep, Holly thoroughly flustered and Taffy looking sheepish. 'You forgot I was coming, didn't you?' said Elsie, shaking her head in amused disbelief as she thrust The Wedding Folder into Holly's hands. 'And I bet you still haven't made a single decision, have you?' She looked around the chaos of their kitchen. 'Or supper, by the looks of it!'

She turned and gave Holly an assessing glance, as though she knew something was up but couldn't quite put her finger on what it was.

Seeing the kitchen through Elsie's eyes, Holly felt an uncomfortable tug of embarrassment. 'I guess we should tidy up the carnage before the cleaner comes.'

Taffy frowned; he was new to the concept of a cleaner, but he was pretty sure it was bonkers to tidy up *before* they came.

'I'm not chastising you, darling girl,' said Elsie, slightly affronted by the very notion. 'I was merely about to suggest that we adjourn to the pub and let Teddy Kingsley do all the heavy lifting in the kitchen.'

Holly's gaze flickered automatically upwards to where the twins lay sleeping.

'Ah,' said Elsie, pressing her hand to her chest in apology, '*la vie domestique*, of course.' She fumbled in her fuchsia Mulberry tote, emerging with a crumpled wad of cash. 'Maybe, Taffy, you'd do the honours and pick up a little something instead?'

'You don't need to pay for supper, Elsie,' Taffy protested. 'Tonight's on me. And—' He reached out and took Holly's hand before she could lose her nerve. 'I'll get some fizz as well. We're celebrating!'

Elsie clapped her hands together in delight. 'We have a plan? Oh thank God for that!'

Holly grinned, as always buoyed by Elsie's infectious enthusiasm for everything. 'We do. We have a plan. But I have to tell you, Elsie, it doesn't involve the wedding.' With Taffy's arm around her shoulders and one hand settled automatically on her stomach, it didn't take much for the penny to drop for Elsie even before the words were out of Holly's mouth. 'I'm pregnant. We're having a baby!'

Elsie, to her credit, barely missed a beat. 'Well, isn't that just the best news! Of course we must celebrate! You clever, clever girl.'

Taffy cleared his throat and Elsie's laughter rolled out across the room. 'And you're a very clever boy too. A little sip of champagne is probably just what the doctor ordered, no?'

She fluttered around, planting kisses on their cheeks. 'It must have been a sign, you know, because when the new Tiffany brochure arrived yesterday, there were all these darling little bracelets and christening cups – I do hope you'll let me be Godmother?'

'Godmother ... Grandmother ... pick your role!' said Holly, so relieved that her news had been so gleefully received all round, she was feeling a little demob-happy and dizzy.

'Although, I assume we'll be looking at a shotgun wedding now?' Elsie suggested, tilting her head to one side to appraise Holly's silhouette. 'If you opt for an empire-line dress you've still got all the time in the world.'

Holly looked at Taffy for support; this was probably a conversation they should have had before Elsie arrived. 'We're not sure just yet,' she hedged, unwilling to mar this special evening with logistics. 'This is breaking news for us too.'

Elsie looked from one to the other as though waiting for the punchline. 'Are you saying you might *not* get married?' she clarified slowly. 'Not even a shotgun wedding? I've already done all the hard work and I was so looking forward to it.'

'How about we organise a scan to get some proper dates and then we'll see,' Holly suggested. 'But I'd quite like to enjoy it too and if I'm throwing up every five minutes ...'

'We could have an evening ceremony,' Elsie persisted gently.

'Didn't somebody mention champagne?' Holly said, deftly sidestepping the issue. 'And then we'll need to talk names. Any gorgeous middle names you don't mind us stealing, Elsie?'

Taffy gave Holly a wink, impressed at how neatly she'd diffused the situation, albeit temporarily. He surreptitiously gathered together The Wedding Folder, along with the newspapers scattered across the table, to clear some space. 'Right, I'm off to get supper – any cravings, ladies? Any little desires?' He held Holly's gaze for a moment, an unspoken conversation across the room, all their love and excitement channelled into a single look, even as Elsie fished out her address book and started reeling off names of her favourite celebrities for consideration.

Chapter 12

'I can't sleep,' whispered Taffy in the darkness. 'I'm too excited.'

Holly reached out and laid her hand on his bare chest, loving the way he always wore his emotions on his metaphorical sleeve. 'Do you think I ought to check again, before we get carried away?' Holly replied, her own thoughts clearly running at a slightly more tentative tangent.

His laugh rumbled quietly through her fingers. 'I think the third test was probably the clincher, don't you?'

It was true – Elsie insistence that they be 'absolutely sure' before she was prepared to concede that a change of plans might be in order had become a farcical series of hilarious trips to the bathroom, Holly being 'topped up' with mineral water by the gallon in between.

'Maybe it won't feel properly real until we see the scan,' Holly suggested, longing for her own rollercoaster of emotions to find a settling point. In her mind, hearing the fluttering, butterfly heartbeat seemed a likely candidate to be that moment.

'Would it be really poor form to pull a few strings and do it early, not wait?' Taffy said hesitantly, knowing only too well how Holly felt about taking advantage of their position for personal gain.

She laughed. 'Don't think I haven't considered it, but with all the recent cutbacks, I'd say that might be taking our impatience a little too far.'

Holly yawned and stretched out – or at least, she tried to.

Their enormous king-sized bed was currently also home to two sleeping twins in gingham pyjamas, complete with a variety of much-loved teddy bears, and a snoring labradoodle. Every night, they were tucked in sweetly into their own beds, Eric's own fondness for a teddy and a bedtime story meaning that his dog bed had now been transplanted into the twins' bedroom anyway. But every night, like clockwork, at around 2 a.m. there would be the patter of tiny feet and paws, and the duvet was no longer their own.

'At least the boys curl up sweetly like dormice,' Holly whispered to Taffy, gently extracting Eric's paw from her armpit, where he'd made a land grab the moment she moved. He grumbled in his sleep at being disturbed, lying diagonally, woven between all four of them; it was a wonder he got any sleep at all.

Taffy caught Holly's hand, pulling it to his lips and kissing her palm tenderly. 'And you're quite sure we've got space for another one in the mix?' he whispered, his voice bubbling with laughter, as though for him that was never in doubt.

'Ooh, are we getting another doggy?' said Tom suddenly into the darkness, making them both jump. 'Ben, wake up!' he hissed. 'They're talking about puppies . . .'

'Puppies?' said Ben, going from deep slumber to bouncing excitement in mere seconds. 'Can I choose? Can it sleep on my bed? Do we have to share this one too?'

'Um—' managed Holly, struggling to keep pace with the barrage of urgent questions that Tom's merest mention of a puppy had provoked from his brother.

'What about if we didn't have a puppy, but maybe someone else to join our family?' Taffy said, testing the water, before Holly could elbow him to stop.

She had no idea how best to tell the twins about the baby, but she was pretty sure it was a good idea to check that all was well with the pregnancy before she got their hopes up.

'Like a kitten?' said Tom suspiciously.

'Erm—' said Taffy, having backed himself into a corner. He needn't have worried.

'Or a little brother?' suggested Ben, ever the more sensitive, tuned-in of the two.

'Well—' began Holly, always a believer in honestly answering whatever questions they threw at her, even if their timing wasn't always the best.

'Oh, no,' cut in Tom, 'we'd *much* rather have a puppy! Wouldn't we, Ben? Babies don't really *do* anything for ages . . .' he informed Holly and Taffy, as though he were the authority on this topic. 'You can play with a puppy straight away.'

'But puppies can't talk, silly. Babies can. Once you teach them,' Ben replied earnestly. 'I'd much rather have something that can talk.'

'Like the Major's parrot?' Tom said, clearly puzzled by his brother's enthusiasm for a tiny human.

'Too flappy,' dismissed Ben instantly.

Holly heard Taffy trying to disguise his laughter in the dark, shoving his fist into his mouth at the boys' outspoken yet logical opinions. Eric yawned and sat up abruptly, obviously annoyed by all their talking. He made a huge silhouette looming in the middle of the bed, even in the darkness.

'Well,' said Holly easily, 'I'm not making any promises; I think this bed is pretty full at the moment anyway. Maybe, before we even think about another living soul in this house, we ought to practise sleeping in our own beds? Maybe, that's something we could work on?'

The mattress twanged as Ben and Tom both bolted for the door at the same time, Eric following hot on their heels.

'You're rather good at this parenting lark,' said Taffy in admiration.

Holly just yawned. 'I have my moments. That was probably the one for the whole week, by the way – I hope you made the most of it?' she said, contentedly snuggling into the duvet.

'There's actually something else I'd rather make the most of,' said Taffy suggestively, patting their suddenly empty bed.

'Hmm, good idea,' murmured Holly sleepily, stretching out like a starfish in relief. 'If we go to sleep now, we can still have a solid six hours.' She wriggled her toes happily, enjoying the space to spread out.

'The start of things to come,' said Taffy, accepting defeat to his advances graciously and with a smile in his voice.

'I love you,' mumbled Holly, rolling onto her side and tucking herself in neatly beside him. All the space in the world, and it turned out she still wanted to fall asleep with her head on his chest.

'And it's a definite no on the parrot, then?' Taffy clarified, as her breathing grew deeper and she nodded off to sleep.

'We're all out of bacon,' said Holly with a grin in response to Taffy's questioning look, as she flipped five pounds' worth of Parma ham from The Deli in a frying pan the next morning.

'How very middle-class,' he said, wrapping his arms around her waist as she stood at the stove, her hunger that morning almost legendary in its intensity.

She leaned back and turned to kiss his unshaven cheek. 'This is very fancy ham from Italy, I shall have you know.

Surely it qualifies as an upper-class breakfast? Parma ham on brioche? The ultimate bacon sandwich.'

'Nah, if it was an upper-class breakfast, you'd have some-one to cook it for you, wouldn't you?' Taffy teased her.

'You're absolutely right,' Holly replied, kissing him again to distract him, as she placed the spatula in his hand and slipped away from the stove. 'Nice and crispy, please, Taffs. I've been craving this for hours.'

She had thought that wearing Taffy's engagement ring had shifted the dynamic of their relationship, both of them committing to the long term and to raising the twins together, but somehow, discovering she was carrying his baby had elevated their intimacy to a whole new level – and not even necessarily of the naked variety. The ease and adoration between them in the kitchen that morning made Holly's heart sing. The very idea of spending the rest of her life bantering with Taffy, raising not two, but three children together? It was as though all her hopes were actually becoming her realities.

She glanced over at the kitchen table, covered as always with various craft projects that the twins had on the go. She noticed with a smile that they'd already been cutting out pic-tures of puppies and sticking them onto a 'mood board' just as Lizzie had taught them – 'Never go into a pitch without a clear idea of what you're asking for.' It was wisdom the boys now used to frequent effect – their as yet unsuccessful Xbox pitch still a work in progress, and stuck on the fridge door to make Holly smile.

Taffy flipped the Parma ham expertly onto Holly's toasted brioche and presented it with a flourish. 'Will there be any-thing else, m'lady?'

'Ooh, I'm sure I can think of one or two things . . .' Holly answered, her libido fighting her ravenous hunger for supremacy, as he leaned in and kissed her thoroughly, leaving her utterly off balance and aroused.

'Maybe we could just—' she began, before the kitchen door was flung open and the twins and Eric barrelled into the room.

'Ooh, bacon!' said Ben excitedly, turning a suspicious gaze upon his mother. 'And you said we'd run out!'

Orange juice, coffee, toast and yoghurt were soon dotted all over the table, as Eric carried his now-empty bowl plaintively around to each of them in turn, imploring for a refill.

'Can I have some eggs?' asked Tom, climbing onto a chair to reach across and snag the last brioche bun.

'No problem,' Taffy said, taking pity on Holly who was finally getting a look-in with her fancy sandwich. 'Boiled, fried, scrambled?'

Tom looked at him strangely. 'For the Egg and Spoon Race. We're practising for sports day.'

Taffy looked blank for a moment until Holly managed to swallow. 'Sounds like hard-boiled might be a less messy option.'

The twins scattered from the table to search out pillow cases for Sack Race practice and unhooked the curtain swags for impromptu skipping ropes, casting expectant glances at their mother occasionally, as though waiting for her to intervene.

'Is this okay, Mum?' Tom asked eventually, unable to believe his luck.

'Looks brilliant,' replied Holly absent-mindedly, chewing her sandwich and clearly away with the pixies.

Taffy stepped forward and plucked Holly's favourite necklace from Tom's hands. 'Maybe hold fire on the Treasure Hunt until I can help you later?'

Tom nodded, the memory of losing Elsie's diamond ear-rings still fresh in all their minds. Obviously they'd turn up one day, it was just that Tom's abilities to find the perfect hiding spots were second to none; his skill at remembering them, on the other hand, still needed a little finesse.

'Do you think we could set up a support group at The Practice?' Holly mused, once the boys had scarpered outside with their sports day practice paraphernalia. 'I mean, as a regular thing? We could offer the doctors' lounge as a private and comfy place to meet, couldn't we?' She looked up at Taffy for his response.

'Help me out, Holls. What are we supporting now?'

'Oh, yes, sorry. I've just been thinking about Molly Giles. I know she's not the only one who needs a little camaraderie. These invisible disabilities are so insidious and mostly they're affecting our younger patients too. Could we look into offering them something informal – probably not even condition-specific – just, well, you know? A friendly gathering to show them they're not alone? There's no way I'm sending Molly to the Parkinson's group at the old people's home!'

Taffy nodded. 'Sounds like a perfect project for the Health in the Community Scheme, don't you think? And it would hardly cost a bean. Unless you wanted a trained counsellor to oversee it?'

'I don't know,' Holly said. 'I just started thinking how lovely it is to feel supported, to be surrounded by people who are on the same song sheet—'

'You got all that from a bacon sandwich?' Taffy teased her.

Holly bit her lip and looked at him lovingly. 'I got all that from living with you.'

'Well, I am rather inspirational,' he said with a grin. 'Even if you're the only one who thinks so. But, seriously, Holls, this is a great idea, if you've actually got the time and the resources to make it happen.'

Holly shook her head. 'Well, obviously, I've got neither. But since when have we ever let that stop us?'

Taffy pinched the last morsel of her 'bacon' and grinned. 'With you, Holly, I wouldn't have expected anything less.'

Chapter 13

The familiar chirrup of an incoming Skype call startled Alice in the dark that evening. She fumbled around for her iPhone, cursing herself for not switching to 'offline' as soon as she'd started to feel sleepy. Even Coco groaned in protest.

'Hello?' Alice said, all irritation disappearing the moment she saw the tiny circular photograph of a Smurf and tapping once to accept the call.

'Ooh sorry, did I wake you?' said Tilly without any obvious remorse, as her beaming face filled the screen. 'It's just we've been waiting for days to get the internet back up and running and it was a pretty safe bet you'd be online.'

Alice smiled. 'Good to see your priorities are as spot on as always.'

'Well, it's not as though I can pop an order through to Ocado now, is it?' She panned her device around behind her so that Alice could get a full view of the jungle that surrounded her best friend. Her remote location probably explained her disproportionate excitement at the restoration of her Wi-Fi signal.

'Are you still living on custard creams?' Alice asked, trying to take in as much as she could from the wildly swinging images.

'Well, in grocery news, I have managed to stomach a roast plantain without wanting to hurl, but I'm light years away from creepy-crawlies.'

As Tilly, Alice's social conscience and all-round Good Egg, travelled the globe, Alice had learned over the years never to complain about her own limited diet. Tilly's cat would always be blacker, but she was just too nice to actually point it out. Alice was also aware that her constant Tales of Tilly and her questing for social and medical equality seemed to have a habit of making her colleagues feel a little staid and underachieving. Sometimes there really could be too much of a good thing, apparently. Not that she really empathised with that herself; if it was up to her, she'd have Tilly on speed dial every single day for a shot in the arm of her zealous commitment and boundless positivity.

'So, what's new in Stepford?' Tilly asked, sipping the local version of Coca-Cola and grimacing at the sweetness. Still, it was better than the local water.

'Larkford,' corrected Alice with a grin. 'And you have to stop calling it that! It's actually really very sweet.'

'Cannot compute,' Tilly said, pulling her khaki jacket collar up higher as a large indeterminate insect buzzed her repeatedly. 'Surely you'd be happier with a *little* nitty-gritty in your life? Are you really ready to be living in a watercolour painting?'

Alice shrugged. 'I tried Bristol. And look how that turned out?'

Tilly scowled. 'But that's like saying, I dated one bloke and he wasn't The One, so I'll give up and join a convent!'

'The thought had occurred to me,' Alice muttered, pulling the duvet up to her chin and suffering Coco's indignant groans at her audacity.

'So how *is* the love life?' Tilly asked, biting into a power bar that looked like compost. Although the setting had long since changed, their conversational habits hadn't really evolved from their student house-share, that and Tilly's habit of making every coffee 'Irish'.

Alice yawned and snuggled in further. 'Well, there's a nice guy in Norfolk? He lives on a houseboat and has three dogs. He's quite fit actually, if you ignore the funny quilted waistcoat he wears.'

'Norfolk-ing chance,' joked Tilly. 'And is he just gorgeous? If you ignore the contraceptive waistcoat?'

Alice paused, unwilling to hear Tilly's inevitable response. 'Well, we haven't exactly met yet. It's just chatting, you know, online. But he has insomnia, so he's often awake when I am.'

'Well, I suppose that's something in his favour. But is this what you're reduced to? Night owls and insomniacs?'

Alice smiled. 'Well, there's always Australians. There's a lovely guy who lives by the beach in Sydney and we have fabulous chats. He's funny. And he surfs.'

Tilly's laugh crackled through their Skype connection and the picture wavered as her iPad jostled. 'Nice to see you're still keeping it local.' She wiped another bug from her cheek and paused. 'Is there nobody in Stepford you like? A nice hunky distraction? I keep telling you to get a hobby—'

'A boyfriend is not a hobby!' Alice protested.

Tilly just tilted her head. 'Then there's a chance that you've been doing it wrong,' she said. 'My current dating pool, by the way, comprises three nuns, two public school boys who seem to prefer each other and Juan Carlos, our "fixer", who is sixty-three, sprightly, but full of filthy intentions, if you get what I mean.' She sighed. 'What I wouldn't give for a sturdy Cotswold farmer to show me his outbuildings about now—'

'Til-ly!' laughed Alice, making Coco jump. 'It can't be that bad? Surely?'

Tilly grinned. 'Nah. I'll live. I'm moving on next week anyway. Over to Belize where there'll be lots of young enthusiastic chaps on their gap year. Come to Mummy!'

'You know it's Doctors Without Borders, not without boundaries, don't you?' Alice countered. 'You, my friend, are turning into a perv!'

'Nun!'

'Dirty old woman—'

'Less of the old, thank you very much.' Tilly chomped on the ghastly power bar for a second. 'How are you anyway?'

'I'm okay,' replied Alice automatically, barely batting an eyelid at the abrupt turn of conversation.

Tilly squinted at the screen in her hand. 'Bollocks. How are you really? Are you still using Amazon as therapy?'

Alice shook her head. 'Nope.' The silence crackled across the ether. 'It's mainly Net-a-Porter these days,' she confessed.

Tilly nodded, for a moment taking in the possible ramifications of that admission. 'Did you suddenly get a huge pay rise that you forgot to mention?' She might live in the jungle, but she wasn't dead. Tilly clearly knew exactly how many pound signs whizzing around that website signified.

Alice said nothing.

'Somebody there needs to know what you're dealing with, Al—' Tilly began.

'I can't. Don't ask me to,' Alice interrupted, even holding up a hand in front of her as though to bat the very idea away.

Her friend was not so easily defeated. 'This is not some dirty secret, sweets; it's your way of coping and there are people who can help. Sod that, there must be somebody in Stepford who'd be only too delighted to help?'

Alice thought for a moment. 'The problem is, the kind of people that want to dive in and "help" aren't always the ones you actually want helping, are they?'

Tilly nodded, knowing only too well that Alice made a valid point. When her father had died during that fateful storm on Orkney, Alice had been inundated with offers of help and support, not necessarily from her best friends though, but often from those seeking a worthy cause to make their own.

'Talking to you helps,' Alice offered.

'Yeah, but I'm a million miles away, so that's no bloody good,' said Tilly tiredly.

'Your geography's shit,' said Alice.

'Ha! Look who it is, Funny's cousin – Not Funny!' Tilly countered. 'Look, this is mad. You should just get on a plane and join me. Come on, come and harass some gorgeous young men with social consciences ...'

Alice managed a smile. 'That's your dream, Til, not mine. Besides, there's Coco ...' At the very mention of her name, Coco lifted her head and sniffed at the screen, giving Tilly an eyeful of chocolatey nostrils and whiskers. She whistled and watched Coco look around in confusion.

'Of course there is,' said Tilly after a moment, the discussion effectively settled.

'Besides,' continued Alice, undeterred and keen to make her point, 'I have to get myself sorted first, don't I? I need to find a level and I'm not going to get that gallivanting all over the globe.'

Tilly nodded sagely. 'Besides, there's no way you could afford the excess baggage charges.'

Alice ignored her. 'I keep telling myself that a nice steady community, regular patients, friendly faces and I'll settle a bit, you know? But now I just seem to spend half my days referring people on to consultants, or A&E, and I never get to just *fix* anyone properly.'

Tilly leaned forward – if she were any closer to the screen, she'd be giving Alice and Coco a virtual hug. 'Are we talking about your patients here, Al, or are we talking about you?' She hummed their favourite Coldplay song that had run on a loop in their student digs. 'It won't be lights guiding you home though, will it, honey, it'll be an online sale! We have to talk about this at some point, you know, before I fly back one day and find that you've been buried alive beneath cashmere jumpers and stylish accessories . . .'

'I am not a hoarder!' Alice protested, ignoring the niggle of doubt in the back of her mind. Her home was indeed more of a storage facility than a cosy retreat, but by God did she have stylish and organised storage.

'I know you're not, sweetie,' Tilly said gently, 'but I so wish I could be there with you, even if it's just to remind you that happiness has fuck all to do with the stuff you own and everything to do with the people you spend your days with, not to mention how you feel about your place in the world. Al – I see women out here who don't have two beans to rub together, they live in what you and I would call abject poverty, but they are surrounded by their family, their friends, their children. And the smiles on their faces . . . Oh, they may not have prospects by any Western measure, but my God are they happy.'

'Fuck,' said Alice, swallowing down a ball of tears in her throat and dashing at her eyes with her pyjama sleeve. Even Coco had picked up on the message that all was not well.

'There must be someone you feel a connection with?' Tilly said quietly.

Alice nodded. 'Of course. But everyone has their own stuff going on, you know, their own friendships.'

'Are you honestly saying that they won't let you play?' Tilly said.

'No, of course not. Grace invited me to her yoga class this evening. But, you know—'

'You said you were busy and took a rain check?' Tilly interrupted, knowing her friend's habit of pushing other people away all too well. 'But, just for a minute, think about this – what might happen if you let her in?'

'To the house?' Alice squeaked.

'You could start with your life?' Tilly suggested. 'A coffee? A panini – oh my God, paninis – I'd forgotten about paninis . . .' She sighed deeply. 'Look, I'm not saying that this Grace has to become your new best friend, your ultimate confidante. She doesn't even have to be someone your own age – in fact a different perspective might be a good thing. I just hate that I can't be there to hold your hand – even if it is just to stop it getting to your credit card! Maybe just while everything with Coco is so up in the air, you know.'

'I know,' said Alice, 'I miss you too. But your way isn't always my way.'

'Obviously,' said Tilly with a snort. Her own go-to setting any time life got tricky was to chuck it all in and start over. Their friendship was a veritable case study in how opposites attract. 'You know what my suggestion is anyway, Alice.'

'Jump on a plane?' Alice smiled.

'Or under a man. You, my darling, need to let off steam a little. All work and no play, etcetera etcetera. Start small. Don't invite anyone home. Just arrange to meet one of these gorgeous men in a hotel somewhere and let your hair down, release a few feel-good pheromones, if you know what I mean.'

'God, no!' exclaimed Alice, instantly on the defensive. 'What if we met in person and there was, like, zero chemistry between us? And they'd travelled all that way?'

'Firstly, shags are not Air Miles,' Tilly said scathingly. 'Be upfront – don't promise anything. Then it's up to them whether they think you're worth the gamble. Besides, I know it's not quite the same, but surely you can tell if there's a connection between you, when you're – well, you know – online?'

Alice said nothing. She didn't need Tilly's voice in her head telling her she was being a prude. After all, Tilly's love life seemed to revolve around sexting and Skype far more than Alice was comfortable with.

'Oh God, you're not serious?' said Tilly, understanding dawning on her face. She shifted uncomfortably for a moment. 'Listen, if you really don't know where to start, I could give you a few pointers . . .'

'You are *not* giving me sexting lessons,' said Alice categorically. 'I mean just because I haven't, doesn't mean I couldn't—'

'Go on then,' said Tilly. 'Stop moaning to me and get on with it. We both know this is a good idea, so don't overthink it. Do it. Right now. I'm hanging up.'

'You have to be kidding—' protested Alice, just as the screen flickered to black and the connection was lost. There was no way she was going to be coerced into this, she decided, pushing her phone away decisively, just as it vibrated to announce an incoming message:

Just get on with it – & call me after
Tx

Alice sighed. It was one thing being cross with Tilly when she was way off base, but when there was a chance she was bang on the money? She quietly stood up and shut Coco outside the bedroom door, much to the little dog's annoyance. 'I'm doing this for your own good, Coco. There's no way you need to hear this ...'

She picked up her laptop and began to type, relieved to see that it was Oliver in Sydney online, rather than Norfolk Neil who, let's face it, needed very little encouragement before he'd jump on his tractor and head straight for Larkford.

'I missed you, A,' Oliver typed. 'Have you been out saving lives?'

'Hardly,' she replied.

'Isn't it way past your bedtime, anyway, young lady?' he typed, giving her the perfect opening.

'In bed already.' She paused and bit her lip, wondering if she had the nerve. 'Can't sleep – too restless. Need to let off steam.'

He dived into the conversation with such alacrity that Alice couldn't help but wonder whether this was what he'd been waiting for all along.

'Only too happy to help you unwind ...' The cursor flashed for a moment – 'I'm game if you are.'

'Where are you?' she asked, wondering how he found time in the middle of the working day for a conversation like this.

'Just got back from surfing. Lounging at home. Talking to you. Imagining you in bed.'

She pushed away thoughts of his apparent unemployment. 'What are you wearing?' she typed awkwardly, only remembering this particular gambit from a dodgy made-for-TV movie she'd watched the night before.

There was a pause and then a photo popped up on her

screen – washboard abs, board shorts and what looked like an enormous erection tenting the fabric. 'More than I want to be!' he typed. 'What about you?'

Alice hesitated. It didn't seem to matter that he was easy on the eye, or that his image was pixelated rather than in bed beside her. It mattered to her that the towel he was lounging on was exactly the shade of duck-egg blue she'd been looking for. It mattered to her that the only question she really wanted an answer to was where he had bought it and did they deliver internationally.

She logged off abruptly, just as Coco decided she'd had enough of the whole scenario anyway and pushed open the bedroom door.

'Well, it's official,' said Alice as she buried her scorching face in the little dog's fur in mortification, before an attack of the giggles overwhelmed her. 'I seriously need to get out more.'

Chapter 14

Dan blinked hard the next morning, attempting to focus on the screen in front of him. Fatigue and worry were playing their twin roles in making his day so much more challenging than it needed to be. After all, he'd had a relatively easy slate so far, coughs, colds and acid reflux hardly testing his medical prowess.

He tapped redial on his phone, a little unnerved that Harry Grant had chosen this week in particular to go MIA. So inherently, boringly reliable, Harry would always record a fresh voicemail message on his mobile even when he claimed a rare half-day. Today though, the recorded message played out once again on the speaker – the number you are calling is unavailable. Dan finished the call in frustration – knowledge was power when it came to the NHS, and right now, Dan couldn't help but feel they were being deliberately kept out of the loop.

He flicked through the online directory and tried Harry's direct line at HQ. The voice that answered, however, did not belong to Harry Grant.

'Derek Landers speaking.'

Dan was speechless for a moment. He cleared his throat. 'Mr Landers. Good morning. It's Dan Carter here, from The Practice at Larkford.'

Derek gave a smug chuckle. 'Oh, I wondered how long it would be before I heard from you.'

'I was hoping to speak to Harry Grant,' Dan continued.

'Yes, well, I'm afraid your lap dog is no longer in the employ of the NHS. It seems that our visions for the future of our Primary Care Trust were not aligned. He seemed to take our proposals rather personally, dropped the ball professionally so to speak. So, I'm afraid I had no choice but to let him go.'

'Well, I'm incredibly sad to hear that,' Dan managed, trying to keep the conversation on track despite a visceral pull of shock and disappointment. 'Perhaps you'd be good enough to fill us in on your plans for maternity provision. Our patients are extremely concerned that their options are being limited, without, it would appear, any commensurate care being on offer elsewhere.'

'The birthing unit at Rosemore was a drain on our finances and, frankly, a risk to our patients. Surely you should know, Dr Carter, that transferring a woman with complications in labour is far from ideal.'

'I'm not suggesting we send our high-risk patients there, Mr Landers,' said Dan, working hard to remain calm. 'But to remove the option of a midwife-led birth, to insist on hospital births, is tantamount to infringing our patients' right to choose. And you, Mr Landers, can surely appreciate the cycle of intervention that takes place in a hospital setting. If you can't appreciate the personal choices of these women, surely you can agree that high intervention equates to high cost?'

Derek harrumphed down the line. 'And you think these hippy-dippy birthing centres are cheap to run? One-to-one support just isn't cost-effective. Besides,' he sounded rattled now, 'we're hardly going to base our policy around a hormonal minority of trouble-makers who can't see further than their own ovaries.' He cleared his throat. 'I think we can agree that their ability to think rationally is somewhat compromised at this time in their lives. I like to think we have their best interests at heart, rather than buying into some feckless fallacy.'

'That's an interesting stance you've taken,' said Dan coldly, 'but since I am neither hormonal, nor in possession of any ovaries, last I checked, perhaps you might take *my* opinion into account? This is an absolute outrage, Derek, and you know it is. Why else would you pull a stunt like an overnight closure? My colleagues and I feel pretty bloody strongly about this, and we'd like to know what your plan is. What do you intend to do? Close down the Air Ambulance facility too? Fire everyone who doesn't agree with you?'

'If only I could,' Derek bit back. 'And this issue is above your pay grade, I'm afraid. Budgets have to balance, you know. You'll be advised in due course of the alternative arrangements available.' With a click, he hung up on him and Dan stared at the phone in shock for a moment.

'You slimy little git,' he breathed in fury.

He blinked hard, trying to find some semblance of composure, before pushing back his chair, his anger and frustration no excuse to let his standards slip and start relying on the intercom. Derek Landers and his scheming would simply have to wait.

'Edward Everett?' he said, spotting his next patient the moment he walked into the waiting room, for Edward and his wife were well nigh inseparable. Indeed, it was rare to find a couple in their nineties who were still so obviously in love. Edward rose slowly to his feet, nodding his head to Dan in greeting, before holding out a gallant hand to Jane. As the two of them edged slowly towards him, Dan couldn't help but smile. 'Morning, you two. You look like trouble.'

Jane laughed sweetly. 'Oh Dr Carter, you are a card.'

'The mind is willing, son,' said Edward with a twinkle, 'the body not so much.'

By the time they were seated in Dan's consulting room, he couldn't help but note that nearly a third of their allocated appointment time had elapsed, but he didn't have the heart to rush them out of the door – the effort involved in getting here meant they didn't trouble him lightly.

'I've been getting night sweats,' blurted out Edward suddenly. 'And I've lost a bit of weight rather quickly.'

'Without trying?' Dan clarified, noting the gaping collar of Edward's starched shirt.

'I've been trying to feed him up,' Jane said. 'But even my steak and kidney pie isn't helping.' She spoke as though her pie was the panacea for any ills. For all Dan knew, she might even be right.

Dan also knew well enough that it was always worth finding out what possible diagnosis was on the patient's mind. Often, he could put their mind at rest, or at least make sure that they included the appropriate testing at the outset, and Edward was no different. 'I'm convinced it's cancer,' he said. 'I saw my dad go through much the same thing.'

'And the tiredness, Dr Carter, some days it's like he's walking through treacle,' Jane interrupted, leaning forward in her seat for emphasis, her arthritic knuckles swollen as she grasped her cane.

Edward nodded in agreement, the sunlight catching the pigmentation on his scalp where his hair had long since given up residence. They both looked at Dan expectantly as though he might have all the answers, their touching respect for him as their family doctor in stark contrast to Lavinia Hearst's verbal abuse last night when he'd called by the hospital after work to see how Jessica was getting on. These two were old school, and as such, they deserved a few more moments of his time than was generally decreed.

'Okay,' said Dan. 'Anything else you've noticed? Any funny moles, or blood in your stools, or pain anywhere?'

Edward let out a short bark of laughter. 'Oh Dr Carter, I'm ninety-two. I've been in pain for pretty much the last decade somewhere or other! But no, nothing new to report.'

'Well, I'd like to examine you first and then I'd like to check your thyroid, your blood sugar and also your blood count – just a simple blood test to give me a clearer idea of what's going on in there.' He stood up and guided Edward Everett to the examination couch, before giving him a thorough once-over, all the while thinking there was every chance Edward was right on the money. They'd wait overnight for the bloods to come back, but Dan had a horrible feeling he'd be phoning Oncology in the morning.

Watching the gentle banter and loving support that Edward and Jane offered each other, shaking his hand in thanks as they left, Dan found himself quite choked up. It wasn't that he knew them particularly well; it wasn't that Edward's health was in immediate jeopardy – it was just the fact that they clearly loved each other so very much. Politely declining their offer to introduce him to their 'beautiful granddaughter', he was touched that they were still thinking about other people's happiness even in the midst of their own personal crisis.

Grace walked towards him down the corridor and he cleared his throat, unwilling to let on how emotional he was feeling, but Grace missed nothing. 'They do have that effect, those two, don't they?'

Dan nodded. 'I wonder what it's like to grow old with your childhood sweetheart?' He had a vaguely romantic notion of them meeting at Larkford primary school and never spending a night apart.

Grace frowned. 'What *are* you going on about? Childhood sweethearts? They met at the grief-counselling group in Bath, ooh, maybe fifteen years ago now, when they'd both lost their spouses. It's rather lovely actually, that they both get another chance at happiness.' She gave Dan a sideways look, realising she'd shattered his illusion. 'Never too late. Don't you think?'

He just nodded. 'I do, actually.' He watched as she walked away from him, distracted by the way her hair brushed her shoulders with every step. He stayed in the doorway until she was out of sight, wishing things were different.

It took quite a lot to impress Dan. It wasn't that he was hard to please per se, but in his line of work he often found that people had a nasty habit of sinking to the lowest common denominator. Whether comparing cigarettes or calories or alcoholic units, his patients tended to justify their excesses by what was the norm in their social group.

But every now and then, Dan would see a patient who defied all societal norms and just focused on the hand they'd been dealt. He scrolled through Matthew Giles's notes and squinted, trying to trick his eyes into seeing between the lines. This young lad had dropped out of university to return home earlier in the year and had been a regular in the surgery ever since.

'So, Matthew, how are you doing?' He left the question deliberately vague, hoping that the patient himself might open up and fill in the blanks.

Matthew just shrugged. He was a living master class in coping strategies. 'Fine. I mean, not fine, but we're coping. Mum's doing a bit better this month, she's taken some time off work, which makes it easier—'

Underplaying the stresses of caring for his mother, Molly, was his go-to setting. Dan could only begin to imagine how an eighteen-year-old lad might struggle with caring for a patient with early-onset Parkinson's, let alone abandoning his education to do so. The fact that Matthew himself was now suffering from chronic migraines suggested that he wasn't coping quite as well as he thought he was. Sure, the fridge was full and the laundry up to date, even the endless forms from the DWP were filled in with Matthew's cramped and somewhat childish handwriting, but what was the true cost?

'What about you, though?' Dan asked. 'Are you sleeping? I think last time we spoke you mentioned that was becoming a problem?'

Matthew nodded. 'Yeah, it's not been great. Mum's having a lot of pain at night – she wakes up about 2 a.m. and can't get comfortable again. But I can't complain, can I? There's lots of parents of newborns getting by on less.' He paused then and Dan wondered if they were both thinking the same thing – newborns grew up; for Molly Giles this was only the beginning of the decline.

'You know,' said Dan, 'I really think we need to get your mum some help with that, because you can't do everything you do every day on so little sleep, Matthew. And these migraines – well, it won't be helping them either. How did you get on with the melts I prescribed?'

Matthew looked uncomfortable. 'Well, I did try them—' His glance flickered towards Dan, hoping that he might intervene, but Dan had learned just to wait. It was a bit like being a journalist; sometimes if you kept quiet then your patient would blurt out the truth just to fill the empty silence. Matthew was no exception. 'They were great actually. But I can't take them. They make me really sleep, I mean seriously, out cold, there's no waking me. And I can't do that.'

He didn't need to explain why. He was, and had been for the last six months, the sole carer in the house.

'Look,' said Dan gently, 'I really don't want to overprescribe for these migraines, Matthew, when I'm quietly convinced that there are situational factors that trigger them. Wouldn't it be better if we took a look at those, together?' He watched the flicker of fear on Matthew's face and moved to reassure him quickly. 'Nothing dramatic. Molly's fine at home for now, but you need some respite too, you know. Being a carer isn't easy, especially for someone so young. Dr Graham and I have been exploring a few options – some home help, or maybe even some day-care or respite facilities for further down the line? I bet your mum would like that too. She must be worrying about you and all the responsibilities you've taken on?'

'It's not that I can't cope, Dr Carter,' interrupted Matthew earnestly. 'We're doing the best we can, you know.'

'I know,' said Dan. 'But we all need a little help sometimes. And there's no shame in asking for it.'

By the time Dan had made a few more calls and set the wheels in motion, The Practice was oddly quiet. The patients were long gone, the only sound coming from the doctors' lounge.

Taffy grinned as he saw Dan walk in. 'Thought we'd lost you there, for a bit.' He gestured at the kitchen table, where a large Fortnum's hamper was in the process of being devastated by Taffy, Grace and several of the nursing staff. 'I hope you don't mind, we started without you.'

Dan picked up the folded card, a printed crest on heavy vellum stock, his eyes widening as he read the inscription inside.

Taffy grinned, his mouth full of luxury cheese puffs. 'Somebody's got a guilty conscience.'

It was true, for this was no thank-you gift from the Hearst family, but rather an apology for Lavinia's outburst at the hospital. Ironically, this lavish display of wealth meant so much less than a simple 'I'm sorry'.

Dan shrugged off the uncomfortable emotion that chased that thought. He was too tired to go there today. 'Did you save me anything?' he teased, laughing as Jade and Jason squabbled over the last crab cake.

'Figs?' offered Taffy. 'Quails' eggs? Marzipan delights?' He rootled around in the depths of the basket, the contents of which would surely have fed the entire staff with some left over. He'd been strangely buoyant and chirpy all day and was clearly up for letting off some steam. 'And nobody much fancied the jam or the tea. The gin is bloody gorgeous though.' Taffy thrust a large chipped tumbler towards Dan, its pharmaceutical logo ironically declaring a drug to treat acid reflux from over-consumption.

Dan took a long sip and then made fast work of building himself the ultimate club sandwich, snaffling a box of Turkish Delight for later, before the locusts could claim it.

'Sorry,' said Grace guiltily. 'Taffy did say it was for sharing though. But I'm sure the apology was mainly meant for you.'

Dan nodded. 'I just wish people engaged their brains a bit before opening their mouths, don't you? I'd so much rather receive a thank-you and skip the bitter aftertaste.'

It was sometimes a thankless task being a GP: he'd refer Edward Everett on to a consultant who would save the day;

or Matthew Giles to a support group who would guide him and hopefully alleviate some of the burden. Even Jessica Hearst would be out of his hands now, as her family's private health care scheme had picked up the baton once she'd cleared Intensive Care. It was a rare thing indeed for Dan to see the whole story through to the ending, happy or otherwise.

'You did good today,' said Grace, clocking the expression on his face and knowing him all too well. 'Don't let a guilt-gherkin throw you off track.' She held out a cocktail stick, with a perfect miniature cornichon speared on the end.

'Ah Gracie,' Dan said, as he ate it in one bite. 'You could restore a man's faith in human kindness, you could.'

She smiled and pinched one of his Turkish Delight from under his very nose. Dan didn't even react. He'd have given her the whole bloody hamper if she'd only agree to going out with him.

Of course, that would be so much more likely if he ever actually asked her.

Holly came into the lounge, looking almost as knackered as he felt. 'Did you know poor Harry Grant's been fired?' she asked Dan under her breath, her subtlety and discretion unnecessary amongst the escalating party atmosphere. 'He just texted me his new phone number.'

'I found out this morning,' Dan said, offering her one of his Turkish Delight. 'And there goes our greatest advocate.'

'I could murder a doughnut,' Holly sighed, looking around at all the fancy food and grimacing.

'Or Derek Landers?' suggested Dan. 'I could work with that too.'

Taffy came over to join them. 'Do we need to have a Partners' Meeting?' he asked quietly, sliding his arm around Holly's waist and giving her a gentle squeeze by way of greeting. Dan simply nodded; there was no point getting into nitty-gritty detail and worrying all the staff until they'd got their facts straight – it was yet another adjustment to responsibility he was having trouble with, preferring as a rule to keep everything out in the open.

It was as though Taffy could read his mind, thought Dan for a moment, as his friend clocked his need for distraction and stepped up as always. Taffy leaned forward and thrust a jar of caviar in his face. 'Tenner says you can't eat this in three mouthfuls. I had a little taste and if this is what shopping at Fortnum's entails, you can sign me up for Lidl right now.'

Dan sniffed the eggs, their glistening blackness oily in the warmth of the lounge. He hesitated, knowing they could all use a good laugh, but in the end sanity prevailed. He swallowed hard and pulled out his wallet, noticing Taffy's face drop as he did so. 'Alright then, Jones,' he rallied, 'if you're so keen. Double or quits.' He waved a twenty-pound note in the air and raised his eyebrows in hope rather than expectation. 'And a rum and raisin fudge chaser—'

'Deal!' said Taffy, grabbing hold of a spoon and diving in, even as Holly turned away, looking nauseous at the very suggestion. The way Dan saw it, there would be plenty of time for regret later on.

Chapter 15

Taffy scratched at his hand absent-mindedly, irritating the skin to an angry red. 'If your hand really itches, doesn't that mean you're coming into money?' he asked, a hopeful lilt to his voice that showed he was only half joking. They'd been up late last night doing the maths on what the new addition to their family might do to their already precarious bank balance.

Holly looked up from the printout of the day's staff training schedule and grinned. 'Sadly, I think it's more likely that you're just allergic to something.'

'Washing up, maybe?' he suggested, his only request for their wedding list having been that they somehow find room in their tiny kitchen for a dishwasher.

'Now that *would* be terrible,' Holly agreed, only too aware how many hours they spent standing at the kitchen sink picking Weetabix off their cereal bowls and that neither of them were really trained for domesticity. 'Do you know, I could be a qualified heart surgeon by now, if I'd spent as many hours in an OR as I have at that sink.' Indeed, it was only the spectre of Cassie Holland and her green army that kept them from abandoning all decorum and filling their kitchen with disposable plates and cutlery. 'It's such a shame the smell of Fairy

Liquid is making me queasy at the moment,' she said quietly, teasing him. 'But what can you do?' She grinned, catching hold of his tie and pulling him in for a kiss.

'That excuse won't last for ever, you know, Graham,' he replied, his voice full of affection. He'd become incredibly tactile and demonstrative the last few days, so much so that Holly had been very strict with him earlier – 'People will begin to suspect,' she'd remonstrated, as he'd brought her fruit salad and a smoothie at her desk. 'Let's have the scan and then we can tell everyone properly.' Lizzie and Elsie had both been sworn to secrecy, but neither were renowned for their discretion, so in Taffy's eyes, they might as well get on and share the glad tidings before they gave the game away themselves.

'Any chance we can whizz through all this staff training by lunchtime and then work on staff morale at the pub? Morale is very important, you know,' Taffy said seriously.

'I do know,' said Holly with feeling, 'but if the debacle at the Country Show taught us one thing, it's that a little more emergency training wouldn't go astray around here. And it might give us all a little more confidence if we're left to our own devices again. Let's face it, if these cutbacks continue and we can't stem the flow, that might be more often than we're actually prepared for.'

'And Alice arranged this, and set it all up, did she?' Taffy said, impressed. He waved around the doctors' lounge at the array of CPR dummies, bandages and defibrillator units. 'I reckon that business with Jessica Hearst has spooked her far more than we'd realised.'

'Thank God Jess is making a decent recovery now,' agreed Holly, having received regular updates over the last few days as Jess's condition had finally turned a corner. Not that she was home free – there were one or two complications that might yet take months to resolve – but there was no doubting that little Jessica Hearst had been incredibly lucky. And Holly could only hope that Alice might now begin to see that her part in that, and of course its legacy with this new training initiative, could only be positive.

Holly frowned for a moment. 'Have you seen the Major recently?' she asked, seemingly out of nowhere, but her mind making connections as she tried not to relive the accident.

Taffy shook his head. 'I don't think I have actually. Not even at the pub.'

They looked at each other in concern, both hit by the sudden guilty realisation that the Major had indeed been MIA since the show. 'I'll pop round later,' Holly promised. 'But it's not like before though, is it, when he wouldn't come in? I mean, we don't need to worry *really*, because if something was wrong, he would have been to see us, right?'

'Right,' said Taffy, not sounding half as convincing as Holly would have liked.

The doctors' lounge began to fill then, as every member of staff turned up for their obligatory training day – some enthusiastically like Alice, others bemoaning the early start, others joining their ranks as amateur volunteers – the more the merrier.

'Aha! Come to see how to do this medicine business properly?' Taffy teased Rupert Hallow, their thankfully good-humoured local vet. 'With the missus up the duff, you'll be wanting to learn how to do things properly, I suppose,' Taffy teased him.

'Well, we can't all take the soft route and specialise in only one species,' Rupert countered, lightly punching him on the shoulder. 'But actually, yeah, the thought of a baby in the house does rather focus the mind, doesn't it?'

Taffy nodded. 'The number of times Ben or Tom have swallowed things—' He gave a theatrical shudder and dropped his voice to a whisper. 'I'd never been terrified of a grape before I moved in with Holly.'

Rupert nodded; Jemima's hard-won pregnancy had been a long time coming and he was taking no chances. He bent down to pick up one of the CPR dummies, which apparently came in all shapes and sizes these days.

'Aw, look, Fat Boy's back,' said Grace affectionately, as she walked up beside them and patted the plump resus-dummy on the head.

Rupert stiffened. 'Now that's hardly fair. I'm just being supportive. Jemima's had all sorts of cravings, so I promised we'd chub up together.' He looked sheepish. 'Really the very least I could do.'

Grace looked mortified, but before Taffy could call him out on so obvious a ploy to up his doughnut intake – or indeed adopt the concept as his own – the CPR trainer strode into the room, earnest expression, lace-up brogues and no-nonsense attitude firmly in place.

'Right, we haven't got long and there's lots to get through, so divide into groups and we'll refresh the basics,' she said, her booming voice ploughing through every consonant. 'I'm Josephine. Any questions, hands in the air, okay?'

'Charisma levels critically low,' whispered Dan in Holly's ear, making her giggle. 'Suggest immediate mouth-to-mouth.'

'Jesus,' sniggered Jason, 'do we have to?'

Josephine strode over, mistaking Jason's discomfort. 'Now, just because your CPR dummy happens to be male, that doesn't mean you should hesitate to get stuck in.'

'Oh, I wouldn't,' Jason said suggestively, with a seductive twitch of his eyebrow. 'I'm remarkably easy either way.'

Lucy turned away, biting on her plait to stifle the giggles, only to snort unattractively and set herself off again. Holly grinned, loving that they really had become a team who worked together and played together as well.

'So,' continued Josephine, shooting their group a look of intense dislike, 'you should take a moment to re-familiarise yourselves with the contents of each defibrillator kit. Check your plan of action, people – scissors to deal with clothing, razor for those with a hairy chest, microbial wipe to – what?'

Around the room, several hands had gone up. 'We don't seem to have a razor in our kit.'

'Or ours,' said Holly, after a moment's searching.

'Ah, now about that—' Jason looked up at his colleagues and blushed. 'Sorry, troops. Forgot to replace them. Had this really big cycling race and—' A volley of latex gloves and bagels rained upon him, as his colleagues were unable to pass up the opportunity to penalise him for his endless vanity.

They soon settled into some semblance of organisation, not least because Josephine was a formidable presence in the room but also, of course, because, however high spirits were running this morning, they actually needed – and wanted – to know this stuff.

'Now,' opined Josephine a short while later, 'who can actually tell me the leading cause of complications following an emergency admission?'

They looked from one to another for inspiration. 'Jarring from transportation?' ventured Alice, no prizes for guessing which case she was thinking of.

'Infection to open wounds?' suggested Holly, Charlotte Lansing's arm still firmly in the forefront of her mind.

'Would it surprise you,' Josephine said as she glowered around the room with her hands on her sizeable hips, 'to learn that it comes down to communication? Have we got our facts straight? Our information accurate? Name? Date of birth? Blood group? Even the nature or causation of the injury or illness itself.'

'It's true,' interrupted Taffy. 'I had a man come into the GUM clinic when I was a resident. Taken too much Viagra. His paperwork said he was circus-sized.'

'Oh my God,' gasped Alice, still easily shocked despite her constant professionalism.

'He wasn't really,' Taffy quickly reassured her. 'I mean, he did have the most enormous stiffy, but they just meant he was circumcised—'

'Oh,' she laughed nervously, embarrassed to have missed the joke that had everyone else in stitches.

Dan couldn't resist joining in. 'My very first consult on the wards – the chart said the patient needed checking anally. No wonder she was surprised when I told her the plan. She'd been expecting her annual hearing check!' He looked inordinately pleased with yet another of his favourite spell-check jokes.

'Yes, quite,' cut in Josephine tartly, without even mustering a smile. 'If you've quite finished with the adolescent – not to mention highly unoriginal – humour, perhaps we can move on?'

'Burn!' whispered Jason to Taffy and Dan as they visibly shrank under her disdain.

Josephine's head whipped round like a bird of prey. 'Excellent suggestion. Let's talk about burns for a moment, shall we?'

Holly slipped away after lunch, confident in her suturing skills, but unable to clear the apprehension buzzing around in her mind. She called Lizzie as she walked across town, knowing that her friend always seemed to have her finger on the pulse of what was going on in Larkford. You could take the journalist away from the glossy magazine, but it turned out you couldn't take the journalist out of the girl. 'I can't talk now,' whispered Lizzie. 'I'm at my reflexology appointment.' She sighed blissfully. 'I'll call you later though, yes—'

She sounded so completely Zen that, for a moment at least, Holly strongly considered booking herself in there and then. Then she remembered exactly *why* Lizzie enjoyed her appointments quite so very much and decided it wasn't for her. Her pregnancy hormones were driving her libido up the wall right now and it didn't seem the time, or indeed the place, to experiment with new erogenous zones. Taffy would simply have to step up and do the decent thing, she thought, smiling to herself happily at the very idea.

She stopped in front of Waverly Manor, the Major's family home since she didn't know when, and the guilt returned like a punch to the chest. The thick branches of wisteria had shed their purple flowers and the bright acid greens of the honeysuckle had taken full advantage to snake in between, its aroma heavy and cloying. It was a stunning yet strangely unwelcoming façade.

She tapped gently on the oak front door, noticing as she did so that all the curtains were still drawn even mid-afternoon. Quite why she hadn't simply called in to see Marion at the Spar she couldn't say – perhaps, she confessed to herself, because she was looking for a slightly more objective report on the state of one Major Peregrine Waverly.

No reply.

She lifted the latch on the side gate, surprised to find it unlocked, and slipped through the archway into the back garden, the Major's pride and joy. But instead of the usual manicured lawns and titivated borders she saw only neglect. You could easily have taken a hay crop off the lawn and the weeds had run riot.

'I wondered if you might turn up,' said a voice from the shadows of the loggia, as the Major stepped forward, hair unkempt, smoking a forbidden pipe and sporting a tattered, yet clearly expensive, silk dressing gown. 'The wife dobbed me in, did she?' he said tiredly, no trace of his dapper charm on show.

'Nope,' replied Holly, trying hard not to stare at his unusual dishevelment. 'Thought I'd pop by for some advice about my garden.' She paused. 'Oh, and I was worried about you.'

The Major nodded; he looked utterly broken. 'Is she alive?' he asked after only a moment's hesitation. 'You can tell me. Did that poor little girl die?'

'Oh Major!' cried Holly. 'No! She hasn't died. She's on the mend, truly. I had a call only this morning. I thought you knew—' She broke off, wondering for a moment why exactly she'd supposed that. Presumably because secrets in Larkford were few and far between, and he was married to the local oracle?

He shook his head. 'I've been sleeping in the study, or trying to. Haven't seen Marion for days – she's up with the lark and I, well, let's say that sleep is a fickle friend right now.' He paused, drawing in a shuddering breath. 'So little Jessica is going to be okay? I mean, properly, truly okay?'

Holly nodded, wondering quite how much to share. 'It might take a little time until she's galloping around the parkland again, but she's a gutsy one alright.'

The Major looked at her appraisingly. 'Head injuries don't go away overnight,' he said astutely, refusing to be mollified. 'How on earth do I look her in the eye, knowing it was my bravado and stupidity that caused all her pain?' He leaned back against the crumbling wall of the loggia, its stonework seemingly bound into survival by clematis vines, just as the tightened belt on the Major's robe seemed to be the only thing holding him together right now. He puffed on his pipe and stared into the distance, his newly sharpened cheekbones highlighted by the glancing sunlight.

He turned after a moment, the pain etched across his face. 'Tell me what to do, Holly? Tell me what to do, to make this feeling go away?'

Holly took his hand and steered him, almost as if he were a child, through the open French windows and back into the kitchen. She poured him a mug of coffee from the pot on the side and sat down with him at the kitchen table.

'You're going to talk to your friends, to your wife, and share with us how you feel. We all know you didn't set out to hurt anyone.'

'But my ego caused all—' he interrupted.

Holly waved his words away. 'Your ego booked a plane. And frankly the pilot should have known better, but this isn't a day in court.'

'It didn't even cross my mind,' he said despondently. 'I mean, the RAF chaps send their helicopters over all the time to dry out the cricket pitches—'

'Major, for now, let's just focus on the fact that you never *intended* to hurt anyone and that accidents do happen.'

'Hmm,' muttered the Major, not easily swayed from his stance that he was the living breathing catalyst for all of Jessica Hearst's current misery.

But she was alive and recovering, Holly reminded herself when a flicker of doubt appeared in her own mind. And whilst the Major's biplane had been sheer folly on his part, it had certainly not been malicious. His culpability was tenuous at best. In her experience, he would end up punishing himself for this far longer than any legal system ever could. In fact, if Lavinia Hearst wasn't quite so litigious and vindictive, then a visit to Jessica might be just the ticket, but there was no way Holly was suggesting that right now, with the Major so obviously broken and fragile in front of her.

'Can you maybe talk to Marion tonight, stop sleeping in the study? Tell her what you've told me and actually get some sleep?'

The Major harrumphed. 'With Marion sleepwalking all over the bloody house, I'm hardly going to get any shut-eye with her wandering around.' He paused and a tiny twinkle of his familiar humour flickered in his eyes. 'But I will say this for her, she's getting ever so fit with all her nocturnal strolling.'

He yawned and leaned forward, the first time Holly could remember having any physical contact with him beyond a firm handshake or a pat on the back. He folded into her arms, rested his head against her shoulder, and allowed himself to breathe deeply for the first time in what must have felt like for ever.

'Thank you, Holly. For coming over, for thinking of me,' he murmured.

Grover leapt up onto her lap and licked her face; it was almost as though the little dog was thanking her too. Holly breathed out slowly, kicking herself for not realising sooner that there was a problem, but mainly with sheer relief that she'd come on a whim today. This was one part of her job that no amount of cutbacks could take away; the part where they knew and valued their patients – foibles and all – as cherished members of their community.

Chapter 16

'Tell me again why we're doing this?' Taffy asked, as he fought with a striped silk tie later that evening. 'I don't understand why I have to get all dressed up like a stuffed shirt just to go and visit an old people's home?'

Holly inhaled sharply. 'Whoa, whatever you do, do *not* call it that! It's an exclusive retirement community, okay? If Elsie really has her heart set on going there, she'll need to provide all sorts of references, if you can believe it. Personal and financial statements. And there's a trial period when they can ask her to leave if she doesn't fit in!' Holly shook her head. When Elsie had casually suggested that they all pop over this evening for a little snoop around Sarandon Hall, she certainly hadn't expected a three-page email from the Admissions Team detailing their expectations!

'And since we're basically Elsie's nearest and dearest, I imagine we'll be under scrutiny a little bit too. So put on the tie.' Holly grinned. 'Pretend you're going undercover if it helps. The name's Jones, Taffy Jones—'

Taffy grinned. 'It does help a little actually. You can be my Bond girl if you like. Hobnobs Galore.'

'Oi,' said Holly, brushing the crumbs off her silk shirt-dress none too discreetly. 'Based on this dress, I'll have to be Plenty O'Toole, don't you think?' She laughed. Holly's ever-expanding bustline was going to give away her pregnancy quicker than anything right now, even Taffy's slightly mooning expression at every baby that had come into The Practice over the last few days.

Taffy frowned. 'I still don't get this, you know. Elsie has that beautiful house, friends on the doorstep—'

'But that's just it,' Holly interrupted him. 'Since Sarandon Hall opened its golden doors, there's a certain section of our community who have jumped ship from their own homes into this place. Elsie's been feeling really left out for months.'

'Oh,' said Taffy quietly. 'I didn't realise she was unhappy.'

'Not so much unhappy, as unfulfilled,' Holly clarified. 'She keeps telling me all about what her friends are up to – the guest speakers, the bridge parties, the culinary events, the wine-tasting, the trips ... It's like all her friends have left for university and she's stuck at home doing retakes. We might have to accept that she's genuinely considering this as an option.'

'Okay then,' said Taffy. 'But if I get one whiff that this place is a scam, or their care isn't up to scratch—'

'Absolutely,' said Holly. 'I'll be right with you. And at least Elsie's being sensible about this and going to look around properly. She was all up for paying a deposit over the phone this afternoon when she heard that a vacancy had come up.'

They were both silent for a moment as they considered how exactly a vacancy at a place like Sarandon Hall might become available. Holly laid one hand on her nascent bump, thinking about the circle of life and trying hard to be as upbeat and positive about this mooted plan as Elsie was. No matter how she thought about it though, even the prospect of Elsie moving into a retirement community – however pricey and luxurious – felt like an admission of defeat.

Leaving Lucy in charge of the twins with a new bumper pack of Play-Doh and promises not to be long, Holly pulled the front door closed behind them.

'Right then, deep breath, smiley faces,' she said as much to herself as to Taffy. 'We're being supportive, remember.' She peeled open a new packet of Polos to quell the wave of nausea that followed, unconvinced that on this particular occasion it was the pregnancy hormones causing her stomach to protest.

Protesting, however, was the last thing on Holly's mind by the time they had collected Elsie, in full evening dress no less, and driven up the sweeping, tree-lined drive to Sarandon Hall. By the time the butler – dear God! – had taken their coats and organised drinks, Holly had taken a moment to look around the stately home. Her only lingering bias was towards the fact that she might be rather tempted to move in herself.

'Bloody hell,' exclaimed Holly under her breath.

'You see,' said Elsie smugly, catching her awed expression as they stood waiting for the Honourable Adeline Avery to show them around. 'Little bit luxury hotel, little bit country club – not too shabby for Elsie.'

Elsie had a valid point – there was no shortage of luxury or facilities, or so it seemed according to the map of the grounds that Holly had picked up as they entered. Golf course, swimming pool, solarium, tennis courts, wine lockers, Pilates studio and a choice of fine or casual dining – assuming of course that one had chosen to eschew the luxury kitchen in one's own well-appointed apartment. Holly felt as though her brain had absorbed a little too much of the brochure's pithy sales patter and her objectivity was in serious jeopardy.

'Are you sure this is your thing, though, Elsie? Are these kind of people really your friends?' Holly offered, as a momentary flicker of nerves passed over her friend's face.

Elsie raised an eyebrow, clearly unwilling to be challenged on this. 'Not everyone will like me, darling, but you seem to forget – not everyone matters. I'm eighty-four: I'm not walking into here *wondering* if anyone will like me; I walk into a room and wonder whose company *I* might enjoy. It's something you gain with a little confidence, later on in life,' she said, patting Holly's hand a little patronisingly, betraying her nerves with each tiny tremor.

She and Taffy hung back a little, as Elsie greeted everyone passing through the hallways, old friends and acquaintances apparently delighted with their rather smug choice of golden years accommodation. She was quickly swept into their midst and Holly felt the first tiny frisson of envy – not for the finery, or the fripperies, but for the company of one of her favourite people.

'Did you see, Holls?' asked Taffy under his breath. 'They have three different private doctors on call and a twenty-four-hour nursing service. There's even a chiropodist on site. How on earth is she going to afford this place?'

Taffy seemed to have missed the obvious assumption that, with an apartment in Sarandon Hall to call her own, Elsie would have no need of the glorious townhouse on the Market Place that had become their second home and place of refuge whenever things got tricky. Holly couldn't quite imagine turning up at Sarandon Hall with a twin on each arm, in search of a spontaneous cuppa and catch-up.

Holly gave herself a little shake, reminding herself that

this was not about her – this was about Elsie and her choices. Either way, though, she couldn't help but feel a little over-whelmed by the reality of Sarandon Hall in the flesh, so to speak – all visions of tired and taupe retirement communities having been swept from her mind.

This? This was almost a little too much, a little *too* grandi-ose for everyday living, surely? But then, if every day might be your last, who wouldn't want to go out with such a lux-urious flourish?

'Do you know,' murmured Taffy, echoing her thoughts, 'I reckon I'd be craving beans on toast and a box set within a week in here.'

Holly couldn't help but agree, a flicker of hope that her friend might feel the same way quickly extinguished as she caught sight of Elsie herself. Resplendent in her sweeping green silk dress, undoubtedly vintage couture – much like the lady herself – her laugh chimed merrily amongst the general conversation, as the residents were escorted through to dinner. With a delicate martini glass in one hand, and a dapper gentleman in a velvet smoking jacket holding the other, Elsie was in her element. The centre of attention. As a young girl in evening dress began a sweeping arpeggio on the grand piano in the dining room, the chatter and hubbub was supplemented by sighs of delight at the tiny plates of foie gras and caviar at each place setting, where the linen was pristine and the crystal sparkling as much as the conversation.

'Jesus,' said Taffy hanging back in the doorway and pull-ing at his tie uncomfortably, 'it's like a scene from *The Great Gatsby* in here. Is it a special occasion, do you think?'

The Honourable Adeline Avery materialised beside them, a neat leather-bound folder in her hands that already bore the name Elsie Townsend embossed on the front in gold leaf. 'Oh no, this is just our Wednesday Supper Club. But we do hold a gala with a string quartet on the first of every month. You see, for most of our residents the notion of weekends and week-days is meaningless now they're retired. So we try to make every day special in some way. Tomorrow, for example, we're having a literary salon. Perhaps Ms Townsend would care to join us and share some insight into the world of publishing?'

'I'm sure she'd love to,' said Holly. 'I have to ask, though, do all your residents enjoy this constant state of decadence?'

Adeline smiled. 'I know what you mean, but to be honest, we have trouble keeping up with demand. Our residents tend to be outgoing on the whole, and wanting to grab life with both hands – as much as the arthritis allows anyway!' She gave a self-deprecating chuckle that told Holly that this rather clumsy joke was actually part of her spiel.

Adeline leaned in confidentially. 'Many of our lady residents truly embrace the opportunity to dust off their diamonds and put their hair up for a change. You won't find any elasticated slacks around here. We have a hair salon and beautician on site, of course. And naturally, we work hard to keep the ratio of male and female residents as even as life expectancies allow. We've even been privileged to hold a few weddings in recent months.'

'Crikey,' said Holly eloquently. She could understand the desire to be surrounded by friends and living the high life, rather than worrying about the state of the roof or whether the boiler needed servicing, but she had to confess Sarandon Hall wasn't quite what she'd been expecting. She revised her earlier assessment that she'd be moving in as soon as she hit pensionable age. She could only hope that if Elsie had indeed set her heart on this, they would be able to leave her an escape hatch, should the cloying perfection become overwhelming.

There was something about the conversations, and by extension the friendships here, that seemed a little brittle to Holly's eye. There would be none of the down-to-earth honesty and loyalty that, for example, the Major and Marion offered their friends. Holly quietly crossed her fingers that Peregrine had taken her advice to heart and, even now, was sharing his anxiety with his wonderfully blunt but incredibly loving wife. Thank God she'd had the presence of mind to pop round, she thought, even if she'd been so distracted of late it had taken her longer than she was proud of.

Elsie gave her a little wave across the dining room, having sensed Holly's scrutiny. Her cheeks were flushed lightly and her eyes were dancing in delight as whatever anecdote she was regaling them with held the full attention of her table-mates.

Holly could only wish that Sarandon Hall offered a little 'holiday package' – permanent residency would certainly be taking a leap of faith on Elsie's latest whim. What if this was like the llama that she had endlessly obsessed about, but bored of instantly once she realised how moody and unaffectionate he was. Poor Monty, Holly thought, consigned to the petting zoo with barely a backwards glance.

If only there was a way for Elsie to dip her toe in the water without absolute commitment, she mused.

Chapter 17

'Are you sure she'll be okay if we slip away?' Holly hesitated in the becolumned portico of Sarandon Hall, music, laughter and the chiming of cut glass echoing out of the French windows into the summer's evening.

'Elsie's in her element, Holls. I doubt she'll even notice until it's time to call it a night and I'll be right back here to pick her up. Promise,' Taffy reassured her.

Holly nodded, feeling a little guilty that she simply couldn't stomach yet another round of *amuse-bouche*, particularly following the platters of oysters that had had her reeling back in her chair at the salty aroma alone. Or indeed another volley of conversational one-upmanship.

Taffy held open the car door and made sure she was settled inside, his natural chivalry having been seemingly ramped up to Defcon 3 now that she was pregnant. 'Home?' he asked. 'Only, we have a babysitter for the night, and an evening at The Kingsley Arms might be just the antidote we both need?'

He made a valid point, thought Holly as they wove through the lush green lanes back towards Larkford. The opulence of Sarandon Hall was almost cloying – stunning, undoubtedly – but leaving one in need of a palate cleanser of normality.

'Chips,' she decided. 'Let's go to the pub and eat chips.'

*

Teddy Kingsley was an astute businessman and an award-winning chef, his bonhomie and flair more than compensating for his almost chronic lack of common sense. Having just returned from Florence, where the temperatures were bouncing up into the forties, he had come home enthused with ideas to help his patrons through the recent hot weather. As the mercury hit thirty in Larkford, even well into the evening, Teddy had decided to employ Italian tactics.

And so, as Holly and Taffy walked into the pub garden, it was to find Teddy, Dan and Jason looping swathes of pock-marked hosepipe through the trees and the rafters over the patio. Teddy had a rather serious-looking spike tucked behind his ear and welcomed them both with a wave and a grin, wobbling perilously up a stepladder.

'Evening! You're just in time to see my new cooling system.' He clambered down to ground level and gave Holly a kiss on both cheeks. 'All the cafés in Florence have them – just a fine mist of cool water in the air. It's genius, really. Cools everybody right down, and I don't know about you but when it comes to this heat, you definitely can have too much of a good thing.'

Teddy attempted to blow his floppy, sun-kissed fringe from his eyes, but it was already plastered to his forehead. 'If you grab a table, I'll get you some drinks. I've got a few new Italian specials on the menu. Maybe a Bellini or a—'

'Just ginger ale and some chips for me, Teddy,' said Holly, glancing up at the loops of hosepipe. 'This is going to be fabulous. You'll have everyone flocking here if this weather continues. Did they talk you through how it works? Is it pressurised or something, to get the tiny droplets atomised?'

Teddy looked wrong-footed for a moment. 'Oh, erm, I mean – well, how complicated can it be? I'm good with this kind of thing – all common sense really—'

Holly and Taffy looked at each other in wry amusement, Holly edging discreetly towards a table that enjoyed less … well, coverage …

'Oh and get Taffy one of those fabulous Cola Coolers—' Dan called after him, as Teddy headed inside to the bar, scratching his head like Stan Laurel as he glanced up distrustfully at his 'cooling system'.

'Why are you two all dressed up in your glad rags then?' asked Dan, perching on the bench beside Holly.

'Ah, therein lies a tale—' said Taffy, about to launch into a somewhat embellished version of the evening's events.

'Taster session for Elsie at Sarandon Hall,' said Holly succinctly at the same time, earning herself a stern look from her beloved.

'Argh, you've just wasted a perfectly good anecdote there, Holls,' Taffy protested. 'The mileage from this evening could have kept Dan here entertained for hours.'

'Sorry,' said Holly, wrinkling her nose apologetically.

Dan just hooted. 'Well then, I guess I owe Holly a drink. Is it as pretentious up there as everybody says? I mean, if you look past the stunning luxury and general fabulousness that I will never afford in a million years?' Dan had rather hit the nail on the head right there, because half of the sniffy opposition to the Hall did tend to come from those who knew it was well beyond their means and therefore tried to eschew all it stood for, whilst at the same time pressing their faces longingly to the glass.

Holly nodded. 'I do hope Elsie knows what she's doing. I know she's missing her friends, but she's no ordinary pensioner, is she? Even amongst that set? She's an individual!'

Dan nodded. 'But if there's one thing we've learned about Elsie Townsend, it's that she knows her own mind. Interfere at your peril, Holly. If she wants to be Queen Bee of the red-trouser brigade, then really it is the only place to be.'

Teddy plonked down a tray on their table, an overflowing basket of chips effectively ending their conversation for a moment as all hands dived in.

'What's in this Cola Cooler thingummy then?' asked Taffy, sipping away and trying to discern what cocktail Teddy had been cooking up behind the bar. 'I mean, it's nice, but it's hardly Italian, is it?'

'Oh, that's not one of mine,' said Teddy, wiping the tray with a flourish. 'That's Dan's secret recipe, that one.'

Immediately suspicious and knowing his friend only too well – especially with that casually relaxed smile on his face – Taffy put down the drink abruptly. It was the merest moment too late, as with each swirl and crack of the ice cubes it became apparent that Dan's recipe did indeed have a secret ingredient: the foaming jet shot six feet up into the air, spewing cola bubbles everywhere in a violent volcanic reaction as the 'special' ice cubes thawed just enough to release the Mentos into the Coke.

Taffy sat frozen, absolutely drenched, cola frothing all down his face, his eyes wide in disbelief. He blinked and then the laughter began. 'You utter bastard,' he managed, swiping away the foam from his eyes and unable to stop laughing, partly as a nervous response to the complete shock of the 'explosion'.

It took both of them a moment to realise that Taffy wasn't the only one covered in froth. Holly scooped the brown foam from her hair and flicked it away, shaking the silk of her 'posh frock' until the foam rolled down to the ground. She looked at Dan and raised one eyebrow as he quailed in anticipation of a major bollocking.

'You, Daniel Carter, are just very lucky my chips are still

dry,' said Holly, with feeling, reaching over to help herself to a handful from the basket.

Taffy laughed louder still at the discombobulated look on Dan's face at Holly's unexpected reaction. He threw an arm around his fiancée's sodden shoulders with pride. 'Told you she was a keeper.'

Despite the slight stickiness that now seemed to accompany her every move, Holly couldn't remember having enjoyed an impromptu evening out more. Their table soon swelled with friends and neighbours dropping by for a chat and a drink. Of course, it was inevitable that another round of Cola Coolers had been ordered, just to demonstrate their tremendous power when extra Mentoed ice cubes were applied.

As Jason, their exuberantly bisexual, triathlete nurse, attempted his own version in his mouth, Holly had a feeling that they were having an awful lot more fun than any amount of silver-service fancification could provide and could only wish that Elsie were there to share it.

'Oh, by the way,' said Jason, his eyes still watering following his discovery that Diet Coke rather exacerbated the reaction, carrying a sting in its tail if taken orally, 'you owe me a tenner, Dan. Mr and Mrs Greaves called it a day and their house is on the market.'

Dan frowned and pulled a ten-pound note from his wallet without hesitation. 'Shame.'

Holly leaned forward. 'And are we betting on the housing market or the divorce rate?'

Jason looked a bit shifty, his eyes flickering to Dan for moral support. 'Well, you know all the arguments in the waiting room—' He hesitated, clearly unsure how much he was supposed to be giving away.

Holly looked around the table, as Dan, Taffy and Jason all fell silent.

'Are there lots of arguments in the waiting room then? Other than with idiots like Jarley?' she asked, uncomfortably aware that she might just be missing something going on under her very nose.

Jason nodded. 'More than I'm comfortable with anyway, but then it's often couples who arrive together who start having a go. They're the worst actually. Sometimes it's just nerves, sometimes we get to predict the next divorce . . .' He blushed, caught out in one of the games he and the nursing team liked to play. He certainly wasn't letting on that there was a chart on their noticeboard running odds on likely candidates.

Taffy grinned. 'I think we're busted.'

'You certainly are!' exclaimed Holly. 'How did I not know about this?' she asked indignantly. 'Can I put twenty quid down that the Lightlys will be finished by Christmas?'

Dan shook his head. 'You can, but I've got thirty that says Halloween.'

It wasn't exactly professional or discreet, but the four of them bantered happily about which cottages in Larkford might soon be on the market; death, divorce and bankruptcy still being the primary motivators for a sale in this desirable market town. Nobody, it seemed, ever willingly sold up once they'd got their foot on the Larkford property ladder; indeed most of the best houses were simply referred to as hand-me-downs around here.

Cassie Holland walked over with purpose, only to hover uncomfortably beside Holly, as though unwilling to interrupt their evening. 'Holly?' she said eventually. 'Dr Graham? Might I have a word?'

Holly stood up, peeling her dress off the bench where the cola foam had somehow solidified to a paste. It was incentive enough not to give her children cola to drink ever again!

'Hi, Cassie. Are you okay?' Holly said, guiding her away from their noisy group to a quieter spot.

'Well, it's just, I'm booked in to see you in the morning, but I don't think I can cope with another night!' Cassie blurted out. 'I'm in such pain. Can you give me something?'

Holly blinked hard; for Cassie Holland to knowingly request pharmaceuticals rather than obscure herbal remedies was almost unheard of.

'And when I say I'm in pain,' Cassie barrelled on, 'paracetamol doesn't touch it. It feels like it's inside my bones, inside my muscles, gnawing away.'

'Beaver pain,' Holly suggested, the double entendre completely eluding her, until she saw the shocked expression on Cassie's face.

'Well,' said Cassie, caught unawares, 'I wouldn't have put it quite like that, and you're a little off geographically, but yes!'

'If it's that severe, Cassie, we really ought to get you over to the out-of-hours so they can do a full exam. I'm a little reluctant to prescribe something stronger until we know what we're dealing with.' All sorts of scenarios were running through her mind, but sudden-onset pain was normally a warning sign that shouldn't be ignored.

'And when did this start?' Holly asked gently.

Cassie glanced down at her watch. 'Ooh I'd say six, maybe seven weeks ago now.'

'Weeks!' exclaimed Holly, blindsided.

'Well, yes,' said Cassie, unfazed. 'That's when I started doing the Couch-to-5k.'

Holly took a deep breath, trying to convince her adrenalin

to stand down; she'd been moments away from leaping in the car and driving Cassie into Bath herself. 'And it's your muscles and joints that hurt? Just your muscles and joints? Not in your abdomen or anywhere else?'

'Isn't that enough?' said Cassie plaintively, seemingly disappointed by Holly's change in demeanour and certainly not placated by the suggestion of some ibuprofen and a warm bath of Epsom salts.

Holly rejoined the group to find their conversation had taken a rather more obtuse turn.

'Well,' said Jason, casting his eye around the pub garden speculatively, 'I guess I'd murder Cassie Holland, easy that one, mangle old man Jarley and—'

'Did I miss something?' Holly asked easily, sliding in beside Taffy, his arm automatically encircling her waist.

'Murder, mangle, malaise,' Taffy said, as though that explained everything.

'Right,' said Holly, mentally flicking through the patients she'd seen that week for likely candidates. It was probably just as well their table was a little removed from the bustle of the pub garden on this sultry evening. It was fair to say that weeks of unbroken sunshine hadn't actually brought out the best in some of their patients.

She fanned herself with Teddy's fancy cocktail menu and breathed out slowly, allowing the banter to flow around her and make her smile; calm, comfortable and content to be an observer on this round.

She frowned as the first tiny droplets of water landed on her forehead, looking up in confusion to the cloudless, twilit sky.

A cheer went up from the bar as Teddy called for everyone's attention. 'You'll thank me for this!' he cried, throwing out an arm to encompass the whole garden. 'Bringing a little slice of Italy to Larkford!'

His waiting staff emerged from the kitchen in convoy, bearing huge platters of crisp, delicious pizzas piled high with rocket and basil.

The barman gave a drum roll on the counter top and Teddy ceremoniously turned on the tap to its full setting. It only took a moment for the tiny droplets to become a deluge, the holes punctured in the hosepipes forcing water out in multi-directional jets, blasting into people's drinks, faces and hair. Hardly the gentle cooling mist he'd been aiming for.

Holly jumped as a spurt caught her shoulders, everyone around her leaping to their feet and the promotional pizzas already swimming. She paused and looked around her, as some ran for cover, others stomped angrily off into the Market Place, but her friends, her true soulmates, remained beside her, twirling in the impromptu fountains and shrieking with laughter.

Taffy caught her in his arms and spun her around. 'At least it's rinsed off all the Coke,' he said with a grin, before weaving his hands through her hair and kissing her longingly.

'I love kissing you in the rain,' she whispered, her penchant for thunderstorm nookie well established in their relationship.

He raised one eyebrow. 'Well, I do aim to please.'

'Get a room, you two!' catcalled Dan through the deluge.

'The man does make a valid point,' said Holly, curling her fingers through Taffy's and giving him a gentle tug homewards. 'We've got at least an hour before picking up Elsie.'

'An hour?' heckled Dan. 'Hey, Taffs, it sounds like all that interval training's really paying off.'

Chapter 18

Alice thanked God for the little dog sitting at her side for the millionth time the next day. As Coco alerted by pawing at her thigh, Alice realised that, in the hustle and bustle of the busy afternoon clinic, the insidious symptoms of a hyper had been gradually creeping up on her. She blinked hard and her heart rate ratcheted up a notch when she saw the readings from the tiny drop of blood that she squeezed from her finger on autopilot. She quickly calibrated her insulin dose accordingly and scruffed Coco behind the ears in praise. It still amazed her that Coco preferred this to any of the other rewards that Jamie advised.

She rested her head on her desk and breathed slowly, allowing the wonder drug to work its magic on her broken system. Some people craved a different nose or a different haircut – both easily achieved with a little pain or a little expense. But a new pancreas, or a new immune system? If wishes were horses, she sighed.

She was tired, so tired of always being on her guard, never able to truly relax. At least she was no longer on the constant symptomatic rollercoaster of guesswork and stress; Coco had brought a little calm and control to the proceedings. But what she would give to sleep all through the night without the bleary-eyed night-time rituals dictated by her blood sugar. At least Tilly had been online last night with tales of her latest Mrs Robinson exploits to keep her entertained. Slightly shocked, but definitely entertained!

Alice started at the gentle knock on her door, barely having time to compose herself before Grace walked into the room. 'Oh my darling girl,' she said, clearly not missing a trick, 'what are you doing in here all by yourself?'

Before Alice could protest, she'd been swept up into a no-nonsense hug. She noticed that Coco instantly lay down and rested her head on her paws as though to say, 'Thank God the reinforcements have arrived.'

'Are you all sorted with this little lot?' Grace asked, nodding towards the insulin kit lying open on Alice's desk.

'Yeah,' managed Alice, still struggling to find her composure. Every time she was close, she would see the affection and concern in Grace's eyes and she'd feel it slipping further away.

'Then let's get out of here for the day, shall we? Come to The Deli with me and I can tell you all about the dishy pilot I met the other day.' She dangled the anecdote as incentive, as though knocking off work early might not be enough.

'But I've still got one patient to see,' Alice protested.

Grace shook her head. 'We thought you'd just overrun so Taffy took Mr Larch for his asthma review. What's the betting he's still a stealth smoker, eh?'

Grace hovered as Alice gathered her stuff together. She could only be grateful, Alice supposed, that it was Grace who had stumbled upon her self-pity-fest. It was hardly the confident, together demeanour upon which she prided herself at work.

Stepping out into the late-afternoon sunshine, Alice

squinted against the light and pulled her sunglasses from her bag. Win–win, she thought, grateful for a little distance.

'Too late in the day for a frothy cappuccino?' offered Grace, as they walked across the Market Place, which was already beginning to fill with pallid office workers seeking out a little daylight after a day staring at a computer screen. They nabbed a spare table outside The Deli the moment it became free and Grace quickly scanned the menu card.

'I'll get these,' Alice offered automatically, reaching for her purse, before remembering that she'd be lucky to find a fiver lurking in there this week. She faltered, wondering whether the hole in the wall would deign to deliver any cash when she was already teetering around her credit limit.

Grace didn't miss a beat, and certainly didn't let on that she'd seen Alice's hesitation. 'You most certainly will not. I've brought you out to cheer you up. And you've earned it, after organising that fabulous training session yesterday. I think we're all feeling a little more confident and informed. So these are on me.'

'A decaf cappuccino with lots of foam would be perfect then, thank you,' said Alice appreciatively.

She barely had time to collect her thoughts and have a little chat with Coco before Grace was back with a tray.

'Here we go. And I ordered some sweet potato wedges and olives and whatnot for us to nibble on – I hope that's okay? I managed to miss lunch today, what with trying to find out the extent of Derek Landers' evil plans for world domination. Dan's on a mission to get all the facts before we make a plan and it's like pulling at a ball of wool . . .'

The wedges arrived, steaming hot and crispy with sea salt, and Alice felt her mouth water. She took one bite and savoured the contrast of salty and sweet before looking up to find Grace watching her astutely. She felt a bit of a muppet then, because Grace was clearly mothering her.

'Aren't you going to have any?' Alice asked. 'Or is this care in the community?'

Grace grinned and plucked the largest, juiciest wedge from the basket. 'Of course I am, and of course it's not. We are allowed to look out for you a little though, Alice.'

They sipped their drinks quietly for a moment until Grace could no longer resist. 'So about this pilot—'

Alice laughed. 'If you like him so much, why don't *you* call him? I'm pretty sure we can rustle up a number for HQ quite easily.'

'Oh it wasn't me I was shopping for! Why would he be interested in me?' Grace protested. 'I thought he'd be perfect for you actually. Very easy on the eye, equally demanding job, seemed to have all the right bits in all the right places . . . If you know what I mean?'

'Grace!'

'Well actually, I thought he looked kind. And you know kind and thoughtful is the new sexy.'

'Is it now?' replied Alice. 'Then you should definitely call him yourself. Would be a shame to let a good one go to waste. Or tell Lucy – her fascination with men in uniform is quite something. You'll only need to say the word "pilot" and she'll sign up.'

'But you—?'

Alice shook her head. 'Not for me. I've got too much else to think about right now.'

'Of course you have.' Grace backtracked instantly. 'All this extra training for Coco and decisions to be made.' She dropped her voice. 'Not to mention, it must be hard living on a junior doctor's salary around here.'

So much for quiet discretion, thought Alice grumpily, annoyed to have been rumbled. Although Grace did make a valid point – all the holidaymakers and London weekenders had seemingly pushed up the price of everything this summer. The much-promised heatwave had gradually arrived and as the temperatures had risen, so had the cost of living.

Grace continued, her tone soft and confiding, and for a moment Alice was sorely tempted to tell her everything. Tilly's voice was in her head, urging her to take the leap—

Thankfully common sense prevailed.

'If you're finding it hard though, Alice, with the rent and the bills – I do know what it's like to run a household on one salary and I'd be only too glad to have a chat – see if we can trim a little here and there to make it easier?'

It was a kind suggestion, a thoughtful, generous offer, but Alice could immediately feel the prickle of anxiety that assailed her every time she let anybody get too close. And how much closer could one get, than poring over her monthly outgoings? Indeed, what would Grace think if she could actually see her credit card statements and bank accounts? There would be nowhere to hide then.

She somehow didn't think that switching tariffs on her heating bill would be quite enough at this point.

'You are so kind, Grace, but I'm good. Really.'

She couldn't help but wonder if she'd sounded half as unconvincing as she felt.

'No problem,' said Grace easily. 'I'm here if you need me though. But don't wait too long on your pilot fella though—'

'Your pilot, you mean,' countered Alice with a relieved smile that they were back on solid ground.

*

Sometimes spending time with Grace could feel like slipping into a warm bath, easing your muscles at the end of a long day and just letting go.

Today was not one of those days, thought Alice sadly. Ever since the topic of money had cropped up earlier on, she had felt under scrutiny, as though Grace were noticing every single nuance of their conversation and judging her. Even when Grace had complimented her on her new bracelet, Alice had felt that nauseated flip-flop of shame that came from attempting to justify the purchase. Of course, the more she tried to do so, the less pleasure the band of rose gold brought her, the initial rush she'd felt on its arrival already faded.

The irony being that Grace *wasn't* pushing her to explain herself; it had been a genuine compliment. It was merely Alice's guilty conscience that needed no accuser.

When Jamie Yardley came ambling across the Market Place towards them, Alice quickly made sure her sunglasses were wedged firmly in place, managing a wave and a smile. She had no desire for him to see her looking, or indeed feeling, this fragile.

Coco, bless her, ever the ice-breaker in any situation, saved her once again by throwing herself into Jamie's arms as he crouched down to greet her. Her little squirming body was always a sight for sore eyes, as her tail thwacked heavily back and forth and the rest of her seemed to carry the momentum.

'Now *that's* a greeting,' said Grace.

Jamie stood up and grinned. 'Isn't she something?'

He pulled up a chair beside Alice. 'How's your day been?' he asked.

She forced a smile, unsure how to answer. 'Bit up and down. But now we have snacks!' Imitating Jamie's upbeat and well-meaning banter was as good a habit as any to have gradually adopted in her quest for normality.

Jamie looked at her in concern, totally unconvinced, but Alice didn't notice, so busy was she handing down titbits to Coco to convince her to settle.

When she did finally look up, it was to catch the tail end of what seemed to be a telepathic conversation of meaningful glances and raised eyebrows between Jamie and Grace across the table. 'What?' she demanded, cringing at the hint of petulant teenager in her voice. If there was one thing she hated, it was being analysed by other people.

Jamie shook his head. 'Nothing. Don't be so grumpy – it's not a good look on you,' he teased. He clocked their nearly empty mugs. 'Let me pop in and get you two another round. Taffy's already inside stocking up on sausage rolls. We're going for a run in a bit and we need carbs. Apparently.' He shook his head, clearly humouring Taffy's adolescent eating habits.

'Let me,' Grace said, already on her feet.

'Sure, thanks,' Jamie said, a little rebuffed by her abrupt tone. 'Am I interrupting something?' he asked Alice. 'Taffy and I can go and grab another table?'

'You're fine,' Alice reassured him, instantly feeling guilty that she was taking her mood out on him. 'Honestly. Just ignore me, Jamie. I'm having one of those sleep-deprived, paranoid days. It just feels like everybody's looking out for me today. It's really weird, being under the microscope.'

'Hmm, you're right, it *is* weird, that – people wanting to keep an eye on you when you look like death warmed up and that insulin kit is being hauled out more often than a sickbag on a cross-channel ferry? Come on, Walker.' He leaned against her casually, almost nudging her shoulder, a gentle teasing smile lighting up his eyes. 'No man is an island and all that.'

Alice couldn't help but smile herself at his earnest reassurances. 'Well, *men* may not be able to cope with a few ups and downs, but I'm pretty sure most *women* can.'

'Why are you so arsey today, anyway?' he asked, throwing his arm around her shoulders companionably. He'd long since learned to take the rough with the smooth when it came to his favourite client. A bad weather warning with Alice normally meant she was frightened, he reckoned. Not that she'd ever admit it. Quite what she was frightened about today was anyone's guess, but it didn't stop him trying to be her friend.

He glanced down at her, recognising all the signs that she was covering again. He only wished he knew how to persuade her that, whilst keeping everyone around her at arm's length would absolutely create the distance she craved, in all likelihood it would be just in time for her to realise she didn't actually want it. Being unwell was a solitary business at the best of times; with a chronic illness like diabetes, that loneliness could be crippling.

He reached down and fussed Coco's ears. Thank God she had the company and unconditional affection that Coco offered to keep her in balance. This, more than anything else, made him realise that Alice without Coco didn't bear thinking about. In fact, if only he could persuade Alice to stop thinking about 'the greater good' and think of herself a little more, then really, there was no decision to be made.

'How do you feel about being bold and bolshy?' he ventured, reaching over and stealing an olive.

She shot him a sideways glance. 'Are you trying to tell me something?'

Jamie laughed. 'Well, now that you mention it—' He reached over and pinched the last of the potato wedges too. 'But actually, I meant with Judith and the training centre. The way I see it, right now the only sacrifice or adjustment is yours. How about we all share the load a little to make things work?'

Alice turned to him, ignoring Coco's puppy-dog eyes for a moment, as they followed the sweet potato wedge's every movement. 'What did you have in mind?'

Jamie shrugged. 'I'm not quite sure. Yet. But something along the lines of everyone giving a little, so nobody has to give a lot. Judith's awfully good at guilting people into doing what she wants; it's part of what makes her so good at the fundraising part of her job actually. But in this case . . .' His words petered out as he tried to convey his train of thought by holding Alice's gaze.

Alice sat firmly on her hands, suddenly overwhelmed by the urge to brush Jamie's tawny fringe from his eyes as the light summer breeze insisted on ruffling it forward. 'I think a team effort might sit more comfortably with me too,' she said quietly, noticing Jamie's eyes flash a little with the deliberate ambiguity of her words.

He leaned across and drained the last of her drink. 'Leave it with me for a few days,' he said. 'And Alice? You're not being paranoid. We *are* all looking out for you,' he added, squeezing her shoulder lightly, before he got up and walked away without a backwards glance, leaving her pulse ricocheting and the beginnings of a complicit smile on her face.

Chapter 19

'Harry!' said Holly the next morning, relief in her voice, as she arrived at The Practice to find Harry Grant fidgeting uncomfortably by the private staff entrance. After days of trying to track him down, she had to confess she'd been a little worried that his dismissal from the PCT meant that they were no longer even on his radar – perhaps a lucrative contract in the private sector had tempted him away. 'I was beginning to think you'd dropped off the face of the earth.'

She kissed him on both cheeks, surprised by how much his arrival had pleased her. He looked pale, she decided, not to mention a little gaunt behind his ever-present glasses and beard.

He laughed, a bitter edge to his voice. 'Well, to be honest, it does rather feel that way. Eighteen years working for the department obviously count for nothing if you disagree too loudly with Derek Landers. Phone, laptop, car – all gone in a morning.' He paused. 'I'm sorry I haven't been in touch properly.'

The restraint in his demeanour was almost visible; obviously the parting of ways had been even more acrimonious than she'd realised. 'I suppose me thanking you for having our backs doesn't mean all that much in the grand scheme of things,' Holly offered sadly.

'Oh, I wouldn't say that, Holly.' He looked around, a furtive hint to his movements. 'Look, to be honest, I've spent the last few days holed up with my lawyer finding out where I stand.'

'Wow,' said Holly. 'Then maybe this is a conversation we shouldn't really have in the car park.'

'Or without coffee,' suggested Harry with feeling, knowing Holly's usual reliance on caffeine, but unaware she was reluctantly making do with lemongrass tea these days.

Holly turned her key in the door and they slipped inside, the cool of the old building an instant relief from the heat already building outside. Enjoying the sunshine wasn't really an option when their working hours seemed to be growing exponentially. Once Derek Landers' cuts were in place, Holly realised, she and Taffy might never get the same day off again. The simple notion of a picnic on the banks of the River Lark as a family was beginning to feel like a pipe dream.

They walked through to Holly's office, where she pulled a cold bottle of elderflower cordial out of the vaccination fridge. 'I reckon we've got twenty minutes until the hordes arrive, Harry,' she said as she poured out two glasses. 'What's on your mind?'

Harry sat down beside her desk and twisted his fingers together. 'Well, you know I got fired because I disagreed with the proposed cutbacks. I disagreed so strongly with the cutbacks because, in my humble opinion, they seemed short-sighted and biased against the rural population. Hardly ideal in the South West.'

'Quite,' said Holly. 'But what I can't work out is the speed. One moment there's talk of audits, the next my patients are being turned away from Rosemore.'

'Exactly,' said Harry, nodding his head fervently. 'No

real oversight, very little consultation, just focusing on the bottom line.' He drained his glass. '"Streamlining" the maternity provision is only the beginning, I'm afraid. The Air Ambulance regions are being reallocated by population numbers, rather than square mileage – so we'll be screwed there as well. There's even talk of trimming oncology care in the community. It's so incredibly short-sighted, I could scream. Eighteen years walking the tightrope, trying to balance the books and keep optimal patient care – and now this! And you can bet your bottom dollar that Derek Landers won't be giving up his company Lexus or his expense account any time soon.' He paused, uncomfortable for a moment. 'Not that you heard any of this from me, legally speaking.'

'I'm so proud of you for speaking out, Harry. This stuff matters. I mean seriously, life-changingly, matters. But I have yet to explain it to anyone in a suit in such a way that they actually seem to understand,' Holly reassured him.

Harry looked up from under his furrowed brow. 'All the press coverage and naysaying in the world isn't going to change their position on this one. They've been given targets and they're meeting them. On paper. The next crisis, of course, will be patient care and they'll move the goal posts again – if it's an election year – but by then the infrastructure will be gone.'

'You can't put the genie back in the bottle,' said Holly, knowing that there was so much truth in his words. 'So no point in rallying the troops for another PR campaign?'

Harry shook his head sadly. 'Not that I can see. Not this time, Holly. Best I can suggest at this point is that you guys do a quick stocktake on how it's going to affect your patch directly. Then maybe some local fundraising to keep things in motion for your patients at least. Focus on your own patch.

Be a little selfish.' He paused, looking over at the door and, seemingly reassured that he wouldn't be overheard, he continued, 'Just keep the wheels turning for a bit and who knows what might change.'

'Harry, what have you got in mind?' Holly asked, intrigued.

He shook his head. 'Plausible deniability for you, young lady. Let me at least explore some options before you all jump in with both feet.' He stood up and paused. 'We can't keep doing this dance every bloody year, can we? You have patients to treat and I have, well, *had* a department to run. We shouldn't be funding our health care with bake sales and sponsored runs.' He leaned in and unexpectedly kissed Holly on the cheek. 'You're doing a great job. Just keep the wheels turning locally and I'll be in touch.'

Even a back-to-back day of patients, in which she had yet to see even Taffy loitering in the doctors' lounge, was not enough to distract Holly from thinking about Harry Grant. She couldn't decide whether she wanted him to go full whistleblower on what he so obviously knew but wasn't currently sharing, or whether she wanted him to put himself and his lovely family first. In his position, Holly knew, she'd be tearing herself to pieces trying to work out the best course of action. Sadly 'for the greater good' so often left the instigator paying the price.

She slipped away to collect the twins from Lizzie's after yet another impromptu playdate had been necessitated by the sheer volume of patients suffering with the heat. Based on how tired and nauseous she was feeling, she was half-tempted to add herself to the list.

'You are officially an angel and a godsend,' Holly announced as Lizzie pulled open the front door. She handed over the Kettle Chips, Pimm's and Magnums that counted as payment in kind and kissed Lizzie on both cheeks.

'Hmm. Well, you might not say that when you see what we've been up to,' Lizzie said, leading the way through to the kitchen where shrieks of excitable laughter echoed around the back garden and through the open French windows. 'Ta-da!' she said. 'It's modern art, isn't it? Well, that and they got bored of just splashing about.'

Holly laughed, more out of shock than anything else. Her two boys and Lizzie's three children were running around the garden in their pants, coloured from head to toe in streaks of brightly coloured paint. It was like a children's adaptation of the Holi festival of colour that Holly and Lizzie had so enjoyed on their student travels through India all those years ago. The paddling pool water was translucent with rainbows swirling on its surface, some of which had been captured on giant sheets of paper that were now hanging to dry on the washing line. Each child bore a beaming smile, a stained body and the noise levels were certainly enough to get the neighbours tutting.

'I'm not saying it's ideal, but it's kept them good for ages,' Lizzie said, as she turned to pull out another tray of ice for yet more drinks to keep the little darlings hydrated. She eyed Holly speculatively and dropped her voice. 'So, come on, am I allowed to let the cat out of the bag yet? It's killing me keeping your secret from Will!'

Holly's face broke into an enormous smile. 'You mean, you haven't even told Will? Oh, Lizzie!' She shook her head in stunned amazement.

'Well it's not my news to share, is it?' Lizzie said, throwing up her hands in amused frustration. 'And you thought I couldn't keep my mouth shut . . .'

It was true; Holly and Taffy had been quietly waiting for

Lizzie to let slip about the pregnancy and for the Larkford tom-toms to start beating.

Holly shrugged. 'Well, we need to wait for the scan and all that, really, before we say anything officially. Make sure the little bean's cooking nicely. But we can tell Will, can't we? I mean,' she pulled an apologetic face, 'I kind of assumed you had already.'

Lizzie shook her head and laughed. 'You mean I've been weird and evasive with him all week for nothing? Right then, Holls, phone Taffy,' Lizzie urged. 'Come on. The kids don't need to know why we're celebrating, do they? We'll have a barbecue, tell poor Will and raise a little glass to bid adieu to your waistline!' She grinned, pressing the phone into Holly's hand and brooking no argument.

Holly hugged her best friend tightly, knowing without Lizzie even saying that this pregnancy was going to impact their friendship in all sorts of ways. Lizzie, after all, had made no secret in the past of how glad she was to be out of the world of nappies and sleepless nights, already looking forward to school plays and music festivals. Her support meant the world and her enthusiasm was a bonus that even Holly hadn't been banking on.

'Come on, seriously,' mumbled Lizzie into her hair, 'you guys have been all work and no play recently. Let me at least cook you supper – let's have some fun.' She took hold of Holly's hand and gave it a gentle squeeze. 'Dan gave me a little hint about what you guys have been juggling at work lately. Stay and take a breath. You can organise your plans to overthrow The Man tomorrow.'

Holly shook her head. 'I am not plotting to overthrow anyone.'

Lizzie glanced sideways at her sceptically. 'Well I've known you a very long time, Holly Graham, and that there is your shit-stirring face.'

Holly laughed. 'Okay, well maybe a teensy tiny bit, but did anyone ever stop to think that a little revolution around here wouldn't be the end of the world?'

'Oh, I'm all up for a scrap, as it happens,' Lizzie said, as she ripped open an enormous bag of salad and emptied it into a bowl. Cooking had never been Lizzie's strong point, but thankfully she'd recently decided to accept defeat gracefully and now confined her culinary activities to 'opening things' instead. 'I'm just saying, take it easy.'

Lizzie's ever-tolerant husband Will wandered in looking exhausted, his immaculate linen jacket slung over one shoulder and none-the-wiser as to how his evening plans were changing. 'Was any man ever so lucky to come home to two gorgeous women in his kitchen?' he said, kissing them both. He glanced out at the mayhem in the garden and barely missed a beat, before stripping off down to his boxers and charging into the fray, belly-flopping into the paddling pool and causing ripples and waves to splash over the edge. He sat up and pushed his hair back off his face, covered head to toe in streaks of primary colours. 'Come on in!' he shouted. 'The water's lovely!'

And the children followed his lead, until all five of them, along with Will and, of course, Eric, were packed into the paddling pool in a Technicolor swirl of giggles and chaos.

Lizzie put her arm around Holly's shoulders and squeezed. 'You're right, you know. You do need a third one to round out your new little family. A mini-Taffy should do the job nicely. Just promise me that we'll keep having times like this. You're my spontaneity fix, Holls. And I'm worried that spontaneity and babies just don't mix.'

Holly nodded with a smile. 'Firstly, I promise. And secondly, what you're calling spontaneity is what Taffy and I call "winging it" and I'm not sure that's ever going to change.' She looked out at the mayhem in the garden, her eyes shining with delight. 'No matter how many children there are in our house.'

Chapter 20

Holly startled awake with her heart leaping into her throat. She stared around in the dawn light in confusion, as Taffy slept deeply beside her and she struggled to work out the cause of her abrupt awakening. She swung her feet round onto the carpet, bleary-eyed, but concern for the twins propelling her from the comfort of her duvet.

The hammering on the front door jarred her with its intensity, clearly not the first volley of the morning.

She grabbed Taffy's sweatshirt and pulled it on over her pyjamas, rubbing her eyes and yawning as she staggered down the stairs, picking up her doctor's bag and car keys on autopilot as she walked through the hallway, assuming that only a medical emergency would bring someone to her door at this ungodly hour.

She peered through the hallway window, just able to make out the shape of Jemima Hallow on her doorstep, fidgeting from side to side.

'Mims? Are you okay? Is the baby coming?' Holly asked, as she pulled open the door.

Jemima was fully dressed, her newly acquired maternity t-shirt already straining to accommodate her growing bump. Her eyes were bright with a peculiar intensity and her hair was already plastered to her forehead with the kind of morning heat that promised a scorcher of a day to come. She held what looked like some kind of road sign in her hand.

'I've decided not to take this lying down,' she declared. 'I'm going to protest and I want you and the other partners to join us. Everyone will take us more seriously if they can see that we have our GPs' support.'

She spun the sign in her hand around and Holly realised that it was a hurriedly constructed placard bearing the slogan:

MY BABY!
MY VAGINA!
MY CHOICE!

'Catchy,' said Holly drily, forcing herself awake properly. 'Look, Mims, come inside and talk about this at least. You're obviously upset, but I'm sure there's been provision made. We're all working on it, I promise you, but let's at least get all the facts, before your blood pressure goes through the roof.'

'But we're *going* to protest,' objected Mims, stepping aside to reveal a gaggle of pregnant women behind her in various states of undress and sleepiness, all of them clearly roused from their beds to rally to the call. Poor Emily Arden, due any day now, was leaning against the railings outside as though they were the only thing holding her, and her bump, upright.

Holly ushered them all into the kitchen, flicking the kettle on as she rootled around for peppermint tea and decaffeinated coffee.

'Emily? Do you need a cushion? If you'd be comfier on the sofa, make yourself at home,' she offered. 'Anyone else? Water? Cushions? Gaviscon?'

Taffy wandered into the kitchen, yawning, wearing only his boxer shorts, and still smeared with stubborn streaks of colour from joining in the modern art fiesta at Lizzie's the night before. He startled slightly at the panorama of bumps around his kitchen table. The volley of wolf whistles brought an embarrassed smile to his face. 'Well, that's one way to start the day,' he said. 'I suppose I'm overreaching to ask if you've saved me any breakfast?' He beat a speedy retreat to find some clothes and could be heard warning Tom and Ben in the hallway that there was stiff competition for the bacon this morning.

Holly paused for a moment as her own pregnancy hormones made their own small protest, clearly thrown by the abrupt start to her day. Obviously the adrenalin had only kept her morning sickness at bay for so long. ''Scuse me,' she managed as she dashed from the room.

Ironically, there was something cathartic about hurling quite so prolifically and Holly returned to the room with a sharper sense of focus and a reasonable plan of action. She was delighted to find that Taffy had admitted defeat on restoring normality and was now churning out rounds of toast to order, her absence barely noted in the whirlwind of his breakfast efficiency.

'I've been doing my research,' Jemima was telling everyone emphatically. 'This is just the beginning. So, if we want to take care of our families, then we have to take a stand!'

Holly didn't like to say that half the women in the group looked utterly exhausted at the very prospect, and that standing around in this heat was categorically not what the doctor ordered.

'And,' continued Jemima furiously, clearly revved up, 'I

spoke to our esteemed town councillor, Malcolm, yesterday.' Her words were dripping with disdain. 'And all he could say was that the right people, who were in possession of *all* the facts, were making the decision. Said it wasn't part of his "purview".' She shook her head disdainfully. 'Smarmy little fucker.'

'Little fucker,' echoed Tom behind her, utterly thrilled with his new vocabulary.

'Oh Tom,' said Taffy smoothly, crouching down to look him in the eye, 'if you're old enough to swear, then you have to pronounce it properly.' Tom nodded earnestly. 'Smarmy little *trucker*!' Taffy demonstrated.

'Trucker, trucker, trucker!' shouted Tom with glee as he ran out of the kitchen to share his new-found wisdom with his twin.

'Dodged a bullet there at least,' said Holly, shaking her head with a smile. 'Look, I genuinely think that the weight of public opinion is vital, you know I do. But I'd also like to think that we can take a step back, to see what else we can productively do, before we go barrelling in unprepared. Knowledge is power, after all. And, I mean,' she hesitated, frowning, unused to a placatory role when it came to standing up and being counted, 'do you need to protest *today*?'

'What are you suggesting we should wait for?' asked Emily Arden from the depths of the sofa.

Holly shrugged. 'I don't really know. More information? A co-ordinated effort? Clouds?'

One or two of the ladies around the table nodded in agreement – this was obviously a knee-jerk reaction and, based on the fact that several of her guests this morning seemed to still be wearing their slippers, they probably wouldn't mind a little more time to prepare.

'No,' said Jemima firmly, still clasping her placard incongruously, even as she sat at the kitchen table sipping peppermint tea. 'Every day that Rosemore is closed is a day too long. Look at Emily!' Everyone turned to stare at poor Emily, who promptly looked as though she wanted to disappear into the sofa cushions. 'She's fit to pop any day. It has to be today and it has to be all of us.'

'How about a compromise?' Holly suggested after a moment, her mind racing about how best to avoid all her pregnant patients being felled by heatstroke. 'How about we head out to the Market Place before it gets too hot, and catch all the commuter traffic? How about we make a little video of the protest, featuring all the support you need, and then you ladies can take care of your health, while the video gets sent to all the news outlets, on message, and doing all your legwork for you?' She looked at her watch. 'If you want to get dressed and gather some warm bodies, we can meet you there in an hour? Give Taffy here half an hour with a camcorder and your work is done.'

There was a hushed excitement at the very suggestion; it was as though she had somehow stumbled upon exactly the right line to tread – protesting-lite for the pregnant lady. Nobody was complaining though.

Jemima stood up. 'I'll handle all the press releases and whatnot and the sending out – if you're really happy to do this?'

'I'll even call the NCT co-ordinators for the region in case they want to send along their members,' said Holly, mollified. 'It's a bit short notice, but get knocking on doors – you won't be short of support.'

As the ladies hustled out into the street, Taffy stood behind her, watching them go, his arms cradled around her waist and his chin on her shoulder. 'Is this your sneaky way of ignoring Harry Grant then?' he asked quietly.

Holly sighed, knowing only too well that, in the past, it would have been her leading the charge. She couldn't decide whether she liked this new status quo or not, but if there was one thing Mims was not short of, it was motivation. Standing down and waiting was all very well and good, but Mims made a valid point: even one day without cover was one day too many.

'This is local though, just like Harry said. We're just keeping the wheels turning, yes?' Holly replied with a shrug, turning round to face him. 'And when Harry can tell us more, then we'll have more to work with. But at least we're doing *something*.'

'Okay then,' said Taffy, kissing her forehead lovingly, knowing her well enough to realise there was little point in arguing. After all, there were but a handful of people in Larkford who knew how emotionally invested Holly was in these maternity cuts. Not that she herself would be off to Rosemore necessarily, more that it brought home so very clearly the notion of choice. After all, what could be more personal than choosing where to welcome the new addition to your family? 'Tell me what you need—'

There was no way that Holly could have foreseen the effect of her suggestion. Somehow, the spontaneity and earliness of the hour conveyed the urgency of the situation far better than weeks of campaigning and invitations might have done. By half past eight, the Market Place was heaving. Mothers and fathers on the school run pulled their cars over to join in. Large marker pens appeared from somewhere and soon people were taking it in turns to write slogans on each other's t-shirts. 'My Choice – My Baby' was popular, although Holly couldn't help but snort when she saw Teddy Kingsley's offering – a somewhat more abrupt homage to Derek Landers: '$%@€ Off Walrus Face!' Although to be fair, he'd also turned up with impromptu bacon butties and soft drinks from the pub, so he could be forgiven almost anything at this point.

Dan made his way through the crowd towards them. 'This is genius. It's like a flash mob!'

Holly spotted within seconds the way Taffy's eyes lit up and she gently put a hand on his arm before he could even suggest it. 'Let them have their moment, Taffs. These women deserve every second of recognition for pulling this together; don't swamp the news cycle with you and Dan being silly buggers.'

Dan nodded. 'Yeah, we can always do that later.' He leaned in closely. 'Anybody else think that Emily Arden looks a little off-colour?' Before Holly could answer, Taffy and Dan split off in a chivalrous pincer movement to rescue poor Emily before her legs gave out entirely.

It gave Holly an incredibly proud moment to see them carrying her so sweetly over to a shady bench; a moment that also didn't escape the stringer from the local press who seemed to have stumbled onto their protest more by accident than design, if the supermarket shopping bag banging against his leg was any indication.

Rupert Hallow appeared at Holly's side, a mixture of concern and pride on his face. 'I'm so sorry if this has put you guys on the spot rather, but there was just no talking to her.'

Holly smiled. 'I'm actually delighted. It's quite nice for somebody else to be leading the charge for a bit. I think I'm getting a reputation as a bit of a meddler.'

Rupert nodded. 'Yeah, just awful having proactive doctors that care about their patients,' he said drily.

Whatever he was going to say next was drowned out by his wife's incredibly vocal rallying cry. In no time at all, she had all four generations of Larkford's residents chanting in unison. This in itself was rare as hen's teeth – possibly the one and only issue they could all jump on board with. Whether it was the Air Ambulance, the Maternity Unit at Rosemore, or indeed the incipient threat of what might be next, it was an oddly unifying moment.

Holly didn't even realise she was crying until Rupert handed her his freshly pressed handkerchief. He sniffed. 'It kind of gets you, doesn't it, seeing Mims pull everyone together like that. She's going to be a great mum.' He wove his way through the crowd and plucked his pregnant wife off her feet, manfully swinging her around to cheers and applause, as he kissed her thoroughly.

Holly swallowed another happy sob as the emotions rolled over her, no longer in control at seeing her beloved community come together in yet another time of crisis. Even if this one happened to be bringing the Market Place to a halt during what passed for rush hour, as the cacophony of hooting delivery trucks grew louder on the outskirts of town, with no idea what was causing the hold-up.

'Dr Graham!' interrupted Gladys Jones, insistently tugging at her sleeve. 'Help me out, love. I was too rushed to put in my hearing aid. What are we protesting about?'

Holly leaned down to the elderly lady amongst the crowd, making sure to keep the twins in sight. 'It's about the Maternity Unit,' she said, enunciating every syllable, 'closing it down.'

'Quite right too,' replied Gladys incredibly loudly. 'Don't want that kind of nonsense in the town.'

Holly paused. 'Maternity?'

'Yes! It's the start of the rot,' Gladys said firmly. 'Those young men aren't at university to party every night!'

Holly just smiled, unable to work out how on earth Gladys had any experience of the controversial new fraternities at the nearby university anyway. 'Come on, Gladys,' she said, offering her an arm. 'Come and get a cold drink from Teddy and you can tell him all about it.'

'You'd think old Gladys would have worked out where babies come from by now,' sniffed Tom disparagingly, as they made their way through the crowd, causing a ripple of laughter to follow in their wake.

Chapter 21

Alice paused on the corner of her road that evening, strangely reluctant to head home just yet. The emotional ripples from the morning's protest had stayed with her all day. And with her patients, come to that; there hadn't been a single person to walk through her consulting-room door who hadn't offered their support in some way and, as the number of photos and videos online began to gain momentum, it had been all anyone could talk about.

It went without saying that the picture of Taffy and Dan carrying poor Emily Arden had been the one to get the most retweets and shares, but then what's not to like about two dishy doctors being chivalrous in the extreme? Even Tilly had managed to comment on that one, from another time zone . . .

Alice had never lived anywhere like this before; where your business was everybody's business, or so it seemed.

She couldn't quite work out how she felt about that either. Seeing everyone rally together behind Jemima and Emily and the rest of the newly anointed Preggie Protesters had been quite the eye-opener. People here cared. Perhaps it was the Cotswold equivalent of the South American communities that Tilly was always extolling?

Alice paused outside The Boutique On The Square, more out of habit than intent, squinting hopefully through the darkened windows and wondering whether a cathartic half-hour trying on designer jeans might be just the salve she was looking for. She felt disoriented and not a little claustrophobic.

Laughter and conversation caught her attention as Rupert the vet and his wife spilled out of The Deli, their paper sack of takeout food wafting its delicious aroma towards Alice as they passed. They waved, Jemima calling out her thanks for Alice's earlier support.

Drawn to the idea of company, without company, she pushed open the door to The Deli and let her eyes travel along the shelves of delicacies. Maybe a little deli-picking would deal with the almost overwhelming urge to buy something, anything really. Hattie waved a friendly hello from behind the counter, where she ladled out casserole for Marion Waverly, with precise instructions for how best to reheat it later. Watching Marion hand over a crisp ten-pound note caused Alice a flicker of guilt. She tried not to think about the effect customers like herself had on a small business's cash flow. But then, she justified, they had offered her the option to run a pay-day tab . . .

'Alice!' said Hattie, as Marion left with a wave and Alice studied a jar of puttanesca sauce. 'I know it's out of hours, and I hope you don't mind, but can I ask you about teething? My twins are getting their molars through and seem to do nothing but grizzle. They're driving me nuts, to be honest.'

Alice put down the jar and saw that Hattie wasn't kidding; she looked tired, drawn and thoroughly pissed off at the thought of another sleepless night. 'Well,' she said slowly, feeling oddly touched that Hattie would ask her, child-free and off-duty. It almost felt as though they were becoming, well, friends. 'If you've tried the gel and it doesn't do the trick, there's some little sachets of homeopathic powder that work wonders—' Alice looked around The Deli for a moment and dropped her voice. 'Although to be fair, I grew up in Scotland, where everyone just rubbed a drop of whisky on their gums. Works a treat, with the added bonus that they sleep like a dream. But you did NOT hear that from me.'

Hattie laughed, instantly looking five years younger. 'And now you come to mention it, I think *my* teeth are a little sore as well.'

The bell above the door chimed and they both looked up to see Grace, who had abandoned all pretence at her usual calm composure and was looking flustered and decidedly pink. 'I give up,' she announced to Hattie. 'I've got nothing to wear and I've just heard that the High Commissioner is on the bloody guest list!'

'Crikey,' said Hattie with feeling. She turned to Alice, sweetly bringing her up to speed on whatever drama was unfolding. 'Grace is going on a date with a hunky pilot, but it's black-tie and she's wigging out.'

'It's not a date!' Grace protested, snaffling one of the individual biscotti from the counter, without bothering with the accompanying espresso. 'Is it, Alice? Tell her.'

Hattie grinned. 'Yes, do let's get Alice's take on this. She can be the tie-breaker. So, gorgeous Chris Virtue called earlier on to invite Grace to be his plus-one at the Regional Air Ambulance Dinner. He *says*,' she couldn't help but smile, 'that it's to give Grace a chance to meet the movers and shakers and see behind the scenes. But you'll note that he hasn't extended the same invitation to Dan. Presumably, because he doesn't look so fetching in a silk evening dress as our Gracie—'

'Oh you do talk rot,' cut in Grace.

'Although Dan has got lovely legs,' Alice mused deliberately, loving their easy banter.

'It's not a date, because it's a *work* do,' Grace said firmly. 'But that doesn't mean I can't look nice.'

'I think he likes you,' said Hattie in a singsong voice designed to torment.

'But does he have to like me in "cocktail attire"?' Grace said peevishly. 'I think Alice here should go instead. I've been trying to introduce them for ages. He's really very lovely and *you've* no shortage of fancy frocks.'

'Ooh,' said Hattie, instantly intrigued, 'waste not want not—'

Alice was distracted for a moment, uncomfortable in the extreme at the very suggestion, and hardly heard the words around her, until Hattie repeated her name.

'Earth to Alice, come in, Alice? I was just saying to Grace how fabulous you always look. Come on – what's your secret? Maybe you could give her some pointers to get an outfit together?'

Alice nodded, caught on the hop; whilst fashion and designers were her passion, it was more of a private, almost secret obsession, and she wasn't sure how she felt about sharing. She looked at the two expectant faces before her – open and affable, and asking her advice. Tilly's voice echoed in her mind.

'Sure,' she said slowly, realising this let her off the hook of stepping into the breach. 'What have you already got? Maybe we can accessorise something to make it more fancy?'

Grace and Hattie both laughed. 'You'll have your work cut out then,' confessed Grace with a shrug, indicating the simple powder-blue sundress she was currently wearing. 'This is my smart dress, or was my smart dress when I had occasion to wear it. Now I just get on and enjoy it. No point saving things for best, is there really?'

Alice suppressed a small wave of bewilderment. It was almost as though they were talking a foreign language. 'Okay then,' she said. 'Maybe we need to take you shopping.'

Grace and Hattie looked guiltily at one another.

'The thing is,' Grace said, 'the dinner's tomorrow night.'

'Oh,' breathed Alice, wondering why Grace wasn't actually panicking more. It hardly occurred to her that, for Grace at least, the dress she would wear was probably the least of her concerns.

Stepping back out into the Market Place, without so much as a bag of fancy pasta in her hand, Alice drew in a steadying breath. If she took even a moment to outline the anxiety she was feeling, Grace would no doubt think her crazy.

She couldn't even put a finger on when this bizarre obsession with keeping things just for herself had begun; it was hardly as though she could blame a sister for borrowing and trashing her clothes, or indeed a shortage of replacements should something be damaged whilst 'on loan'. No, she decided, it was just one more step in the direction of being an official nutjob – or whatever the technical term actually was for someone who bought more clothes than they could ever reasonably wear in a lifetime? Of course, she'd watched the programmes on television about hoarders, and she'd been comfortably smug that she would never let her own home get into such a state of disarray. No indeed, because Alice's collections of books and clothes were all catalogued and cared for – no unsightly heaps for her – just a spare bedroom filled with hanging rails and indexed storage boxes stacked neatly in every available space.

The very idea of lending Grace something to wear was one thing; inviting her into her own personal space was even harder. She felt a sweaty, clammy wave of discomfort prickle over her chest, even as Grace chatted easily beside her. How on earth had a longing for something special for supper ended up like this? She couldn't even really recall how the conversation had morphed into her making the invitation.

'You are very sweet to offer, you know, Alice,' Grace said after a moment, perhaps picking up on Alice's uneasiness, 'but if you've got other plans for this evening, you only have to say.'

Alice thought for a second. Well, she did have plans. There was Neil from Norfolk to chat to online, a sale on matchesfashion.com and a new instalment of her latest Netflix box set – yet somehow all of those things felt a little hollow now, compared to the laughter and bonhomie in The Deli.

'Nothing that can't keep,' Alice said quietly, determined to push herself out of self-imposed exile. There was no need to point out to herself that she could equally well do all of those things in the wee small hours, when Coco nudged her awake to check her blood sugar as it plummeted.

Besides, she was almost intrigued to see Grace in such a tizz. It was so out of character that Alice wondered if it was Pilot Chris – as Hattie had anointed him, as though he came straight out of a children's cartoon – who had got Grace's pulse racing. Maybe he really was just that wonderful? Which would be a shame really, thought Alice, as she'd harboured a secret hope that Dan and Grace would one day look up and actually notice each other.

'Your aunt said you'd picked up an interest in interior design,' Grace said, as they turned into Alice's road. 'Spotting fabulous bargains at the Antiques Market and restoring them?'

Alice shook her head. 'Sadly my aunty Pru has a big mouth and a severe case of wishful thinking. She keeps threatening to drag me to Ikea to get organised.'

Grace shuddered, earning herself immediate Brownie points from Alice. 'What fresh hell would that be? And who wants to live in the same identikit house as everybody else anyway?'

'Quite,' said Alice, secretly surprised by Grace's vehemence on the topic.

'And is she still calling it Eekoo? I do love your aunt and her malapropisms; she told me she was after joining some flamingo classes when I saw her last week.' Grace smiled. 'She only wants the best for you, Alice – probably just wants you to settle in, put down a few roots so you're less of a flight risk,' she said, adopting Dan's spot-on phrase.

She made a valid point, thought Alice, but Grace continued. 'It can take a while to settle anywhere new. And you do spend so much time at work, and with your gorgeous Jamie . . . I guess Pru just wants you to feel at home here.'

Alice nodded, overcome by the entirely unfamiliar, but increasingly nagging, urge to share. 'You do know he's not really *my* Jamie.'

'Oh,' said Grace, her voice laced with understanding. She stopped walking for a moment. 'You could just tell him, you know,' she said gently.

Alice shook her head. 'Too messy.'

Grace opened her mouth as though to say something and then stopped, satisfying herself with a supportive look.

'Maybe there are easier ways to appease your aunt,' she offered. 'Buy a bookcase, maybe? I mean, how many books could you possibly have that it's causing her such concern?'

Alice pushed open the door to her cottage, where the cat-alogued boxes were stacked neatly against one whole wall.

'Eight hundred and ninety-three,' she replied simply, ushering Grace inside and wondering whether her surprised expression boded well for what she was about to see upstairs.

'Cool,' said Grace after a beat. 'Well at least I know where to come when I need reading advice.'

Alice was grateful that she hadn't immediately said what most people did: either they expressed disbelief that anyone could need, or indeed read, so many; or they made jokes about using her as their local lending library. Alice breathed out slowly, trying not to relive how pissed off she'd felt at having her beloved Jilly Coopers returned with corners folded down and coffee rings on the cover. In Alice's world, her books were treasures to be enjoyed again and again as new, not merely coasters for the nearest hot beverage.

'So,' she said, as the front door swung to behind them and she perched on the back of the sofa, 'what look are you going for? Professional interest or super-sexy?'

Grace blushed. 'Somewhere in between? I mean, it would be lovely to feel a bit swish, wouldn't it?'

'And this Chris? Is he just lovely?' Alice felt she needed to ask. If she was going to give up on her ideas about Dan and Grace, then she felt an odd responsibility to vet this potential suitor. It was madness really, and certainly none of her business, but she couldn't help notice that Grace seemed relieved to have someone discreet to talk things through with. Grace held up her iPhone, tapping on the Safari icon, and an image quickly filled the screen.

'Crikey,' said Alice, a little taken aback at the image of a smiling man in his flight suit.

'Quite,' said Grace. 'So you can see why this isn't a date. What would someone who looks like that see in someone who looks like me? Are you quite sure *you* won't go?'

It was her endearing insecurity that made the decision easier for Alice in the end. Chris Virtue was one of the good guys – he could be flying in the private sector and earning a bundle, but he'd chosen the Air Ambulance. And what's more, he'd obviously looked at Grace, with her yoga-toned body, but endearing lack of guile, and decided she was worthy of his attentions.

Alice paused at the top of the stairs, wondering how to make her request. In the end, she opted for transparency, ignoring the clammy swell of apprehension at letting anyone into her world. She couldn't help thinking Tilly would be proud. 'Grace,' she said, 'can we agree not to talk about this with anyone? It's just, well . . .'

She pushed open the door to her spare room, to the rails and rails of dresses and jackets and blouses, to the hooks bearing necklaces and bracelets and scarves. She shrugged, the ache of vulnerability making it hard to speak. Quite why she'd decided that tonight was the night to bare her soul she couldn't say. Was it Jamie's total belief in her and the confidence that conveyed, or Hattie's proffered hand of friendship, or perhaps simply that she'd reached the point where the secrecy was wearing her down?

'Bloody hell,' said Grace, turning her wide grey eyes on Alice in surprise. 'No wonder you always look so stunning. I had no idea you were a fashionista.'

Right then, in that moment, Alice would so easily have hugged her: fashionista sounded so much healthier than compulsive shopper.

She stepped forward and pulled a cobalt blue halter-necked dress from the rail nearest her. 'I thought this would frame your shoulders perfectly,' she said, as though it were the most normal situation in the world.

Grace leaned forward and gave Alice the lightest of kisses on her cheek, herself a little emotional. 'Thank you, Alice,' she said with feeling. The honour of this vulnerability was not lost on her. 'It looks beautiful.'

Alice managed a smile. 'Oh, we've barely started yet.' She watched Grace's eyes flit around the room from rail to rail; it was about time she started having fun with her trophies, rather than sequestering them away in shame. Perhaps helping Grace might prove to be the first step on the path to helping herself, she thought, as she pulled out another two dresses and laid them in Grace's arms. 'What are you waiting for? Let's see how they look!'

She pulled out her iPhone from her pocket and hit play on her summer playlist and as the sultry tones of Tracy Chapman rang out in her cottage, Grace slipped off her sandals with a grin.

'I'm not doing this on my own,' she said. 'Get that gorgeous green tunic on you, madam, and let's see how you look.'

Chapter 22

Grace tried not to stare when Alice arrived at work the next day. The carapace of co-ordinated clothing no longer seemed quite so incongruous in their rural bubble, but rather clarified so many little questions that had been in the back of Grace's mind for months.

'Hi,' said Alice simply, hesitating for a second, as though just waiting for Grace to blurt out her secret. 'Are you excited about tonight?'

'More nervous than excited, but the dress is just wonderful, Alice, thank you. So even if the evening is a bust, there's that at least.'

Alice laughed, the shutters lifting slightly. Everybody knew Grace was the soul of discretion, but Alice obviously had morning-after-the-night-before reservations.

'I'm going to skip out for a bit and get my hair done too,' continued Grace. 'Can hardly let the dress down, now can I?' She gave Alice's shoulder a gentle squeeze, making the most of this rare moment of privacy. 'And then you and I are going to have supper together one night and get some plans in motion, okay?'

The feisty, self-sufficient part of Alice clearly wobbled at the very thought; the exhausted part, the solitary part, seemed to recognise a reprieve. 'That sounds lovely,' she said.

Grace could only feel relief at her simple capitulation. She had spent half the night tossing and turning, worrying about this wonderful young girl with the weight of the world on her shoulders. There had been a certain amount of bravery in letting her in last night, Grace had decided, and she was determined not to let the moment pass. As far as she could tell, there was very little support in Alice's young life and God knows she needed it more than most. She was certainly adept at putting on a front though.

Grace thought back to her first year at med school, sharing a room with Suzie Rogers. Putting aside all the crude jokes they had made at the expense of her name, she had been Grace's best friend throughout that awkward freshers' year and someone she would never forget. Suzie, like Alice, had been a Type One diabetic, and seeing what she went through every night had been quite the eye-opener. The disrupted sleep, the checking and calibrating ... But Suzie had chosen the opposite path to Alice; she talked about it to her friends, who in turn then found it easier to check in with her, to tease her even, but most importantly, to be there for her on the days when things seemed unmanageable.

Alice? Well, as far as Grace could tell, Alice had her aunt Pru. And as wonderful as Pru Hartley was, she didn't seem to grasp the severity of Alice's condition, still turning up with sticky buns and 'gat-ox' from the bakery to 'cheer her up'. And, Grace decided, if Pru really was convinced that all Alice needed to do was to pop to Ikea and 'unpack', then clearly she hadn't been allowed into Alice's inner sanctum either.

She wondered who really knew what was going on in Alice's life. Jamie? One of these online 'boyfriends' she occasionally spoke about?

What was it about Larkford, Grace thought, that it seemed to collect those who needed to heal? Besides her aunt Pru, she'd never heard Alice mention any family at all and the only friends she referred to seemed to keep in touch via status updates and Skype calls rather than visits — what a miserable generation of lonely kids, she thought. Although to be fair, Elsie the silver surfer was much the same these days. Perhaps Grace herself was the anomaly, spending so much time with 'tech' during her working day and for her hobbies that she longed to keep her personal interactions personal?

Speaking of which, her heart gave an involuntary flip as she saw Dan Carter walk past the doorway. Perhaps Alice wasn't the only one in denial, though, about how their life was actually playing out?

Alice reached into her soft leather handbag and pulled out a velvet box. 'I thought this might work with the dress?' she offered, blushing slightly and regaining Grace's attention.

Grace popped open the box and a fabulous necklace of twisted silver leaves, pearls and filigree lay nestled inside. 'Alice! It's beautiful.'

Alice grinned. 'And you don't need to worry about breaking it or losing it, it's really nothing fancy.'

Grace raised an eyebrow in disbelief, the delicacy of the workmanship directly contradicting that statement. 'It's far too precious, Alice. Honestly, I'm so grateful for the dress, I couldn't possibly—'

Alice shook her head. 'And you say *I'm* stubborn. Just wear it, enjoy it; it deserves an outing. And if it all falls apart on the dance floor you can blame me, because I made it, okay?'

'Are you serious?' said Holly, ambling into the room with

a pain au chocolat in one hand and a vast glass of orange juice in the other. 'You are such a dark horse, Alice Walker!'

Grace nodded, wondering how Alice had managed to have them all so convinced that she was a straight-cut pillar of professionalism and composure. Whilst in reality, beneath every layer there lay another one awaiting discovery.

Alice blushed. 'It's just a hobby. I have rather a thing for craft shops, so I had to find a reason to visit!'

Grace smiled at her proudly. Baby steps, small admissions of her vulnerability.

'Well, I think it's stunning and, if you truly don't mind, I'd love to wear it tonight,' Grace said with feeling.

Holly nodded, the flakes of pastry fluttering around her. 'God, Alice, if I'd known we had the next best thing to Tiffany's in our very midst, I'd have been pestering you to make me something for the wedding months ago!' She flustered then and flushed. 'Not that I'd be expecting a freebie, and it would probably take months . . .'

Grace narrowed her eyes as she watched Holly dissemble. She'd put money on the table her discomfort had absolutely nothing to do with Alice or her jewellery-making skills. She watched Holly take a long sip of her orange juice and that in itself just played into the wired and weird atmosphere that surrounded her. Where was the omnipresent double espresso? Where was the—? Oh. Grace paused, unable to conceal the smile that spread across her face. She turned away and busied herself answering the phone. All in good time, she thought to herself, all in good time.

Later that day, with her freshly blow-dried hair falling neatly into place and Alice's necklace resting gently on her collarbone, Grace pulled her front door closed behind her and stepped into the street. She'd already sent Alice a selfie of herself all dolled up and was gratified by the enthusiastic response. It was just as well really, as she was starting to have a little wobble. Somehow, without even realising it, she had agreed to her very first date since Roy had died. She wasn't sure whether to feel awful that she hadn't really noticed the milestone, or just plain nervous at how out of touch she might be on dating etiquette.

She swayed slightly for a moment, unaccustomed to such high heels, but under strict orders from Alice that the dress demanded them. The silky fabric billowed for a moment around her legs at a sudden gust of wind and Grace heard a wolf whistle echo between the houses.

'Come and give us a twirl,' hollered Taffy from the grass bank outside the pub.

She looked up in confusion. As far as she could tell, Dan and Taffy were lining up rows of Babybel cheeses at the top of the slope.

'You look absolutely stunning,' Dan said, as though he couldn't quite believe it.

Whilst she could admit to being secretly thrilled at the obvious admiration on his face, Grace felt a moment's pique at the underlying note of surprise.

'Dare I even ask what you're up to?' she said, checking her watch.

Taffy grinned. 'Poor man's cheese-rolling. Couldn't get to Gloucester, so we thought we'd recreate. Look, we've got Ben's Action Men for scale.'

For a moment, Grace couldn't help thinking that this was so much more appealing than a night of champagne and self-congratulation.

Teddy Kingsley walked over to join them. 'Daft buggers,'

he said fondly. 'Blimey, Grace. You scrub up okay! What's the occasion?'

With a perfection of timing that Grace could only be grateful for, Chris Virtue's Volvo pulled up beside them. Gentleman that he was, he hopped out and opened the passenger door for Grace, kissing her lightly on the cheek.

Dan stumbled to his feet. 'Hey, Chris? I have to ask, mate—' The 'mate' had a slightly belligerent tone to it. 'Who's funding all this champagne and revelry? Gracie told us about your shindig tonight. Shouldn't we concentrate on getting that second helicopter up in the air rather than dishing out awards?'

Chris stiffened slightly, giving Grace a tight smile. 'You don't know what you're talking about. Mate. It's a sponsored award, so please don't think we're just frittering money away. Tonight is about morale. I would have thought you, of all people, would understand that.'

He checked that Grace's dress was clear and closed the passenger door. Grace looked up and saw the anger on Dan's face. Whatever his thoughts on fundraising, or even not being invited himself, it seemed rather disproportionate to her.

Grace was almost grateful that Dan couldn't see the sheer luxury of the country house hotel where the awards ceremony was being held. It would only feed into his assumption that the money could be better spent elsewhere.

For a moment, even with Chris's hand in the small of her back guiding her towards the sweeping staircase, Grace had the uncharitable thought that, as their inside man – strike that, inside woman – it was probably a good idea to find out the truth of the situation.

'So, did Dan have a point?' Grace asked quietly, as she took in the opulent floral arrangements around them, and the waistcoated waiters with silver platters.

Chris shook his head. 'I can see why he might think that, but honestly, this is one of our most profitable fundraisers – and a valuable boost to morale. We have one corporate sponsor who provides the awards to the various crews and then every table is sold at a sixty per cent profit; the hotel do the catering at cost and we get loads of coverage in the glossy lifestyle section.' He shrugged. 'I do get that it's counterintuitive, to spend money to make money, but a lot of people around here don't like the idea of suffering for a cause; they won't run a marathon but are all too happy to contribute an absolute fortune for a little fizz and hobnobbing.'

As they picked up flutes of champagne and began to mingle at the edge of the vast ballroom, Grace couldn't help but notice several furtive glances thrown her way. Women in particular seemed to spend a lot of time looking at Chris Virtue, their eyes lingering on his broad shoulders as he passed, before flicking down towards Grace appraisingly.

It should have felt wonderful, to realise that she was here as Chris's guest; he was obviously quite the catch. Not to mention charming to boot, she realised, as his attentive and considerate nature became increasingly apparent. Quite why she couldn't let go and enjoy herself, she didn't know.

'Let's find somewhere to sit, unless you'd rather mingle,' he suggested, as Grace's heels made her a little unsteady on her feet. Collapsing back into a heavily upholstered sofa, with Chris beside her, Grace felt herself begin to relax. The evening so far felt as though it were happening at a remove: the dress, the necklace, even the venue – it felt as though she were wearing a costume and playing a character whose role was as yet unclear.

Chris's arm around her shoulders provided a little clarification. As did his ever-attentive concern that she was having a nice time, pointing out people from his crew and giving her amusing little back stories for each. If she didn't know better, she would have thought he wanted her to feel as at home in his world as she did in her own.

So why did her thoughts keep returning to Larkford? Was it the little worm of a notion that this might be how Alice felt every day that was proving so distracting? It was easy to be fooled by Alice, and to forget how young she was. Grace wondered how often she too felt out of place, or out of her depth – was that where the need for designer 'armour' came in?

Was Alice actually the only one dissembling at work, she wondered, thinking back to Holly's highly unusual, and therefore suspicious, lack of caffeine? She didn't dare hope that it meant what she thought it might.

Or was it simply that, for Grace, evenings arsing about in the pub with her colleagues felt so much easier and more comfortable than this overstated luxury? She could certainly identify with Holly's concerns about Sarandon Hall now.

The invitation from Chris had actually taken her by surprise, and part of her still wondered if she'd been right the first time and this was actually a professional outing, despite all his actions to the contrary. She had no idea how to find her feet in the new dating landscape; the last time she'd been in the market for a boyfriend it was easy: turn up to bar with like-minded students, apply alcohol, repeat as necessary. This? This was a whole new ballgame. And however much she may have protested in The Deli last night, it was now obvious that

Chris had singled her out for his attentions and invitation. This was personal.

As their bodies were naturally thrown together by the deepest sofa cushions that Grace had ever encountered, she decided to simply go with the flow. Just because they were having dinner together in public didn't necessarily make them an item. Or did it?

Chris leaned in further. 'Would you mind if we went and talked to my boss? I'd love him to meet you.'

His tone, his affection, the gentle way he brushed her hair from her face made Grace's heart skip a beat. If they had been alone there was no question he would have kissed her. As it was, they escaped the sofa's clutches and made their way through the crowd to make small talk with the head of Air Ambulance South West. His hand in hers and his smile so intoxicating, it felt a little as though they were going to Meet The Parents.

'Ready?' asked Chris.

Grace only smiled; hoping his question was rhetorical.

In her mind, she wasn't actually sure she was ready for any of this. Or indeed, whether she ever really would be.

Chapter 23

The next morning Holly was on a roll, and had never been so delighted about having so many no-shows. Normally it was her bête-noire, running figures about wasted time and overhead costs in her head. Today, she simply didn't care.

Ever since Elsie had casually mentioned that her annual check-up with the stroke consultant had been brought forward, it had been preying on Holly's mind. Elsie had been decidedly cagey about whether this was simply a case of getting a medical report for her Sarandon Hall application or something more worrying, but either way, everything felt a little out of kilter. Maybe it was her own pregnancy hormones – projecting her nerves about next week's hurriedly scheduled prenatal scan perhaps? – or maybe it was some sixth sense she just couldn't put her finger on?

Taking advantage of this unexpectedly free time, she picked up her car keys and, double-checking with Grace that she actually was done for the morning, Holly impulsively headed for Bath. With a bit of luck, she could at least be there when Elsie came out of her appointment with the Big Cheese of Stroke Consultants.

Pulling up outside the leafy Georgian mansion that was the private clinic made Holly pause, wrenching the complaining

Golf into reverse and gingerly parking with extra concentration between a Jaguar and a Mercedes. Both of them, she noticed as she climbed out, were sporting Hospital ID badges in the windshield. She tried not to throw her morals and her beliefs out of the window, as her traitorous mind pointed out that this was the very medical path she had always shied away from on principle, the very path that would mean their financial concerns about having this little bean could be a thing of the past.

Even the rarefied atmosphere in the waiting room was so different from the squalling, sometimes even brawling, situation at The Practice that Holly was taken aback. She helped herself to a cappuccino and sat down to wait, flicking through this month's – *this* month's – *Country Living* magazine. She sipped at the cappuccino, the delicious scent making it irresistible, but gagging slightly as the coffee turned to sawdust in her mouth. Old habits died hard.

She felt unaccountably guilty, as though she were betraying her NHS roots simply by sitting here, decadently flicking through magazines and sipping frothy coffee. She breathed out slowly, her eye immediately caught by the photo shoot on the pages in her lap. A beautiful summer picnic was laid out on a river bank, canoes festooned with flowers, and petals floating on the water. Now that, thought Holly, was the kind of wedding she could get on board with, even if it did rather resemble a scene from a Flower Fairies book. Hardly the stuff that Taffy's dreams were undoubtedly made of. Although he might be more up for it if they had matching dragon boats and the theme from *Hawaii Five-0* belting from the river banks!

The gust of air as the huge double doors from the consulting rooms were pushed open made Holly look up to see Elsie making an entrance, looking decidedly peeved. She clocked

Holly's presence without even blinking and didn't bother to wait until she was within twenty yards to start talking loudly. 'Well I always thought you paid peanuts and got monkeys, but apparently these were just more expensive peanuts!'

Holly stood up and walked towards her, laying a finger on her lips in an attempt to get Elsie to turn the volume down. 'Hello, gorgeous. Surprise!' She linked her arm through Elsie's. 'So, did the doctor you paid tell you what you wanted to hear?'

Elsie gave her a scathing look. 'It's my money, darling. I can fritter it away on a second opinion I might actually prefer if I choose.' She sighed deeply. 'But apparently even at three hundred pounds an hour the diagnosis is the same. Previous mini-stroke equals high-risk and no bloody fun.'

'Were you secretly hoping he'd give you a clean bill of health and full permission to do whatever the hell you like?' Holly asked, voicing the suspicion she'd harboured ever since Elsie had first mooted the suggestion of going private.

'Well obviously,' said Elsie with feeling.

The automatic doors hissed open, disgorging them from the cool and rarefied environment into the heat of the car park, where wafts of petrol fumes were trailing in the wake of an expensive sports car.

'Scuse me,' managed Holly, before peeling off abruptly and heaving into the shrubbery.

'Jesus,' said Elsie, holding out her small bottle of water, 'are you okay? Is this morning sickness, or should I be giving you a very wide berth?'

Holly put her hands on her thighs and breathed slowly. She nodded. 'It'll pass, if last time's anything to go by. But I've been a bit worked up about one thing and another the last few days though. I'm sure that isn't helping.'

Elsie didn't look impressed – in fact she was rather piqued at having her thunder stolen. 'You can take empathy too far, you know.'

Holly nodded. 'Sorry, Elsie.' She managed a smile. 'You go ahead and puke too if you need to.'

Elsie just huffed, as Holly pivoted towards the bushes again. Elsie waved away the luxury sedan that had been idling outside waiting for her, the chauffeur looking incredibly relieved as the retching from the shrubbery continued. 'We'll go in your car,' Elsie announced.

'Jemima's protest really made me think about your wedding,' said Elsie, as they drove into the Market Place. 'Even with this baby on board, I still think we need to go big or go home.'

'Well, here we are! Home at last!' said Holly with a grin, timing it to perfection as she pulled up outside Elsie's Georgian townhouse. 'I guess that answers that then.'

Elsie, to her credit, managed a chuckle. 'I'm not giving up that easily, darling. Oh—' Elsie stopped and blinked, leaning forward to squint through the rather dirty windscreen. 'Oh, well this should be interesting.'

Holly followed her gaze, to see a rather alarmingly tanned-to-the-point-of-orange woman in designer clothes standing on tiptoe to peer through Elsie's sash windows.

'You'd think I'd get some warning that Hurricane Harriet would be turning up sniffing around,' said Elsie, sounding suddenly exhausted and not at all pleased.

'Harriet? Your *daughter*, Harriet?' Holly clarified in surprise. Said Harriet seemed to have spent most of Holly's acquaintance with Elsie in and out of various exclusive rehab facilities in America – it was almost as though this woman enjoyed the process of getting clean, more than the promise of sober living.

'I know. It's hardly cause for celebration, is it? I wonder how much she wants this time?' Elsie popped open the passenger door before turning back to Holly in a rare moment of weakness. 'Come in with me, darling. I'm not feeling on top form and Harriet's never an easy person to say no to. Come and be my moral conscience for a while?'

'There you are, Mummy!' cried Harriet, as Elsie walked towards her. 'I was worried I'd missed you and you were already set up at Sarandon Hall!'

For the record, Holly thought, Harriet actually looked anything but worried; thoroughly pissed off might be a more accurate statement.

'How on earth did you hear about my little visit there?' Elsie said crossly, as she unearthed her Tiffany keyring from her handbag and let them all in.

'Visit? You mean, you're not moving into a home?' Harriet persisted, by way of a greeting, as they all made their way inside.

'How lovely to see you too, darling,' said Elsie. 'Do join me and Holly for a little lunch.'

'Lunch with the staff?' sniffed Harriet, peeling off a delicate cashmere wrap and discarding it on the table, as she glanced around at her mother's possessions hungrily. 'Really?'

'Dr Holly Graham, do meet my daughter Harriet. Please excuse her manners, she's just stepped off a long flight from California, but I'm sure she'll remember herself momentarily.' Elsie fixed her daughter with such a hard look that even the most insensitive of offspring would surely have registered her displeasure.

It seemed to flow over Harriet's bottle-blonde head like quicksilver. Her lips were plump with fillers and her forehead strangely immobile; indeed the only similarity to her mother was in the striking depth of colour in her eyes. She rummaged through her designer handbag and popped a couple of tablets without missing a beat. They looked suspiciously like melatonin and Holly bristled at the notion of such casual dosing.

'Dr Graham? I presume you're here to assess my mother's mental competency? I gather she's been frittering away the family possessions with little or no regard as to their true value, or indeed line of succession.'

'Oh, do get over yourself, Harriet,' Elsie chided her. 'We're not the Royal fucking Family. There is no "line of succession" and we're hardly short of enough to go round. And by the way, Holly may be a doctor, but she's also my best friend, so perhaps a slight adjustment in your approach is in order. This isn't LA, darling. We're in the Cotswolds, so take a breath, have a cup of tea and, for the love of God, stop popping random pharmaceuticals as though they're Smarties.'

'Nice to meet you, Holly,' Harriet said after a pause, in which mother and daughter seemed to hold eye contact in a duel for supremacy. Harriet turned and stared at Holly with such intensity that Holly actually felt a prickle at the back of her neck, the way she did in Pru Hartley's house, where the ghost allegedly walked.

'Pleasure,' said Holly easily, flicking on the kettle and delighting in Harriet's *dis*pleasure that she was quite so famil-iar with her mother's kitchen.

'But I did get a call,' Harriet said, like a dog with a bone, as Holly poured the tea. 'The family solicitor – Arnold something? He specifically wanted me to know your plans. As your next of kin.' She was whining now, as though she had been promised a treat, only to have it snatched out from under her very nose.

'Ah, it seems the rustle of money can even cross the Atlantic. Useless man. He ought to know better by now.' Elsie's tight control of her voice only served to highlight just how very furious she was.

Holly knew only too well the battles that Elsie had fought with her children over the years, maintaining that being born into a life of money and privilege had actually been the ruination of them. Her darling Ginger had died too young, living fast and loose. Otto, a boiled egg on legs, puffed up by his own self-importance, only featured in his mother's life when he needed a handout, or to patronise her about how she was running her financial affairs. And then there was Harriet: poor, weak-willed, utterly spoiled Harriet. She was certainly no oil painting, yet the promise of wealth seemed to attract a carousel of unsuitable men, each break-up inevitably triggering another relapse into addiction.

There was something shrewd and underhand about the way Harriet's gaze skittered about the room though, that made Holly think of that *Cash in the Attic* programme that Elsie loved so much. At this point, she was mindful not only of Elsie's blood pressure, but also her own. She was pretty sure that this was not what the doctor had ordered for either of them.

As Holly prepared a simple salad and Elsie fought to keep her temper in check, it was obvious there was no love lost between mother and daughter and Holly couldn't decide which was worse, leaving the two of them alone, or staying here as the gooseberry at the lunch table.

Harriet wandered around the room, trailing a hand across the furniture as she did so. When she turned it was as though she had flicked a switch from angry and accusatory to sulky and flouncing. 'I was worried, Mummy. You have no idea what it's like to get a phone call on the other side of the world that your mother has been moved to a nursing home.'

'Or that there might be a Georgian townhouse going begging?' Elsie finished for her. 'Am I not allowed to plan my estate the way I see fit, Harriet?'

The spoilt pout of Harriet's enhanced lips, even though she was nearing her fifth decade, clearly indicated that was exactly how she felt.

'I honestly thought that the property in Los Angeles would keep you and your brother quiet,' Elsie said sadly. 'Surely twenty acres of prime Beverly Hills real estate is enough for you two. Find a way to share it, Harriet. And then let me live my life over here the way I want to. There's nothing here for you.'

'But this house—' cut in Harriet, glancing around with a kind of possessiveness that made Holly feel as though she were thoroughly intruding.

'Is mine to do with as I wish, being of sound mind and body,' Elsie said sharply. 'It's hardly as though you're going to move to the English countryside, now is it? You'd just parcel it up and sell it off to the highest bidder.'

'My father—' began Harriet forcefully and Elsie's face darkened.

'Your father gambled away every penny of my savings. Your father left me with three small children and no roof over my head,' Elsie reminded her curtly.

'But there must be something left,' Harriet persisted.

Elsie looked around appraisingly. 'There's a sweet but worthless painting in the morning room. One of his own.'

Holly noticed that Harriet made no move to go and look.

'Or there's Toby,' Elsie offered, waving a hand at the ugly-jug that had housed Elsie's beautiful Montblanc pen collection for as long as Holly had known her. His ugly little face all mushed up reminded Holly of a baby about to launch into a major tantrum and she'd always had rather a soft spot for him. She felt unaccountably annoyed at the very thought of him in Harriet's clammy custody.

'He's ugly but priceless,' Elsie continued, Harriet's head shooting up at the word and then sinking back again as she clocked the hideously malformed ceramic features. 'If memory serves, Toby here was the beginning of the end of my marriage to your father,' Elsie reminisced. 'He drove off to a poker game in my gorgeous Aston Martin and came home with Toby here and some chump change instead. I've always kept him as a reminder never to let a man near my financial affairs again. Like I said, Toby has value beyond bricks and mortar.'

Harriet's lip curled and she stood up abruptly. 'Do I look like a fool to you?'

Elsie turned to Holly, eyes twinkling, sotto voce, 'Do you think she wants me to answer that?'

Harriet picked up her voluminous handbag and her cashmere wrap and glared at her mother. 'I'm going to check into a hotel. I can see I'm not welcome here. We'll talk about the house when you've had some time to come to your senses.'

'You're welcome to come back when you have control of yourself,' said Elsie coolly. 'But for the avoidance of doubt, my love, even over my cold dead body, this house will never be yours. Last chance on Toby here? Are you quite sure?'

Harriet slammed out of the kitchen and sucked the air with her, creating a kind of vortex in her absence.

'Bloody hell,' said Holly. 'I think she's been watching reruns of *Dynasty*, don't you?'

Elsie shook her head. 'And she was so sweet. Until she learned to talk.'

'Maybe she was worried, nervous, you know?' Holly offered magnanimously. 'She thought you'd moved into an old people's home.'

'Hmm. Maybe. Maybe not. Besides, I don't expect you to dislike her straight away, Holly. You've only just met – give it a little time, get to know her, just let it evolve naturally.' She sighed. 'I'm all too aware of my failings as a parent every time I see that girl.'

'But you're so wonderful to me. Please don't sell yourself short,' said Holly with feeling, knowing only too well that, without Elsie's love and guidance, she herself might not be enjoying this wonderful renaissance with Taffy.

'Ah, but it's easy to love *you*, Holly. You have no drowning expectations, no agenda, no ability to *constantly* make me feel as though I'm letting you down in some way.

'My children grew up with a life of privilege and expecta-tion. I ruined them really: all they do is take, take, take and then complain. They have no ability or desire to make their own way in the world. Even with a beautiful property of their very own. The scope for that alone is enormous, but of course it would involve some effort on their part. I always thought it would make a glorious hotel complex.'

'You know, you've never mentioned you had a house in LA, let alone a humongous one,' Holly pointed out.

'Didn't I?' Elsie replied innocently.

'And you've never even visited, in all the time I've known you.'

'Darling, it's LA – why on earth would I?' Elsie chastised her. She sighed and sipped her tea, grimacing at the coldness.

Holly got up to put the kettle on again, feeling herself relax a little and hoping that the worst of Hurricane Harriet had passed. Maybe seeing her mother in fine fettle, rather than dribbling on the damask, would be enough to put Harriet off? Obviously it wasn't ideal that Elsie had chosen this week to grab a lift home from the fit young police sergeant, feigning confusion, because she couldn't be bothered to walk across town in her new suede shoes. If Harriet heard about that, then all manner of questions might yet be asked.

Chapter 24

Holly poked her head into the waiting room for the start of her afternoon clinic, wondering whether Gladys Jones had actually heard Lucy's calls that she'd slotted her in for an appointment now, due to yet another no-show. Holly was about to call out herself when she noticed Gladys deep in conversation with the Major and his snooty neighbour Richard le Grange – a more unlikely trio you would be hard-pressed to find in Larkford, their only thing in common undoubtedly their age, but with the advent of Sarandon Hall, it was actually rather cheering to see them gossiping together, a little community contact going a long way towards keeping them engaged and sane, in Holly's expert opinion. She couldn't pretend that she wasn't delighted that the Major had finally made it in, before she'd been forced to make another impromptu house call.

'I was thinking of playing a little golf later,' Richard le Grange opined, his social background given away by the very redness of his trousers, and possibly his nose.

'Bit windy, isn't it?' asked the Major.

'Thursday, I think,' Gladys chimed in, pleased to be helpful for once.

'At least my memory's still up to par, even if my golf game isn't,' Richard said, knocking on the wooden arm of his chair.

'Me too. It's this weather,' Gladys nodded.

'Isn't anybody going to answer the door,' interrupted Richard, 'or are we supposed to do that ourselves now too?' He looked around and spotted Holly in the doorway. 'Bloody NHS,' he muttered.

Holly could barely suppress her laughter long enough to winkle Gladys away from her debonair, if slightly dotty, companions. 'Come on through, Gladys,' she said, making sure to enunciate clearly. 'We're just through here.'

Gladys sat down with a heavy sigh, fishing out her mobile phone and squinting at the screen. She waved it in Holly's direction. 'Is this important? I haven't got my reading specs on.'

Holly looked at the text:

FWIW – GHA – L8R

Even though she read it three times, she couldn't make head or tail of it. 'Erm, is it possible your friend wasn't wearing her glasses either?' Holly suggested in the end, as she read the text out loud.

Gladys hooted with laughter. 'Ooh, just type in ATD for me, would you, Dr Graham, and I'll talk to her later.'

Holly did as she was told but couldn't resist asking, 'Gladys, have you and your friends got your own texting etiquette now? I thought I'd finally caught up with Taffy and his abbreviations . . .'

Gladys grinned, delighted to have one up on the youthful Dr Graham. 'Well, all that text speak was no good for us, was it? How often are we out dancing and carousing? So this is ours. FWIW – Forgot where I was, obviously. ATD – At the doctor's. Easy. And a great time-saver.'

Holly nodded, silent laughter making it tricky to speak. 'And GHA?' she managed.

Gladys shrugged. 'Got heartburn again. Or was it haem-orrhoids? I'll find out when I pop round later.'

Holly took a deep breath, relieved that Sarandon Hall hadn't crushed all of their senior citizens' social lives. 'Now, what can I do for you today, Gladys?'

'You tell me, Dr Graham. You're the one who invited me in.'

'You mean, you didn't want an appointment?' said Holly in confusion, scrolling through her itemised screen only to find a notation from Lucy: 'No idea why Gladys Jones is here, but I don't think her hearing aid is working . . .'

'I think we were going to take a look at that hearing aid, weren't we, Gladys?' said Holly, reaching forward, only to find a Bluetooth earpiece nestled in Gladys's ear where her hearing aid should have been. She deftly unclipped it and held it up for Gladys to see.

The old lady may have been deaf but she still had most of her marbles, paling as she recognised it immediately. 'Ooh my Lord,' she said, 'my grandson is going to be *so* cross.'

Holly ushered her back out to the waiting room, only to find that the Major had disappeared. Cursing herself for not calling him in first, she summoned Richard le Grange instead, determined to follow up with panicky Peregrine later.

After a very long day, which at times had tried Holly's patience to its limits, she was actually relieved to head over to the pub for Dan's hurriedly organised call to arms that evening. Provoked by Jemima's efforts and Grace's feedback from the fundraiser, they had all decided there was little point in holding back. Holly told herself she was just keeping her promise to Harry Grant – keeping it local.

She was quietly thrilled to see such an excellent and, dare she say it, effectual, turnout: Chris Virtue was there, trying to focus on Grace, but with their receptionist, Lucy, seemingly hanging on his every word; Rupert and Kitty – both of Larkford's vets-in-residence – were there with notepads at the ready; even the Major was now tucked away in the corner with Grover and a pint of Guinness, deliberately avoiding her gaze.

It was Grace who was taking charge of the meeting though; Dan was simply standing beside her, looking proud as punch to have served as her opening act.

'Well, you've all been absolutely wonderful in rallying such support so quickly. I'm sure we all know one or two people already who are being affected by these cuts and, I'm sorry to say, all the car boot sales and coffee mornings in the world are not going to be enough this time to stem the tide of closures.'

She glanced over to Chris Virtue as though to double-check she had his permission to share what they had gleaned at the party. He nodded, his gaze flickering back and forth between Dan and Grace at the front of the room. Whether he looked quite so piqued because of the news they were sharing, or the obvious chemistry between the two speakers, was hard to say.

'It seems as though we aren't just fighting for funds any more – it's politics behind the scenes – and the figures involved are simply eye-watering. I firmly believe now that we need to fight in the court of public opinion. Let's stand up and make sure that our voices are heard: let's find a way to show them that government needs to be by the people and for the people.'

Grace sat down, flushed, to a round of applause and some whoops of encouragement from the triathlon squad arriving at the last minute, upping the body count by at least fifty per cent.

'So,' Dan said, stepping forward, 'if anyone has any ideas, suggestions or indeed contacts, we're all ears.'

There was a wave of muttering and scuffling in the pub, a few volleys of laughter at obviously inappropriate suggestions, and then silence.

Elsie stood up and fixed them all with her querulous gaze. 'I think we need to make a statement. We can raise some money, of course – we've done that before – but I feel like creating a few waves, don't you?'

'More like a tsunami to fix this bloody mess,' grumbled Geoffrey Larch wheezily.

Elsie rounded on him instantly. 'Listen, Geoff,' she said forcefully, 'the way you're going through those secret cigarettes and inhalers, you'll be grateful we made an effort in a few years' time!'

He shrank back away from her gaze, not the only person in the room to be shocked by her intensity.

'Look,' Elsie continued, 'it's easy to be laid-back about all of this when life is good and your health is great, but as we saw at the Show, it only takes a moment for all that to change. So, are you going to sit on your backsides, or are you going to help me organise a star-studded auction – antiques, celebrity contributions, bequests from our local community? Come on, you lot – don't you ever watch *Cash in the Attic*?' She flashed them with her mesmerising smile. 'Now, who's with me to make some serious noise?'

Elsie sat down to a round of tumultuous applause that knocked Grace's restrained contribution into a cocked hat. Elsie looked quietly triumphant and Holly couldn't help but wonder whether it was Hurricane Harriet's visit that had provoked this demonstrative response. It was typical of Elsie to want to up the stakes and, naturally, to make any event an excuse to gather the area's A-listers together on her watch.

Grace rose to her feet again. 'Well then, unless anyone else has a better suggestion, I say we jump on board. Let's stand out, shall we? Let's be remarkable. Financially, our goal is to cover the repairs to the second Air Ambulance and one midwife for our local area, working independently of the regional maternity unit. From a PR perspective, let's make some serious noise. A little politics isn't beyond us.'

'Is this just something we do now?' called Mary Darnley from her habitual corner booth of the pub. 'Isn't it time for someone else to stand up and take some responsibility around here?'

Grace nodded. 'Wouldn't that be lovely! But would you rather wait around and hope, or would you rather be pro-active?' She shrugged. 'I haven't noticed any of the other medical centres locally doing more than complaining, have you?'

'Bloody Framley,' cursed Teddy Kingsley behind the bar. 'Every time there's a problem, they're nowhere to be seen, but when there's benefit to be had—'

A groundswell of murmurs rumbled around the pub, the animosity between Larkford and Framley well established over the years. They'd even had to put a halt to their intra-mural rugby games when the injury count became too high. Calling it a grudge match didn't come close.

Holly settled back in her chair, the weight of responsibility easing slightly on her shoulders. She knew only too well that it would normally be her up there, waving her notebook around and making impassioned pleas for support. But the honest truth right now was that her support had to be in name only. She just didn't have any reserves left to give. It was enough, surely, that she'd offered to be the main point of contact for Mims and the rest of the self-named Preggie Protesters. She'd even managed to wangle Mims a highly coveted slot on a local phone-in radio show. And Molly Giles had been over the moon at the very suggestion of some solidarity. But right now, that was about all she could muster. She needed and wanted to focus on having a healthy, happy pregnancy. Unless . . .

She leaned forward in her seat, her pregnancy hormones for once proving useful and clearly leading the charge. 'Chris,' she hissed. 'Chris.'

He looked round, confused. 'You okay there, Dr Graham?'

'How do you feel about taking your shirt off for a good cause?' she asked him bluntly.

'Oh dear God,' managed Mims faintly, sitting beside her and clearly similarly afflicted.

Chris just shrugged with a grin. 'I'm game if you are.'

'Oh, don't be ridiculous,' said Holly dismissively, sounding an awful lot like Elsie. 'And what about the rest of your team? Are they quite easy on the eye as well?'

'Oooh,' said Mims. 'I like where you're going with this.'

'Where *are* you going with this?' asked Taffy, completely discomfited by the turn in conversation.

Holly paused for a moment. 'Any sexy midwives in the area, do we know?'

Teddy's Vulcan hearing was highly tuned to anything involving the word 'sexy', apparently, and he was keen to join their discussion. Grace's end of the room were deeply involved in allocating tasks for the auction and discussing which local celebrities might yet be persuaded to part with their valuables.

'There's that gorgeous Kiwi girl who delivered Hattie's

kids. Is she still around, because she's just lovely,' he volunteered, batting away the slightly strange looks that the women in the vicinity gave him. 'What, so Lucy's allowed to go ga-ga at the merest sight of a pilot, but I'm not allowed a few thoughts about naughty nurses? That's a double standard,' he complained, aggrieved by the injustice of it.

Lucy coloured instantly, glaring at Teddy even as she attempted to laugh off the accusation. It wasn't until she dared look over at Chris that she realised he actually looked rather taken by the idea. He leaned in towards her, his voice low and intimate: 'So, any pilots, or just the ones who flew Chinook rescue missions for the RAF?' He grinned, blushing at his own audacity and clearly unused to blowing his own trumpet. 'Sometimes you have to be your own wingman,' he clarified.

'So that's official then,' Holly said thoughtfully. 'We can have a lovely photo shoot to send out with our press releases. A calendar, maybe? Chris's abs alone ought to provoke a few column inches.'

Mims tittered slightly at the double entendre, even before anyone else caught on or Holly realised what she'd said. 'That's *not* what I meant,' she said categorically when Taffy gave her a dirty look.

Chris just blushed a vivid shade of fuchsia pink. 'You only said it would be topless!'

'Hey!' called Grace from the front of the room. 'Any chance you want to be involved with this auction, or have we lost you to the sleazy side of tabloid journalism? Not that I'm complaining, it's just that we've got a few more things to organise before we start objectifying our workforce. I need a volunteer to be our public spokesman, or woman. And it needs to be someone independent.'

She looked hopefully around the room, carefully allowing her gaze to skim past Cassie Holland, who looked a trifle too keen for a moment in the limelight to be effectual.

'I'll do it,' Dan said, as if it were no big deal.

'I hardly think that's appropriate,' said Malcolm Bodley pompously, their much maligned and wholly ineffective local councillor, who had been sitting silently at the bar throughout, nursing the same warm bottle of Stella. 'I don't think you, or any of the staff from The Practice, can be seen to be objective at this point.' His voice was a monotone and as charismatic as wilting lettuce.

'Then I'll do it,' said Chris, clearly loving the feeling of being part of something bigger than himself. It was an addictive feeling, no doubt, and his military background probably meant that he, like Dan, would always be willing to step up.

Malcolm shook his head. 'Of course, if you need me to pick up the baton, to speak for all of you when I say that—'

'I'll do it,' said a voice from the back of the room and everyone turned in their seats. 'Call me invested in how this all plays out.'

'Harry!' cried Holly, leaping to her feet with as much elegance as a baby elephant.

'Holly! My favourite troublemaker at it again,' Harry laughed in response. He grinned and pulled her into an avuncular hug.

'I'm so thrilled you're here,' Holly said when she'd come up for air. 'We just decided to get on with it and seize the day. We hadn't heard from you, so we're keeping it local, like you said.'

Harry shrugged guiltily. 'Well, to be honest, I had fully intended to get on a plane and lick my wounds on a sunny beach somewhere. But it turns out that I hold a grudge. Who knew? So, I don't think I can truly enjoy my pina coladas until we've brought Derek Landers down a peg or two and righted a few wrongs in the process.' He beamed. 'It's somewhat liberating actually, being on the side of the Rebellion. I've always been rather Establishment up until now.'

'Brilliant,' said Taffy happily, shaking him by the hand. 'Harry Grant's gone rogue.'

'Can we have call signs and everything?' Harry asked, clearly swept up in the excitement.

'Like in *Star Wars*?' Holly asked drily, the first to catch on to his train of thought.

'Ooh yes,' said Harry. 'And if I'm the spokesman for the Rebellion, can I be Rogue Leader?'

'No problem,' said Grace with an expansive smile; this was obviously better than she'd even hoped for. A proper inside man. 'But the budget won't stretch to a Millennium Falcon, okay?'

Harry tried not to look utterly affronted. 'I think you mean X-Wing Fighter,' he muttered under his breath so that only Holly could hear, as he sat down beside her and raised a glass to their joint endeavour.

'So, tell me, what have you got planned?'

Chapter 25

Alice fiddled with the rose quartz lanyard around her neck the next morning, before allowing it to fall back into place. There was always a moment of hesitation when she wore something new for the first time; did it truly look as beautiful as the online pictures promised, or indeed make her feel wonderful and complete? Of course, she knew she was looking in all the wrong places for that feeling of acceptance and belonging, but right now something had to be better than nothing.

With ten minutes until her morning clinic began, and with it a deluge of problems to be negotiated, Alice tapped refresh on her internet browser again; it had become a nervous habit when she felt uncomfortable, to torment herself with Facebook posts of her friends' wonderful photogenic lives. Far from being soothed, all she felt was a hollow emptiness as she scrolled through holiday photos, engagement photos, wedding photos . . . Didn't anything bad ever happen to these golden people? Was it even humanly possible to look *that* glamorous after a transatlantic flight?

And then, for the first time in a long time, the penny slowly dropped. If she was running her own life through a filter, then what was to stop them doing the same?

She pulled up her own Facebook page and looked at the

posts she'd made: ecstatic pictures with Coco at the training facility (no mention of the heartbreaking decision facing her); gooning faces at the pub with Taffy and Dan (no mention of the harrowing afternoon trying to resuscitate an elderly patient on a house call); and a 'what shall I wear?' dilemma when she'd already spent three hours whittling down her choices to the three that looked incredible.

She shoved the mouse away from her with a force that embodied the sudden wave of bitterness that overcame her. When had all her friendships become as deep as the proverbial puddle, she wondered, clicking through to Skype for a fix of irreverent Tilly-humour to keep her balanced and sane.

Ten minutes later, despite her Tilly-top-up, Alice knew exactly why her first patient of the day was making her feel quite so uncomfortable. 'We'll start with an antibiotic,' Alice said calmly, 'but you'll need to be seen in the foot clinic every day this week for them to change the dressing and keep an eye on things.' This entire scenario was basically Alice's worst nightmare and a little glimpse into her future.

Carol Wainwright sighed. 'But it was just a blister, Dr Walker. I don't understand how it can have got so bad so quickly.'

Alice nodded sympathetically. 'I know it probably didn't seem like much at the time, but with diabetes you just can't afford to ignore your feet. Your annual assessment can only tell us so much, because a lot can change in a year. That's why we ask you to be vigilant yourselves.'

Carol looked embarrassed. 'I do remember reading that somewhere actually, but I didn't think it applied to me.'

Alice tilted her head as she evaluated Carol Wainwright. Non-compliance wasn't something you'd normally expect from the Carols of this world – well-to-do, beautifully turned out, obvious care taken with her appearance ... 'How are things generally?' It was one of those open questions that could lead anywhere and, in Alice's experience, tended to be the most fruitful. It was so much better than putting her on the spot and asking about the state of her marriage, or how she was coping with redundancy.

'Fine,' said Carol with a slight wave of her hand. 'Everything's fine.'

'Okay then,' said Alice slowly. 'Because if there was anything, you are always very welcome to come in and talk to me.' She smiled. 'I'm not sure you could say anything I haven't heard before.'

Carol forced a smile. 'So antibiotics and lots of check-ups then?'

Alice nodded, making no effort to move or indeed to start typing the prescription into the computer, her sixth sense still niggling.

Carol picked up her handbag – Italian leather with a Pucci scarf tied loosely through the handle – and Alice was convinced her hunch was right. Someone who took this much pride in their appearance would never neglect their feet, not with the spectre of diabetic complications hanging in the ether, let alone sandal season in full swing. Not unless there was something else claiming their attention.

Carol held the bag to her chest as though it were a shield, and her voice, when she spoke, was barely a whisper: 'I think I might be going mad, Dr Walker.'

Alice nodded. 'Okay ...'

'And not like PMT, or forgetful when I'm tired – I'm talking batshit crazy.'

'Ah, the technical term,' said Alice gently. 'Are you aware of any particular triggers?'

Carol looked up at her through her eyelashes, as though fully expecting Alice to mock her. 'Crisps, cereal, apples, muesli bars … Anything crunchy really.' She paused and managed a small smile. 'I'm not making much sense, am I? But it's become so distracting, I can barely think about anything else. It's just the sound of someone eating, chewing, masticating—' Carol was clearly working herself up and Alice laid a soothing hand on her arm.

'Just eating sounds?' she queried. 'What about breathing?'

'God, yes!' said Carol with feeling. 'All night long – my husband is breathing like a fucking walrus. It's a wonder I haven't smothered him in his sleep.' She stopped. 'It's not snoring though, you understand, just normal breathing. But it never used to be so, well, loud.'

'Has it been keeping you awake at night then?' Alice asked, trying to get some measure of how badly Carol was affected.

Carol nodded, pausing for a moment. 'And I've stopped going out for dinner, going on the train – anywhere people might be eating and I can't get away.' She looked aghast at having to share what she clearly felt was bonkers behaviour. After all, she'd come in with nothing more than an angry inflamed blister that refused to heal and prevented her wearing high heels.

'Well, the good news is, you're not going mad,' Alice said gently. 'What you're describing is a condition called misophonia. We will all experience it to some degree in our lifetime. For some people, it's that nails-on-a-blackboard-type situation, but for a few it can develop to include all sorts of sounds. And,' she said, gauging Carol's reaction, 'for some it's not just about disgust, but actual rage. Does that sound familiar to you?'

Carol nodded; the red flush mottling her chest was inching its way up her neck. 'Fury,' she said quietly. 'As though they're being deliberately loud just to piss me off.'

'Do you think the eating sounds and the breathing are louder than normal, or is it possible that you're aware of it now, so you might be expecting it?'

Carol fiddled with her handbag. 'I downloaded an app. It's a decibel meter. I was beyond surprised, to be honest, when even the bloody crisps hardly registered. That's when I decided I must be losing the plot.'

'I'd like to consider a few options for this. We can think about using some TRT, that's Tinnitus Retraining Therapy – basically it's designed to improve your tolerance of certain noises, maybe even with a little positive deconditioning. But since it's so important that we get you balanced and focused, so you can maintain your at-home diabetes care, I'd like to suggest we also try a course of mild antidepressants.' She held up her hand before Carol could protest. 'Although I'm not suggesting you're depressed, just that they have been shown to help. We can also talk about white noise, just in the background to decrease the contrast – if you hop online there's all sorts of behind-the-ear noise generators; it's trial and error mainly.'

Carol was breathing normally again now – the panicked shallow breaths had relaxed. 'It has to be worth a try.'

'And cut yourself some slack,' Alice suggested. 'Have supper in front of the TV. Maybe find a show you really enjoy so you start looking forward to mealtimes again?'

Carol's face broke into a smile, a relieved smile. 'Are you basically saying it's doctor's orders to eat on the sofa watching *Gilmore Girls*?'

Alice grinned and pulled open her drawer to find one of

the old-school green prescription pads and scribbled a note to that effect. 'Take three times a day or as necessary,' she said. 'And I want to see that foot again in three days. And every day with the foot clinic, yes?'

Carol nodded, her body language totally different now.

Alice stood up. 'This whole diabetes thing is enough of a bastard without adding sore feet and miserable mealtimes to the mix.'

Carol caught Alice by surprise as she pulled her into a spontaneous hug, untangling her hair from Alice's necklace.

'Beautiful lanyard, Dr Walker,' she said as she left.

Alice allowed the quartz stones to run through her fingers and smiled. For the first time in ages, one of her pick-me-up purchases had actually served its purpose. In this case, to remind Alice that whatever might be falling apart in her personal life, when it came to her job, her instincts were still second to none.

Back in the doctors' lounge after morning surgery, Alice was still on a high. Misophonia ticked all her boxes for the quirky and unusual. She filled up her mug with hot water, dunking an Earl Grey tea bag to give just a hint of flavour.

'For God's sake,' said Dan, as she tossed it into the bin, 'at least make a decent cuppa with it.' His voice was oddly irritable and Alice frowned for a moment, confused, until she followed his gaze and saw Grace. Grace looking hungover and tousled. Obviously the plotting session in the pub last night had run on much later after Alice had left.

Alice sipped at her mug and went to sit beside her. 'Morning. Should we all be whispering today?'

Grace managed a smile. 'It wouldn't be the worst idea. I thought you weren't supposed to get a headache with champagne. Chris's idea, so it's all his fault, really.' She grimaced, recognising how spoiled that sounded. 'First World problems, eh?'

Alice laughed, even as the sound made Grace wince. 'That Chris Virtue knows how to spoil a lady – first it was fancy ballrooms and fine dining, now it's late-night champagne at the pub. I'm liking his style. Did you have a good time? With Chris, I mean.' Alice was aware that she was fishing, but couldn't resist. After all, she'd been gradually baring her soul to Grace for weeks now; it was high time the current flowed both ways.

'Chris was, well, I guess you could call him the perfect gentleman,' Grace said quietly.

'Not too perfect, I hope,' Alice teased her.

Grace just blushed prettily and flicked her eyes across the room to make sure nobody was listening. 'Not too perfect. Just lovely actually. Even if—' She broke off abruptly. 'Never mind. And actually, the champagne gave me one or two ideas about how we might be able to raise a little extra money ourselves . . .'

'Grace,' Alice chided, 'I hate to tell you, but this wasn't a busman's holiday, it was a date. A second date, really.'

Grace shrugged. 'So I mixed a little business with a little pleasure. It was easier that way; otherwise it might have been a little overwhelming, to be honest. I hadn't realised the dinner the other night was actually my first date since—'

'So it *was* a date then,' Dan interrupted, having somehow made his way silently across the room. 'And is Chris the model of Virtue – or is he just another pilot, going for the prettiest girl in every room?'

Alice froze, unused to Dan being anything other than friendly and professional. She always forgot about his stint as an Army medic and guessed he must have come across one or two pilots in his time, who merely had to click their fingers and have all the girls come running.

Grace said nothing, her confusion evident in the hurt expression on her face. Alice shook her head; it didn't seem fair for Dan to rain on Grace's parade, particularly since he'd had all the time in the world to make a move himself. Sour grapes because of Chris Virtue seemed a little petty and immature to her.

'I'd take the compliment, if I were you, Grace. Dan here obviously thinks you're the prettiest girl in this room.'

Grace's smile was forced and tight as she stood up to leave. 'I think I need some paracetamol,' she said.

Alice turned to watch her leave. 'Jesus, Dan, what was that all about? Do you know something about Chris Virtue that we don't?'

Dan just shrugged and left the room, leaving Alice feeling as though she were back in the Sixth Form Common Room.

'So,' said Maggie into the uncomfortable silence, 'I gather you've been having all the interesting cases this morning? Misophonia? That's a new one on me.' As their resident pharmacist, Maggie had the reputation of being widely read and well informed on almost every medical topic. That and having the cleanest, most sanitised space in the building. 'Is that why I want to club people who eat with their mouth open?'

Alice sat down beside Maggie, the tension between Dan and Grace leaving her oddly rattled and grateful for the distraction. She shook her head. 'Nah. I think that's just because it's plain rude and disgusting, don't you?' She was almost pleased to find that she wasn't the only one checking herself against the parameters for the condition. It was all too easy to become a hypochondriac in this profession. Only last week, she'd been adamant that she had an emerging case of argyria, the so-called 'Blue Man' disease, before she'd discovered the leaking blue ink pen in her pocket.

'Still,' said Maggie, as she wiped down the table top in front of her with one of her omnipresent antibacterial wipes, 'it must be nice to diagnose something like that, even if it's not what she came in for. I suppose only time will tell if those antidepressants help?'

Alice nodded. Truth be told, she was convinced the TRT and the white noise were a better bet, but Carol was already showing a few symptoms of mild depression anyway, so there was no harm in trying a multi-faceted approach.

She took one of Maggie's proffered oatmeal and raisin cookies with a smile. This morning had been just the timely reminder she'd needed as to why she'd chosen general practice over a speciality. Even though it had been driving her crazy of late just to feel as if she were a glorified triage and traffic director, with her only responsibility being to point patients towards the consultant that could actually help them, today had reminded her of the truth. Being a GP was actually a greater challenge – to see the whole person, mind and body, from cradle to grave. It was a responsibility and an honour, she decided, and one that shouldn't be taken lightly or dismissed, whatever some of her med school friends might imply.

She looped the rose quartz lanyard around her fingers again and sat back in her seat, while Maggie filled her in on all the latest gossip and the nurses played a loud and filthy rendition of snap in the corner, with what appeared to be a selection of gruesome Polaroids of skin conditions that had passed through their clinic.

Being a GP, getting to know her patients' foibles and idio-syncrasies, suddenly felt like the greatest and most fascinating challenge she could have. And maybe, who knew, maybe she might get to know herself a little in the process.

After all, who knew that an oatmeal and raisin cookie could actually taste this good?

Chapter 26

The sound of crockery smashing onto the flagstones made Holly jump that afternoon as she dropped by to update Elsie on their progress with the auction plan. She pulled out her front door key and let herself in. 'Are you okay? Elsie? It's me, Holly.'

'I'm fine, just fine,' called back Elsie, her voice barely audible above the television that was blasting from the kitchen. Dumping her bag, Holly rushed through, blinking to adjust her eyes as she went from the darkness of the hallway to the sunshine flooding the kitchen, its French windows flung open into the garden.

Elsie was standing in front of the enormous oak kitchen dresser with her hands on her hips, a determined set to her face and broken crockery scattered across the flagstone floor. 'I never did like that soup tureen anyway, so let's not get too emotional about a little slip.' She gave a large broken handle a dismissive kick with her foot.

Holly passed through relieved, on to confused, before settling somewhere between the two. 'Shall I just turn the television down a notch?' She walked over to where *Antiques Roadshow* was building to its denouement and hesitated, surprisingly keen to see whether the stuffed shirt in a tweed jacket was about to be delighted or humiliated by his confident offering to the experts.

Elsie walked over to stand beside her. 'You just hope it's a knock-off when they look that self-satisfied, don't you?'

Holly smiled, familiar with Elsie's well-developed sense of schadenfreude and wondering if it was contagious. Sure enough, the florid gentleman in question was slowly deflating as the ceramics expert quietly pointed out all the ways that his 'six-figure vase' turned out to be flawed.

Elsie flicked the television set to standby and pulled at Holly's arm. 'Come and see this. You see, I was watching earlier on and they did a wonderful piece about vintage ceramics.' She waved her hand at the dresser, its laden shelves groaning and its cupboard doors flapping open like wings to reveal even more treasure within. 'And Grace had got me thinking with all her suggestions. You know, we're both rather excited about my auction idea! I've been going through the china looking for something fabulous to donate.'

Holly felt a little piqued. She'd been secretly looking forward to doing that with Elsie herself, knowing and privately sharing her true and abiding love for *Antiques Roadshow*.

Elsie frowned. 'Honestly, Holly, don't look so blank – you can't have pregnancy brain already. We all need to find a little something special.'

Holly laughed at Elsie's insistent tone; Elsie on a mission was a force to be reckoned with. 'I think Taffy and I might struggle on that front,' she confessed, thinking about the heaps of mismatched china and melamine that comprised their 'dinner service'.

Elsie didn't contradict her, knowing full well that Holly's house had become a triumph of domesticity over style the moment the twins had arrived. She merely nodded in agreement. 'Well, maybe there's a little something around here you could contribute instead,' she offered.

Holly yawned and stretched, the slight tightening of her waistband making her smile. There was a little part of her that wanted to ignore everything else in the world right now and focus on the fluttering feelings of nerves and excitement about her pregnancy. It was proving one of the hardest secrets she'd ever had to keep and, if she was honest, it was one of the reasons she'd popped round to see Elsie – at least with her, and with Lizzie, there was no need for pretence. She just wanted the peace of mind from her scan before she started spreading the happy news.

Holly picked up and examined a bone china curiosity, turning it this way and that to try and divine its purpose. 'Don't you think it would be nice though, Elsie, if just one year could go by without some big drama or catastrophe?' she asked thoughtfully.

Elsie shook her head. 'Pish-tosh. Don't you know it's the drama that keeps a community together? And it keeps me young! Don't wish that away, will you?' she said with a laugh.

Holly hesitated, unable to jump on board with Elsie's ebullient enthusiasm for a crisis. 'I know, I know, but I wouldn't say no to a little happy-ever-after about now, would you?'

'You're a fine one to talk,' smiled Elsie, shaking her head. 'All that work to plan the perfect wedding and you're talking about putting it on hold. So what if you look a little spherical in the photos, darling? It could still be wonderful—'

Holly laughed, actually rather entertained by the notion of her as a Weeble-in-a-wedding-dress. 'Scan first, wedding talk after,' she said sternly. She paused. 'You know, if Taffy and I did sneak away to Italy, you could always come too?'

'Oh my darling girl, you've rather missed the point by a

country mile. If you two skulk off and get married, it seems as though you have something to be ashamed of – although to be fair, that could just be the Fifties in me. Have a celebration! Have the whole bloody town there to witness your union, darling. Bump or no bump. After all, this one's for ever, right?'

'Right,' agreed Holly, wondering why she'd never thought of it quite that way before. Weddings, in her mind, had little to do with celebration, but were inextricably linked with stress and manipulation. Marrying Milo had been no picnic right from the start. Even the very thought—

'So tell me about all this china then?' Holly said, by way of distraction from her own tumbling thoughts.

'Well,' said Elsie, as ever needing very little encouragement, 'this dinner service here was actually from my first marriage. Beautiful. Probably quite rare now, to find a complete set. So that might be worth a bob or two? And this one, I never really liked. It's from my second marriage – awfully vulgar taste that man had. But still, I gather from the chap on the telly just now, it might be a collector's piece. So that's nice.'

Holly crouched down in front of the cupboard and picked up a lone cup and saucer in the most delicate design. 'This is just stunning.'

Elsie blew the air out from her cheeks. 'And that's the tragedy of it. My favourite dinner service, and at one time, my favourite husband. But by the time the divorce was finalised, I'm afraid most of it had been collateral damage to our arguments.'

'You threw plates at each other?' Holly asked, shocked at the mental image that thought provoked.

'Plates, bowls, glasses too. It was one of those relationships that proved you can have too much of a good thing – with passions running that high, it was always going to end explosively.' She reached forward and took the cup and saucer from Holly's hands, lovingly placing them onto the shelves where she could see them. 'Such a waste,' she mused, and Holly was unclear whether she was referring to the relationship or the dinner service.

After Elsie had spent the best part of an hour giving Holly a full guided tour of her china and ceramics collection, they had both relaxed into a routine – Holly would appreciate and marvel at each piece, while Elsie gave her the backstory.

'By the way,' Elsie said out of nowhere, pressing a packet of small red stickers into her hand, 'I was hoping you'd have a little wander around. And if there's anything you'd like, just stick one of those red dots on it. Or for Taffy. I've decided that this auction is the perfect excuse to get my affairs in order.'

'I couldn't,' said Holly, stunned. 'You're very generous and thank you, but I just couldn't. It would feel too—'

'Greedy? Grasping?' Elsie offered with a grin.

Holly shook her head. 'I was going to say maudlin and defeatist.'

'Bugger that!' exclaimed Elsie. 'We all know I'm going to die one day, right? Well I'd rather shuffle off this mortal coil knowing that my favourite, most beloved people had some benefit from the whole enterprise. At least it will stop an unseemly scuffle for all my best bits when I'm gone and all the grasping relatives and tragedy tourists start circling for a handout.'

'What on earth is a tragedy tourist?' asked Holly in confusion.

'Oh, you know,' said Elsie airily. 'There's always a few people you barely know who start circling like vultures when there's calamity looming. They just love the idea of being in the inner circle of gossip and news.'

'Seriously though,' said Holly, trying not to smile at Elsie's vehemence, 'what about your children, Elsie? What about Harriet? Has she even been back to see you? Maybe there's still time to build some bridges.'

'Don't be ridiculous, darling,' Elsie replied. 'You saw how they all came running when I was unwell last year – not a peep! Well, stuff them. I'd rather leave all this to the dogs' home before they got a dime out of me.' She held up a hand to signal that Holly's interjections would be falling on deaf ears.

'Besides,' she said, with an enigmatic smile, 'I've had a few thoughts on that front already.' She leaned back against the kitchen worktop and gazed out at her beloved garden, her expression almost wistful. Holly couldn't quite believe she would even consider trading this idyllic spot for some pokey apartment at Sarandon Hall, no matter how prestigious, luxurious or sociable it was over there, and was about to say just so—

'I'm quite serious, you know, Holly,' Elsie said suddenly, snatching the stickers from her and waving them in the air, making Holly jump. 'This is what will make me happy. I want *you* to get the pick of my belongings. I fully intend to flog the rest. I mean, how much stuff do I actually need? Look at me! I'm delightfully petite and decidedly low-maintenance.' She struck a pose and gave Holly a cheeky smile.

Holly couldn't help the snort of laughter that escaped her. 'Low-maintenance?'

'Well I am,' Elsie pouted, her mood that afternoon decidedly mercurial. 'I mean, I could be stamping my foot and insisting you get married, couldn't I? After all that planning! But instead, I'm offering you priceless antiques and a chance to help save that little maternity unit in time for your latest arrival.'

She dropped the packet of stickers onto the counter and pulled Holly into an embrace that barely left room for oxygen. 'You know I only want you to be happy, my darling girl,' she whispered against her shoulder.

'I know,' said Holly gratefully. 'And we want you to be happy too.'

Elsie turned away, her eyes decidedly moist, and poured out two glasses of pink lemonade, pressing one into Holly's hand. 'It's not quite a toast without proper fizz, but I wanted to mark the occasion somehow.'

She paused and looked at Holly appraisingly, as though weighing up how much she wanted to say. Perching on the kitchen stool beside her, Elsie looked Holly squarely in the eye. 'I think that I should rather enjoy seeing you settled, Holly. And I don't just mean married to that gorgeous specimen of a man. I want to go to sleep at night, knowing that you're content and have a wonderful life ahead of you. And there's only one way I can do that and still be around to see it happen: I want to leave you this house. And I want you to move in as soon as you'd like.'

'Oh Elsie,' breathed Holly in shock, completely blind-sided. 'You're so generous, and so thoughtful, but I couldn't possibly—'

'I thought you might be a little reluctant,' Elsie continued, as though she hadn't even spoken, 'but I drew up the documents as soon as I knew you were expecting. It's the only logical solution. The house will be yours one way or another. I would just *so* much rather I was still around to see you and your boys enjoy it. You do so much for other people, my darling, please let me do this for you.'

Holly was unable to formulate a sentence as the magnitude and affection of this gesture overwhelmed her. She simply reached out and clasped Elsie's hand, her eyes filled with love for this wonderfully feisty, outspoken woman who had influenced her life in so many ways. 'This is just so very—'

Elsie nodded, seemingly content that her wishes could not be ignored. 'Take a little time to think it over. But you can't stop me. The deed is done. All we're really talking about now is logistics.' She paused, her face lighting up with a smile, as she sat back, looking incredibly pleased with herself.

'Elsie, you're so kind and I can't even begin to tell you how touched I am. But your family—?' Holly began, as a whole gamut of emotions overwhelmed her. Even the vague prospect of raising her family in this beautiful house – a house that cried out for the hammering of tiny feet on the stairs and laughter in the garden – was like something from a dream. But, for her, the dream always included Elsie.

Elsie shrugged. 'Family means different things to different people, Holly. You should know that. And for me, family means the people I love who are there to hold my hand, in good times and in bad.' She grinned mischievously. 'So I'm calling dibs.'

Holly laughed, as always amused when Elsie picked up one of the twins' turns of phrase. 'Dibs?' she queried.

'Yes, dibs,' replied Elsie with conviction. 'You're my family, Holly. More so than Harriet and her grasping ways, more so than my boiled egg of a son who can barely pick up the phone once a year. Dibs. I'm calling it.'

Elsie glanced over at the packet of stickers on the counter, which was still sealed shut. 'So you see, I wasn't going quite mad when I suggested you pick out a little furniture, because you'll need a few pieces to get you started. I dare say Ikea can fill in the gaps for the children.'

'Well—' managed Holly, before her eyes widened in mute surprise and her hands flew to her belly. 'Oh my God, that's the first time I've felt the baby move!' She caught Elsie's hand and laid it on her nascent bump. At the second fluttering, she laughed with joy, quickly becoming a sobbing, hiccuping mess.

Elsie shook her head, pleasure at Holly's exuberant reaction lightening her face, and looked incredibly smug. 'Well! I think we can all agree that means you're out-voted, Holly, don't you? Two to one. The house wins.'

Chapter 27

Holly walked home through the streets of Larkford as though in a dream. The tiny streets that radiated from the Market Place like a cobweb had been her home for the last two years and her life had changed so much in that short time that really, what was one more change? One more adjustment?

'Holly!'

She startled from her thoughts, looking around to see who was calling her, and was delighted to see the Major striding towards her forcefully, little Grover having to run to keep up.

'Evening, Major,' she said. 'How's tricks?'

'Andy McLeod is dead,' he said abruptly. 'Rather puts things into perspective.'

'Oh Major,' said Holly, reaching out to clasp his shoulder – as close to an affectionate hug as this bluff old gentleman was generally comfortable with. Andy McLeod, his best friend and long-time adversary when it came to dodging the doctors. 'Are you okay?'

The Major gave her a funny look. 'I'm not the one who's dead, dear. Bit of a wake-up call, though. Poor old sod.' His gruff delivery did nothing to hide the pain in his eyes. 'So I thought, hang it all, I'm going to visit little Jess.' He held up a hand. 'And I know, I shall have to face her ghastly mother, but it's the right thing to do. Honestly, it's the only thing to do.'

Holly nodded. 'You might feel better once you've seen her. By all accounts, she's making an excellent recovery. It's just going to take a little time.' She couldn't help but admire the Major's bravery; even feeling so bleak these last few weeks, he was still thinking of others and doing 'the right thing'.

The Major harrumphed a little. 'I wanted to say thank you to you too. For coming over the other day. For not judging me.'

'Oh Major,' said Holly, 'we all make mistakes.'

'Well, I reckon my Andy would have given anything to be around for a few more mistakes. So, I think the time for doubt has passed. I've every intention of living life to the fullest until my time's up.' He strode away then, before the thickness of his words could spill over into tears.

Holly stood still for a moment, watching as the shadows of Larkford church spire grew longer across the Market Place. There was something to be said for the older generation in Larkford; they seemed to weather their experiences well and always come out fighting. Thoughts of Elsie's house were obviously still uppermost in her mind and the Major's senti-ment seemed to echo Elsie's own wishes.

She looked up to see Amanda Lightly running circuits across the parkland in the dappled sunlight, stopping every now and again to sip from a large bottle and wipe the perspiration from her brow. Even from here, it was obvious that this was a beau-tiful woman enjoying the prime of her life and certainly not suffering from depression as her husband had implied.

Holly had discreetly asked around after Gordon's visit to The Practice – Amanda was popular and well-liked, even if her husband was widely considered a bit of an arse. In fact, last she'd heard, Amanda was shagging Dishy Dad – renowned local Lothario and triathlete – on the quiet. Quite why Amanda didn't ask for a divorce if she was so unhappy at home, Holly couldn't say, especially as she watched Dishy Dad sprint out of the woods towards his mistress and openly swing her around in his arms, making her squeal in delight.

There was an awful lot to be said for seizing the day, Holly decided as she walked home, even as she mentally wrote off the twenty-pound bet she'd placed on that marriage lasting until Christmas.

Letting herself in through the front door, she was greeted by whoops of laughter from the back garden, where Taffy was obviously entertaining the troops. She glanced around her cramped kitchen, unable to resist drawing comparisons with Elsie's stunning conservatory. She felt the first prickles of excitement that this move might even be a possibility, for the first time her better angels shouting down the voice of responsibility and reason in her mind. This could actually happen, she realised; all she had to do was say yes.

She swallowed her own whoop of excitement that sprang unbidden to her lips just as the back door was flung open with such force that it ricocheted off the kitchen worktop, barely missing giving Tom a hefty black eye. 'Can we have tea in the playhouse, Mummy, Mummy, can we?' He played his best card, turning the full blaze of his Disney-sized eyes on Holly, having somehow clocked that she was increasingly becoming a soft touch these days.

Taffy stepped inside behind him before Holly could even reply. 'Do you think that you and Ben could collect all those little twigs from around the garden and build a little pyramid with them in the fire pit? I'll come and light it when you're done and we can cook up some baked beans on the campfire.'

The door swung shut behind him as Tom departed with alacrity, shouting the news to Ben as they set to on their mission. Taffy grinned. 'That should keep them good for a while. Hello, you.' He leaned in and kissed her lightly on the lips. 'Big day tomorrow.' He smiled at her and, even as a yawn overtook her, she leaned into his solid warmth for support. 'Do you think we should find out if it's a boy or a girl? I feel weird saying "it", don't you?'

Taffy's excitement about the scan was utterly endearing. Even though he knew perfectly well they were unlikely to discover the sex of their baby at this early stage, it hadn't stopped him talking about it endlessly. 'I just call it Beany,' Holly said easily, still in two minds about finding out – this might be one surprise worth waiting for.

She paused and looked deeply into his eyes. 'And Beany is clearly an overachiever, by the way – I felt the first movements earlier. Kind of a fluttering.'

'Are you serious?' Taffy knelt down and put his hand on her tummy. 'Come in, The Bean. This is your dad calling. Come in, Beany ...' He paused in anticipation, looking up at Holly as though this were somehow within her control. 'Do whatever you were doing last time – orange juice? Laughing?'

'Ah,' said Holly, glancing out of the window to make sure the twins were safely gathering kindling and out of earshot, 'about that.' She took Taffy's hand and sat down at the kitchen table, pausing for a moment to gather her thoughts. She still had no idea how she truly felt about Elsie's life-changing suggestion, swinging ambivalently from delight to discomfort every few minutes.

'Elsie wants to give me her townhouse,' she said simply in the end and watched Taffy's face slacken in disbelief. 'She wants to be at Sarandon Hall, apparently, and she wants us to move in as soon as possible.'

'I don't understand,' Taffy said slowly. 'Do you mean as tenants, because the rent on that place would be—'

Holly shook her head, emotion bubbling in her voice. 'No, as in, she wants to *gift* me her house – leave it to me, technically, I think. But she made it pretty clear: she wants to see us settled and enjoying it. All the more so with another one on the way.' She gave a nervous laugh. 'I don't know how to react – it's like all my dreams coming true, but I can't quite get over the feeling that I'm turfing my granny out of her house!'

'But ... I mean ... Well, I—' managed Taffy, still trying to get his head around the idea.

'Do that for another hour and you'll be where I am now.' Holly laughed. 'It is honestly the most wonderful, incredibly generous thing that anyone has ever offered to do for me, so why does it feel as though I'm taking advantage ...? Oh God, I don't know! And then I feel downright ungrateful for even questioning it!' Holly sank her head in her hands, knowing full well that Elsie would be furious that her offer had triggered anything other than absolute joy.

'It's a beautiful house,' said Taffy. 'A proper family home.'

'I know,' said Holly, biting her lip, barely daring to let the threatening smile escape. 'That's what Elsie said. She reckons it should be filled with laughter and sticky fingers and fairy cakes – her words, not mine.'

'You know,' Taffy said equably, 'we could all move in together. I for one would be only too happy to help out with Elsie if that's what she's worrying about. Joining a retirement community is a big leap.'

'I asked her about that.' Holly laughed as she recalled Elsie's emphatic response. 'She said she thought we might cramp her style, if we all lived there together, and that the move to Sarandon Hall was all about keeping her independence and her social life, rather than losing it. That visit really clarified things for her, apparently.'

'Oh,' said Taffy succinctly. 'She probably has a point there. We have become couch potatoes of late.'

'So what do you think? I'm so conflicted I can't see the wood for the trees. Part of me cannot quite believe that we would get to raise our children somewhere so utterly heavenly – I mean, that house is like something from a novel, isn't it? But the other part still feels like it's cheating somehow.'

'You didn't earn it, so it's not really yours?' Taffy said, nodding, understanding immediately what Holly meant. 'And then I suppose you have to think about who the rightful heirs should be – I mean, Elsie has children in America, right? That Harriet character for one. Which probably means they'd think nothing of taking a litigious approach to any disappointment on that front. I mean, Elsie is in her eighties – they might suggest she's not of sound mind and a court case like that would be just hideous for all concerned.'

Holly nodded. 'So you see why I'm not dancing around the kitchen? Which in itself is awful, because that's what Elsie intended for us – she wants us to dance around the kitchen and to sleep at night knowing we have space and the wherewithal to raise our children in Larkford.' Holly stopped. 'You know, she was remarkably up to date on maternity leave legislation as well. Kept mentioning how nice it might be for me to work part-time after this little one arrives. It's like she's got my life all planned out for me!'

'Tricky,' said Taffy.

'You'd think,' replied Holly happily. 'But actually it was just wonderful. Knowing that she cared enough to take the time, to take the interest. She's so invested in our family, Taffs, it knocks my mother's pathetic efforts into a cocked hat.' Holly's mother was a spectral presence in their lives at best. Always travelling around the world, often with a new boyfriend in tow, always moaning, always complaining, never showing any interest in her grandchildren beyond the odd bragging postcard from wherever she happened to be that month. It was one way to live, and obviously it was her choice, but it hardly made her grandparent of the year when she saw the boys so rarely that she could never tell them apart.

'I think we should just do it,' said Taffy after a moment's thought. 'I mean, we're renting here anyway, and it's hardly perfect for our needs. So let's take the adventure, jump in with both feet and enjoy it the way Elsie intended. I mean, when somebody loves you so much, Holly, to make such a phenomenal offer, it might actually be more upsetting to her if you said no.'

Holly nodded. 'Plus it turns out, with the prospect of leaving, that I really and truly hate this house.'

'You do?' Taffy was astounded. 'But you wanted to stay here after Milo left?'

Holly shrugged. 'Only for a little while so there weren't too many changes at once for the boys, but then life got busy and the months flew by and,' she held up her hands, 'here we are. Still living in Milo-Land.'

'Oh for God's sake!' laughed Taffy. 'What a pair we are. You know I hate this house too – I just thought you were committed to it, so I made it work.'

Holly blinked hard. 'But you said how convenient it was for work—'

'Well I had to find something positive to say, didn't I?'

Holly shook her head, starting out laughing and suddenly finding there were tears pouring down her face. 'This is mad.'

Taffy nodded, swallowing a little hard himself at the sight of such emotion on her face.

'So we're actually doing this?' she queried, her hands pressed to her lips as though to restrain herself.

'I know it'll be a wrench to leave all this luxury behind,' said Taffy with a smile, 'but I think we'll manage.' He paused. 'Is it weird that I still wish Elsie was staying put, though? I quite like the idea of an eccentric granny on hand for words of advice and killer cocktails.'

'Me too,' replied Holly. 'You know what, though, I think it's good that we've started to share our little foibles.' She shook her head. 'I can't believe we would just have stayed in this bloody house for ever, if Elsie hadn't started the conversation for us.'

Taffy frowned. 'Hang on, though. Elsie knew I hated living in Milo's shadow.'

Holly leaned forward. 'And she knew I hated feeling stuck here, waiting to move on.'

Taffy raised one eyebrow. 'Well, I can think of cheaper ways to get us talking to each other than giving you her townhouse.'

Holly grinned. 'But none of them quite so very effective.' She kissed him gently on the lips. 'You know this means that you'll have to build a proper treehouse?'

'For me and Dan?' Taffy teased her.

'Why not?' she said, as Ben and Tom appeared breathlessly at the door, their clothes and hands utterly filthy but their faces beaming.

'We're ready for fire!' Ben announced.

'And beans,' Tom chimed in.

Taffy squeezed Holly's hand. 'Well then, it's decided; it looks like we're ready for anything!'

Chapter 28

Alice pushed her chair back from her desk the next afternoon and watched Susan Motherwell make her way tentatively across the room to the examination couch. With a name like Motherwell, there had to be a certain expectation about how you raised your five children. Five children? The thought didn't bear countenance, yet on every other occasion that Alice had met Susan she had been calm and funny and seemingly in control of her various offspring, whose ages ranged from nine to nineteen.

Not so much today.

Today, Susan was clammy with a cold sweat and apologising for herself with every step she took, 'I'm so sorry, Dr Walker. I really feel like I might be wasting your time, but I've felt so unwell all night—' She finally reached her destination and heaved herself up onto the couch as though it was taking every ounce of her strength to do so.

'Tell me again,' Alice said, as her mind worked itself through the symptoms that Susan had been casually dropping into their conversation one by one, until Alice felt as though she was trying to piece together a jigsaw puzzle in her head to find the clearer picture.

Susan gave an uncomfortable laugh. 'Well, like I said, it

just feels as though there's this heavy weight on my stomach and the pain at about 3 a.m. was just awful. And this morning my jaw is so sore – maybe I was grinding my teeth together when it hurt?'

'And when did this cold sweating begin?' Alice asked gently.

'About breakfast time. I couldn't eat anything. I felt too sick. Do you think it's an ulcer, Dr Walker? We have been having a pretty stressful time lately, what with Nathan and his troubles.'

Downplaying Nathan Motherwell's issues as 'troubles' was so typical of Susan. The poor lad had been caught up in the bombing of a tourist resort on his gap year and had been lucky to escape with surface injuries and an over-whelming case of survivor's guilt. Even as Susan alluded to it, Alice watched another spasm of pain cross her face as she doubled over.

Alice pressed the intercom button on her phone to request another pair of hands. She didn't want Susan to overhear the phone call that needed to be made. It was one thing to tell a previously healthy fifty-year-old woman that she was having a heart attack, it was quite another to do it so far from hos-pital treatment.

It was only when Alice knew for a fact that the emergency transfer was pulling into the Market Place that she gently sat down beside Susan and outlined her concern.

'A heart attack?' Susan said, confusion all over her face. 'Oh Dr Walker, I think you've got that wrong.'

'It's different for women,' Alice explained. 'Women erode; men explode. Their heart attacks are more aggressive – sudden onset, arm pain, chest pain ... For women, we need to look for different signifiers and I'm sorry, Susan, but we really need to get you checked out. The team in Bath know you're coming. I think we can all be grateful that you did the right thing and popped in this morning.'

Alice didn't dare think what the alternative might have been, if Susan had chosen to push on through, as most mothers normally did. It was a mystery to Alice how few women actually knew what a heart attack might feel like for them, rather than their husbands.

Seeing Susan safely into the rig and briefing the paramedics left Alice feeling strangely off balance, as though she had some part of herself invested in Susan's recovery.

She was almost relieved to see her next patient arrive with an angry boil on his back. A nice, simple, easy fix. Disgusting, no doubt, but predictable. Taking a certain amount of satisfaction in the procedure, Alice lanced the swelling caused by a curled, in-grown hair and swabbed the area clean. If only everything in life was as easy and rewarding to deal with, she thought. Wondering how she might deal with the metaphorical carbuncles in her own life, she was only too pleased to call it a day.

'Fancy a run later?' Alice said to Taffy, as she picked up her habitual clobber from the doctors' lounge. 'I haven't forgotten about our Three Peaks idea, you know, so I hope you'll be match fit when we get around to it.'

He shook his head. 'Ye of little faith, Walker. I'm ready when you are. But I can't run tonight anyway. Popping into Bath with the missus-to-be.' He looked strangely excited at the prospect.

'No worries,' said Alice. 'Have fun.' She couldn't help being a teensy bit envious of the ease and affection that Taffy and Holly brought to their relationship. She'd yet to see any cross words between them, except that time when Taffy tucked into the cupcakes Holly had ordered for the twins' birthday party, but even that had been tempered by her obvious struggle not to laugh. Their relationship might not be perfect, but it was as close to a role model as Alice was ever likely to find.

She pulled her phone from her pocket as she left the building. There was no hesitation, no self-analysis – she just needed to hear a friendly and supportive voice. 'Jamie? Do you fancy a walk with me and Coco this evening?'

'That sounds great,' he said with his usual enthusiasm, 'but I can't stay long. I've got plans later.'

'Anything exciting?' asked Alice, an awkward sixth sense protesting that she'd even asked the question.

Jamie hesitated, the few beats of silence stretching through the ether. 'Just a date. A blind date, actually. Judith at the training centre thought we might be a good match.' He paused. 'I'm not really sure about blind dates, but beggars can't be choosers.'

Alice got off the phone and began to wonder whether there might be a lurgy doing the rounds; her stomach was lurching in a most disconcerting way. Perhaps it was the very idea that somebody as lovely as her friend Jamie, all six foot four of tousled charm, might consider himself to be a beggar on the dating scene. She daren't think where that left her.

Alice walked through the Market Place and felt whispers of that insidious sense of detachment that had dogged the last few months. She'd been trying so hard to move forward, but something was holding her back. Certainly when she'd moved to Larkford last year, she had been filled with good intentions, enthusiasm for a fresh start and with the hand of friendship outstretched. It had been somewhat galling to discover that she had brought most of her problems with her and her 'new life' was very much a case of same-shit-different-location.

'Alright, tiger,' said Jamie, slamming the car door of his knackered Subaru with just enough force to get the door to catch. 'Lovely to hear from you. Was beginning to think that young Coco was avoiding me and you'd jumped on the political bandwagon. I'd half expected to see you two on the evening news wielding a placard.'

He leaned in and kissed Alice on the cheek and the warmth of his face against hers made her hesitate. She knew that, on so many levels, she would be lost without Jamie – after all, he was the one who had helped her through all these months of indecision about Coco. On the other hand, she held back. The idea of being so reliant on one person for anything frightened her. If she closed her eyes against the late-afternoon sun, her friendship with Jamie looked conceivably like all her eggs nestled firmly in one basket.

That's why a little distance was good, she told herself.

She was doing just fine.

Publically.

No need for him to know that she was drowning.

After all, he obviously had dates and girlfriends requiring his ear and his shoulder; pulling him under with her could only have one possible consequence. And life without Jamie's friendship didn't bear contemplating.

She didn't like to consider that she might be doing him a disservice, not crediting him with the emotional reserves he might need to cope with what her mother called The Full Alice. She daren't stop to imagine his reaction if she threw open her front door and aired all her dirty laundry. And she certainly didn't need anyone to point out that a friendship built on half-truths and secrets wasn't actually much of a friendship at all.

'Not quite, well, not yet anyway. But there's an idea for an auction afoot. We're all a bit shell-shocked about the cutbacks, to be honest.'

Jamie nodded. 'I can see why. It's going to put an awful lot of pressure on your team if you're expected to fill in the gaps.' He paused, realising that he didn't seem to have her full attention. 'Just let me know if I can do anything to help, yes?'

'Of course I will,' Alice replied distractedly. 'So,' she said with an imperceptible sigh, noting that he was wearing his best blue shirt – the one that made his eyes look like cornflowers – 'tell me about this blind date then?'

Jamie looked uncomfortable. 'I don't know much. I don't really know why I'm going.' He paused and looked at her. 'I'm not sure I'm cut out for blind dates.'

Alice nodded, trying to muster some sympathy. 'It'll be fine. Judith wouldn't set you up with anyone too hideous, now would she?'

Jamie's brow furrowed. 'I suppose not. But one man's idea of funny and entertaining is another's idea of shrill and boring.' He sighed, already seemingly preparing himself for an evening of stultifying conversation.

Alice nodded, a little taken aback that it was possible boredom that concerned him, rather than what his blind date might actually look like.

'At least we know she likes dogs and she works in the countryside. I could never go for one of those women whose idea of a great weekend is schlepping round the shops! How shallow is that?' Jamie said with feeling.

'Quite,' breathed Alice quietly. His dismissive tone had told her everything she needed to know about Jamie's ideal woman. And it didn't take a genius to point out that Alice needn't worry her head about applying. Not that she ever would, she told herself firmly, even as she fondly watched him being conned out of doggy treats every twenty paces and stopping to scruff Coco's tummy with affection.

'What are you up to this evening?' he asked, as they stopped in a patch of sunlight to lob Coco's tennis ball across the parkland.

'Just catching up with a few friends,' Alice parried, seeing no need to spell out that she'd be chatting with Tilly online and not in person. And that guy from Norfolk was sweet and funny and charming, even if he did keep sending her pictures of him shirtless on his narrow boat. Maybe she'd even consider his request to meet in person – not in Larkford, obviously, the very thought made her feel claustrophobic – but somewhere in between, like Tilly had suggested. And there was always Ollie Turner in Sydney, as the night wore on.

'And is that a euphemism for getting ratted in Bath and dancing on tables?' Jamie teased her, as though she were still a student who partied the night away. 'Don't tell me there isn't a hot date on your horizon?'

Alice turned her head away and called Coco back out of the shrubbery she'd been exploring. Just because *he* had a date lined up for once, did he really need to put her on the spot and make her feel so inadequate?

Alice swallowed down her angry retort and forced an easy smile. 'Not tonight; I'm saving myself for a weekend in Oxford.' She let the innuendo dangle and would normally have taken pleasure in the flash of pique in his eyes. Two could play at that game, she thought in annoyance.

'Hey,' he said, catching her arm, even as she was tempted to pull away. 'What's going on, Al? I don't hear from you for days and now this. What's got you so grumpy?' He paused, waiting for her to fill in the gaps.

She shrugged. 'I don't know.'

She did though.

She knew that the very thought of him on a date – a blind date, any date really – was enough to make her want to cry.

He lifted her chin gently with his finger, concern etched all over his face. How had she never noticed before how one of his eyebrows bore the faintest trace of a scar, or that his deep blue eyes had flecks of yellow around the pupil? She was aware that she was staring, but somehow couldn't bring herself to break contact. The warmth of his hand on her face was addictive.

'I'm glad you called,' he said. 'I've been thinking about you since we spoke the other day.'

Alice swallowed hard. 'Me too. About you, I mean.'

He smiled and let go of her face. 'You see? We're in sync.' He guided her to a sunlit bench and sat down. 'And I think I've found the perfect way to keep Coco with you and still allow some scope to explore the cancer side of things.' His gaze was intense and his energy was focused exclusively on her, on her reaction to this news.

Alice blinked hard, trying to change gear.

They were talking about Coco – of course they were. He'd been thinking about her – and Coco. Because that was his job. She felt a hot flush of embarrassment prickle the roots of her hair and she swallowed hard. 'Well, that's just fantastic. Tell me everything.'

He leaned forward and clasped her hand with excitement, much as he had a hundred times before. And on none of those occasions had Alice been aware of every single touch and movement on an almost visceral level. He grinned. 'So, I was thinking about what we said at The Deli the other day, about how you were the only one making a sacrifice, and I realised that isn't strictly true. For Coco to have the confidence and continuity to explore her new skills, she needs you too – you guys have a symbiotic relationship, you see,' he explained.

Alice blinked, willing herself to listen to his every word; this was no time for distraction. 'So, I go with her?' Alice queried.

Jamie sat back and smiled. 'Kind of. Coco lives with you and goes to work with you, okay? That's Step One. Then comes the magic: we apply for funding from the centre – and maybe a little fundraising ourselves – and then for one day a week, we run a clinic out of The Practice, or from the Oncology Department if they prefer. But you get to double up as doctor on duty *and* Coco's handler.' He paused for a moment, his brow furrowing. 'The only thing I don't know is how she would react if you were having a hypo and a patient presented as a positive. But these are hurdles we need to hop over – none of this is going to happen overnight. And my feeling is that the more low-key we keep everything, the more successful it could actually be.'

Alice nodded, completely engaged with the notion, any bruised feelings pushed into the background where they belonged. 'So if I just blocked out one day a week at The Practice to do nothing but see potential cancer patients with Coco, then we'd be working as a team? I'd get the tests ordered and the medical history, while Coco here was sniffing around.'

'Exactly. Low-key, low-tech—'

'No drama,' finished Alice for him. She smiled, daring to allow herself to hope that this might possibly work. 'What about Judith?'

He shrugged. 'How do you think I got lumbered with a blind date? I'm doing everything I can to keep her sweet.' He paused. 'She scares me a little bit, to be honest. But this whole business is new, right? We're all learning as we go. Ten years ago, we didn't really know that dogs could smell cancer. Five years ago, it seemed like a pipe dream. Even last year, we didn't think that dogs could just spontaneously acquire the skill without extensive training. Why *not* try this? Worst-case scenario, you get to keep your spaniel and your sanity, and there's too much conflict for her – but at least we tried. Best-case scenario? Well, if you ask me, you and Coco are stronger as a team and, if this is going to work, it will work better with you two together.' He paused, suddenly uncomfortable at the emotion in his voice as he spoke. He cleared his throat and looked down at the sleeping dog between them. 'At least, that's what I told Judith.'

Alice leaned forward and kissed him gently on the cheek. 'Thank you,' she said. 'You have no idea what it's like to have lost all faith in yourself, only to find that someone else has your back.' It was possibly the first truly honest thing she had ever said to him.

He blushed. 'Oh Alice Walker,' he said. 'If only you could see what we all see, when we look at you ...' He stood up, tugging uncomfortably at the cuffs of his smart shirt. 'Right, now I've got you sorted, I hope you realise the sacrifice I'm making on your behalf, madam. I'm off for an hour of awkward conversation with a total stranger.'

He walked away towards the pub, leaving her sitting on the bench staring after him, the whole dynamic of their relationship suddenly in flux. Alice leaned down and kissed Coco on the top of her head. 'What do you think then, Coco? Are we feeling brave and a little bit bonkers?'

Chapter 29

'I swear to God, if they don't let me pee soon, I'm going to lose my rag!' Holly said through gritted teeth that evening. It was all very well asking her to drink two whole litres of water before her scan, but the pressure on her bladder was now excruciating and bringing her to the verge of tears.

Taffy quietly and discreetly put down his cup of coffee for fear of making any sloshing noise that would tip Holly over the edge. 'I could go and ask how long the wait might be?' he suggested, also clearly out of his comfort zone but for different reasons.

Holly shook her head, attempting a smile that looked more like a grimace, trying to put Taffy at ease. After all, this was a happy day and she may have done the whole pregnancy fandango before, but she had to remind herself that this was an entirely new experience for him, sitting in a roomful of pregnant women, the air thick with pheromones and emotion.

'They don't make you wait with a full bladder on purpose,' Holly reassured him. 'If they had to rush somebody in ahead of us with an emergency, then we simply have to wait. And a full bladder gives us a much better view, so—' She squirmed in her seat and pulled at the ever-tightening waistband of her jeans. Well, not technically *her* jeans, but the pair she'd given in and bought on the cheap in a larger size, when she couldn't quite bring herself to buy maternity clothes just yet. She saw it with her patients all the time: the first pregnancy, they were into the jersey-panelled jeans almost as soon as the stick turned blue, excited and full of anticipation; the second time around, they clung to their 'normal' clothes, their hard-won denim jeans, as long as it was feasible to sit down. By the third pregnancy, she'd noticed without judgement, their 'normal' clothes were still maternity clothes. She wondered where she fell on this spectrum, having popped out two bouncing baby boys in one go.

She gave a slight shudder. 'Popped out' didn't really do justice to the marathon labour and paralysing fear of her first delivery that had ended in an emergency C-section. At least that was one decision off the table, she thought with relief; nobody would be pushing her to have a traditional birth after that fiasco. Frankly they'd been lucky to all escape unscathed.

'Holly? Holly Graham?'

She looked up expectantly, a surge of relief that this discomfort would soon be over and she'd be allowed to have a wee – oh, and she'd get to see her baby too, she corrected herself. But there was no lovely smiling nurse with a clipboard to appease her pain.

Jemima Hallow stood in front of her, her ever-expanding bump encased in a tent of striped linen and a look of embarrassment on her face. 'Oh God, I'm so sorry, I bet you thought you were being called and the purgatory was almost over.' Jemima fidgeted from one foot to the other. 'Nobody warns you, do they?'

Taffy gallantly stood up to offer Jemima his seat in the crowded waiting room. 'Hi, Mims,' he said, kissing her on both cheeks. 'You're looking well.'

Jemima snorted at the GP's tact and diplomacy. 'If by well you mean a chipmunk that swallowed a beach ball, then thank you.' She turned to Holly, virtually dancing in excitement, although to be fair she was probably just desperate for a wee. 'Oh, I'm so thrilled to see you here! Don't worry, my lips are sealed but ooooh—' She clapped her hands together. 'I couldn't be happier. How far along are you? No wonder you were so supportive of our little protest. And you can join us officially now!' She breathed for a moment. 'Although obviously you're keeping it under wraps, or the whole of Larkford would know already.' Jemima on full excitement was an unstoppable barrage of enthusiasm.

Holly laughed – there was something infectious about Jemima's bouncy zeal for everything in life. In fact, ever since Mims had married Rupert, their local vet, Holly had been struck by what a lovely couple they made. Seeing them through their battles with infertility had only cemented that opinion. 'It's early days for us yet,' Holly confided, truly delighted to share the news; it was killing her not to be shouting it from the rooftops, but nevertheless caution had prevailed, just in case. 'We haven't even got a due date confirmed.'

'Well, once you're through the pukey stage, give me a call and we can have a cuppa and a natter one day.' Jemima stood up, unable to sit still for long. 'This GP's a lovely chap, but he doesn't have a clue about the mood swings.' She gave Taffy a twinkly smile and patted his arm. 'Although I imagine that might change soon.'

'Mood swings?' Taffy queried, looking sideways at Holly. 'We're not going to bother with those, are we, Holls?'

The two women looked at each other and smiled. 'No, I thought we'd definitely opt out,' Holly replied reassuringly.

'We're ready for you now, Dr Graham,' the nurse interrupted them, 'if you'd like to follow me.'

Holly leapt to her feet, amusing Taffy no end with the undignified walk she needed to adopt, simply to avoid weeing herself. Yup, Holly decided, this whole pregnancy was going to be one steep learning curve for her gorgeous fiancé.

Taffy held open the door to the sonography suite, solicitously making sure that Holly was settled. He barely perched on the edge of the seat beside her, fidgeting in anticipation. 'Why do I feel so nervous?' he asked Holly in a whisper.

She reached across and squeezed his hand. 'Because this matters. And it's exciting. You're going to be a dad.' No matter how hard he blinked, Holly could tell that Taffy was already wearing his emotions on his sleeve. She couldn't wait to see the look on his face when they heard the heartbeat for the first time. In fact – she shifted slightly on the bed, turning to look at him rather than the screen. She wanted to make sure she was fully in the moment herself – no distractions, no squinting at the screen with her doctor's hat on. She wanted this moment to be etched in her memory for ever.

Holly gave a slight shiver; she would never get used to that first chill of the jelly on her tummy no matter how many scans she had.

'You okay?' Taffy asked, gripping her hand a little tighter and not missing a trick.

Holly nodded. 'I'm nervous now too.' She turned to smile at the sonographer, who was routinely clicking away at the screen, seemingly oblivious to the momentousness of the occasion for them, as indeed it must be for every couple through her door.

'And when did you say your last period was?' the

sonographer asked, frowning as she angled the screen slightly away from them, so they couldn't see the images even if they wanted to.

Holly felt a tiny flicker of alarm, but nevertheless duly ran through the dates yet again in her head, convinced that their treehouse escape had been their only real opportunity for conception.

'Okay, then just bear with me one moment.' The sonographer stood up and walked to the door.

'Quick,' whispered Holly, a sudden wave of anxiety roiling in her stomach, 'look at the screen.' She was lying on her back, with paper sheets tucked into her pants and the conductive jelly glistening on her tummy; she herself was going nowhere fast.

Taffy, though unencumbered, stared at her blankly. Frozen to the spot, he looked from Holly to the machine to the door swinging closed. 'But I—' he began, worry darkening his eyes as the possible ramifications of this sudden scuffle sank in.

The door swung open again and Holly's ob/gyn walked into the room with an easy smile. 'Well, you two obviously have more restraint than I do. I had a tenner on the table you'd have grabbed a sneaky peek.' His smooth banter and Irish charm always put Holly at ease and the tiny, protective part of her brain that had switched to high-alert paused for a moment. Would Cormack O'Brien really be this upbeat if there was actually something on that screen to worry about? Nevertheless her grip on Taffy's hand tightened imperceptibly.

Cormack flipped the tails of his jacket backwards like a concert pianist as he settled on the sonographer's stool as she herself remained standing, murmuring in a low voice and pointing at the screen. Cormack looked up and gave them both a reassuring smile. 'Don't go getting worried, there's no

cause for alarm – we just need to double-check a few measurements. There's a chance your dates are a little off.'

'Jesus,' muttered Taffy, breathing out in a rush and
scowling at the sonographer, 'is that all?' He stood up and
hovered awkwardly.

Cormack clicked so many times on the screen that
Holly began to wonder if he was playing Solitaire on there.
'Cormack?' she prompted, after a few minutes had passed
in silence.

'Right, yes. Sorry about that. Just wanted to make sure
we'd got all the information we needed.' He swivelled around
on his stool and smiled. 'Grab yourself a seat there, Taffy, and
I can talk you through.' He cleared his throat. 'Well, firstly,
you're quite a bit further along than we'd originally thought.
Not that unusual to have a little breakthrough bleeding and
mistake it for your period. Your measurements suggest you're
actually at sixteen weeks already, so no wonder you've been
feeling so tired and emotional. Obviously that means it's a bit
too late to do some of the pre-natal testing we'd normally
do, nuchal folds and suchlike, but from what I can see on the
screen there is nothing to worry about unduly.'

Taffy leaned in to kiss Holly lovingly on the forehead as
they both exhaled in relief. 'Not so long to wait after all.'
He swallowed hard. 'And we can tell people now too, Doc,
yes? How great is that, Holls? It's official – we're having a
baby!' He batted away the tears that were threatening to spill
over onto his cheeks and sniffed. 'Can we hear the heartbeat, Doc?' They were both poised for the main event but
Cormack hesitated.

'There is just one other thing I should probably mention . . .'
Cormack said, a nervous smile on his face as he turned the
monitor slowly towards them. 'You're having twins.'

'Oh my God!' gasped Taffy, giving up all pretence of calm. He leapt to his feet and pulled Holly into his arms. 'You beauty—'

Holly laughed, partly from relief that all was well, partly in shock at this latest bombshell. Hearing those words out loud made her well up, not in fear, or trepidation, or even just excitement, but with a deep-seated feeling that this was all meant to be. Her and Taffy and their four children. Her family would at last feel complete.

'Taffs—' she managed, laughter trembling behind her words. 'We're having two babies—' She kissed him gently on the lips, tasting the salt of their tears mingling together.

Cormack chortled happily beside them, swinging from side to side on the sonographer's stool. 'Well that does tend to be the definition of twins. But this can't have come as a complete surprise?'

Holly paused for a moment, still trying to adjust to the seismic shift in her life – you'd think she might have realised. She shook her head. 'I was utterly convinced this time felt different.'

'Well, it probably doesn't help to say that every pregnancy is a little different. Maybe it's down to how you feel about the pregnancy, or indeed the make and model you're working on. Shall we take a closer look?' Cormack was like a kid at Christmas, whizzing through all the fancy toys on his ultrasound machine. To be fair, thought Holly, he probably only got summoned to the sonography suite for the problem cases – it must be quite a pleasant change to be in here for a celebration. Not to mention two parents who were seemingly unfazed by the prospect of a multiple birth.

But then perhaps she'd spoken too soon. She felt rather than saw Taffy sink into his chair, eyes wide and unblinking.

'There's two babies in there, Holls,' he said, staring at the screen. He tilted his head to get a better view and Holly followed suit. The two babies were curled around each other, like a mini yin-yang symbol, and Holly could see their tiny fingers flexing, almost as though waving to her.

With a flick of a switch, fast butterfly beats filled the room in stereo and she was spellbound. 'They're so fast,' she murmured, still somehow surprised.

'Jesus,' said Taffy, still entranced by the screen. 'Two little people in there,' he repeated. 'No wonder you've been tired.'

Cormack guffawed. 'Just wait until they get here!'

Holly felt a moment's unease – how on earth were they going to juggle two newborn babies, two excitable boys and two careers? Something was clearly going to have to give. A twang of elastic as Holly shifted slightly to get a better view of the screen made her laugh out loud – at least it was her knicker-elastic not her sanity. So far anyway.

'Can you tell what sex they are?' she asked, feeling a sudden impatience to be holding her babies, to feel those tiny hands clasping around her fingers, and to watch Taffy meet his children. 'Are they identical or fraternal?'

Cormack clicked the screen again, enlarging parts of the image for them to see. 'It looks to me as though they each have their own placenta, so it's more suggestive of fraternal, but as you know, about a third of the time that's also true for identicals. On the other hand, fraternals do run in your family, do they not?' He chuckled. 'I still can't believe you had no idea! And you a doctor!' He clicked again. 'Are you quite sure you want to know the sex?'

'Yes,' said Taffy fervently, at least three shades paler than when he'd entered the room. 'I mean, that might answer the twin question too.'

Cormack pulled up several images from different angles. 'Well, there's a possibility of one little girl in there, but it's far from clear. I certainly wouldn't bank on it. And I'm afraid her womb-mate is giving nothing away. I guess you're in for a surprise.'

He clicked 'print' and a scroll of photographs began emerging from the top of the machine. He smiled at Holly and Taffy. 'I'd say congratulations and a few lie-ins are in order. Pop next door with me now and we'll run a few basic checks and get you booked in for a delivery date.'

Holly took one last look at the screen and slowly sat up, her hand automatically resting on her stomach. Two babies. In only four or five months' time. The ground seemed to shift beneath her feet as she went to stand up and she sat back heavily. 'Oh my God, Taffy,' she said, 'we're having twins!'

Cormack shook his head in amusement. 'I thought you were altogether too cool about this.'

Holly had reached the stage of shock where blinking was a challenge, just as Taffy seemed to be bouncing back.

'There'll be four children in our house before Christmas!' Holly whispered, a ball of excited tears blurring her words.

Taffy stopped, her statement so much more a reality than a grainy image on a screen. His smile lit up the room. 'Just as well we're moving house then,' he said gently, as they walked next door to pick a date that would change the rest of their lives together.

Chapter 30

'Bloody hell!' said Taffy with feeling, as they walked back to the car. 'Talk about efficiency. You walk in expecting one baby and ninety minutes later, you've got two on delivery and ahead of schedule! And they say the NHS is unproductive.' He swung Holly's hand gently as they walked along, a lightness to his step that made him seem even taller.

'You could put that on a poster for Reception if you like?' Holly volunteered, still veering alternately between shell-shocked and over the moon. It wasn't so much the prospect of twins that had floored her, as the accelerated time frame. How on earth had she not known she was pregnant for nearly four months?

'Well this certainly explains the obsessive Hobnob consumption,' Taffy said, almost as though he was reading her mind. 'I've never seen anybody cry when they ran out of biscuits before.'

Holly laughed. 'I'm afraid there's more of that to come, if last time is any guide. I sat on the floor and sobbed because we'd run out of cherry tomatoes, if memory serves.'

Taffy scowled. 'So you're basically saying that Ben and Tom were healthy eaters even before they were born, but my offspring are already addicted to junk food.'

How quickly they had slipped into talking in the plural, Holly realised as she slid into the passenger seat, content to let Taffy drive until the latest wave of nausea passed. 'Yup,' she said easily, unable to resist the opportunity to tease him. 'They're already addicted to KitKats and Pringles as well. What I can't work out is, if there are two of them, and they are each fifty per cent you, then why aren't they kicking up a storm already?' She laid a hand protectively on her tiny bump; the same little bump she had assumed to be partially sponsored by Cornettos and tubular snacks. Given her dates, though, she was actually now worrying about them being underweight. Pregnancy the first time around had made her go out at the ears and in at the ankles. This time, she looked more like a Tasmanian Devil, with slim arms and legs and a definite absence of waist.

'You heard Cormack – every pregnancy is different. Or maybe you're just harbouring two girl babies under my shirt.' He grinned, rather touched that Holly had snaffled one of his soft, faded cotton shirts as her chosen pregnancy attire. With her hair tousled into a ponytail, she barely looked her age and she was certainly glowing, although she swore up and down that that was just perspiration from the regular vomming.

'Do you think we should make an official announcement?' Holly asked as they wove through the outskirts of Bath towards Larkford. 'I reckon I've got another two weeks of just looking porky before this bump pops out and there's no fooling anyone.'

Taffy nodded. 'Let's make sure we tell Dan, Grace and Alice before they hear it elsewhere, though. I don't want them worrying about what this means at The Practice, even if we haven't got it all figured out yet.'

'How do you think they'll react?' Holly asked.

'They'll be thrilled, because we're thrilled,' Taffy said firmly, as though any alternative was simply unthinkable. And in his world of simple male camaraderie he probably had a point. It obviously had never occurred to him that there was a certain politics when it came to pregnancy, a certain discretion depending on who you were talking to. The thought reminded her of Jemima, who had endured four cycles of fertility treatment to conceive their longed-for child.

'Mims was looking well, wasn't she?' Holly said. 'And her baby is due in two months so there's hardly an age gap – perfect playmate already.'

'Maybe you can persuade her of the benefits of a hospital birth while you're chatting. She's absolutely convinced that a midwife-led water birth is the way forward.'

Holly didn't answer. She'd wanted much the same herself the first time around, before it became obvious that, with twins, it would have been madness. 'If everything's straightforward, then why shouldn't she?' Holly offered. 'It's just such a shame about Rosemore. I know she'd prefer it. In fact, if it was still open, I'd be keen for a few days there after these little tykes are born. I can't tell you what a difference it makes getting off on the right foot: feeling supported and having a little extra help while you're feeling so sore.'

Taffy frowned. 'Wouldn't you want to get home straight away?'

Holly shrugged. 'I'm just saying that it's something to consider. If it's even an option any more, that is. Those first few nights—' She blew her fringe out of her eyes with the force of her exhalation.

Taffy silently signalled and took the Larkford exit, a flicker of concern passing across his face as he glanced sideways at Holly. 'I'm beginning to wonder whether everything I thought I knew about pregnancy is purely theoretical,' he said quietly.

Holly's hunger for Teddy's salted potato wedges had taken on dangerous proportions by the time they reached Larkford and, as they pulled up outside The Kingsley Arms, they were both in buoyant mood. They'd logged in with the babysitter and, taking advantage of whatever sorcery she'd employed to get both Ben and Tom off to sleep in record time, they decided to make the most of the glorious summer evening.

'No time like the present to share our news . . .' Taffy said, noticing Grace and Dan huddled in conversation in the pub garden. 'Are you ready to meet your public, girls?' Taffy said, one hand automatically reaching for Holly's bump.

Holly hesitated for a moment. 'Shouldn't we wake the boys and tell them first?'

Taffy guffawed. 'And I thought I was the newbie! Never wake a sleeping child – isn't that what you told me at orientation?'

A tap at the window made them both jump.

'You two look incredibly suspicious in there,' Grace informed them. 'Are you so starved of quality time that you have to make out in the car park?'

'Yup,' said Taffy, popping open the door and coming round to let Holly out, the twins having somehow engineered the child locks to be stuck on every door. 'In fact we were just coming over to join you, if we may?'

Grace grinned. 'The more the merrier – you can help me persuade Dan that having an office parrot is a health and safety risk.'

'I would LOVE a parrot,' Taffy said, his ears pricking up at the very notion.

'See,' said Dan amiably, as Taffy and Holly sat down at the table. 'Just think of the fun we could have teaching it to talk to the patients. Besides, the Major's already done the hard work for us. Phillip can say about two hundred words apparently—'

'None of them clean,' interjected Grace, glancing at Holly for support.

'Phillip?' Holly queried, wondering whether she really wanted to pursue this line of questioning.

'The Major's African Grey,' Taffy clarified. 'Crikey, I can't believe he wants to give him away.'

Dan blushed. 'Well, to be fair, it's more a case of Marion putting her foot down. Every time Phillip sees her, he comments on the size of her bottom.'

'And you want this bird at The Practice?' Grace exclaimed.

'Seems a shame for him to leave Larkford just because he enjoys an ample derrière. He moved here as a chick, you know,' Dan protested, ever the softie.

Grace rolled her eyes affectionately. 'And now he's getting broody for a parrot. Somebody get this man a puppy!' It was widely known that Dan's loudly ticking biological clock had been at least partially instrumental in his break-up with Julia Channing.

'Talking of broody—' Taffy blurted out.

'Actually, since you're both here—' Holly began at the same time, before catching Taffy's eye and laughing. 'We have a little news of our own.'

Dan grinned widely. 'Oh thank God, you've decided to elope after all and save me the bother of renting a morning suit?'

Taffy laughed. 'Never say never, mate, but actually—'

'I'm pregnant,' interrupted Holly, determined to be the one to share the news.

The grin on Grace's face said it all. 'But then you already suspected that, didn't you, Grace?' Holly realised.

Grace leaned in and kissed her. 'Well, you did practically rugby tackle Lucy for the last KitKat the other day, so I may have had my suspicions. But oh – how wonderful this is! Congratulations, you two. You have quite literally made my day. When's the baby due?'

Dan shook Taffy's hand vigorously, rather too vigorously in fact, seemingly short of words that would make a coherent sentence. Holly could just about make out the words 'bloody well done' but the rest was a mystery to her.

'Ah, well, that's the other thing.' She rested her hands on her shirt and Taffy smiled at her with so much adoration that she too found herself lost for words.

'We're having twins!' Taffy blurted out. 'That's two babies!'

Dan guffawed with laughter then. 'We know what twins are, you muppet. The question is, do you have any idea what's in store for you?' He clapped Taffy on the back. 'Now this, I have to see!'

Dan pulled Holly into his arms and hugged her, dropping a little kiss on her forehead. 'Well played, Holls. Well played.'

'You make it sound as though I did this on purpose. But you do have to admit, it is very efficient. One pregnancy, one Caesarean, a lifetime of chaos and nappies ahead.' She grinned. 'I honestly can't wait.'

Dan froze for a moment. 'You're going to want time off work then?'

They all turned to look at him as though he had sprouted a second head.

'It is traditional,' offered Holly. 'But we've plenty of time to sort out maternity cover. It'll be fine.'

'It'll be fine,' repeated Dan, as though in a trance and if he said the words often enough, he might actually mean them.

'It will be more than fine; it will be just wonderful,' interrupted Grace. 'I am honestly so chuffed for you two. You deserve a little magic. Have you thought what you'll do about the wedding?'

'Oh crap, the wedding!' Holly exclaimed, as the reality of a twin pregnancy dawned on her. She'd be breezing down the aisle like a ship in full sail at this rate.

'Just what every bridegroom wants to hear,' said Taffy, shaking his head. 'Maybe Dan had a point and we should just elope before we need to roll you into church?'

'Well, you're braver than me,' interjected Dan. 'Who's going to tell Elsie that her big country wedding is off?'

'It's not off,' Holly said with feeling. 'We might just need to postpone it a little, add a few . . . tweaks?' She squared up her shoulders at the very thought. 'You know what, though? I don't want to think about that today. There's plenty of time for worrying about the logistics of work and weddings and whatnot. Today is for celebrating! Let's track down Alice and we can all have lasagne at ours.'

Dan shook his head. 'You're all quite mad, but I happen to be thrilled to bits for you and I love lasagne, so count me in.'

'Alright, Garfield,' teased Taffy. 'Now, let's talk about my paternity leave, shall we? I can't help noticing that these babies are due during the rugby season, possibly during the All Blacks tour, no less.' He clapped a hand on Dan's shoulders as they walked across the pub garden and Holly had honestly never seen him so happy.

Chapter 31

Ben and Tom fidgeted impatiently at the breakfast table, desperate to be off. Since they had shovelled down their cereal at record speed, Holly's notion of a misty-eyed romantic announcement was fast evaporating, somewhat compounded by the debris from their impromptu supper last night.

'Taffy and I have some news,' she began again, making sure she caught their full attention this time.

Tom looked smug. 'Told you. We're getting a puppy,' he told his twin bossily.

Taffy pulled a face at Holly, this constant line of barter for another four-legged friend in danger of making their own momentous news splutter on landing like a damp squib.

Holly shook her head with a smile and crouched down between them, laying out the ultrasound photo on the kitchen table. 'Can you guess what this shows?' she asked gently. 'Can you see who's coming to live with us?'

'A potato?' asked Ben drily.

Taffy snorted with laughter and Ben grinned cheekily. 'Only jokesing – it's my baby, isn't it, Mum?' He turned to Tom. 'I win.'

'Well actually, you both win—' said Taffy excitedly, loving their easy banter.

'Because it shows not one, but two babies,' Holly finished.

'One each?' clarified Ben with a frown. 'We don't have to share?'

Holly nodded. 'Kind of. Two babies for us *all* to share.' It was a little surreal how this conversation was developing, but if Holly had learned one thing with her properly switched-on boys, it was to let them follow their own train of thought and work things out for themselves.

'Can they sleep in our room?' Tom asked, intrigued despite himself, squinting at the picture with great concentration.

'Once they're a little bigger, maybe. To begin with, they might not sleep as much as you do,' Holly replied easily. This was hardly the time to drop the moving-house bombshell to boot. One surprise at a time was plenty, she figured.

Ben just nodded. 'Cool.' He elbowed his twin. 'Can we go and play now?'

And they were off, hurtling through the back door into the garden, elbowing and nudging each other for right of way.

'That went well,' laughed Holly as she watched them flinging plastic balls at each other in a rather violent rendition of 'tag' as though nothing had actually changed.

'Better than expected,' Taffy agreed amiably, forever thrown by these two boys and their ability to adapt to almost any changes in their lives with ease, so long as they had each other. He walked over and wrapped his arms around Holly, the boys' excitable shrieks providing the perfect soundtrack to their morning – although probably not to their neighbours'. 'I feel weird that I haven't seen Elsie to say thank you about the house,' he pondered. 'I daren't think how we'd be feeling about this little bombshell if we didn't know there was a little more living space in our future.'

Holly nodded. 'We'd be flipping a coin to see who got to

sell their soul to private practice, I reckon. Based on the ratio of Mercedes and Lexuses in the clinic car park the other day, there's money in medicine if you know where to look.'

'Ah, but could you look at yourself in the mirror?' Taffy said with feeling. 'Knowing you'd sold out on your principles, wouldn't every measly pound be tainted?'

'Not so very measly,' Holly replied, mentioning an annual stipend that made Taffy's eyes go wide and unblinking, 'but I take your point. That's not how we do things, right?'

'Right,' he replied. 'Nothing wrong with a few hand-me-downs and beans on toast.'

Holly kissed him gently, not wishing to point out that, thanks to Elsie's incredibly lavish gesture, they really weren't doing too badly on the hand-me-down front! And he made a valid point: they were able to celebrate right now, and enjoy this blindsiding news, because of Elsie. They weren't pulling out their hair and tapping numbers into a calculator in a state of anxiety, they were content to roll with the punches and their principles – the NHS and state schools all the way.

Swinging by Lizzie's house on the way to work, Holly was fizzing with excitement. If only Elsie had answered her phone, Holly would have been able to tell all her nearest and dearest in one fell swoop. Elsie's recorded voicemail message had made Holly snort with laughter – *'I'm sorry I can't come to the phone right now, but I don't want to talk to anyone. Even you. Leave a message and I might call you back – no promises.'*

She knocked on Lizzie's door, braced as always for Eric to come bounding out and knock her flying. Instead it was a doleful Eric who greeted her, lead firmly attached and a guilty expression in his dark brown eyes. Lizzie was still in her pyjamas and clutching a large espresso. 'Don't be nice to him; he's been rogering Mrs Jennings's pedigree miniature beagle already this morning. She is not a happy bunny.'

'Mrs Jennings or the beagle?' quipped Holly tactlessly, earning herself a very stern look from her friend.

'I'm phoning Rupert later. We can't let him become the sex pest of Larkford, can we?' Lizzie said sadly, miming a pair of scissors. 'Even though Missy was so whipped up by her hormones she broke into our garden and presented herself for servicing, Mrs J is majorly on the rampage. Don't suppose Tom would like a crossbreed puppy, if it comes to that? Might be rather cute?'

Holly shook her head. 'No puppies for us. We'll have our hands full already.'

Lizzie blinked hard. 'Oh God, shoot me now, Holls. I can't believe I forgot – how did the scan go last night? All hale and hearty and we can start spreading the news?'

Holly couldn't help the grin that spread across her face as she silently passed Lizzie the photo, the yin-yang babies crystal-clear to her now well-practised eye.

Lizzie looked up and then down again, checking that her eyes were not deceiving her. She seemed to swing from shocked, to delighted, to falling about laughing within moments at the prospect of what lay ahead. It seemed to be a common theme, this amusement at how Holly and Taffy might juggle two new arrivals at once, Holly realised.

'Oh my God!' Lizzie shrieked in excitement, startling even Eric from his self-imposed purdah of shame. 'This is just brilliant. What did Taffy say? Did he cry? Did you cry? When are they due?'

Holly laughed. 'We're both completely over the moon and utterly shell-shocked. Not to mention the fact that I'm already sixteen weeks gone!'

Lizzie clasped her arms and leapt about like a mentalist spaniel. 'This is going to be hysterical! And, erm, obviously, lovely and wonderful and—'

Holly shook her head, laughing. 'Between you and me, hysterical is probably more like it. I'm trying not to think about the practicalities and just wallow in the excitement, to be honest.' She grinned. 'And now I have to go to work and pretend I don't secretly want to curl up in my office and sleep.'

Lizzie pulled her into a rib-crushing hug and Eric insinuated himself around her ankles. 'I'm so bloody happy for you,' she whispered.

'Me too,' replied Holly gleefully, not feeling even a scrap of guilt at her hard-won contentment.

Walking into the doctors' lounge, Holly felt a sudden wave of nerves overcoming her; there was no way she was going to make an official announcement at work until she'd tracked down Elsie. In her mind, it would be the height of rudeness to leave her beloved friend out of the loop, even if that meant yet another day of walking on eggshells.

She needn't have worried.

Grace was bustling about sticking task allocations for the auction preparation on the staff noticeboard and Taffy and Dan seemed to be fighting with the new coffee machine.

Grace saw her come in and paused. 'Morning,' she said with a subtle smile. 'How're you feeling?' she asked quietly, no need to be briefed about discretion.

'Queasy, excited and terrified in equal measure right now,' Holly replied, her eye falling on the sheaf of papers in Grace's hands. 'Going up or coming down?' she queried.

Grace blushed. 'Coming down. Quite what Jason was

thinking putting up all these photos of himself without his shirt on—'

'Aw,' said Holly. 'He was probably feeling left out not to have been invited to be in the "paramedics and pilots" calendar. Bless him – maybe these were his audition shots?'

Grace flicked through them again. 'Oh God, I think you're right. Although, to be honest, some of them are a little X-rated.' She discreetly flipped over one of the photocopies, only for Holly to get an eyeful of Jason's admittedly pert and well-rounded buttocks in all their naked glory.

'Well, at least he's committed to raising morale,' Holly offered, feeling all unnecessary. 'Maybe we should offer him December after all? He does look rather good in that Santa hat.' The fact that the only thing he was wearing was said Santa hat, plus a come-hither smile, whilst clutching a gift-wrapped package over his, well, package, made Holly wonder whether she was the only one who found the image both mildly erotic and a trifle distasteful at the same time.

'Hmm,' said Grace darkly, 'I think raising morale might not be uppermost in his mind, to be honest.'

'Well, I bet Chris Virtue won't let the side down, photo-genically speaking anyway,' teased Holly, watching Grace blush. 'He seems to be such a lovely chap, Grace. And God knows he's rather useful when it comes to getting the full story about what's going on over there.' Holly grinned. 'I think we all appreciate you taking one for the team there.'

Grace looked aghast and Holly realised how her ill-chosen words might have come across. 'Not that you're taking one, I mean, not that he's . . . Oh God, you know what I mean . . .' Holly's words petered out as she tried to dig herself out of the hole.

Grace shook her head. 'I know exactly what you mean.

Relax. And yes, he is a really lovely chap—' There was a but just hanging in the air between them, Holly thought, and she didn't mean Jason's photo. There was a reservation in Grace's voice that suggested her gorgeous pilot-suitor might not be quite the catch they all assumed he was. At least, maybe not for Grace—

A shout of laughter echoed across the room and both women looked up in surprise. 'They've been fannying about with that new coffee machine for ages,' Grace said in confusion. 'It's not exactly rocket science – go and give them a hand Holly, would you? I've got a million and one phone calls to follow up from my data request. But I mustn't grumble, it's just wonderful how many rural trusts are jumping on board.'

Holly nodded and wandered over, only to find Dan almost crying with laughter as Taffy took yet another go at securing his morning espresso.

'One es-press-oh,' he said, sounding out each syllable precisely, but unable to avoid the Welsh lilt to his voice.

The coffee machine sat stubbornly silent.

Holly leaned forward and read the instructions affixed to the machine: 'Simply press the red button and speak clearly into the microphone.' There followed a list of the coffees available, ranging from a simple espresso to a caramel cappuccino with extra foam.

'Try something more complicated and see if that works?' suggested Dan.

Taffy frowned and pressed the red button firmly. 'Mak-ey-ah-to.'

Nothing.

'It's your wonky accent,' said Dan, shaking his head. 'Here, let me try.' He stood in front of the machine and cleared his throat. 'One espresso,' he said, never having sounded more plummily English in his life. The coffee machine obligingly erupted into life, pouring a heady stream of thick black coffee into the little cup, a perfect crema settling on top.

Holly turned her head away, biting hard on her bottom lip to stop herself laughing, knowing that Dan had perfectly angled himself to prevent Taffy seeing the flick of the all-important power switch on the side, before pressing the red button. Dan flicked the machine to 'off' again. 'Here, have another go and try to speak clearly this time—'

Taffy frowned, leaning forward to read the instruction label one more time.

He paused, then narrowed his eyes, the top corner of the label beginning to peel fractionally away. 'You utter bastard!' he guffawed, knowing he'd been had, knowing deep down that there was no such thing as a voice-activated coffee machine, knowing that Dan was always a little bit faster on the hoof. It didn't stop him chasing him right through the lounge and out into the car park though, until both of them were breathless with laughter.

Chapter 32

Dan rubbed one hand over his eyes and yawned; it had seemed such a good idea to have an impromptu celebration the night before that none of them had considered how they would feel twenty-four hours later, at the end of an extended day. It had seemed the very least he could do, to volunteer to cover Holly's evening surgery.

He was thrilled for his friends, of course he was, but he couldn't help wondering how their new arrivals – and of course they had to be in the plural – would affect the delicate balance they had worked so hard for at The Practice. If these cuts really were the harbinger of things to come, then surely they needed more hands on deck, not fewer.

He read through the oncology report for Edward Everett, his suspicions about prostate cancer all too sadly accurate. How his wonderful wife, Jane, would cope was anyone's guess, but it did rather put things in perspective. Their marriage was one of equals and it endured; he could only wish the same for his two best friends. Happily-ever-after apparently wasn't an open-ended state of affairs, and that alone made all his concerns seem shallow and superficial.

Taffy poked his head around the door, looking almost as rough as Dan felt. 'Are you sure you're happy to stay? You don't want me to stick around for some company? Try out some fancy coffees from the new machine?'

Dan shook his head. 'Nah, I think you'd better get home to Holly and rub her feet or something. Isn't that what you're supposed to do?'

Taffy grinned, pushing open the door and sitting on the edge of Dan's desk. 'Nah, she's too ticklish for that. Not to mention your daft cousin has filled her head with nonsense about feet being the new erogenous zone.'

They both gave a theatrical shudder.

'So,' Taffy said after a moment's pause. 'Are we going to talk about the parrot?'

Dan looked up in surprise; he'd only been joking when he suggested it. 'We can't really have a parrot at work, Taffs, you know that. I was just winding Gracie up.'

Taffy looked at him sceptically. 'You do seem to spend an awful lot of time winding her up these days. Had you considered just asking her out?'

It wasn't often that they were so frank with one another, preferring the ease of their long-established bantery relationship, but obviously impending parenthood had trimmed away another layer of familiarity.

Dan frowned, but responded with honesty: 'I think we have to accept that I missed the boat there, Taffs. We don't all get our happy-ever-afters on the doorstep, you know.'

Taffy grinned. 'Are you likening my wife-to-be to a takeaway pizza?' He stood up. 'Pop round when you're done – we can have a few beers in the garden and plot the downfall of Chris Virtue if you like.' He paused. 'Failing that, you could be the sexy doctor with the pet parrot – it could be your USP for online dating.'

'My Utterly Sexist Parrot?' Dan clarified with a grin,

punching Taffy on the arm by way of affection. 'That might work. If in doubt, be eccentric, right?' Eccentric sounded so much better in his head than just 'single'.

Ten patients, three hours and a demanding heap of admin later, Dan clicked 'print' on his last referral letter of the day and sighed. He really didn't want to intrude on Holly and Taffy two nights in a row – no matter what Taffy said, they needed some couple-time to adapt to their big news – but he had to confess he'd do anything to just talk about cricket and nonsense with his mate for a bit.

He couldn't even bring himself to go for a run, even if running with the Larkford Harriers always gave his self-esteem a little boost. He did try to ignore the obvious flirtations and increasingly skimpy Lycra that some of the female triathletes had adopted, but he was only human after all. The pity was that he could no longer even see the attraction in a pointless one-night hookup; Lindy Grey had cured him of that.

He picked up the notebook that Grace had bought for him last week, the light bulb on the front cover hinting at the genius fundraising ideas he was supposed to be drafting inside.

So far, he had a list of the Air Ambulance crew and a few doodles of helicopters with faces. The name Chris Virtue seemed to leap off the page and Dan barely suppressed a shudder of irritation. Grace had been annoyingly chipper for the last few days, full of chit-chat about the poncy dinner, all the little nuggets of information she'd gleaned, and now this new suggestion of an auction. By the sound of it, any contribution he personally could make would only be a drop in the ocean of funding required. It was enough to make a man feel a little irrelevant – on every level.

Dan closed down his computer. It had almost been worth staying late to clear up his overflowing inbox, but even that accomplishment seemed hollow and unsatisfying tonight.

A loud crash from Reception startled him; he was out of the door and running down the corridor even before his logical brain could kick in. There was another clang as something hard and metallic fell to the floor and the skin at the back of his neck prickled a warning as he took in how eerily deserted the building was.

He slammed open the door to Reception, hoping to take the intruder by surprise, only to freeze in the doorway for a split-second, as his brain struggled to compute what he was seeing.

Old man Jarley was puce in the face and shouting at Grace, as he held her pinned against the wall. An angry bruise was already erupting over her eyelid and she was begging him to stop. With one hand he held her wrists above her head and with the other he was waving a knife in front of her face. 'Just give me the fucking key!' he hissed, his eyes glazed and pupils dilated. There was no doubt that he was high as a kite.

The remains of a smashed lamp and computer were scattered all over the room; it was clear that Grace had been fighting him off with whatever she could find to hand.

With just two steps Dan was across to them, barely giving Jarley a chance to react. In a bizarre turn of the tables, Jarley was just as hobbled as Grace, with both his hands otherwise engaged. Dan didn't hold back; he brought his fist forward with such force that Jarley flew across the room and slammed into the wall, crumpling like a rag doll, blood oozing from his nose and the corner of his mouth.

Convinced that Jarley wasn't going anywhere any time

soon, Dan stepped forward just as Grace fell mutely into his arms. It wasn't that he expected her to be sobbing, but there was something about her utter silence that frightened him more. As though she had somehow logged out of the situation.

He bent forward and caught one arm under her knees, swinging her fragile frame up into his arms. He walked through to the waiting room in search of water and a chair, pressing his lips into her hair and murmuring reassuring words that made no real sense. The salty taste on his lips confused him for a second, as tears ran down his own face in shock and horror at what might have been, if he himself hadn't been such a lazy bastard in letting his paperwork pile up. The image of that knife glinting so close to Grace's face was imbedded in his mind's eye.

'Grace?' he said gently, as he sat down and she automatically settled in his lap. She made no sound, other than a tremulous keening that was barely audible, as though her scream had been caught unspoken in the atmosphere. With one hand he slipped his phone from his pocket and dialled. 'Chief Inspector? I need you at The Practice. Now. There's been an assault.'

Whether it was the thought of the police, or the word 'assault', he couldn't tell, but Grace bent double in his arms, her cries no longer frozen, as she moaned in pain and disbelief. 'I was just locking up—' she managed, raising her head to look at Dan. 'And he wouldn't believe me. I told him I didn't have the pharmacy keys, but he wouldn't believe me.'

He tried so hard not to look shocked at her appearance, but perhaps she saw herself reflected in his eyes, as she dropped her face instantly into his shoulder and sobbed. 'I'm so stupid. Why did I even let him in? But he said he needed to drop off a letter—'

He kissed her hair once more, and then her forehead – lovingly, gently, with completely honest adoration. 'Oh Grace,' he murmured, 'my poor Grace. You're so trusting, that's all. And so brave.'

She shook her head. 'It still wasn't enough though. He didn't believe me. And he was so strong.'

Dan sniffed back the tears he seemed incapable of controlling, the tears that sprang unbidden to his eyes at the very thought of anything ever happening to the woman in his arms. The woman, he could now clearly see, for whom he would give up anything and everything. And not a scrap of Lycra in sight! He tried to smile at the thought, but it only set him off again.

Grace slipped off his lap and onto a different chair, holding Dan's hand the whole time, as though she would never let it go. 'What would I have done if you hadn't been here? We all dismissed him as just some old perv, the local stoner, but Dan, he meant it when he threatened me—' She sobbed and her words became strangled. 'He really meant it.'

Time became elastic after that and Dan had no idea how long he and Grace had sat entwined, waiting for the police to arrive.

Even after Mr Jarley had been handcuffed, groggy and abusive, and driven away. Even after both their statements had been taken, there was still a feeling of time being suspended. Of an alternative path for how this evening might have ended, but for a few different choices. Grace kept rubbing at her neck, where the knife had grazed the skin as she struggled, stroking it almost hypnotically.

'Let me take you home, Gracie,' said Dan quietly. 'We can clean up those bruises, get you a drink. A brandy might help with the shock.'

She shook her head. 'I don't want to go home.' She looked at him plaintively, the tears welling unshed in her eyes, the swelling unhalted by the ice pack they'd applied as Chief Inspector Grant had sensitively quizzed her about the evening's events. Dan could only be grateful that his own witness statement would be enough to avoid any semblance of doubt about Jarley's drug-seeking intentions.

If Dan had anything to do with it, old man Jarley wouldn't be free to walk the streets of Larkford again for a very long time. Rehab at this point was actually too good for him. But right now, none of that mattered. 'Come home with me. I'll sleep on the sofa. But you'll have company nearby if you need me? Or,' he said, kicking himself for not thinking of it sooner, 'we could call Alice or Holly? In case you'd rather—'

Grace shook her head. 'Maybe Alice could pop by, but, Dan, please don't go. I don't want to be – I can't be – on my own.' She offered him a feeble smile, so feeble in fact that it almost achieved the impossible and made her smile for real. 'I guess there's no point using puppy-dog eyes when I look like a hammered steak, is there?'

Dan held both her hands and looked her squarely in the eye. 'You look beautiful, Gracie, you always do. And to be honest, just knowing that you're okay and—' He choked at the memory that had assailed him in those few brief seconds, the very thought of anything happening to her.

'Hey,' interrupted Grace, 'I thought it was my turn to fall apart here. You're bogarting the emotional breakdown.'

He stood up and held out a hand. 'Well, maybe we could just skip over that bit when we tell the others; focus on your Ninja lamp-throwing skills and my sensational rescue instead?' He was teasing her and she knew it; right now, neither of them gave two hoots what anybody else thought.

They'd been there. They knew the truth of what had happened. And what were a few tears between friends anyway?

'Do you want to call the counsellor the police recommended?' Dan carefully avoided using the phrase 'victim support'; he had no desire to play into any scenario where Grace considered herself a victim of anything.

'No,' she said simply. 'I would like a shower though.' She looked vaguely around Dan's bedroom.

On the walk over, he'd almost lost his nerve. There was no way on earth that he wanted Grace to associate his home, his bedroom, his bed – goddammit – with what had happened to her today, but it seemed that Grace was craving comfort and support. He supposed he should be honoured that she considered his pokey flat met those criteria.

So, instead of all the ways he'd ever imagined Grace in his home, Dan found himself sitting on the floor outside the bathroom door while Grace took a shower with as much peace of mind as he could provide right now.

He picked up his phone again and pressed redial. 'Chief Inspector?' His voice was low enough to be drowned out by the running water. 'Is he okay?' He hadn't dared voice his fears in front of Grace – after all, what could he possibly say? But an Army-trained punch was a punch with power and as much as he'd personally like to kill old Jarley, he'd much rather see him stand trial. Let's see how much he enjoyed spending his twilight years in prison, rather than tormenting the population of Larkford.

Chief Inspector Grant cleared his throat before answering. 'I won't lie to you, Dan, and it seems to be a clear case of aggravated assault with intent to obtain prescription drugs, but—' He hesitated. 'Look, we've taken him for some X-rays, under police guard of course, but now he's awake, he's angry. There's been talk of having *you* up for assault. Just, try not to worry, okay?'

Easier said than done, thought Dan, as he hung up the phone. Assault charges and medical licences didn't tend to go hand in hand. He hung his head despondently and ran the scenario yet again in his mind. Had he used excessive force? Did he really care?

To save the woman he loved from being held at knifepoint, wouldn't he do the same thing all over again?

The sound of Grace's tears pulled him back into the moment. What's done is done, he thought, as he tentatively tapped on the bathroom door. 'Grace?' he called gently. 'Gracie?'

She pulled open the door, her hair swaddled in a towel-turban and his sweatshirt and pyjama trousers dwarfing her. She looked tiny and lost and utterly beautiful.

She stepped forward into his arms and rested her cheek against the flannel of his shirt. 'Thank you,' she said. 'I forgot to say thank you.'

'You're welcome,' he replied seriously. 'Let's order some pizza and take a look at that black eye, shall we?'

He stopped in the hallway, trying to feel his way through this situation – to focus more on Grace's needs than his own. God knows, a bit of tactless Taffy therapy would be welcome at this point.

'Do you want me to call anyone?' he offered. 'Holly? Alice?' He paused and took a deep breath, trying to be the bigger person. 'Chris Virtue?'

'No,' she said, with the tiniest shake of her head. She pushed the sleeves of his sweatshirt up over her tiny wrists and leaned back against the doorframe, watching him intently. 'I only want you.'

Chapter 33

'Jamie?' said Alice, as she attempted to fill Grace's coffee machine with one hand early the next morning. 'I'm so sorry, but something's come up. I have to cancel.'

The silence at the end of the phone was just long enough to make Alice wonder if they'd been disconnected.

'Are you sure?' Jamie said in the end. 'I mean, I would understand if you were losing your nerve a little, but we need to talk to Judith as a united front. I can't do this without you, Alice.'

Alice automatically looked down at Coco, who was watching her with inquisitive eyes, probably wondering why they were here, in Grace's kitchen, at this ungodly hour.

'I know. I do. And it's not that,' Alice protested, even though a tiny part of her brain registered that she'd been only too pleased to postpone her plans to go to the training centre this morning when Dan had asked for her help. 'Something horrible happened at The Practice last night. An intruder. Everybody's okay, but Dan called me to ask if I could stay with Grace until she's feeling a little more settled. It must have been terrifying for her, Jamie. And I guess, since I had the morning off and they've all got patients ...' She was aware that she was rambling, over-embellishing what should have been a simple conversation.

'Alice?' Jamie said softly. 'It's okay. It sounds like you're in the right place. And I'm sure that you're the right person too – not just because you've got the time, but didn't you do that trauma-counselling course? Don't put yourself down.' He paused and she could hear him flicking the kettle on; she'd never met a man who liked his morning cup of tea so much. 'Why don't I come and take you both out for lunch? If Grace is feeling delicate, she might appreciate some company and maybe we can talk some more about Coco's plans? Really get our ducks in a row before we face Judith?'

Alice could feel herself mentally logging out of the conversation; it didn't seem to matter how empathetic and supportive Jamie was being about the whole thing, she simply couldn't cope with that right now. Hell, she could barely think about it without feeling nauseous. What had seemed like the perfect solution in the park a few days ago – sensible, credible, acceptable – now felt like a leap of faith.

'Maybe,' she hedged. 'Let's just see how Grace is feeling.'

She hung up and turned her attention to the coffee, Grace padding silently into the room behind her and making her jump.

'I hope you're not letting that poor lad down because of me?' She was pale and drawn and still wearing Dan's oversized sweatshirt. Even the simple act of coming home this morning seemed to have taken it out of her. Sitting down at the kitchen table, Grace seemed to have shrunk overnight.

Alice shook her head. 'You're doing me a favour actually. I couldn't quite face the fearsome Judith at the training centre today. The way she goes on and on about Coco being her Star Pupil – well, it's a little possessive and kind of irksome. I need to be on top persuasive form to deal with her.' She shrugged. 'I'd much rather be drinking coffee with you.'

'Irksome,' smiled Grace weakly. 'Now that's a word you

don't hear every day. I rather like it. I may even borrow it.'
She stared at the cup of coffee that Alice placed in front of
her as though she barely registered what it was.

'Would you rather have tea?' Alice offered. Somewhere in
the back of her mind was the advice not to smother people
after a trauma, hovering around them and infantilising them,
but on the other hand she firmly believed that making small
decisions paved the path back to making bigger ones, like getting dressed or leaving the house. But it was early days and the
tremor in Grace's fingers showed that she was still in shock.

'I keep thinking about the noise Jarley's head made when
it hit the wall,' said Grace instead. 'It was kind of a thunk.
Different, I suppose, to what you hear in the movies.' She
picked up the coffee and took a thoughtful sip. 'I don't know
what I would have done if Dan hadn't been there.'

'But he was there, and you're safe,' Alice reassured her. 'But
if you want to, I'm happy to run a few alternative scenarios
with you. It can really help, actually, to know that you had
options that didn't require a burly knight on a white horse.'

Grace nodded. 'I keep wondering whether he would ever
have taken no for an answer, would ever have believed that
I didn't have the bloody keys! Maybe he was just too out
of it?' Grace's voice rose to a higher pitch than normal and
Coco broke all protocol to walk over and lay her head on
Grace's lap, nuzzling at her as she sensed the distress behind
those words.

There was silence for a moment, as Grace stroked the fur
back from Coco's compassionate gaze and then leaned forward to drop a kiss on her head.

'Your Jamie is wonderful – you do know that, don't you?
I'd be so sad if you kept him at arm's length all this time
without realising that.'

Alice frowned. 'I don't keep him at arm's length. We're friends, that's all. Kind of colleagues, when it comes to Coco. So it's complicated.'

'But we all have to start somewhere. And good men like Jamie Yardley don't grow on trees, Alice. And whatever you say, you two clearly have chemistry. Don't cloud your feelings for him with how you feel about the Coco situation, will you?'

'It's almost one and the same thing though, isn't it?' Alice responded. 'Besides, he's dating and I have a career. Not to mention a time-consuming and rather boring lifestyle commitment. We're hardly love's young dream.'

'But this is real life, not a fairy tale. And do you know what? When I had that knife pressed to my neck, Alice, I wasn't thinking about work, or yoga, or whether I should have skipped the mayo on my sandwich. I've been existing, not living, for years. All these ideas about my big fresh start? They're just ideas. And maybe it took being terrified out of my skull to show me that, but I will tell you this, I'm not waiting for the "right time" any more – the right time has to be now, doesn't it? Because what if now is all there is?'

Alice nodded slowly, blown away by the conviction in Grace's words. 'Does that mean you and Dan . . .?'

Grace nodded. 'Maybe. Probably.' She genuinely smiled for the first time that morning. 'Hopefully.'

It was just a knock on the door.

That was all Alice could think, as she watched Grace's hard-won resolve not to let these shocking events affect her shatter.

From their easy conversation over a second pot of coffee and, hang it all, a slice of cold pizza for 'breakfast', to a shaking, fragile Grace with eyes wide and full of fear.

Alice squeezed her hand gently. 'I'll answer it. You stay there with Coco.'

Grace could barely nod as her teeth chattered uncontrollably and Alice was torn as to whether she should even be leaving her side, whoever might be knocking at the door.

'Floral delivery for Grace Allen?' called a young woman's voice and Alice immediately felt Grace unclench. Whoever she'd been imagining at her door clearly had a much deeper voice.

The bouquet, if such a vast arrangement could even be called that, took up most of the kitchen table. Alice passed Grace the accompanying note, but lingered beside her, ready to deal with any eventuality.

'Well that's nice,' said Grace without feeling, reading the card as though it were simply a circular about bin day. She passed the note to Alice, who took a moment to decode the signature:

Darling Grace – I heard about what happened and I'm so sorry I can't be there with you
   All my love Chris xx

'Oh,' Alice said, seeing all too clearly that, as stunning and thoughtful as these roses undoubtedly were, they were simply from the wrong man.

'Oh indeed,' replied Grace, as she stood up and walked over to the window, presumably so her view included something other than half of the local florist. 'Will you come out with me, Alice?' she asked suddenly, turning to face her. 'There's something I need to do.'

For some reason, Alice had it in her head that they were going to see Chris, or Dan, or possibly even the police for an update. She certainly hadn't expected Grace to direct them out of town and to pull up here.

'Are you sure?' Alice said gently. 'It might just be a knee-jerk reaction to last night. And it's a big commitment.'

Grace shrugged. 'One day, some day, maybe? No, I'm not doing that any more, and I'm not going to let some angry, vile man in a dirty mac with a carving knife make me start jumping at shadows. I won't feel unsafe in my own home, Alice. Not to mention, this is something I have always wanted. So why not today?'

Her assurance was absolute. This was clearly no whim.

Alice pushed open the car door and watched Coco tilt her head from side to side as she took in the new sounds and smells, before leaping to the ground with alacrity. Grace smiled. 'You see. Even Coco thinks this is a good idea.'

She pushed open the main door and Alice and Coco followed her inside, allowing her to take the lead and uncertain exactly what she had in mind.

Grace simply smiled at the woman who greeted them. 'I do hope you can help. I'm here to adopt a dog. I'm not fussy about what breed, but I'd like to feel safe in my home again and I'd love a little company.'

The lady nodded and held out her hand. 'You've come to the right place then. I'm Patsy. Come and meet some of our residents.'

As Alice followed behind them, Patsy and Grace talking nineteen to the dozen about how the Dog Defence League worked, and how Grace's life might accommodate a furry friend, she quietly took in their surroundings. Coco trotted neatly at her side, almost as though, in the presence of so many unwanted dogs and puppies, she was counting her tiny canine blessings.

Grace walked straight past an Alsatian, a Vizsla and a soulful Boxer, all of whom would have made excellent guard dogs, but Alice could tell from the intent expression on her face that Grace had something very particular in mind.

Patsy stopped by a pen containing a litter of Labrador puppies, fluffy and Andrex-y and utterly adorable. Grace merely shook her head.

'Perhaps something a little more portable then?' Patsy suggested, as she walked over to a small Jack Russell terrier who was pressing himself tightly against the wire front to his pen in a quest to be noticed.

A sharp yap from the end of the room echoed loudly and Grace's head turned immediately. Cutting Patsy off mid-sentence, she walked towards the sound, which seemed to be echoing in stereo.

As Alice watched, Grace sank to her knees in front of the end enclosure and pushed her fingers through the wire netting. The yapping stopped immediately.

Patsy turned to Alice with a look of concern on her face. 'Would your friend be a first-time dog owner? Only dachshunds can have incredibly strong personalities. She'd need to be clear from the start about who was boss.'

Alice thought about the last twenty-four hours, about Grace's strength in the face of adversity and her resolve to make the best of the whole fucked-up situation. 'I don't think that would be a problem. And we have an excellent dog trainer on hand if she needs support.'

Patsy looked a little comforted. 'Okay then. I just didn't want her falling in love with the idea, only to struggle with the reality. Dachshunds may be small, but they have delusions of grandeur.'

They walked over to Grace and Alice did a double-take,

quite literally, as there were two perfectly formed and perfectly identical wire-haired miniature dachshunds looking up
at her, their eyes like tiny mirrors to their souls. Already it
seemed that Grace was the centre of their world.

Her eyes shining with unshed tears, this time from happiness, Grace looked at Patsy for understanding. 'I couldn't
possibly separate them,' she said, nodding towards the little
note on the wall.

Twin brothers. Eight months old and already abandoned.

Patsy managed a smile, choking back her own obvious
emotion at Grace's reaction. 'That's exactly what we've been
hoping for for them.'

Grace sat cross-legged on the floor as Patsy opened the little
gate and the two boys tumbled excitedly out. They barely gave
Alice or Coco a passing glance, before burrowing onto Grace's
lap and making the most of Dan's vast sweatshirt for comfort.

Patsy turned to Alice. 'And as far as safety goes, these little
chaps won't let anyone within ten feet unless you want them
to. Their bark can be quite off-putting, but with the right
training your friend will have the most wonderfully affectionate companions.'

Alice watched Grace's shoulders relax and her eyes widen
with joy as one of the puppies snuffled into the palm of her
hand, warm breath and whiskers tickling her skin.

'Now then, I think you can be Noodle,' she said to the
puppy, kissing him lightly on his tufty little head. 'And you
can be Doodle.'

Alice crouched down beside them. 'I think they're just
beautiful,' she said.

'Gather ye rosebuds,' said Grace quietly. 'What a load of
bollocks. It should surely be "Get thee a puppy and thine love
will be eternal"?'

With Noodle and Doodle in Grace's arms and Patsy rushing through the paperwork, it was hard to imagine that such a wonderful day had begun in such a dark and frightening place. It only went to show what a little personal honesty and authenticity could achieve, thought Alice, if only she too could be brave enough to try it.

Chapter 34

Holly arrived at work to find the car park full of white vans and tradesmen in logoed polo shirts crawling all over The Practice. The very sight brought home the reality of what Dan had told her and Taffy earlier that morning when he'd stopped by the house. She was still in a state of shocked disbelief. In fact, if Dan hadn't delivered the news in person, if she hadn't seen the drawn exhaustion on his face and the broken skin on his knuckles, she would have been convinced this was some kind of wind-up.

Based on the new security equipment being installed, this was no laughing matter.

Based on how Grace had sounded when Holly had phoned, this was no storm in a teacup either. It certainly wasn't lost on Holly that Grace's primary concern right now seemed to be whether Dan might be facing charges himself.

'Morning,' said Holly as she walked into Reception to find Lucy staring wordlessly as one of the workmen touched up the paint where Jarley's blood had stained the wall. She clasped Lucy's hand for a moment, both of them inevitably thinking that it could so easily have been Grace's blood, rather than Jarley's. Suddenly a Perspex screen for their protection didn't seem quite such a preposterous idea.

'You okay?' asked Dan, walking into the room with a clipboard and immediately clocking Holly's pallor. She nodded, swallowing a wave of nausea; it was hardly the time to share her news with the rest of the team. All she could think about was Grace.

'I've called in every favour I can think of to get things done today,' Dan said, checking the annotated list in front of him. 'I just want everyone to feel safe. Even if we are shutting the door after the horse has bolted.'

Lucy stepped away to answer the phone and Holly leaned in, dropping her voice. 'Why didn't you tell me you might be facing charges, Dan? This is just awful. Poor Grace stuck at home and terrified, and now you're in trouble for saving her!'

Dan shrugged, his handle on his emotions clearly tenuous at best right now. 'What can I say? Alice is staying with her this morning while we're all on duty and I'm off to the police station to give another statement later. It is what it is, I guess.' He paused, looking around at all the enhanced security measures that were being hurriedly implemented. 'I can't help feeling this was all avoidable though.'

Holly pulled him into a hug and they stood there in silence for a moment. 'I'm so incredibly proud of you,' said Holly.

He pulled away. 'It could have ended so differently. Imagine if I hadn't covered your shift?'

Holly's hands flew to her stomach instinctively; somehow in all the rollercoaster of emotions this morning that salient fact hadn't occurred to her. 'Then if you think about it, you're a hero twice over,' said Holly. She leaned in and kissed him on the cheek. 'And I can't think of a better godfather or role model for these babies.' She turned away before he could see the gamut of emotions flitting across her face and made for her consulting room, in a vain attempt to ready herself for morning surgery.

It was hardly the ideal day for the inaugural Invisible Disabilities Support Group meeting, she thought, toying with the idea of cancelling. She glanced out of her window, to see that Molly Giles and several other patients were already congregating in the car park, their faces expectant and nervous, even as Jade ushered them inside. Thank God she'd had the presence of mind to bring in a professional counsellor for these sessions; she was hardly in a position to be offering insightful and empathetic advice herself this morning. Molly looked up and spotted Holly at the window and waved enthusiastically. Whatever else was going on at The Practice today, Holly thought, life went on. Their patients needed them, and they could only do their best.

'Oh!' said Holly, trying not to look shocked as she peeled back the dressing on Charlotte's arm; it was hardly the ideal sight this morning of all mornings, while they were all feeling so fragile.

'Vile, isn't it?' Charlotte Lansing said in revulsion as she looked down at her arm as though it were something she'd found in the trash.

Weeks in hospital and two, rather invasive, operations had saved the limb, but Charlotte's physical well-being was actually the least of Holly's concerns right now. Previously buoyant and outspoken, the woman who sat before her today was cowed and distant, as though barely able to engage.

'It's going to take a while to heal,' Holly said reassuringly. 'It really is early days and after such a virulent infection—' She guided Charlotte's fingers through their limited range of motion; it was perfectly obvious, even to her, that her patient had not been doing the physical therapy she'd been prescribed. 'As all the layers of structure in the arm begin to heal, it's more important than ever that we keep you moving. Without the physical therapy, there's a risk of foreshortening and you'll end up with a limited range of movement in the long term.' Holly worked hard to muster a smile. 'And I'll bet you can't wait to get back on a horse?'

Charlotte just shrugged. For a woman whose life began and ended with the well-being of the horses in her yard, long before the family's needs were even considered, it was a worrying reaction. 'I think we both know that's not going to happen. I've told Rupert to keep a lookout for some good homes for them.'

'Oh Charlotte, no!' exclaimed Holly, shocked out of her professional role and personal anxieties. '*Please* don't do any-thing rash. I know you will come to regret it and it's barely been a month. With some commitment to the physio, we can make all the difference and—'

Charlotte looked up at Holly, oddly dislocated from any reaction. 'I just don't seem to care any more. And my horses deserve more than that, don't they?'

'*You* deserve more than that,' Holly insisted. However ambivalent her feelings towards the Lansing family's equine obsession, her commitment to Charlotte's recuperation was absolute. 'And it's perfectly normal to want to make sweeping changes after a trauma – but we always, always, advise against it. I'd so much rather make a plan with you about tiny steps we can take, together if you like, to get you back to feeling like yourself. Now, tell me, how are you sleeping?'

Listening to the usually eloquent Charlotte communicate in disjointed, distracted sentences was a red flag for Holly. Sure, it took a little time for such potent medication to clear the body, a single general anaesthetic causing enough woolly-headedness, let alone two – but this? 'Charlotte?' Holly said gently, after she'd stumbled to a halt yet again. 'Can you talk me through your medication regime again, just so I can write it all down?'

In the first instinctive reaction since she'd walked through the door, Charlotte's face flushed a vivid red, her eyes scudding to one side over Holly's shoulder, fixing on the noticeboard behind her. 'Just, you know, the antibiotics and the painkillers.'

Holly nodded, jotting words on the scratchpad beside her. 'And what about the diazepam?'

Charlotte looked at her sharply. 'I haven't been prescribed anything like that.'

Holly nodded and waited. She really didn't want to call Charlotte on her suspicions, the whole conversation being so much easier if she were to confess on her own. Of course, Holly knew perfectly well that her husband had exactly such a prescription for his back spasms and that he seemed to have ordered a repeat prescription remarkably quickly. And of course there were the other telltale signs of distraction, inability to focus and the edge of hostility in Charlotte's words.

'I might have borrowed some from Henry when I couldn't sleep the other night,' she muttered. 'We were both at our wits' end.'

Holly nodded without judgement. 'And this is why it's so good we get to talk. The medication that's good for Henry might not be what you need. Diazepam is never a long-term solution, but it's great for back spasms. Now, let's talk about what *you* need.'

By the time Charlotte Lansing left, clutching her own

personalised prescription, Holly had a faint hope that they might have turned a corner. Perhaps she could even get Rupert to stand down on looking for alternative homes for the Lansing horses. With a little more time and commitment to the physio, Holly remained hopeful that Charlotte would be back on a horse, bossing the Pony Club around in no time. God knows, the Larkford Flower Festival would be in complete disarray this year, without her steady hand on the tiller, arbitrating petty rivalries and grudges before they could escalate.

It was a timely reminder of how fleeting all their favourite amusements could be and, inevitably, her thoughts turned to Elsie. To Sarandon Hall and to Number 42. It was one thing for her and Taffy to feel uneasy about taking ownership of Elsie's beautiful home, it was quite another to stymie her attempts to make the very most of her golden years. And who was to say what the right course of action was? If Elsie was finding the house to be more of a burden than a blessing, then wasn't it up to Holly to support her choices and her bid for freedom?

If today had shown them anything it was that a little carpe diem went an awfully long way. Holly signed out of her computer and walked towards the door.

'Oh Gracie!' said Holly, spotting her in the car park immediately. 'You're here. We were just on our way to see you.' She thrust the hurriedly purchased bouquet of flowers and box of chocolates into Taffy's arms and gathered Grace into an enormous hug. It was hard to say who was seeking more comfort at this point.

Grace's face was heavily bruised and one eye partially swollen shut, but both Holly and Taffy were stunned to see that she was smiling. Alice hovered beside her, trying to transmit some form of message by semaphore but it sailed right over Holly's head.

'You'd think I was the only one avoiding work today,' Grace said. 'And please don't look so traumatised. I want you to meet my twins.' She paused. 'I'm determined to find the silver lining in this hideous situation, so you need to go with me on this, okay?'

Holly and Taffy exchanged confused glances, but complied anyway, intrigued. Grace gestured towards the ground and Holly's gaze dropped to take in the dachshund puppies straining at their leads. 'Your twins!' she said, as comprehension dawned, and she crouched down to scruff them behind the ears, laughing as the bossier one rolled onto his back for a tummy scratch.

'Meet Noodle and Doodle,' Grace said proudly. 'They're my guard dogs.'

'Ferocious,' commented Taffy drily, nevertheless won over by the limpid pools of chocolatey eyes that Noodle, or was it Doodle, had fixed upon him.

Grace laughed. 'I know it's a bit mad but—' She gave a shudder. 'I didn't like the idea of being home alone.'

'I don't understand,' Taffy said, looking to Alice for support and finding none. 'How are two miniature puppies going to make you feel safer?'

Grace smiled – a genuine smile that actually reached her eyes. 'It's not just about the safety, although I'm assured they'll be an excellent deterrent. This is just something I've always wanted and I couldn't put it off for another moment.'

'What are these little guys going to do, lick an intruder to death? What you need is a goose,' said Dan, striding across the car park towards them.

'A goose?' clarified Alice, still not used to Dan's oblique humour.

Dan nodded. 'I'm not even making that up. Geese make excellent guard animals; they're very territorial.'

Whilst it was true that Dan had rather a soft spot for Larkford's resident goose, Gerald, and that said goose was incredibly defensive of his nest, Holly couldn't quite see how a twenty-pound bird would benefit Grace's quality of life, except perhaps at Christmas.

Grace just smiled. 'They're just learning. And they are pure wire-haired miniature dachshunds,' she said proudly. 'Alice's Jamie is going to help me train them.'

'Well okay then,' said Dan. 'At least you've got a plan.' He turned to Alice. 'Thank you so much for stepping in this morning. I hope I didn't ruin your morning off too comprehensively.'

'It was my pleasure,' said Alice, before colouring instantly. 'I didn't mean pleasure, just that, you know – you're welcome.' She looked so flustered that Holly's heart went out to her.

'Well, you seem to have the measure of us,' said Holly quietly, as Grace proudly got Noodle and Doodle to sit and stay on command. 'I'm sure Grace is more shaken up than she's letting on. Adopting a couple of dachshunds is probably the most sensible reaction I've seen to trauma around here lately. Thank you, Alice.'

Grace interrupted. 'I hope Dan mentioned that I was going to take a little time off, Holly? I'll keep working on the auction plans, of course – I don't want to leave you in the lurch – but I have to say, even the thought of coming back here right away—'

Holly nodded and scooped one of the wriggling grey

puppies into her arms. 'Take as long as you need, Grace. We're all just so sorry that this has happened to you. And, once the new security system's fitted, there'll be posters that pharmacy access isn't possible out of hours. I know it's not much, but—'

Taffy frowned. 'It seems like the equivalent of "No tools are kept in this van overnight", if you ask me.' He caught the look on Grace's face and backtracked immediately. 'But obviously if it helps, then all to the good.'

'Well, that's why I'm here, actually,' Grace said. 'Dan thought it might make me feel better to see it in action.' Her tone was doubtful in the extreme and Dan looked uncomfortable.

'I just thought, you know, knowing it's there, versus seeing it's there,' he said. He reached out for Grace's hand and Noodle and Doodle instantly began barking. Dan dropped down on his haunches. 'Only me, guys.' He held out his hands in supplication and they ran over to give him a thorough once-over. 'Only me.'

Grace smiled, seeing them together. 'Clearly twins are so on trend this year.' Noodle and Doodle had managed to wind themselves around Dan's legs in an instant, creating an intricate cat's cradle of leads and legs. Dan gave in and simply sat on the ground, the two puppies leaping onto his lap in a frenzy of excitement.

'Are we all just skiving off and playing with puppies today then? Because I could actually get on board with that,' Dan said with feeling, obviously dreading his impending trip to the police station.

Taffy grinned. 'Count me in, mate. I've got a hellish asthma clinic all afternoon. Fiver on the table says half of them can't use their inhaler properly.'

The boys shook hands before Holly could interject that, technically, it was their job to ensure that wasn't the case.

Just as they were about to disband, Maggie burst out of the front door and across the car park, flapping her hands in a panic. 'That bloody robot has locked me out of the pharmacy again! It's only been three hours, but it's clearly taken against me.'

'Did you type in your password to reset?' Dan asked from under a heap of dachshunds.

Maggie nodded. 'I must have used the wrong one though, because then it initialised total lockdown.'

'Ain't technology grand?' said Taffy flippantly. 'Come on, Mags, let's go and conquer the robot overlord.' He flung his arm around her shoulders as they walked back towards The Practice, the others tailing behind them. 'Now I always find that a handy password is one that you can't possibly forget.'

He stopped in front of the security panel and swiped his ID, tapping simply one number when his password was requested. When the screen flashed up in front of him, he grinned. 'See? Password is incorrect.' He began to type: I – N – C – O – R

'You didn't?' Dan said, shaking his head in disbelief.

R – E – C – T

'Why not?' said Taffy. 'Handy reminder every time.' He looked simply delighted with this latest life hack.

'These twins of yours,' whispered Grace to Holly. 'They're not going to be identical, are they?' She nodded towards Taffy meaningfully. 'Because if they are, you might want to consider getting them tagged.'

Chapter 35

Holly turned sideways and eyed her silhouette in the mirror. Who was she kidding? There was no way that she could keep a twin pregnancy under wraps for another few weeks – frankly even days was probably pushing it. They had to start telling people straight away before the rumour mill got started. Telling Elsie was today's priority.

Julia had the right idea, she thought, having opened a gushing email only last night about her plans to adopt a Ugandan baby – the email had come complete with a photo of Julia herself, all bright eyes, burnished skin, and not a dent in her perfect, untrammelled physique. She really was on track to become the next Angelina Jolie, Holly thought, tugging at her ever-tightening waistband and thinking of the glorious apartment Julia now owned overlooking the shores of Lake Geneva and of her growing role as humanitarian superstar.

Holly tripped on a Nerf gun as she made her way through the hallway, giving it a hearty kick for good measure. All of this clutter and crap brought to her in less than two hours, she realised. She was only grateful that Elsie wasn't here to see it, in case it gave her second thoughts about the house.

The House ... For surely it deserved a capital letter in her mind.

It had become all Holly could think about in the wee small hours last night. Focusing on the prospect of a family home with room to breathe had certainly been better than worrying about Grace. Or Dan. Or Dan's expression when he'd said the words 'maternity leave'.

Holly cast one last glance around the gloomy hallway and pushed open the front door to allow the light to flood in. She couldn't help but feel that Elsie was fast becoming her guardian angel – the prospect of another set of twins all the more exciting for knowing she wouldn't be raising them here. It was as though the stars were aligning to make this pregnancy a joy rather than a strain. It was amazing what a fundamental difference that feeling of support made to Holly's state of mind.

Even as she walked through the streets of Larkford, the sun seemed a little brighter, the sky a little bluer, the heat haze already shimmering over the valley. Her focus was singular. Cutbacks, auctions, abusive patients all consigned to the back of her mind, as the smile spread across her face. By Christmas-time, she'd be pushing a double pram along these selfsame streets, Taffy and the boys at her side, and coming home to this—

She stood in front of Elsie's townhouse, its pastel façade in direct contrast to its funky front door. Could she truly be fortunate enough to call this home?

'Only me!' she called, as she made her way through to the kitchen at the back of the house.

Elsie lay on a chaise longue, a silk dressing gown swathed around her and an eye mask draped across her face. She waved a hand in greeting. 'Do me a favour and make me a Virgin Bloody Mary, would you? Maybe I can trick my mind into imagining the vodka.'

Holly did as she was bid on autopilot. 'You okay there, Elsie? Bad night?' It was something she hadn't really stopped to consider for her feisty friend – God knows the heat was affecting a lot of her elderly patients; she just hadn't thought to put Elsie in that category.

'Oh the night was fine,' said Elsie with a filthy laugh, flinging her eye mask across the room. 'That young physio chappie does fuel the imagination, I'm finding. It's the morning that's gone to pot.' She swung her legs around and sat up stretching, surprisingly limber of late. 'Harriet popped in again at sparrow's fart. Inconsiderate girl. Just because she has jetlag doesn't mean I want visitors at 6 a.m.!'

'Is she making life difficult?' Holly asked sympathetically, handing over her drink, an acid-green stick of celery slicing through the lurid red tomato juice. 'Maybe she really is just worried about you?'

Elsie snorted unattractively. 'Oh my darling girl, your naïvety knows no bounds.' She cast a hand towards the kitchen table, where a number of brochures were skewed across its surface; brochures for low-rent retirement communities in every sense of the word. 'Harriet has been doing a little research on my behalf.'

Holly was aghast; some of these places looked bordering on the institutional. Nobody who had ever exchanged more than three words with Elsie would deem them suitable. 'Stay here then,' she blurted out, the shock eclipsing any thought of her own situation. 'If it's ruffling so many feathers. Forget Sarandon Hall and stay at home.'

Elsie shook her head. 'Ah, but it's not my home any more, sweetheart. It's yours. Your baby needs light and love and space to move around without tripping over an arsenal of toys.' She raised an eyebrow at Holly's shocked expression.

'Just because I don't comment, darling, doesn't mean I don't notice.'

'Oh,' said Holly succinctly.

'The situation with Harriet does require a little thought, I'll grant you. But I promise you this, it won't be me, or you for that matter, making the compromises. Now, are you going to keep me on tenterhooks about your scan? Do we have a firm date? I have all your wedding arrangements positively poised for the get-go.'

Holly reached into her handbag and wordlessly passed Elsie the printed screenshot showing beautifully the two babies nestled together. They say a picture is worth a thousand words and Holly held her breath as she waited for Elsie's reaction.

Elsie blinked, held the photo at arm's length and squinted. 'Am I missing something, Holly? You appear to have a litter of puppies on the way.' She tilted her head to get a better angle. 'Two babies, darling?'

Holly nodded, partially holding her breath; Elsie's opinion was so incredibly important to her.

Elsie raised her glass into the air, her eyes shining. 'Well this changes everything,' she said. She patted the seat beside her. 'Come and tell me all about it. I may not be medically trained, but there appears to be a distinct lack of penises in this picture – are you saying I'll have two little girls to take to the ballet next Christmas?'

Holly smiled. 'Well, technically, you can take them this Christmas but they'll be fresh from the oven. And we're really not sure if they're girls or boys – they were both frustratingly shy.'

'Well, boys can enjoy the ballet too – I'll have no bias, thank you very much.' Elsie stared at the scan once more. 'Your dates . . .?'

'All quite wrong,' said Holly happily. 'I'm just over sixteen weeks gone already.'

'Not, in fact, a treehouse baby then?' Elsie clarified.

Holly shook her head. 'Nope, just two regular babies. Who knows when they first made an appearance – it's not as though we were planning it this way round.'

They both paused, unwilling to bring up the spectre of the wedding. The dates, the multiplying factor, the prospect of a house-move – it was as though everything was conspiring against Elsie's bucolic vision of matrimonial perfection.

'Hmm,' said Elsie after a moment. 'Well I think we can forget a corseted dress, don't you?' She looked at Holly, waiting for some sign that she had a plan for this contingency.

Holly's awkward hesitation, however, spoke volumes as they held each other's gaze.

'But wouldn't you rather be married?' Elsie ventured. 'What if you're all bloated and shouty and hormonal? Isn't it better to get the legal "I do" in place?' she said, in one last-ditch attempt to convince Holly to go ahead with their plans, any plans.

'I don't think he's going to change his mind,' Holly said gently, affection laced into her every word. 'We're building a family and a life together. And in many ways, that's more important than one day. A day that can easily wait until next year.'

Elsie looked instantly chastened. 'You're absolutely right. I deserve to be shot.' She took Holly's hands in her own, the left one still struggling to take a grip even after all these months of physio. 'Congratulations, darling. Twins! I couldn't be more thrilled for you both. Taffy will be wonderful, attentive and generally fabulous. You will be serene and beautiful throughout, even when you look like a Zeppelin. I have no doubt.'

'And I am sorry,' continued Holly sincerely. 'I know how much effort and energy you've invested in our wedding, but I happen to remember how stressful weddings can be from the first time around and I'm not doing anything that would put these little monkeys at risk. My blood pressure tends to have delusions of social climbing when I'm pregnant anyway.'

Elsie looked duly contrite. 'I didn't think of that.'

Holly shrugged. 'I'm probably just playing it safe.'

'Well, why wouldn't you?' Elsie said with feeling, leaning in to kiss her cheek. 'That's precious cargo you've got there.' She was, of course, the consummate actress, but on this occasion, even Elsie was unable to disguise the whisper of disappointment behind her congratulatory smiles. 'I guess I'm all out of excuses not to help out with the bloody Flower Festival now, though. I've half a mind to take you down with me, Holly – if it weren't for your reputation of being a plant murderer.'

As she worked through her list of patients later that morning, Holly felt the relief of having finally had that conversation with Elsie and, perhaps more importantly, that Elsie had seemingly come around to the idea. Sure, there was a frisson of guilt that she was taking Elsie's longevity for granted – it had been the unspoken comment in the room. How easy it was to put things off until next year, when the concept of next year was a given.

Holly turned her attention to Percy Lawson, lying on her treatment couch and stubbornly refusing to give her the full story.

'You don't have to tell me, Percy,' said Holly tiredly, as she gingerly applied an antiseptic solution to his legs, 'but it would be really helpful to know just how you did so much damage to yourself.' She swallowed another wave of nausea as she took in the carnage on the treatment couch in front of her.

Percy just looked shifty and embarrassed. And it took quite a lot to embarrass Larkford's resident adrenalin junkie; his ineptitude had long been legendary. Whatever he'd been up to this time, both of his knees and shins were virtually skinned to the raw and the angry areas of flesh that survived were discoloured and lividly inflamed.

'If you came off your motorbike,' Holly persisted, 'then I need to take extra precautions to make sure there's no gravel or tarmac lurking in the wound. The last thing you want is for an area this large to get infected.' Even as she said the word, her stomach heaved in protest.

Was it psychosomatic, she wondered, but ever since she'd discovered she was expecting twins, she had felt doubly sick and doubly exhausted. Or had the scan results simply given her permission to stop pushing on through the worst of it, putting on a brave face that sapped her energy even more? Maybe now was the time to admit that she might need to start taking it easy? After all, she reasoned, stifling a yawn, she was four months pregnant already – nearly halfway through growing *two* people.

'I don't have the motorbike any more,' Percy confessed petulantly. 'I had a little, erm, incident with it and the insurance people thought it was better just to write it off.'

'Maybe not such a little incident then,' Holly said gently, quietly breathing a sigh of relief that Percy and his red BMW bullet would no longer be terrorising the streets of Larkford; the man was a liability.

'Still, all's well that ends well, because they sent me a cheque and I went bungee-jumping in Australia instead.

Bit of white water rafting. Bit of scuba.' He frowned. 'For some reason they wouldn't let me do the base jumping I had planned. Something about a risk assessment? But anyway, it was a fabulous trip. I just need to save up for the next one now.' He winced yet again as Holly ministered to his wounds, his knuckles white as he gripped the edge of the treatment couch, but not uttering a word of complaint.

'So,' Holly prompted, 'how *did* you get your legs in such a state?'

'I was trying to make a bit of cash,' he confessed in the end. 'Did you know a decent treadmill montage on YouTube can make you megabucks? But it has to be new and fresh. You know, daring.'

'Right,' said Holly, struggling to comprehend why someone would risk life and limb, apparently, for a few clicks online. 'Should I even ask?'

Percy shrugged, his face beginning to gain a greyish pallor that told Holly the adrenalin was wearing off and the pain was kicking in. 'You know how you can bounce a mountain bike on its back wheel? Well, if you do that on a treadmill then—' He waved his hand at his mangled legs.

'Jesus,' sighed Holly. 'You do know you're a liability, don't you, Percy? At this rate, we ought to send you on a health and safety risk assessment course!'

'No need,' said Percy. 'I can weigh up the cost-benefit of every stunt myself.' He exhaled sharply as Holly began to dress his injuries, layering gauze to keep the antiseptic in situ.

She wobbled for a moment, her face matching Percy's in an attractive shade of apple-white. 'Give me a sec,' she said, turning away to slowly sip some water and willing the queasiness to pass. 'You know, if this had been only fractionally worse, I'd have been referring you to the hospital. They might even have wanted to do some skin grafts – this kind of friction burn is almost as destructive as an actual burn.' She struggled to put this in a way that would limit Percy's thrill-seeking: 'They would have taken skin off your backside to patch your legs.'

She felt a small moment of relief that something she had said had got through to him, as an expression of revulsion flickered across his face. He cautiously swung his feet off the couch and lowered them towards the floor. 'Okay, point taken,' he said, clearly annoyed. 'Now while I'm here, Doc, can you do me a favour and whip off my sock? Since I got back from my trip, I have a sneaking suspicion there's a fungus among us.' He grinned his best little-boy-innocent smile. 'My girlfriend reckons my athlete's foot is the only truly sporty thing about me.'

Holly gently pulled off his hi-tech, super-wicking, extra-outdoorsy sock and gagged instantly. 'Percy, if you got back from Australia a week ago, how on earth can you have missed the fact that there's sea urchin embedded in your foot?' she exclaimed.

Professional courtesy be damned, Holly clamped her hand over her mouth and dashed from the room, only just making it to the ladies' before the sickness caught up with her. It was all very well saying she could carry on business as usual, but even her resolute control of her hormones was not designed to cope with the onslaught that was Percy Lawson.

Chapter 36

Alice pushed her hands deeper into her pockets and watched as Coco looped the loop around the ancient horse chestnut trees in the Larkford parkland the next morning. At this hour, even the hardiest of the local dog walkers were probably still tucked up in bed. It was definitely worth the extra resolve to get out of bed just to have such a magnificent space all to herself, she decided, even as an enormous yawn ambushed her.

She needed time to think, space to find some clarity – and with the best will in the world, her terraced cottage would never qualify as spacious, even without all her boxes. And therein lay the cause of her bad mood that morning. She'd woken to the dawn chorus and lain in bed mentally cataloguing the boxes in her bedroom, then in her euphemistically named 'dressing room' – even though there wasn't even enough room to put on a pair of trousers in there without causing a tsunami of accessories.

Jamie's absolute faith in her and his willingness to stand beside her in the negotiations about Coco had certainly given her pause; it was a long time since anyone had given her such cause for self-reflection. Sure, Tilly liked to tease and prod her into action occasionally, but there was never a moment where Alice felt that their friendship was in jeopardy if she didn't take action.

With Jamie, she was navigating different waters.

How could he possibly look at her with such trust and affection if he knew the truth, thought Alice, as she threw Coco's tennis ball unnecessarily hard. But more than that – more than wanting his good opinion of her – his faith had given her the resolve to make some changes.

As the sun began to filter through the foliage above her, creating stripes of light and shade, Alice breathed out slowly. This parkland was her favourite place in the world right now and it didn't feel right to contaminate it with her bad mood. She stood under the largest and presumably oldest of the horse chestnuts and ran her fingers over the crumbling bark. How long had this tree been hearing the joys and woes of Larkford's residents, she wondered, feeling comforted at the very thought.

'I see I'm not the only one confiding in the trees these days,' Grace said quietly as she ambled towards her, Noodle and Doodle straining at their leads. 'It always seems such a shame that they can't talk back.' Grace was pale and the bruise on her face now bloomed in Technicolor.

'Morning,' said Alice, blushing lightly at having been caught ranting at the trees. 'I thought you'd be having a lie-in.'

Grace shrugged. 'I was too tired to sleep, if that makes sense?' She hesitated and that flicker of hesitation told Alice the real story. No doubt nightmares had been her constant companion since the attack, even with Noodle and Doodle at her side.

'You know, I still keep hoping these trees will come up with the answers . . .' She deliberately let the idea float. Somehow it felt incredibly important to Alice in that moment that Grace realised she wasn't alone in her fight with the nightly vigil of insomnia, even if she didn't know how to say it.

As the dogs circled and played around them, Alice and Grace both leaned back against the sturdy tree trunk. 'I've spent so much time with Mr Google at night in the last week, it might just mean we're in a committed relationship,' Grace confessed.

Alice smiled. 'Even if it does, it wouldn't last. Can you imagine going out with such a know-it-all?'

Grace laughed, the sound echoing under the branches, and seemingly giving them both a lift. 'All information, no application,' she mused. 'He'd just be suggesting recipes for fancy food with no intention of mucking in.'

'Or washing up,' Alice joined in.

'Bastard,' said Grace with feeling.

'Cut him loose,' agreed Alice, 'before it goes too far.'

'But he's excellent company at two a.m., right?' Grace said astutely, clearly one of the very few in Larkford not to fall for the competent image of Alice that she normally worked so hard to portray.

Alice nodded. 'Every night since I can remember,' she confessed quietly. She watched Coco leap and frolic between the tree trunks with Noodle and Doodle and corrected herself. 'But it's a bit better now, since I got Coco. I don't have the fear about missing a hypo in the night.'

'I guess it's one less thing to worry about,' said Grace gently. 'And if nothing else, it's a bloody good excuse to have the dog sleep on the bed. Not that I need an excuse, although Noodle there does snore like a heathen.'

Alice laughed, even though the notion of a bed without Coco in it was something she couldn't begin to contemplate this morning. She was only too happy that Noodle chose that moment to roll in something disgusting, Grace running towards him with her arms flapping and a choice range of vocabulary tumbling from her lips. As soon as sanity prevailed once more, Alice was quick to change the topic. 'Any news on whether Dan's being charged? He said he was due at the station *again* last night. Why are they dragging this out?'

Grace shook her head. 'He won't find out what's going on for a few days. Jarley's got some amazing legal bod apparently, although how he's affording it, I couldn't tell you. I wouldn't put it past him to use the threat of an assault charge as a bargaining chip.' She gave an almost imperceptible shudder. 'I just want it all to be over, really.'

Alice nodded – she could well empathise with the notion. It seemed incredibly unjust that Dan might yet be prosecuted for saving Grace under the remit of 'unreasonable force'. Just how much force, Alice wondered, would have been considered 'reasonable' in the circumstances?

There was silence between them for a moment, both caught up in their own thoughts as Noodle, Doodle and Coco continued to 'let off steam' around them, seemingly intent on making them both laugh. In reality, this involved a number of cartwheels and other gymnastics as the three dogs hurtled through the lush grassland and yapped at each other in excitement. Coco's tongue lolled out of her mouth as she panted and tried to keep up with the younger dogs, whose euphoria and energy seemed boundless.

'I'll have what they're having,' Grace said, shaking her head at their antics. 'You'd never believe they were ever miserable and wan, would you?'

Alice stretched and plonked herself down onto the grass and smiled. 'You did a good thing there, Grace.'

'Alice Walker, please tell me you're not sitting in the mud in a pair of Armani jeans?'

Alice shrugged. 'They're not new ones.'

'Easy come, easy go,' sighed Grace as she sat down beside her, before looking aghast. 'Oh my God, I'm turning into my mother! Did you hear what I just said? And I was about to launch into a lecture about appreciating what you have . . . This is just awful!'

'Your mum kind of has a point though, doesn't she? I mean, how many pairs of jeans does one person actually need? It's not as though they have magical powers to boost your mood, now is it?' There was a shadow of bitterness in her words. Alice leaned back on her hands and watched the dogs hurtle in a loop. 'They've got the right idea, haven't they?'

Grace was silent for a moment, but Alice could feel her gaze.

'I was thinking I might redecorate my cottage while I'm off work,' Grace said eventually. 'Give the house a bit of a spruce. All the clutter is driving me crazy.'

'Good idea,' said Alice, plucking nervously at the daisies around her, wondering if she had the nerve to— 'We could do a car boot sale together if you fancied it?' she blurted out suddenly. 'I'll bet between us we could fill a carload.'

'I would love that,' Grace said simply. 'I've still got stuff from when Roy was alive and the boys' kit seems to multiply with every passing visit. I feel like my house is a glorified storage locker some days.'

Alice began to thread the daisy stems together wordlessly, running Grace's comments in her head again, listening to the heartfelt tone of her admission. Perhaps they were all dealing with the same baggage to a greater or lesser degree – both literal and metaphorical?

'Maybe I could help you?' Alice offered, only too aware of the irony of the suggestion.

'Maybe we could help each other?' Grace countered. This time there was no missing the understanding in her eyes. 'It seems to me as though baby steps might be required all round.'

Alice focused determinedly on a tricky daisy that refused to submit – it was easier to talk without eye contact. 'I wouldn't know where to start. I actually have a box full of books about decluttering and streamlining my life, did you know that?'

Grace blew two bursts on the whistle and all three dogs came running for a morsel of chicken. If only people's behaviour was so easy to train, thought Alice.

'And what do these books say? Is it the usual bollocks about "Have you used it in the last year?" because honestly that winds me up. I mean, I haven't been skiing in ages, but I'm hardly going to chuck out my salopettes, am I?'

'And after a while, doesn't high fashion just morph into vintage anyway?' Alice added.

'Well, I can't speak for high fashion but I have given up saving things for best. When Roy died, I sort of had a "fuck it" moment and just got on with it. Why not enjoy a lovely handbag every day, or pretty pyjamas?' Grace said with feeling.

'When I add up how much I've spent on stuff to make me feel better, when I look at my credit card statements, I could actually vomit,' Alice blurted out, her usual defences somehow missing in this conversation.

'Not so easy to give things away when technically you're still paying for them, is it?' Grace agreed, no trace of judgement in her tone. She leaned in. 'I gave our sofa to Cancer Research after Roy died and still had to keep paying instalments for the next year. But it was worth it, not to look at that grey upholstery and not to see him sitting there, moaning, with a can of lager in his hand.

'But it sounds to me as though a car boot sale might be doing you a disservice,' Grace continued matter-of-factly. 'Maybe we should find one of those pre-loved boutiques and you could pay off your cards with your share of the proceeds? Would it feel better, do you think, to have less stuff and no debt? Or would you simply want to replace it all?'

The thought of clearing out the house made Alice's pulse race erratically and she drew in a deep breath as though she were drowning. This was what she wanted, she reminded herself, even if it was so painful. She swallowed hard, flinching slightly as Grace laid a hand on her arm.

'Let's do this together,' Grace said, refusing to sway from her suggestion, even in light of Alice's emotional reaction. 'And honestly, you'd be doing me a favour too.'

'How on earth do you figure that?' Alice was defensive, but on some level she couldn't help but feel intrigued.

'Well, I think we both know I'm kidding myself if I thought adopting two puppies would take my mind off what happened completely.' Grace automatically touched the bruising on her face that was already turning a vile shade of ochre. 'So I have plans to keep busy. And I know, I know, going back to work is the only real way to confront all this fear head-on, but,' she blew out a lungful of air, 'I just can't do that yet.'

'Bloody hell, Grace,' said Alice with feeling, her heart going out to this woman beside her – this courageous and thoughtful woman who had never deserved to feel violated in the sanctity of her workplace. For the first time Alice noticed the tremor in Grace's hands and the effort it was taking her to remain upbeat and positive.

Grace shrugged, almost angrily. 'I can't tell you how stupid I really feel. For letting that bastard in when he knocked, yes, but mainly for letting it affect me so badly. I know everyone's looking at me, wondering why I haven't gone back to work. I just can't bring myself to tell them how much the thought of it scares me.' She chucked a handful of daisies in the air. 'If I could just get past the nightmares, then maybe?' She sighed. 'There's only so much busy I can fit into each day; I'm beginning to wonder if the fear will ever really fade.'

'What can I do, Grace? Really? Let's stop talking as though getting rid of a few jumpers is going to fix this. What would *really* help?' Alice said helplessly.

Grace shrugged, scruffing Noodle and Doodle's fur as they tumbled over her lap. 'I honestly don't know.' A look of devilment flitted across her face. 'Unless you fancy dating a sexy pilot? I'm pretty sure he's utterly wonderful, but he's not the man for me. I just haven't had the heart to tell him that yet though.'

Alice leaned against Grace's shoulder in a rare moment of physical intimacy, following her lead. 'Are you trying to offload your sloppy seconds on me, missus?'

'Oh,' said Grace with feeling, 'there is *nothing* sloppy about Chris Virtue. In fact, I probably need a lobotomy for not falling instantly in love with the man – he's basically Action Man in a flight suit – but love is a fickle thing . . .'

They sat in silence for a moment, both of them with their thoughts caught up by where exactly their affections truly lay.

'So, I either have to sort out my house or date a sexy pilot,' Alice said in the end, with the merest hint of resignation. 'It's hardly Sophie's Choice.' She sighed. 'So why do both options seem so horribly challenging? Perhaps it's me who needs the lobotomy?'

'Well, Chris may be gorgeous, but he's also very local,' said Grace perceptively. 'And it's no secret that you prefer your men a little more, shall we say, international in flavour. I'm assuming that's the only reason you're holding that gorgeous Jamie at bay?'

Alice didn't respond; she didn't know what to say. The spirit of honesty decreed that she confess, but the words were like cotton wool in her mouth. Yet Grace continued to surprise her.

'Of course, if you felt a little more, erm, settled at home, it might not seem quite so daunting inviting somebody in – oh, Doodle! Don't eat that. That's disgusting!'

Alice gratefully leapt to her feet to help. The very least she owed Doodle for her reprieve was a nice piece of chicken, rather than the unthinkably disgusting tissue he had unearthed in the long grass beneath the trees. But as tenacious as Doodle was with his new-found treasure, his owner was much the same once she had an idea in her head. 'You and Jamie are a perfect match, you do know that?'

'I can't have a relationship. Not really,' Alice said quietly.

Grace stayed silent, waiting for her to explain, waiting for Alice's sudden obsession with her fingernails to subside.

Alice took a deep breath, suddenly desperate to bare her soul, to have someone understand her dilemma. 'My health is my priority, right? And then Coco. Obviously. And then, well, I'm a doctor, so my career is kind of important. So what am I really offering? Hey, fancy being number four on my list? Fancy always, always coming last when I have to make a choice? It's hardly a romantic or reasonable proposition, now is it?'

She'd barely drawn breath and she swallowed hard, her eyes swimming even as she made a joke of it.

Grace's sympathetic expression was actually enough to tip her over the edge, thought Alice, when she finally did look up.

'Oh you daft, sweet girl,' said Grace, taking her hand and squeezing it. 'Is that what you really think?'

Alice nodded. 'That's what I *know*. No bloke is going to put up with the nightly crap I have to deal with. Or stick around when I lose my sight, or my leg, or my figure . . . You forget, Grace, this runs in my family. I've seen the end of this movie and it's not pretty. So I need to make my time count – it's why I became a doctor. And going on dates with random men doesn't seem like a good use of time, does it? Particularly since you know they're going to run a mile anyway.'

She didn't want to think about the time she wasted.

She didn't want to consider that Grace might have a point and that Jamie Yardley might be something different, something special.

Because if she thought about it for too long, then she would realise how skewed her logic was.

Right now, having Jamie as a friend for the rest of her life seemed so much more valuable than a fling that was destined to implode.

'Let me help. Just a little. You'd be helping me too,' Grace said quietly as they gathered themselves together to leave. 'I know it's hard, Alice. Please trust me when I say that, but I also believe that life is genuinely too short to spend it hiding – from love, from addiction, from true friendship.' She squeezed Alice's hand and, for once, Alice didn't feel the overwhelming urge to pull away. In fact, if she were pushed to name the uncomfortable emotions assailing her, she might just have to call them the first tiny pricklings of possibility.

Chapter 37

'Morning! I hope you don't mind me waiting,' said Dan, tentatively hovering by the Cotswold-stone wall that framed Grace's garden and holding out a bag of warm croissants as an offering. 'I just wanted to—'

He never got to clarify what it was he wanted to do, because Noodle and Doodle clearly recognised him and rushed over to snuffle him to death.

'How're they settling in?' Dan asked, kneeling on the lawn, having been thoroughly frisked for doggy treats and come up wanting. 'Are they sleeping on the bed yet?'

Grace laughed. 'Oh yes. Although they do rather hog the duvet and Doodle here really shouldn't eat cheese before bed.' She gave a single burst on her whistle and both dogs flashed to her side and sat, expectantly waiting for a little piece of chicken. 'I hate to say it, but I think they've raised the IQ level in the house considerably. They seem to learn everything the first time I show them.'

Dan nodded. 'If only humans were the same. I wonder whether I need to be hit around the head with a brick sometimes before I'll take a hint.'

He looked up at her and Grace felt the air still between them for a moment, neither of them confident enough to address their feelings head-on. It was one thing to wait for Dan to recover from his split with Julia, Grace had realised, but then it was as though the moment had passed and they'd slipped into the friend zone. If the other night had shown them nothing else though, it was that friendliness was only half of the picture.

'Come in,' Grace managed in the end. 'I've got your sweatshirt for you.' She pushed open the front door and the two dachshunds hovered in the doorway, waiting for her to go through first.

'Have you been teaching the boys to be chivalrous?' asked Dan with a smile.

'Nope. It's all about being the alpha dog, apparently. Alice gave me some basic dog-training tips and Jamie's going to help me with the more advanced stuff. For now though, I just need to let them know who's boss, apparently, take the lead and all that.'

She picked up Dan's sweatshirt from the kitchen table and held it to her chest – without even realising it, she was taking a last breath of the warm, comforting fabric.

'You should really keep that,' Dan said softly, watching her. 'It looks much better on you than it ever did on me.'

There were mere inches between them, but a mile of emotions.

'Dan—' began Grace, just as Dan spoke.

'Grace—'

Everything Grace had just said to Alice about seizing the day sprang into her mind and suddenly it didn't seem to matter who made the first move. The lingering kiss they'd shared after the attack was one thing, born of fear and a need for security. This? This was different.

Grace closed the distance between them with one step, dropping the sweatshirt to the floor and sliding her hand up to caress the back of Dan's neck. Their lips touched and Grace felt a sigh of relief and recognition somewhere in her body.

Dan groaned as their kiss deepened and he dropped his hands to her waist, lifting her slightly onto her tiptoes towards him. Whether moments or minutes had passed, Grace couldn't tell as she cleaved into his embrace with abandon. All these months of stepping around each other at work, in the town, watching and waiting – wondering if this very moment would be a mistake she would come to regret.

But how could something that felt so right possibly be a mistake?

Grace pulled away and looked into Dan's eyes, overwhelmed by the affection and desire that pooled there. 'I—' she began.

'Don't question this, Gracie. Surely we've both done enough thinking to last us a lifetime?' He grazed his hand along the side of her neck, dropping kisses along her collarbone and stopping every now and again to look up, to reassure himself perhaps that he wasn't the only one swept away on this tide of longing. He drew her into his arms and kissed her deeply, sliding one arm around her shoulders and the other under her knees to lift her easily off her feet, much as he'd done the other night, but for wholly different reasons. 'Do you have any idea how beautiful you are?' Dan asked, watching Grace's eyes fill with unshed tears. 'I really think you should know that.'

Grace leaned in and kissed him again, unwilling to stop even to hear such wonderful sentiments.

Dan took a few steps towards the stairs, pausing for a moment only to be sure. 'Do you want to—?'

Grace smiled. 'What was that you said, about not taking a hint?' She kissed him again, making her own intentions perfectly clear, and revelling in feeling the quickening of his breath.

A sharp knock at the door shattered their fantasy.

They froze and Grace laid a finger across Dan's lips. She honestly didn't care who was on the other side of that door; they had procrastinated long enough.

Of course, she hadn't accounted for Noodle and Doodle, whose cacophony of barking would have alerted even the most oblivious of visitors.

'Grace? It's me, Taffy. I come bearing gifts.'

By tacit agreement, Dan slowly lowered Grace to the ground, reaching out for one last kiss, before reality could be allowed to intervene.

Grace pulled open the front door to find a bouquet so large it appeared to have legs. Taffy peeked around it. 'Don't go getting ideas – they're not from me.' He walked into the kitchen and hefted the flowers onto the kitchen table, beside the last lot. 'The delivery girl was lost in the Market Place so I said I'd drop them off.' With his legendary lack of boundaries or tact, he waved the accompanying note in the air. 'I guess that pilot is super-keen.'

Dan and Grace exchanged uncomfortable glances, unable to hide the intimate smile that passed between them when it became obvious that Taffy was here to stay for a while.

'Ah,' said Taffy. 'Poor bloke. Waste not, want not though; you'll make young Lucy's day if she finds out he's available.' He sat down at the kitchen table and picked up Grace's jottings from the night before, a brief outline of the auction and how it might work. 'This is looking rather professional there, Gracie. Are you quite sure you haven't missed your calling as a political activist?' He didn't even question Dan's presence in her kitchen at this early hour. As far as Taffy was concerned, anyone who locked their front door and didn't welcome spontaneous visits was a little bit uppity – they had all long since accepted that you could take the boy out of Wales, but you couldn't take Wales out of the boy.

Dan pulled up a chair beside him and they were soon batting fundraising ideas back and forth. Their constant one-upmanship was really rather sweet when you chose to see it that way, Grace decided, as their suggestions for activities became ever more hazardous.

'Maybe,' she said, plonking down her huge cafetière so that it sloshed alarmingly, 'we should stick to ideas that don't involve risking life and limb? It would be just too ironic if we needed to call out the Air Ambulance to deal with the casualties, don't you think? Please don't give up on the auction idea already. We can surely rope in a few big names locally to give it a boost and a little extra pull to the public? Elsie's completely on board, by the way.'

'Oh, we're not suggesting we drop the auction,' said Taffy with feeling. 'We're just thinking of ways to *supplement* it – things that everyone can join in on, even if they haven't got a Picasso stashed in the attic.'

Grace nodded, appeased. 'I really loved the auction of promises at The Duck Race last year. Do you think we can just incorporate something like that into the main event? Keep the focus on the auction?'

Grace watched Dan and Taffy, as though she was at Wimbledon, as they picked up the idea and debated it back and forth. She felt ridiculously excited by the idea of a project so dear to her heart. The fact that she was so busy seizing the day on so many different fronts at once that she was in danger of overcommitting herself didn't even occur to her. Anything to keep thoughts of old man Jarley at bay.

'Has anybody heard from Harry Grant?' she asked, as she

gave Taffy a stern look for feeding Doodle bits of croissant from the table. 'I was hoping he'd be a fount of all knowledge as our inside man, but he's gone awfully quiet.'

Taffy nodded. 'I spoke to him last night, just briefly though. He says he's on the case, but to be honest he sounded awfully upset. He kept muttering about needing to talk to a man—' He took a slug of coffee and sighed. 'There's another rumour afoot, apparently, about a wider remit for "centralising care"—' He said the word 'centralise' as though it left a foul taste in his mouth. After all, everyone in the rural sector knew only too well that such ideas only led to benefits for urban centres.

He took a huge bite of croissant, spraying crumbs across the table. 'So,' he continued, 'we have to work out whether it's money or politics that are really swaying the decision. Because right now, some of the opinions Harry's relaying can only have been thought up by somebody who has never lived in a rural environment. I'd lay odds they've never ventured beyond the M25 actually. Certainly the distance-to-care figures that are being bandied about were as the crow flies, with no reference to terrain or weather implications.' He looked up and his eyes were full of a righteous indignation. 'So, whilst the fundraising is amazing, there's every chance it will never be enough.'

'What can we do?' asked Grace simply.

'It's a shame Julia isn't here,' Dan said, possibly without thinking how it might make Grace feel. 'This is just the kind of story they would love on that doctors show she did.' He looked furious at this latest update. 'Do you ever feel, when it comes to the NHS, as though the left hand just doesn't know what the right hand is doing?' he asked in frustration, banging his hand down on the table and flinching as he caught the bruising on his knuckles.

Grace picked up his hand and examined it, the broken skin

still red and angry. 'Alice said you'd been back to the station last night?'

'Seriously, are they still grilling you over this?' Taffy asked in disbelief.

'That's what I came by to tell you actually,' Dan replied, looking a little discombobulated that this could ever have slipped his mind. 'I gave a notarised statement last night and they've decided not to press charges. I believe I have the photos of your bruises to thank, actually, Grace. Chief Inspector Grant took one look at those and managed to persuade Jarley that it really wouldn't further his cause. So, I'm off the hook.'

He shrugged, as though this rather momentous news meant very little in the grand scheme of things, but Grace knew otherwise. She knew exactly how horrific the consequences of his heroic actions could have been to his career. Forgetting herself for a moment, she breathed out slowly, all the tenderness of her feelings for him spilling into her gaze as she clasped his hand. 'That's fantastic news.'

Taffy cleared his throat uncomfortably. 'Er, guys? Do you need to be alone?' He didn't wait for the answer though. 'It's only that, whilst obviously I'm thrilled that Dan's not going to be hauled off to jail, I rather needed a little advice myself this morning.'

There was an awkward pause as both Dan and Grace visibly struggled to change gear. Taffy was normally so sensitive to these things that clearly whatever he needed was no trifling matter. He seemed almost oblivious to his gooseberry status, in fact.

'I've done something incredibly stupid and I don't know how to tell Holly.'

Chapter 38

Later that day, following Dan and Grace's instructions to the letter, Taffy guided Holly through the hallway of their cottage, the twins running loops around her, their little nylon book bags serving double time as effective weaponry.

'Washing up's all done, supper's in the oven and also, this!' He pushed open the kitchen door with his hip: 'Ta-da!'

Holly glanced around the kitchen in confusion, where it appeared that every single soft drink currently in production was lined up in serried ranks. 'So, however bad your morning sickness gets, there'll always be something you fancy to drink!' Taffy declared, seeming inordinately pleased with himself. 'Although I have to give Dan some of the credit. He's doing something similar with the local ciders, but with you feeling so sick every day—'

Holly reached forward and kissed him, partly to thank him for being so thoughtful, but mainly to stop the stream of words that were gathering speed and making her head spin. She didn't like to rain on his parade of beverages, to tell him that sipping iced water seemed to be the most effective way to combat her sickness and avoid dehydration. Although she was quite sure that Taffy's fondness for sugar would ensure that nothing went to waste.

'Right,' she said gently, pulling away after a moment, 'are we going to talk about what's making you feel so guilty or do I have to guess?'

Taffy fidgeted from one foot to the other. 'Are you sure you wouldn't like a drink first? Any drink?'

Holly just raised one eyebrow and fixed him with a no-nonsense stare; it was the same look that Elsie always used to excellent effect and Holly was all up for practising any chance she got.

'I've invited my parents to stay,' Taffy blurted out in the end, a high colour flushing his neck. 'And I know, I should have checked with you first, what with everything going on at work and you being quite so doubly pregnant, but—' He frowned. 'Why are you laughing?'

Holly held up a hand while she caught her breath, thumping him on the arm. 'I thought you were going to tell me something really awful, you sod. You had me so worried for a minute.'

'But I've invited my parents to stay, without asking. Grace tells me this is basically a cardinal sin! A relationship-wrecker. Not that I didn't already know that – I mean, I didn't need her to tell me that—'

'Ah, but what Grace doesn't realise is that I actually *like* your parents,' interrupted Holly. 'Although where we're going to stack them, I do not know.'

'Well, that's the other thing,' Taffy said haltingly. 'When Dylan found out they were coming, then he wanted to come too, and then Bobi said that, erm . . .' He hesitated.

'Taffy?' Holly asked, shaking her head, 'is this your cack-handed way of telling me the whole bloody Jones clan are turning up on our doorstep?'

He nodded and held up his hands in surrender. 'Aldwyn

went online and he's rented them a house nearby. They're all ridiculously excited about it. Apparently Mum had been watching re-runs of *Gardeners' World* and they featured last year's Larkford Flower Festival. And then Mum went online and got all of a dither about seeing it ... You know how she gets about a floral display. Plus, you know, it's good timing actually because we can tell them about the babies when they're here.'

'Well okay then,' said Holly easily. 'How lovely that they've found a house to rent. I think the novelty of playing sardines in here would wear off fairly quickly, don't you?' She looked up to see that Taffy still looked thoroughly shifty. 'So, what aren't you telling me?'

Taffy wrinkled his nose, in a gesture so reminiscent of Tom in trouble, it was actually hard to imagine that they weren't blood relatives – strike one for nature over nurture. 'Well, the thing is – I mean, the house they rented isn't available until Monday and they all fancied coming a bit sooner, while the flowers are at their best, apparently ...'

'Taffs, are they all coming to stay here?' Holly said, completely unsurprised by this mob mentality and unco-ordinated planning. This was, after all, the family who had booked a villa in Granada, Spain and flights to the island of Grenada, in the Caribbean. Apparently that tiny difference had eluded the entire family until they touched down after a ten-hour flight – including stopover! – with nowhere to stay.

Taffy nodded. 'They'll be here tomorrow.'

Holly looked around at the utter chaos that was their cottage, at the heaps of folded laundry still waiting to be put away, and mentally started counting beds and sofas in her head.

'You don't need to worry too much though, because I thought my brothers could just camp in the garden,' Taffy offered, as if that solved everything.

Holly stepped forward and gave him a hug. 'Darling, I love you and I love your family, but I'm not going to spend the weekend living like squatters while I feel this queasy. How about I ask Elsie if we can borrow a bedroom or two?'

'For my parents?' Taffy said, brightening immediately, as always desperate to please his adored mother.

Holly hesitated, before the twins shifting in her newly, more obviously rounded bump gave her a timely reminder of her priorities. 'No. I was thinking more for the four of us. They're very welcome to take over the whole house for the weekend – heck, they can even clean it if they like. But I'm going to sleep in a comfy bed and hurl in a toilet without a queue at the door.'

Taffy paused and Holly could see the conflict on his face. For once though, as much as she did love his family, she didn't feel particularly moved to sacrifice her own comfort. The thought struck like lightning – how much more secure she was in this relationship than she'd been with Milo, where she would probably have offered to sleep in the garden herself just to appease his demanding mother. She grinned. 'Once your mum discovers there's not one but two grandchildren on the way, I'm pretty sure she won't begrudge me a comfy bed.'

Taffy smiled. 'When you're right, you're right. She is going to be so excited. They all are.'

Holly looked down at her bump, which seemed to have doubled in size overnight. 'I think we should take the opportunity to have a little baby shower while they're here, don't you? A lovely little party, keep it small, and then maybe we won't have your mum and Elsie constantly bemoaning the lack of wedding in our future.'

*

Holly smoothed her hand lovingly over the acorn finial at the bottom of Elsie's staircase the next morning, running her fingers over its weathered oak contours and wondering how many lives this house had witnessed. The sunlight streamed through from the conservatory at the back of the house, making hazy stripes along the hallway.

She couldn't help thinking that it had been a stroke of genius to come straight over and stay with Elsie after her conversation with Taffy last night. Even though she was working today, after a night on a memory foam mattress with gazillion thread-count sheets, she felt as though she were on a Cotswold mini-break. She'd left Taffy to sort out the house for his family's impending arrival and was surprised to find she felt not one jot of guilt about this. She was actually thankful she and Elsie had managed an uninterrupted evening of plotting and planning for the auction, time running away from them on that front, as they all attempted to juggle their personal and professional lives.

She sighed happily; at this ridiculous hour of the morning, she revelled in having the house to herself, a house she was falling irrevocably in love with, even despite the insistent whispers in the back of her mind still pointing out that she was taking advantage.

Holly stepped through into the kitchen, questing for something stodgy to eat to ease the quailing vestiges of morning sickness that still marked the start of every day. She stopped dead, shocked to find Elsie sitting at the kitchen table in her hot-pink velour tracksuit and sipping fruit juice. She had a glow to her face that could only mean one thing: Felice had already been.

'Jesus, you gave me a scare,' Holly exclaimed, clapping her hand to her chest. 'Have you seriously already had your physio session?'

'Good morning to you too,' said Elsie drily, raising one perfectly pencilled eyebrow at Holly's outburst of questioning. 'And yes. I find a little session with Felice always sets me up for the day rather nicely.' She couldn't resist a cheeky smile, adding a somewhat lascivious tone to her comment.

Elsie recapped her fountain pen and popped it back into Toby, the ugly-jug. But Toby wasn't the one holding Holly's attention this morning, no matter how much she loved him; there was something rather furtive about the way Elsie had so deftly folded her fancy writing paper in two and slipped it into her Smythson leather folio.

'Sit yourself down before that gravity-defying bump of yours tips you over. How you can possibly stay like that for another three or four months defeats me,' said Elsie, deftly changing the subject.

Holly laughed. 'It's only going to get bigger from here. I'll be in need of scaffolding by the end, if last time is anything to go by.' She didn't look unduly fazed by the idea, merely resigned. An uncomfortable few months was a small price to pay for two happy, healthy babies. She reached forward and plucked a piece of toast from the toast rack beside Elsie, not even stopping to add butter or jam. Her hunger, when it came, was immediate and greedy.

'Did you sleep well?' asked Elsie.

Holly nodded, her mouth full of toast. 'Like a dream,' she added as she swallowed. 'For the first time in months, actually. It's such a beautiful bedroom, Elsie. All those stunning sculptures and that pair of sketches above the desk – well, I could have been in Paris at the George Cinq!'

Elsie smiled. 'It is rather special, isn't it? In fact, that used to be my room, before I became practically nocturnal and moved to the back of the house away from the street lights.'

She fleetingly squeezed Holly's hand across the table. 'I'm so pleased you like it.'

Holly buttered a second piece of toast, marvelling at the small niceties that made staying with Elsie such a joy – the roses on the table releasing their heady scent, the tiny silver spoon in the marmalade, even the crisply folded copy of *The Times*. She had no delusions that her own life could ever be managed this way without considerable forethought, planning and sacrifice, but it was still nice to enjoy it and savour the luxury while she could.

'Those sketches in your room are the ones I'm donating to the auction actually,' said Elsie. 'I shall rather miss them, but between you and me, I can't resist the chance to make an impact.'

Holly smiled – the sweeping curves of the nude ballerinas were bound to cause quite a stir and she knew full well how much this would delight her friend.

'It turns out we owe Harriet a thank-you on that front, actually,' continued Elsie. 'If it hadn't been for her stalking my every move, I would never have thought to get the insurance chappie round to make sure there was a full inventory of the house.

'I always thought those sketches were rather beautiful, but not really worth anything – just rather lovely art, you know? Some minor protégé of Degas, we always thought ... Anyhoo—' She sipped her juice again blithely and Holly had to restrain herself from shaking the news out of Elsie. 'It turns out they might actually be preliminary sketches from the Master himself. The poor chap from London nearly had a cow when he saw them and then, obviously, all hell broke loose for a couple of hours, because they're woefully under-insured, of course.' She paused, impish delight making her seem decades younger. 'He seemed most upset when I told him my plans for them.'

'Wow,' Holly said, still slightly reeling from the cavalier way that Elsie had shared her news. To think she'd been sleeping under the gaze of such priceless historical pieces. She was rather pleased she hadn't known, to be honest, as she doubted she would have slumbered quite so peacefully.

'Well, anyway, the whole insurance thing got me thinking. Not to mention the spectre of Hurricane Harriet's return. She's gone to London – shopping apparently, but you can bet she'll have swung by the family lawyers while she's there – she seemed rather attached to the notion that I'd lost the plot. Her meeting my darling Felice while she was here was hardly ideal – lots of spluttering about the age gap. Am I supposed to have a geriatric physiotherapist, do you think?' Elsie meandered off topic with such regularity these days that Holly had become accustomed to simply sitting her out until she got back on point.

'Look,' said Elsie thoughtfully, as Holly returned to the table with a fresh pot of tea, 'I've decided that, if the vultures are already circling, we'd better do things a little differently. I don't want any questions left unanswered – surely no inheritance is worth it, if it also unleashes Harriet on you?' She popped a morsel of toast into her mouth and chewed for a moment, holding up a hand to stop Holly interrupting. 'So, what I'd like is this. To keep things straightforward – Holly, will you buy my darling Toby jug from me? A sale, pure and simple, and then I know he's in happy hands. None of this inheritance tax bollocks.'

Holly laughed, humouring her. As though Toby was going to be the inheritance tax issue at hand! But if it made Elsie happy, then why not? She flipped open her phone case and tugged out her emergency tenner. 'Of course I will. The twins adore him. Will this do?'

'Haven't you got anything smaller?' Elsie protested.

'Nope. But he has to be worth ten quid, doesn't he? Even to make the boys smile? And you know I'm rather fond of his smushy little face anyway.'

Elsie reached forward, a slight tremor in her hand, and firmly shook Holly's. 'Deal,' they both said at once.

'Well thank God for that,' Elsie gasped. 'I've been holding my breath about him for days. I've barely slept since Harriet turned up.'

Holly gave her a sideways look. It was natural to want your prized possessions to pass down into loving hands, but Elsie seemed to be taking the notion to the extreme where Toby was concerned. 'And I promise to remember the lesson he brings,' Holly reassured her. 'No giving all my money to gambling husbands, I promise.'

'Yes, yes,' Elsie interrupted. 'But now to the crucial matter at hand. Toby is now, officially, yours. Bought and paid for. Yes? And according to the lovely man on the television last week, not to mention the insurance valuer chappie, he's worth roughly the same as this house . . . I did say, didn't I? Ugly but priceless.' She paused and fixed Holly with an impenetrable stare. 'So, I'd like to propose a trade. You buy this house fair and square and pay for him with Toby. No more endless soul-searching of your tiresome moral code required. Everything above board and I get to do what I want with my things.'

Holly's mouth was open in shock. She could barely compute what Elsie was suggesting, let alone respond coherently. 'Is that even legal?' she managed eventually.

'I have a man in a suit with lots of fancy letters after his name popping round in an hour who says it is.' She looked utterly delighted with herself. 'So typical of Harriet not to look beyond the aesthetics. But she can't say I didn't offer now, can she?'

'I don't really understand,' Holly confessed.

'Am I going too quickly for you?'

'I think you might be actually – I'm really missing my coffee; ginger tea doesn't really wake up the brain cells, does it?' Holly breathed out slowly.

'Well, I've decided that the Degas sketches will sort me out rather nicely. Sell the pair together and split the proceeds. One half can go to the Air Ambulance thingummy and the other half ought to cover a five-year lease at Sarandon Hall – and frankly even that seems rather optimistic. So, Holly darling, do pay attention. If I kick the bucket before it expires, I want you to pick your favourite pensioner from work and install them instead. Okay?'

'Okay,' said Holly faintly, tears threatening. 'I'm a little speechless.'

'Oh my darling girl, I do hope those are happy tears? This is something I really want to do – you mean the absolute world to me.'

'And you to me,' Holly managed. 'I'm so incredibly grateful, Elsie. This will quite literally change my life. But do me a favour? Please stop talking about a future without you in it. I keep hoping you'll change your mind and we can all live here together—'

'Just one big dysfunctional happy family?' Elsie said, a little choked herself.

'Exactly,' said Holly. 'Although we might need to agree a code for when your physio comes round. I'm not sure I want to walk in on your yoga practice again—' She sniffed inelegantly and just about managed a tremulous smile.

'Don't you just love it when a plan comes together?' said Elsie happily, gently dabbing her eyes with a lace hanky. 'You know, I'm not normally one for delayed gratification, but I have to tell you, Holly, this moment really was worth waiting for.'

Holly smiled. 'I didn't even know this was what I wanted, until it was a possibility.'

Elsie nodded. 'You can pop that in your notebook, darling. Words to live by – don't ever give up on what you want most, in favour of what you want right now.'

Holly hugged her and dropped a kiss onto her papery cheek. 'Then I'm incredibly lucky, because for once in my life, they're exactly the same thing.'

Chapter 39

Alice opened the front door to Grace later that morning looking sheepish. 'I know I said I'd get started—'

Noodle and Doodle were through the doorway and making themselves at home before she could say any more and she was relieved to see that Grace wasn't the least bit cross. It was one thing for Alice to give up her rostered day off to tackle her impending life-crisis, but when Grace had offered to help her — no, insisted on it, then the nerves had really started to kick in. After all the times Alice had attempted this process before, only for it to end in abject failure and self-recrimination, she couldn't help but think of herself as a lost cause.

Grace held up Grande coffees from The Deli in one hand and a giant roll of bin bags with the other. 'Don't look so doubtful; I've come prepared,' she grinned. 'I even have stickers.'

'Well,' said Alice with an anxious smile, 'what could possibly go wrong if you've got stickers?' She hesitated, unsure whether to let on that she'd been pacing her house since the wee small hours, picking things up and putting them down, fretting about how to take this seemingly enormous step and successfully let go a little. Wandering through to the kitchen, she gestured at the kitchen table, where she'd got as far as labelling the three enormous cardboard boxes she'd collected from the supermarket – Auction, Car Boot, Recycle. Naturally, they were all still empty.

Grace plonked her roll of bin bags beside them and the quadrumvirate was complete. She walked over and pulled Alice into a gentle hug, murmuring her support into Alice's hair. It was a timely reminder for Alice that, despite there being barely more than a decade between them, Grace had already raised two full-grown sons. There was a chance she actually knew what she was doing.

'You are a wonder for helping me with this,' Alice began, before Grace shushed her.

'Well, you've had a little time to get your head around the idea and we've a fairly decent motivation on the table, don't you think?' Grace said gently, seemingly well aware of how challenging this day was going to be. 'Just close your eyes and think how amazing it would be to not only be debt-free but also to have made a difference to such a wonderful cause.'

Alice nodded – she quietly hoped that her pledge to offer several lots to the auction would be incentive enough to quell her outspoken demons.

'And of course,' continued Grace, 'think about how much fun lies ahead in making your house your home, rather than your storage facility.' The gentle teasing was layered with affection and there was no doubting Grace's commitment to helping with this.

Alice could only pray that her own inability to let go wouldn't slow them down. 'Right then,' she said tentatively. 'Where do we start? Hardest first, or build up to it? Tilly says we should just dive into the middle!' Typical Tilly advice, to be fair – why have a plan when you can just dive in and wing it?

Grace nested the boxes neatly inside one another. 'You grab the coffee. We're starting in your bedroom. If we only achieve one thing today, it will be making that room somewhere restful so you might actually get some decent sleep.' This was obviously something she'd given some considerable thought to.

Opening the door to her bedroom, as the sun shafted through the windows and across the bed, Alice felt almost winded. Seeing her room through Grace's eyes was an unwelcome revelation. How naïve she'd been to think that making the bed neatly this morning and throwing a few cushions on top would make a scrap of difference. Two chests of drawers, one double wardrobe that wouldn't close, eight – she double-checked – yes, eight enormous storage boxes and, somewhere under a pile of shopping bags and parcels, there was an antique armchair that rarely saw the light of day. She couldn't even bear to think about the 'dressing room' next door and its rows of weighed-down hanging rails, not to mention the wall of pigeonholes crammed with shoes and bags.

She felt weighed down too, by the scale of the task ahead of her. 'I don't think—' she began, her words buckling in her throat.

Grace took her hand. 'This isn't saying goodbye, Alice; this is a beginning, your new beginning. And, if the fundraising works out, then maybe another chance for so many other people. Not to mention if you imagine all that money you're paying out in interest every month – you could probably swing a flight to visit Tilly for the same amount. You see, more carrots than Mr McGregor's garden! Now, don't let's overthink this. Just pick out one item that you truly love and makes you smile.'

Alice's eyes widened in fear. 'To get rid of?'

Grace smiled. 'Nope. We're not doing things that way round. Too much negativity, thinking about all the things we don't want. What on earth would Elsie say? We're going to make sure that your house is filled with things you love. *Only* things you truly love.' She paused to give Alice a reassuring squeeze. 'They've written loads of books about it. It has to be worth a shot?'

Alice tried to ignore the sweating prickly feeling that was gripping her chest at the very idea of tackling this behemoth of a task – at confronting head-on all the waste and profligacy that had characterised the last few years of her life. Not to mention all the time and effort it had taken to keep everything organised, clean and sorted – that being perhaps the only way she could continue to differentiate between her own behaviour and that of a more committed hoarder. Nobody could accuse her of that, she reasoned, as long as every item was beautifully packed, presented or displayed. It was a justification she returned to with worrying regularity.

For some reason, with Grace standing beside her and the spotlight falling on the magnitude of her belongings, that argument didn't quite hold water. Looking around at all her possessions now, she realised she had only actually postponed the problem. Swallowing hard, appreciating the restraint it must be costing Grace to remain patiently, silently, awaiting her first move, Alice reached out and plucked a vintage Chanel suit from the wardrobe. 'This,' she said. 'My grandmother bought this in Paris for her going-away outfit. It fits me perfectly.'

'Wow,' said Grace, stepping forward to marvel at the fabric and the stitching and the fluidity of the skirt. 'It's an absolute treasure. And, do you know, I've never once seen you wear it.' She laid it reverentially on the bed and Alice realised that Grace had a point – with so many clothes and so many options, the true gems were never getting to see the light of day, eclipsed by the newest, shiniest baubles to join the ranks.

She smiled, a frisson of pleasure surprising her as she looked at the suit laid out so beautifully. In a quick, almost subconscious, one, two, three, she pulled out a tailored Dior 'Le Smoking' jacket, a slim pair of jet-black trousers and a maxi-length cashmere cardigan in the softest smoky blue. She glanced at Grace for a little encouragement and was quietly thrilled to see the look of surprise and appreciation on her face.

'Well,' Alice said quietly, 'I know I can't wear them for work – can you imagine? But it makes me so happy just to know that they're there.'

Grace nodded. 'I can see that. Maybe you could have your day-to-day clothes in one cupboard and we can put your vintage and occasion items next door. Whittle them down until you can actually see what you've got and make it a feature in your study. That is still the plan? To have the other bedroom as a study with bookshelves and a sofabed?'

Alice nodded. It seemed ridiculous to have a two-bedroom house and yet nowhere for her friends to come and stay. She had to keep reminding herself that personal relationships would bring her considerably more happiness than a rail of dresses ever could, but looking at the small selection on the bed, even she had to concede that may not be true for everyone in her address book. Still, everything in moderation and a little bit of what you fancy does you good. See – she had been listening when Elsie had been waxing lyrical in The Kingsley Arms the other night.

She picked up a knitted cashmere dress and held it out in

front of her to appraise. There was no polite way to say this –
it was vast.

'Whose is that?' asked Grace. 'It's beautiful fabric.'

Alice felt herself colour slightly. 'It's mine. I mean, it was
mine, when my weight was a little more—' She stopped,
hearing the mean comments of her fellow med students
echoing in her head and half expecting Grace to make some
snide remark.

But Grace herself was cut from different cloth. 'Well,
there's no way we can get that tailored in without ruining the
line. So I guess it's time for someone else to enjoy it.'

Alice felt her grip tighten on the hanger, watching her
fingers go white. What if she needed it? What if she suddenly
put all the weight back on and it was the only item in her
wardrobe that fitted? What if—? She paused, remembering all
too well the struggle with her weight before Coco had come
along, sweetly innocently demanding a walk three times a
day, whilst offering companionship and unconditional love.
The need to comfort-eat had disappeared almost overnight.

Grace sat down quietly on the end of the bed, patiently
waiting, saying nothing, not a word of judgement passing her
lips. 'I like to keep something lovely for Christmas in a bigger
size,' she said after a moment, 'just in case all the mince pies
get the better of me. But just in the next size up, you know?
I think sometimes hanging on to clothes or jewellery from a
difficult time in our lives only serves as a reminder, and not
always in a good way.'

Alice nodded; Grace made a valid point. She checked the
label and nearly laughed out loud. Four whole sizes bigger –
she would need to eat an awful lot of mince pies for this to
become her 'just in case' dress. 'It's Mulberry though, so I'm
not sure it's car boot material?'

Grace nodded. 'Do you know, I was thinking that just now. The auction is for the antiques and vintage originals. Knick-knacks can go to the car boot sale. But where do we put the in-betweens?'

Alice shrugged. 'And now you see my dilemma: too good to ditch but no use to me. Every time I look at that dress I remember how much I paid for it. It makes me feel a little queasy actually, but I was so desperate for something to wear that made me feel good, at a time when anything with a waistband wasn't an option. Splurging felt like the only way to deal with the problem.' As she spoke, she didn't look at Grace. It was almost as though she were processing out loud, the closest she'd ever come to therapy.

'I still do that, you know? When I feel down,' she confessed quietly.

Grace reached out and took her hand. 'Maybe we can find you something new to do when you need a pick-me-up? Something a little less financially draining?'

Alice nodded. 'It's emotionally draining too, though, you know? The expectation, the adrenalin rush, the guilt, the denial – oh it's a whole bundle of laughs shopping with me! It's why I always shop alone.'

Grace stood up and reached out for the cashmere dress. 'Well that's one thing that's easy to change. I'm perfectly happy to be your wingman. But somehow, I'm not sure you need to go shopping for a little while . . .' She ran her fingers over the baby-soft drapes of the dress. 'But I also think we need to set you up with your own pop-up shop.'

'My what?' asked Alice, thrown by the abrupt change of direction.

'Not a physical shop. Or you'd end up paying rent. But I can put together an online boutique for you to sell this kind of thing. You can still split the proceeds the way you wanted to originally, and you'd need to charge postage . . .'

'Vintage by Alice,' murmured Alice under her breath, her frown turning to one of concentration. 'Do you think anyone would buy this kind of thing online?'

Grace raised an eyebrow. 'Do *you* buy this kind of thing online?'

Alice laughed. 'Good point, well made. But we'd need to photograph everything . . .'

'Hmm,' said Grace, teasing her slightly, 'if only we knew somebody who's fabulous with a camera and really tech-savvy. Someone who really wants to help?'

'You would do that? For me?' Alice clarified, sounding rather overwhelmed – whether by the generosity of the offer or the scale of the task ahead was anyone's guess.

She sank down on the end of the bed, scarcely missing the bundle of dogs, where Coco, Noodle and Doodle had apparently snuggled up on siesta setting. 'I genuinely want to throw up when I think about how much money is hanging on these rails and in these drawers. Money I couldn't afford. Just to give myself a boost.'

'What about now though?' Grace asked gently. 'Does looking at all this stuff still give you a boost or . . .?'

'I feel like I'm drowning,' Alice murmured. 'I feel like my stuff owns me, rather than the other way round! I mean, I'm renting a two-bedroom house for one person and a spaniel just to accommodate all this—'

'Okay then,' said Grace. 'You know this is progress, don't you? Last time we spoke, you didn't feel that way.'

Alice shook her head. 'I didn't *admit* to feeling that way,' she corrected. 'And last time, all I could think about was paying off my debts and giving up my things. This time, with the auction, I get to actually do something constructive.' She grabbed the cashmere dress from Grace's hands and hung it on the back of the door. 'Every one of these we sell might make just enough difference between somebody living and dying, right?'

'Right,' said Grace. 'But let's still approach this in a way that makes you feel good. All the books say the same thing – focus on keeping what you love, rather than letting go. So—'

She stood up and with a momentary glance at Alice, she scooped everything out of the wardrobe and onto the bed, half covering the slumbering dogs. She pointedly picked up the four items that Alice had originally rescued and hung them on the empty rail.

'I firmly believe that the fewer the things hanging on this rail, the more outfits you'll have to wear – outfits you truly love and make *you* feel good – and you'll actually be able to see them. More space, less guilt, and let's ditch all the crappy memories while we're at it.'

'I don't know if I can change that much,' Alice said quietly.

'Change is pretty black and white – you either have or you haven't. It's not a question of degree. And even doing this with me now is a change. You have to start somewhere, right?'

Alice breathed out slowly. 'Does this mean I can never go shopping again?'

Grace shook her head. 'Of course not. But let's buy less and value more, okay? See this beautiful silk scarf with the hole in it? Let's mend it and you can actually wear it. I think for you, a healthier goal would be to be more selective about what you actually buy. You have the most wonderful sense of style when you allow yourself free rein.'

'Only buy something if I utterly adore it?' Alice clarified.

'And I'm not convinced that only applies to shopping,' Grace smiled. 'Why do anything that will make you unhappy, if you have the choice? Clothes, food, people ...'

'It's all about the choices,' Alice said slowly. Her eyes danced for a moment with the myriad of possibilities, lightening the doubt and insecurity. 'Okay then, let's start in here and see where it takes us.'

Chapter 40

'Oh my goodness! Look at you!' squealed Taffy's mum in delight as she took in Holly's decidedly rounded form. 'You're positively radiant!' She chucked her bag in the hallway and marched through to envelop Holly in an enormous hug. 'You have no idea how excited we've all been to come and visit. Like a whirlwind, it's been.'

Holly, as always, was blown away by Patty's affection. Being back at the house as a welcoming committee had definitely been the right thing to do, no matter how knackered she was after a day at work.

Taffy's dad bustled in with a wave of grandchildren around his legs, carrying easily enough luggage for a fortnight's stay. Predictably Aldwyn and Bobi were bickering outside about who deserved the solitary parking spot – both cars currently blocking the narrow road as bag after bag was unloaded, ferried inside by a procession of mini-Joneses. It was like an invasion, as the fridge door already hung open, tiny hands grasping for sustenance. Dylan was already raiding the snack cupboard and Holly would lay odds that those same cupboards would be bare by this time tomorrow.

Greeting everyone in turn and accepting their congratulations was one thing, but everyone also wanted to touch her bump to 'introduce' themselves to the latest recruit. By the time Taffy's brothers and their children had all said hello, Holly was feeling like a much-loved pass-the-parcel.

'Well, you've timed it perfectly,' Holly said, tactfully wrapping her cardigan over her bump. 'The Flower Festival starts tomorrow and you'll wake up to see the town in full bloom. Absolutely the best time to see Larkford in all her glory.'

Patty frowned. 'But there's no flowers in the Market Place at all. I did wonder if our Aldwyn had got the dates wrong.'

Taffy stepped in, before Patty and Aldwyn could lapse into their infamous bickering. 'Definitely tomorrow,' he confirmed. 'It's rather sweet actually – a local tradition. There's nothing to see at all and then the Flower Committee stay up all night and set up all the displays, the hanging baskets, the river floats – we all wake up and there it is!'

Patty clasped her hand to her ample bosom. 'Well isn't that just delightful – it's like a fairy tale.'

Holly and Taffy exchanged glances. 'If you mean there's a darker backstory to it, then yes,' Holly laughed. 'Apparently they voted to introduce the overnight reveal because everyone got so competitive, the whole town ground to a halt in the lead-up.'

'There was even talk of sabotage,' Taffy said darkly, knowing only too well his mother's fondness for a bit of intrigue. 'Gladys Jones's cousin lives in Framley,' he said with heavy portent, as though that explained everything.

Dylan wandered over, already demolishing a family-sized bag of pretzels. 'But *we* don't have to stay up all night?' he clarified, looking less than impressed. 'Coz you know I like the flowers and all, but not that much!'

Holly grinned; in her imagination Dylan was becoming more and more like his namesake in *The Magic Roundabout*.

'It's not just about the flowers though, Dyl. The whole morning is like one big fiesta – breakfast pastries and local produce, a little local cider maybe—'

'Well, now you're talking,' he said, turning to punch Taffy habitually on the arm. 'Good to see your lady has her priorities right.'

'She does,' agreed Taffy. 'And since you're all here, we thought you might like to hear our news—'

'Oh thank the Lord, you've set a wedding date!' said Patty with feeling. 'I didn't like to nag, but with that babi on the way . . .' Her words petered out as she clocked the awkward look between Holly and Taffy.

'Actually,' Taffy continued, 'we wanted you to know something even more special.' He paused, making sure that all his brothers were in hearing distance. 'We're having twins!'

The roars of excitement must have been heard on the other side of town. Holly quickly found herself swamped by hugs and kisses and, of course, another round of meet-the-new-recruits. There was enthusiasm, she thought happily, and then there was Jones-family enthusiasm – somewhere on a par with a springer spaniel being offered roast chicken for dinner. Even laid-back Dylan was practically bouncing.

'This is bloody brilliant,' said Aldwyn – normally the nominated pain-in-the-arse of all family gatherings. He gazed at Holly in awe. 'You're going to be huge,' he told her, as though this was breaking news.

Holly just nodded cheerfully – she knew the form. Glancing out of the window, she saw that Ben and Tom had also taken the opportunity to share the news with the younger generation, as there was much squealing and merriment amongst the girls as well. As far as an impromptu celebration went, it didn't get much better.

'Tell them about the baby shower,' Holly whispered to Taffy amongst the chaos.

'Oh yes,' Taffy said, raising his voice above the melee. 'So we decided that, since you're all here and the Festival is the perfect backdrop, we're going to throw an early baby shower tomorrow afternoon. We're going to take over Elsie's garden and have a proper afternoon tea.'

Bobi let out a guffaw of laughter. 'And you won't need to shell out for any flowers, right, bro? Thrifty.'

Patty was mumbling something to her husband, flashing glances of concern in their direction.

'Come on, Mum. You know you love a scone,' Taffy said after the briefest hesitation.

Patty nodded and rallied. 'Of course I do, my love. And I'll even whip up some proper Welsh Cakes for the occasion.' She glanced at her husband. 'No news on the wedding front then?'

In the end, it had taken quite a while to persuade Taffy's family that their terraced cottage could no more cope with that many inhabitants than Holly could fit her ever-expanding bump into her longed-for slender lace wedding dress. The Jones clan were mostly mollified by the prospect of a party nevertheless, and Holly, Taffy and the twins had escaped to Elsie's with only a shadow of fuss. Only the vague spectre of Patty's disappointment still whispered in the air.

Stepping into Elsie's townhouse after the short walk across town felt like stepping into a blissful oasis, compared to the crowded and boisterous chaos they'd left behind. A vase of pink roses and variegated foliage adorned the uncluttered hall table and somewhere a scented candle filled the air with white jasmine and mint.

'Oh God,' said Taffy under his breath. 'When we move in here, we're going to ruin it, aren't we?' He looked distinctly uncomfortable and Holly felt her burst of exuberance flag a little.

When *she* walked into Elsie's house, it felt like home. Not because it was always immaculate, or because there were vases of fresh flowers instead of wilting, neglected orchids, but because there was a vibe of happiness and frivolity in the air that appealed to Holly on some deeply fundamental level. It was as though the house had a voice that cried, 'Sure, life can be tricky and hard work too – but, hey, pull up a chair, let's get you a drink and put some soothing tunes on the wireless!'

She shook her head slightly, wondering if the last twenty-four hours of rushed organisation had tipped her over into insanity. That feeling only intensified when the echoes of chiming glass and laughter drifted through from the conservatory. 'Hellooo?' she called, blushing slightly as they dumped Taffy's kit in Elsie's hallway in an unfortunate mirroring of what had so infuriated her at home earlier, swallowing the words 'we're home' even as they came immediately to mind.

They wandered through into Elsie's conservatory, Holly's eyes widening in surprise as she took in the scene. So much for a quiet retreat.

'Come and sit down!' called Elsie. 'We're one drink ahead of you and plotting your party.' Holly smiled as she took in the gaggle of women sitting around sipping cocktails: Lizzie, Grace and Alice had all clearly been roped in to help. 'Well,' shrugged Elsie guiltily, 'you shouldn't have to plan your own baby shower, now should you?'

Holly did as she was told and sat down, revelling in the comfort of her favourite rocking chair in the world. Apparently it was some Danish designer that Holly had never heard of and was probably worth a fortune, but none of that was important right now, compared to the warm feeling of contentment from having all her favourite people together in one place.

'Well, this I could get used to,' she sighed happily. 'Taffs, do you want to join in and have your say? After all, this party is for everyone, not just the girls.'

Taffy frowned in thought for a moment, hovering uncertainly in the doorway.

'You are okay with the baby shower idea though, Taffs?' Holly asked, concern flitting across her face at his unusual reticence.

'I honestly think it would make my mum's week,' he reassured her.

'But what about *you*?' she pressed. 'Would you actually enjoy it?'

'Any chance to celebrate with you, Holls, and you know I'm all in,' he said, walking over and leaning in to kiss her. He held her gaze for a moment before letting her go and the smooth pendulum movement of the chair made her squeal. 'I just – well, it won't be too fancy-schmancy though?' Taffy said. 'I mean, there will be doughnuts too, yes? We have to think of the priorities here, Graham.'

'Lots and lots of doughnuts . . .' Holly agreed easily, once she'd rediscovered her centre of gravity. 'Speaking of which, is it awful that I'm starving again?'

Taffy grinned. 'And is this an ice-cream-starving or a banana-sandwich-starving?' he checked, well accustomed of late to the vagaries of Holly's appetite.

Holly frowned. 'I don't know,' she said, wobbling for a moment. 'Is it really weird to be wanting pickled onions and Marmite?'

'Yes,' said Elsie and Alice firmly in disgusted union.

'I'll join you,' said Taffy easily, no snacking combination as yet too peculiar to put him off his food. 'Womb service here we come,' he joked, flinging a napkin over his arm.

Holly leaned back contentedly into the rocking chair and looked out across Elsie's garden, watching the boys as they swung delightedly on the tyre swing that Brian, Elsie's gardener, had installed as a surprise. There were flurries of butterflies darting around the buddleia and the summer evening was lightly perfumed by Elsie's well-stocked flower garden. In short, it was paradise.

'I should have moved you lot in months ago,' sighed Elsie with feeling. 'It's just heaven hearing the house come alive. And look, that tree over there would be perfect for a rope swing too, wouldn't it? Or even a treehouse?'

Taffy nodded his agreement, as he returned bearing Holly's disgusting snack, cheerfully surrendering any downtime for the foreseeable future to yet another project to keep the twins entertained.

'And of course,' added Taffy with a grin, 'if you want the boys to really enjoy the baby shower, we could always rent a bouncy castle.'

Elsie, to her credit, barely flinched at the very notion of such a monstrosity adorning her beautifully manicured lawn. She was learning to relax around the cycle of constant motion that Ben and Tom created, but she clearly wasn't there quite yet. 'Well, let's pop it on the list as a maybe,' she suggested tactfully.

Taffy leaned down and kissed Holly on the top of her head. 'I'm a little outmatched down here. Okay if I take the kit up and get things a bit sorted?' Holly nodded, well used to Taffy code for please-God-don't-make-me-stay. He dropped his voice to a whisper: 'I might pop round and see Dan too, keep a weather eye out at The Kingsley Arms. If the Major and Richard le Grange start fighting about their dahlias and delphiniums again, it'll be all hands on deck, especially if my brothers get involved!'

Holly was only too aware that Taffy and Dan hadn't exactly enjoyed a lot of downtime together of late, although she wasn't convinced that policing botanical barnies was the path to relaxation and enjoyment, however emotionally heated they might become. 'Go to the pub, talk bollocks and put the world to rights,' she suggested. 'Stay out for a curry if you like?'

'I knew I liked you for a reason,' he said, kissing her lightly once more and making a break for it.

'You're looking a bit perkier,' commented Elsie, as she took in Holly's flushed complexion. 'It's a healing house, this. I told you it would do you the world of good.'

Holly didn't like to say that, since they'd been there all of five minutes, it was unlikely to be the house that had wrought this noticeable change, but then who was she to judge?

As Lizzie and Grace argued over the best theme for the baby shower when Holly had given them no clue as to the sex of the babies, Holly couldn't help thinking they were in for a long night. She absent-mindedly picked up Elsie's Wedding Folder from the table beside her, all the research for Holly and Taffy's abandoned Big Day neatly filed away. Holly wondered how long it would be before they dusted off the mothballs and had another go. Sometime after breastfeeding and fitting into clothes without elastic, she thought.

She flicked through the pages, some of them printed, some of them scrapbooked, all of them thoughtfully, sweetly, inherently 'Holly'. She swallowed hard, barely taking in the excitable chatter around her. 'We could use some of these ideas for the shower? Like the choux pastry buns, or the butterfly decorations – even the cocktails ... Who knows what will be in vogue by the time I've hatched these two.' She looked to Elsie for her support on this; if they used these ideas now, it would be back to square one for the wedding plans.

'Let's do it,' cried Elsie in delight. 'I can pull *that* together in a few short phone calls. And money's no object, darling. I insist. I've never thrown a baby shower before, but I find I'm rather taken with the whole idea – if we ignore the fact that it's rather *American*.'

'Well, let me cover the flowers at least,' Lizzie insisted, completely confused when everyone jeered. As the penny slowly dropped, she grinned. 'Maybe not the flowers exactly, but please let me contribute something. It's almost a shame Eric's illegitimate offspring won't be around for the sheer cuteness factor; I'm dying to see what a miniature-beagle-labradoodle-cross might look like.'

'Rather delightful, one imagines,' Elsie opined. 'I think I should quite like one of those. Seeing your darling dachshunds, Grace, rather got me thinking. They're so divine, already devoted. And there's no such thing as too much devotion, have you noticed? So maybe I should adopt Eric's illegitimate offspring in my decline?' She paused, her brow furrowing in thought. 'But then, what if the puppy's tiny and I sat on it accidentally? Nobody deserves to go like that. Maybe a wolfhound would be a better choice?'

Grace caught Holly's eye and they both tried not to laugh; Elsie was well known for her fleeting obsessions. They could only hope this one would pass without incident.

'And if we're making this baby shower more official, I could help with putting together a gift list for the twins, so you don't end up with twenty-seven romper suits?' Alice suggested, attempting to bring them back on message. 'Seriously, it would be quite rewarding to be shopping for somebody else,' she countered, holding Grace's concerned gaze with a reassuring smile.

Grace just nodded. 'It's going to be beautiful,' she said. 'Why not let me co-ordinate on the day so Elsie can relax and enjoy?'

Elsie settled back into her armchair, slender ankles crossed on a pouffe and a pitcher of low-alcohol margaritas within easy reach. 'Then it's a plan. It's perfect. A little baby shower to celebrate Bert and Ernie—'

'I am *not* calling them Bert and Ernie,' Holly interrupted with a laugh, and not for the first time. 'It's not sodding *Sesame Street*!'

'Siegfried and Roy? Cagney and Lacey? I do hope you won't be too deadly prosaic when you come to name these little cherubs?' Elsie shook her head in mock-disappointment.

'We don't even know for sure what sex they are yet!!' Holly protested. 'And when we do, we promise to at least discuss some of your ideas – how's that for a deal?'

'Deal,' Elsie said happily, sipping at her cocktail. 'And tomorrow will be perfect, darling. You won't have to lift a finger. Except to turn up looking beautiful. I've got dear Ozney all booked in to take some photographs. Afternoon tea will never have looked so stylish!'

Holly blanched as she considered the need for something to wear. She'd considered the children, the relatives, the food and decorations. How, in all of that, had she forgotten to consider herself? What did *she* need? She took a long swig of iced water and considered her options, as the evening birdsong ramped up a gear and she slowly began to relax, her eyelids growing heavy with the chatter and laughter around her. Strangely enough, once she let go, the answers came thick and fast as she watched the boys spin hypnotically round and round.

Chapter 41

Holly rolled over in bed and stretched, the memory foam mattress having worked its magic for the second night in a row. No matter how much she'd tried to stay awake to talk to Taffy when he got in, she'd been fighting a losing battle as soon as she got into bed.

The dawn light filtered through the trees outside the window and Taffy lay beside her, fast asleep, his eyelashes long and dark against his cheek. She had to restrain herself from reaching out and touching him, looking so angelic in repose.

She could hear the scurrying of the Flower Committee on the Market Place below, almost comical in their attempts to be quiet, often the shh-ing and giggling making more noise than the flower buckets and ladders. She had no desire to peep outside and ruin the surprise though. Half the pleasure of the Larkford Flower Festival was in that first reveal.

'Pst!' she whispered quietly. 'Taffy – are you awake?'

He murmured something incomprehensible and she wondered just how late he and Dan had called it a night. Based on the text she'd received at ten o'clock, when Taffy's brothers had joined them, it was unlikely to have been before midnight. Still, some things just couldn't wait.

'Taffy,' she murmured, dropping gentle kisses onto his

shoulder and stroking his back in a way that she knew only too well guaranteed an awakening of sorts.

'Morning, gorgeous,' Taffy said sleepily. 'Too early.' He reached out for her and wrapped her in his arms, still too drowsy to make much sense.

'Taffy,' whispered Holly insistently, unable to wait a moment longer to share her revelation with him. It had been hard enough last night to resist the urge to pull on her shoes and race over to The Kingsley Arms.

When you know, you know, right, she thought to herself joyfully. She just needed her partner in crime to wake up so she could share the news.

Taffy smiled lazily, knowing only too well that once Holly was awake there would be no peace for him. 'What are you so excited about at this ungodly time in the morning?' he asked.

'Well,' said Holly, working hard for nonchalance, 'I wondered if you fancied getting married today?'

Taffy blinked hard and sat up suddenly, the duvet falling away to give Holly full sight of his sculpted torso. 'Today?' he clarified, his smile now matching her own and his eyes twinkling with delight, all thoughts of sleep forgotten.

Holly nodded, biting her lip in nervous anticipation. 'Everyone's here. There'll be flowers everywhere you look. And little pastries. And fancy drinks – and I'd so much rather have a wedding afternoon tea than a wedding breakfast. It's just perfect, don't you think?'

Taffy slid one hand under her hair at the nape of her neck and kissed her thoroughly. 'I do,' he said tenderly, after a moment.

They both stared at each other in suspended disbelief at what they were suggesting, the morning birdsong providing the perfect soundtrack as the soft white voile curtains wafted inwards with the breeze. It simply didn't get any more romantic than this.

'Do you think we should warn them?' Holly said, hesitating briefly at the notion of a madcap spontaneous wedding.

Taffy shrugged. 'Why spoil the surprise? We might need to rope in a few co-conspirators though?'

'Reverend Taylor's always up for a lark,' Holly reassured him.

'I'll need a best man,' Taffy said. 'But Dan will always step up, so do we really need to say anything?'

'Lizzie might squeal about being kept out of the loop, but I know she'd be Maid of Honour in a heartbeat.' She paused. 'Actually, the people that truly need to know are the ones least likely to keep the secret—'

'Elsie—' said Taffy, just as Holly said:

'The twins—'

They both laughed, their hands entwined in this wonderfully impulsive scheme.

'You know this is exactly what I wanted,' Taffy said, 'without even knowing it. I get to be married to you without spending the next three months discussing napkins and seating arrangements. I get to be your husband before I become a father and, until then, we get to celebrate the litter of puppies you're apparently smuggling under that t-shirt,' he said with a laugh, as one of the twins gave a hearty kick against his hand.

'Are we really doing this?' Holly said, her words dancing with affection and excitement.

'I think we really are,' he confirmed. He grinned suddenly, humming the theme from *Hawaii Five-0* under his breath. 'Now, I'm assuming you're *not* up for arriving on a flower-laden canoe?'

'Nope,' said Holly easily, tucking herself in beside him, fitting their bodies together like jigsaw pieces having found their true place, 'but you can if you like?'

It was taking an almost superhuman restraint not to blurt out their secret over breakfast. It didn't help that Elsie's eagle eye missed nothing and she kept glancing between them in consternation.

'You look different,' she accused Holly, as they loaded the dishwasher together while Taffy took the boys out into the garden to let off steam. Already the heat was building and it promised to be a scorcher later. They'd deliberately stayed away from the front of the house, the town covenant dictating that, on this Sunday, nobody was allowed out into the Market Place before the church clock struck nine. Holly glanced at the large station clock on Elsie's kitchen wall. 'Ten minutes,' she said, 'and then we get to see the big reveal.'

'Hmm,' said Elsie astutely, not buying Holly's diversion for a moment. 'All this smug serenity – am I given to understand that your morning sickness has passed?' She was fishing and they both knew it.

'I'm just really excited about the baby shower,' Holly said, leaning down to kiss Elsie lightly on the cheek. 'I'm so grateful for everyone pulling together to make this happen. It feels like the perfect welcome to the community for them, you know? After all, these are Larkford babies born and bred.'

'They are, aren't they?' Elsie agreed. 'And actually, it's rather wonderful to have a little celebration, you know, in lieu of the main event—' She'd stopped making little digs about the wedding ages ago, once the prospect of Holly's vast twin bump had kyboshed any hope of a sleek sophisticated dress, Holly realised, but that didn't mean she wasn't feeling the lack of it. Hopefully that meant she'd be all the more delighted come this afternoon.

Holly blinked suddenly, realising what she'd forgotten in her excitement. 'And I still have no idea what I'm going to wear.'

Elsie patted her arm fondly. 'I wouldn't worry too much, darling. We can give your bump centre stage and nobody will be looking at your outfit.' This was so totally out of character for Elsie that Holly was nearly thrown off balance. Perhaps that was indeed Elsie's intention?

'But the photos—' Holly managed.

'Ah, yes. Well, we've got all morning to have a rummage upstairs, haven't we?' She eyed Holly's bump warily. 'Although, to be honest, my darling, there's only so much leeway in a von Furstenberg wrap dress.'

The first chime of the church clock rang out in the Market Place, Holly literally saved by the bell from blurting out her real reasons for wanting the perfect outfit.

Taffy and the boys hurtled inside from the garden. 'Can we go now?' bellowed Tom in excitement, his volume knob having recently become stuck on maximum.

'We can,' said Holly, taking Taffy's hand as they all surged into the hallway and Elsie threw open the front door. It was almost as though the houses lining the Market Place were serving as a giant cuckoo clock that morning, as with each chime more glossy front doors flew open and more residents emerged outside.

'Oh!' exclaimed Holly, tears quickly glistening on her lashes as she took in the scene. It was almost as though the Flower Committee had taken a secret peek inside her Wedding Folder. Rather than the usual riot of mismatched colour, the whole of the town was decked out in shades of white, silver and green. Acid-green fronds stood out in pale relief against lustrous dark leaves that were almost sculptural in their beauty. Carpets of tiny white alpine flowers curved around the bases of the trees and in small crevices in the Cotswold-stone walls and creamy alstroemeria bowed their silky heads in silver buckets of blooms. Heavy barrel planters had appeared overnight outside each shop-front, tall white agapanthus bobbing lightly in the warm breeze.

Taffy's hand in hers was all the catalyst she needed to let the tears flow. But it wasn't as though she were alone. As more and more people arrived in the Market Place, the gasps and cries of astonishment echoed against the Georgian townhouses.

With the final strike of the church bell the applause began, rippling through their community to honour the ten souls who had been up all night and had wrought this magic in their town. As they stepped forward to take a bow, Holly was stunned to see they were all holding hands. After months of bickering and feuding, which had necessitated this curfew and reveal, they were all united in their creation. But it wasn't until they stepped aside that Holly fully understood the reason why.

The clapping grew to a crescendo, punctuated by whoops and hollers of delight. The banner was simplicity in itself, bordered by lush green foliage:

SAVE LIVES, NOT MONEY

The Auction Fund had been voted their charity this year by a landslide, it seemed. No room for personal agendas or sniping when it came to an issue so close to all their hearts.

The Major stood proudly beside the banner, saluting neatly

to Holly as she caught his gaze. 'Thank you,' he mouthed at her across the Market Place. It was all Holly could do not to run across and hug him, standing there in his ceremonial best, proudly contributing to their community again. It took a moment for her to register the young girl beside him in a wheelchair. It was only when young Jessica Hearst took the Major's hand in her own, broadly smiling and clearly delighted to be there, that Holly realised who she was.

'Is that Jess?' exclaimed Taffy beside her, having no such compunction about bolting across to say hello. Holly followed on behind, delighted to see that, whilst Jess might not have the energy to walk far, there was nothing wrong with her speech or recognition.

It was turning out to be the perfect day.

Grace and Alice fell into step beside her, Alice's aunt Pru accompanying them, and their trio of dogs on incredibly best behaviour. It put Eric to shame a little that he would spend the morning in Lizzie's garden, for fear of him cocking his leg on every single flower arrangement he passed, or indeed finding himself yet another 'lady friend'.

'Are you excited about this afternoon?' Grace asked. 'It seems as though the whole town is turning out to celebrate Larkford's latest additions, even if, you know, they're not technically here yet.'

Ben tilted his head, looking quizzical and oddly like Eric. 'Where are they then? Because one of those babies kicked me when I hugged Mummy.' He looked rather put out. 'I've told them that won't wash with me when they come outside.' His oddly mature turns of phrase were often cause for hilarity in their house, as the older he grew, the more he began to sound like a little old man, or possibly a chip off the block that was Elsie Townsend.

Grace, Pru and Alice manfully held back their laughter as Holly tried to explain and Ben quickly lost interest. His main excitement about the pregnancy currently seemed to stem from the fact that one of his little school friends had been given an Xbox when his baby sister arrived. Ben wasn't slow and he'd quickly calculated that two babies meant that great things were in store for him and his brother.

'I've had such fun putting together your baby gift list, by the way,' said Alice. 'Are you quite sure you don't want a say?'

'She's done wonders,' agreed Pru. 'Even using that little bou-tick-you in Bath.'

Holly shook her head, knowing exactly the pricey children's boutique that Pru was attempting to refer to. 'I quite like a surprise present, to be honest. And your way is the best of both worlds for me. We won't get piles of duplicates and I still get the surprise!' Holly paused for a moment as a thought occurred to her. 'You're always so beautifully stylish, Alice. Any chance you've got something that might work for me this afternoon? In all the excitement, and with Taffy's family turning up, I can't believe it slipped my mind—'

Alice did indeed look suitably astonished that such a thing could happen. In her world, no doubt, the outfit came first and everything else followed.

'What about the pale blue Armani?' Grace suggested, her familiarity with Alice's wardrobe since their big clearout, coupled with her almost photographic memory, an obvious boon. 'Was that on the rail for the pop-up shop?'

Alice nodded, appraising Holly as she did so. 'It might be just perfect, if a little dressy for a baby shower, but hey – it's your special day, right?' Why don't I pop over in a while with some options and you can try a few things on, see what works?'

Grace nodded. 'And don't forget that ivory shift; it would look perfect over some palazzo pants.'

Alice grinned. 'Grace Allen, we'll make a fashionista of you yet!'

'If Holly doesn't want the par-laz-oh pant thingummies, I'll have them,' volunteered Pru. 'I do love me a bit of Dolsey and Cabbanos.'

Holly smiled, enjoying their banter and their friendship, not to mention Pru Hartley on word-mangling form as ever; it made her so happy to see this lighter, easier side of Alice. 'Sounds like a plan. Thank you. And you are bringing Jamie this afternoon, yes?' Colour immediately flooded Alice's cheeks and Holly rushed to let her off the hook. 'I mean, with half the canine population of Larkford in attendance, we'll definitely need someone to keep them in line.'

'And you honestly *found* this in the back of your wardrobe, Alice?' Holly said in delighted disbelief, a few hours later, turning this way and that in front of the mirror.

'One of the few upsides of never getting rid of anything,' Alice said modestly, even though her face beamed with delight at being able to make such a significant contribution to the day. She stepped forward and smoothed the soft blue fabric, cut in layers to fall from an empire line under the bust. 'I bought it to wear to a christening when I was a bit bigger. But it works, doesn't it? I mean, the way the fabric drapes, it makes your bump look really neat. You deserve to be the star of the show at your own baby shower, after all, before these two come along and upstage you.'

Holly nodded, slightly emotional for a moment. She honestly hadn't known it was possible to feel this beautiful whilst pregnant. Her hair was glossy and full, her skin suddenly radiant. And who knew that an empire line could be so incredibly forgiving? There was definitely something of the Jane Austen about this dress. 'I'm so grateful, Alice. Thank you.'

She pulled the younger woman into a hug, even then noticing how Coco tiptoed amongst the dresses and shoes scattered on the floor. Clearly a dog of many talents, she obviously had respect for Alice's fashion fetish.

Taffy knocked discreetly on the door. 'Are you two decent in there?'

'Of course not,' replied Holly, 'but we have got all our clothes on, if that's what you mean.'

He came in shaking his head at her daft humour and stopped in his tracks, absolute adoration on his face and, for once, completely lost for words. He simply held out his hand for hers.

Alice discreetly slipped away with a smile and Coco at her heels; her work was done.

'You, Holly Graham, look absolutely stunning,' said Taffy after a moment, as his eyes ranged over her body, drawn back time and time again to where the fabric draped easily over her stomach. 'I can't believe there are two tiny humans in there. I mean, I understand the process,' he laughed. 'But there's a moment, isn't there, where it feels more like magic than reality?'

Holly nodded. 'I think so. Somehow even more so with twins.' She leaned forward and kissed him on the lips, lingering for a moment in the warm, familiar sensations that overcame her. 'I'm so glad we're doing this today. It just feels so right, doesn't it? Spontaneous and easy, for the kids, as much as for Elsie. It's the best kind of surprise, because everyone has been wanting the same thing. We're just doing it our way,' she said, knowing full well that she wasn't the only one who would be more at ease without the formality that always threatened to overshadow many a happy occasion.

It had been an easy decision, in the end, not to tell a soul except Reverend Taylor – secrets in Larkford had a way of not staying secret for long, after all.

'I'm beyond excited actually,' Taffy confessed. 'And not just about those profiteroles I saw arriving on my way upstairs.'

Holly leaned her head against his shoulder, delighted that they'd finally found time to talk in bed that morning, whispering to each other under the duvet like a pair of teenagers. Laughing and giggling as the babies' little kicks gained enough momentum to give Taffy a nudge, as he curled around her.

'It's going to be perfect,' he whispered, kissing along her collarbone and knowing exactly the effect he was having on her.

'Our kind of perfect,' she agreed.

Chapter 42

Holly hovered by the French windows into the garden and looked out at the scene before her. It was easy to see the love and attention that had gone into planning this baby shower. Fairy lights were strung amongst the trees that lined Elsie's garden, with tiny pairs of yellow booties suspended amongst them. Three tables in the shade groaned under the weight of all the tasty morsels and delights awaiting them. Posies of fresh flowers artfully tumbled across the small round tables dotted around the beautifully manicured lawn, and several of the large agapanthus planters from the Market Place had miraculously reappeared around the edge of Elsie's patio. It genuinely seemed as though the entire population of Larkford had spruced up and turned up to celebrate her babies.

Little did they know, thought Holly happily, hugging the secret to herself, even as Taffy winkled Dan away from the crowd to clue him in on his duties for the afternoon.

The Reverend Taylor was also caught up in the delight of springing a surprise wedding on her flock and was completely unfazed by the prospect of an al fresco ceremony, even one that seemed to have a largely canine contingent. 'I think this is the most beautiful wedding I've seen in a long time,' she whispered to Holly. 'Everyone is so happy and relaxed – look! Not a stressed bunny among them. Good thinking, Holly.' She clasped her hand briefly and couldn't help but smile at the excitable bride beside her. No nerves, no dramas, just absolute delight that her clandestine plotting was falling so simply into place.

She watched as Taffy whispered in Dan's ear and his head shot up in surprise, followed by a burst of laughter and much backslapping. To anyone watching it was simply a case of boys being boys; no doubt they would now be on the lookout for today's wager, but Holly knew otherwise. Dan looked across the garden and caught her eye, raising his champagne flute and mouthing 'well played'. She nodded in acknowledgement, unable to formulate her thoughts.

Holly took a moment to stand in the doorway and just 'be' – watching all her favourite people in the world, decked out in their summer finery, laughing and joking and joining together to celebrate her babies' start in life. 'Wish me luck,' she said to Reverend Taylor after a moment's hesitation, and then she stepped out into the garden. They'd decided earlier to let the baby shower play out just a little before they announced the change of plan.

It was a good decision. It seemed that the very idea of two sets of twins had entranced all their guests, for equally as many gifts were being presented to Ben and Tom as to the excitedly awaited arrivals.

Despite Elsie's earlier concerns on the issue, this baby shower was the epitome of pastoral English living, with an abundance of flowers, scones and Pimm's, and barely an Americanism in sight. Unless you counted the 'Guess the weight of the baby' game that Dan had rigged up by filling a babygrow with little bags of rice and popping a dolly from the waiting room on top! Holly did a small double-take as she saw money changing hands and realised that, of course, the competition didn't just have a prize, but also a wager. Although to be fair, Dan was looking incredibly distracted now he was in the loop and kept glancing over in her direction, waiting for his cue.

'Ten pounds and nine ounces,' Taffy whispered in her ear, as he walked over to join her on the shaded patio. 'I checked.'

Holly winced at the very idea, grateful for once that her babies were coming 'out of the sunroof'.

He fidgeted beside her, eager to get started. He leaned in. 'Come on, Holls. Let's do this,' Taffy said. 'If we wait any longer, *I'm* going to be the one to give the game away.' It was true; his face was lit up with affection and anticipation. He literally couldn't tear his gaze away from her and his hand found hers at every opportunity. As their hands touched and his fingers automatically sought the diamond engagement ring on her finger, there was a moment when it seemed they were alone in the garden, the only point of focus in a Monet haze, the moment when their new family truly began.

'Absolutely,' she whispered, stepping out from the shade into the sunshine and barely noticing Ozney snapping away on his hi-tech Nikon camera, capturing her radiant smile.

A gentle round of applause grew into whoops and cheers at the sight of Holly's stunning dress and the proud look on Taffy's face. Ben and Tom looked up in shocked amazement, a doughnut in each hand and sugar smeared on both of their faces. Holly didn't even miss a beat when they both ran over and pressed themselves against her legs, desperate to be included in the celebrations.

'Lady with a baby, coming through,' cried Lizzie in delight, only too happy to have the chance to quote one of her favourite movies. Holly laughed, even more so once she clocked Taffy's bemused expression.

'It's *Grease*,' she whispered.

He looked down at the small sticky handprints on her dress. 'Yeah, but it'll wash off.' To be fair he looked even more confused then, as both Holly and Lizzie dissolved into laughter.

Elsie rushed over, looking incredibly pleased with herself, and slopping champagne over her wrist in her enthusiasm. 'Didn't I tell you this would be a wonderful way to celebrate these babies?'

Holly kissed her on each cheek, choosing not to remind Elsie that at seven o'clock that morning she'd been sweeping through the house proclaiming their baby shower a 'disaster' because they had no baby bottles in which to serve the champagne.

Holly was presented with a tiny bottle of Babycham with a straw and the twins clamoured for their very own. Ozney clicked away happily, under strict orders from both Elsie and Lizzie that black and white candids were the only way to go for that spontaneous, thrown-together look.

Elsie pressed a small envelope into Holly's hands. 'There's a little something in there for you. Not for the babies. For you. You deserve to have some beautiful maternity clothes to make you feel special.'

Holly clasped her hand. '*You* make me feel special. You've already been so generous. Save your money, Elsie, please. A hug is all I need.'

'Pish-tosh,' exclaimed Elsie in disgust. 'Taffy, do you even realise that your fiancée refuses to go shopping? You have no idea how lucky you are!'

'Oh, I don't know,' said Taffy slowly. 'I think I know

exactly how lucky I am.' He laid a hand on Holly's bump and a small kick bounced his palm away. 'Assuming I can get past the guards here.'

Lizzie tinged her cake fork on the side of her champagne flute and cleared her throat. 'I'd like to make a toast! To Holly and Taffy, Ben and Tom – wishing you all the very best for your new arrivals. To Thelma and Louise!'

'What?' cried Holly.

'Ant and Dec!' called Dan.

'Mary-Kate and Ashley!' hollered the Major, surprising everyone, even himself.

Holly turned to Taffy in confusion and he blushed guiltily. 'They're not convinced I don't know the sex of the babies, so they keep trying to catch me out.'

'You can tell me, you know,' whispered Elsie conspiratorially. 'You know I can keep a secret.'

Holly, Taffy and Lizzie burst out laughing, knowing only too well that Elsie's tongue could be loosened by the merest drop of champagne.

'Speaking of which—' Holly said, stepping forward and raising her own glass for silence.

'We do actually have a little news to share,' she said, beaming and laying a hand protectively on her bump.

'Oh my, is it actually triplets?' Patty asked faintly, looking completely overwhelmed by the joyous and slightly unruly atmosphere of the party. Even Taffy's brothers were on their best behaviour in sight of all this decadence.

'God no!' exclaimed Holly with feeling. 'We definitely feel that four is enough. Don't we?' Holly turned to Taffy for clarification, but he just shrugged, unfazed.

'Jesus Christ, that's a whopper,' said the Major into the silence, as he hefted the poor floppy 'baby' and attempted to guess its weight. He looked up in alarm at his unintended outburst. 'Sorry, Reverend.'

'Couldn't matter less,' said Reverend Taylor easily, turning back to focus on Holly.

Taffy took Holly's hand once more and gave her a supportive smile. This was her secret to share, after all. 'I hope you don't mind,' said Holly with a tiny nod of her head, 'but there's been a slight change of plan.'

Reverend Taylor took one step forward, and turned to face the expectant faces before her. 'Dearly Beloved, we are gathered here today—'

Elsie's squeals of surprised delight nearly drowned out her words and the garden was thrown into complete pandemonium. Dan leapt forward with alacrity, fully intent on being the very best Best Man. He shook Taffy's hand more firmly than was strictly necessary. 'Proud of you, mate,' he said gruffly.

Holly turned to Lizzie, whose hands were clapped over her mouth in absolute shock. 'Would you be my Maid of Honour?'

Elsie fanned herself vigorously with a linen napkin. 'Oh, Holly! My darling girl! You absolute rotter!' Her face was wreathed in smiles, her eyes filled with tears, and it was obvious she was utterly delighted at being outsmarted for once. She couldn't resist stepping forward to hug her tightly. 'You are the most beautiful bride I could ever imagine. And so serene.' She squeezed her tightly. 'Clever, clever girl.'

It was the work of moments, but the entire impromptu congregation realigned themselves accordingly. The Major appointed himself chief usher and soon had the residents of Larkford settled into place by way of polite officiousness – he was in his element. Cassie Holland surprised them all by standing discreetly to one side and singing the most soulful and pitch-perfect Ave Maria that Holly had ever heard, the goose-bumps springing up on the back of her neck and her emotions threatening the artful make-up that Alice had so sweetly applied earlier. She glanced up to see that it was too late for Patty, the tears now streaming freely down her face as her other three sons quietly joined Cassie, their Welsh tenors lending her performance depth and resonance.

Taffy squeezed Holly's hand tightly, clearly fighting his own emotions at the sight of this outpouring of support and affection for their impromptu union. The whole garden was entranced by the four stunning voices, even Ben and Tom's attention captured and held – the spontaneity of this *a cappella* rendition making it all the more exquisite in the serenity of the garden, the soft floral scents caught on the light breeze and lifted by the occasional clink of champagne flutes.

As they drew to a close, Reverend Taylor lifted her arms and the congregation, as surely that is what the guests had now become, all rose as one. Ben and Tom proudly flanked the bride and groom under the looping clematis arbour that provided Nature's own cathedral.

Elsie, for once, was now speechless, and merely found herself a prime viewing spot and sank into a chair, occasionally dabbing her eyes with a lace handkerchief, her face lit up with excitement at the undeniable romance of the scene.

'Do you, Meirion Aled Selwyn Jones, take this woman to be your wedded wife?' Reverend Taylor asked, herself a little choked up by the delighted and enthusiastic response. After all, one never really knew how surprise weddings were going to go down with the couple's nearest and dearest . . .

'Say yes!' insisted Tom in the least discreet 'whisper' of all time.

As they exchanged their vows, with Ozney discreetly capturing their first kiss as husband and wife, Holly found herself alternately laughing and crying, overcome by such an intense feeling of happiness that it could only in part be attributed to her hormones.

She felt the smooth band of rose gold on her finger, and the warmth of Taffy's hand in hers. It seemed so fitting, somehow, that their wedding be as spontaneous and loving as their relationship. Everybody she loved in one place, supporting her children, supporting her marriage, and never for one moment doubting their ability to find that elusive happy-ever-after.

As kisses and congratulations flew around her, Holly sought Taffy's gaze. 'I love you,' she said, confident that he could read her expression if not her lips. His face creased into a grin and he replied in kind.

She looked around for the boys, only to find they had taken the initiative and were stacking glazed doughnuts into a precarious pyramid in lieu of a wedding cake.

The Major was walking around, simply shaking every one of Taffy's family members by the hand and saying, 'Jolly good show,' over and over again.

'This is the best bloody wedding I have ever been to,' said Elsie, to nobody in particular.

And Holly couldn't help but agree – all of the beauty and emotion, without any of the draining build-up and negotiations. She had everything she wanted for her special day right here.

Alice skipped over breathlessly and kissed her on both cheeks. 'Thank God you liked your dress!' she exclaimed, obviously unable to comprehend how someone might leave something so important as a wedding dress to chance.

Holly laughed. 'I have to confess, it was rather a bonus.' She smoothed the silken fabric again. 'At least this time I can have the photos out on the mantelpiece without dying of mortification. Wedding dresses aren't really all they're cracked up to be, Alice. Any garment that requires assistance to help you pee is a non-starter in my book.'

Alice snorted with laughter at her bridal irreverence and Holly was delighted to see that her lovely new friend seemed to be more relaxed than she had been in ages. Maybe they had all needed an impromptu reminder of how wonderful their little world of Larkford truly was?

'Are you ready to cut the cake, Mrs Mummy Jones?' said Tom, stumbling over what to call his newly married mother, but beaming from ear to ear, completely swept up by the occasion. After all, hadn't they been nagging for this all summer long? He tugged at her hand urgently, pulling her down so that he could whisper in her ear. 'Mummy, when the babies come, will they call Taffy Daddy?'

'As soon as they can talk,' Holly replied, unable to resist kissing him on his little chubby cheeks, and not even minding the sticky sugary sheen that transferred to her lips.

Tom thought for a moment, his brow furrowed in concentration. 'Do you think Taffy would mind if we called him Daddy too?'

Holly swallowed hard, her mascara no longer even standing a chance. 'I think he would really, truly love that,' she replied, pulling him into a hug and kissing the top of his head until he squirmed.

'And a family shot for the album?' called Ozney, bemused beyond measure as half the congregation surged towards him, pooling around the bride and groom, lifting the twins up easily into the frame.

'Best wedding ever,' managed Elsie yet again, as they all did jazz hands for the camera and fell about laughing.

Chapter 43

Grace watched the happy couple from the shaded rose garden, sipping thoughtfully at her glass of champagne. Holly's beatific smile and happiness were in sharp contrast to how Grace had felt on her own wedding day, all those years ago. Pregnant and terrified, dropping out of medical school, she had never really stopped to explore her motivations for marrying Roy: they were having a baby together and it was as simple as that. How many times over the course of that soul-sapping relationship had she wished she had only been a little braver?

Seeing Holly getting married now, equally as pregnant, but noticeably more besotted, was a sharp reminder to Grace that her actions, her choices, had the ability to influence so much more than her own happiness. She had no desire to see her fourth decade frittered away, like her twenties, with cowardliness and indecision.

'Are you hiding out or just bogarting the best sticky buns?' Dan said with a teasing smile as he wandered over to join her. Grace couldn't deny that their budding relationship had brought a spring to her step and a sparkle to her eye that she hadn't felt in years. When he leaned in to kiss her on the lips, it was so natural, so wonderful, that she couldn't help wondering what exactly they'd been waiting for.

'How would you feel if I wanted to tell my boys about us?' she ventured tentatively, leaning in to his chest as he wrapped his arms around her.

Dan pulled back for a moment, confusion on his face, and she felt her heart lurch with disappointment that she might have misjudged whatever 'this' was. 'Oh Gracie,' he said, concern etched into his every syllable. 'I didn't realise.'

She pulled away too, forcing a smile, shaking her head as though it didn't matter. But it did. 'It's okay,' she managed, distractedly noticing that her hands had begun to shake. Maybe some people just didn't get their happy-ever-after, after all.

Dan stepped towards her. 'I'm so sorry. I just didn't realise we were keeping it a secret.' Grace looked up, blinking hard to recalibrate. 'I mean, I don't know about you, but I've been so ridiculously happy the last few days, I couldn't really hide it. Taffy knows. Holly knows. God, I think even Pru at the bakery knows – she caught me whistling while I bought our breakfast the other morning. I've told everyone I can possibly think of.'

Grace allowed a small sob to escape. When would she stop anticipating the worst eventuality at every turn? 'So you mean—'

'That I want *everyone* to know we're together? God, yes.' He leaned in, one hand slipping behind her waist to pull her in closer. When he kissed her, she felt her whole body relax, all the tensions erased by the promise in his kiss.

A cacophony of whoops broke into her awareness. 'I think the cat might be out of the bag now anyway,' she whispered.

'Perfect,' he replied, barely missing a breath, before kissing her as though his life depended on it.

Ambling over to join the others later, Grace couldn't wipe the smile off her face. The bride and groom were circulating, their hands never parting, even as Patty began fussing with Taffy's hair for the photos. Even Ben and Tom seemed determined not to miss a trick and were hovering beside Holly like a fidgety shadow, only breaking away occasionally to replenish their cake supply.

Elsie appeared to have recovered from her initial shock at the impromptu wedding and was now swinging into gear as the hostess with the mostest. 'Oh Grace,' she exclaimed as she bustled by with yet more posies of sweet peas for the photographs. 'I'm really *most* pleased with you.' She stopped and gave Grace's hand a delighted squeeze. 'You can fill me in on all the scrumptious details later. And don't spare my blushes, darling girl. I'll need to know everything.'

'Please don't,' begged Dan quietly, trying not to laugh at the lascivious look Elsie had shot his way.

'Wouldn't dream of it,' replied Grace, becoming accustomed oh-so-easily to their intimate banter; that feeling of solidarity that people had talked about in their relationships, but she herself had never before experienced.

She wanted to tell him how she felt, but every time the words came to her lips, that little catastrophising voice in her head, the one that had been haunting her all week, would point out that maybe Dan's highly developed White Knight complex was all that was throwing them together.

'Do you have any idea how long I've loved you?' Dan asked, his hand still warming the curve of her waist, but moving with imperceptible tenderness.

Grace blinked in surprise. It was as though he'd heard her doubts and countered them before they could take hold. 'Tell me,' she whispered with a smile.

'Er, guys?' said Rupert, seeking them out with some urgency. 'I'm so sorry to interrupt, but we have a bit of a situation.' He was flushed and uncomfortable, unable to stand still, and he wasted no time pulling on Dan's arm and setting off towards the kitchen. 'She didn't want to interrupt the wedding, you see. We both thought we'd have ages. I mean, that's what they say in all the books, isn't it?' He was running on with a stream of consciousness that bore no interruption, but was certainly giving Grace a clear idea of what they were dealing with.

Pushing open the French windows into the kitchen, it was immediately apparent that Rupert's concern had actually been an understatement. Poor Mims was clutching at the edge of the kitchen table, doubled over in pain, sweat sticking her hair to her forehead as she groaned quietly. The effort not to bellow was clearly taking its toll, her knuckles white and her whole body shaking.

'How far apart are the contractions?' Dan asked, gently taking Mims's pulse on her wrist.

'Um, I don't know, not long,' Rupert flustered. As if to answer his question, Mims spasmed again as yet another contraction caught her in its vice. 'Two, three minutes?'

'Make it stop,' begged Mims, panting as the wave subsided. 'It's too early. I'm not due until next week. I thought it was just Braxton Hicks.'

Rupert shook his head. 'I even told her it was, during the ceremony.' The guilt on his face was almost palpable. 'I was going to call an ambulance just now, but she begged me not to.' He turned to Dan, professional to professional. 'I know I can't *make* her go to hospital if she doesn't want to, but can you persuade her? Please?'

Dan shook his head and Grace could see the conflict on his face. 'Rupert mate, it's too late now anyway. Unless there's complications you haven't told me about, she might be better staying put.'

'We were supposed to be going to Rosemore,' Mims wailed. 'I had a plan!'

Grace wrung out the clean tea towel she'd been running under the cold tap and gently pressed it against Mims's forehead. 'Plans are great, but the babies never listen, Mims. We just have to follow their lead.' She turned to frown at Dan and Rupert, who seemed to have been caught up in some heated debate about the best plan of action. 'Guys,' she said firmly. 'We're in a kitchen during a wedding reception. I don't think Holly and Taffy need to know, do you? Can we at least find somewhere a little more private while you work out what to do?'

They waited until the next contraction had passed, alarmingly close to the last. Even tackling the first flight of stairs was no mean feat and Grace could only be grateful that she was bringing up the rear rather than physically supporting poor Mims. She quietly plucked her mobile from her pocket and tapped out a message to Chris Virtue. A little part of her mind already covering their bases and wondering just how slammed the Air Ambulance team were today, just in case.

She ducked around them as they came to the landing, pushing open the first bedroom door they came to and watching Rupert and Dan give in and carry Mims to the bed, as yet another contraction crashed over her. It was only as they were plumping up cushions to prop her up and make her comfortable that Grace clocked all the flowers and candles decorating the bedroom. Apparently Mims was about to give birth in Holly and Taffy's bridal suite.

'Bugger,' said Dan, as he clearly noticed the same thing. He dropped his voice as he leaned in to Grace. 'Nothing about this is ideal, Gracie. But maybe you could muster up Alice, some towels and an idea of how busy they are in Bath?'

She nodded and dialled as she ran down the stairs, cursing the twinkly muzak as her call was diverted again and again. When finally it was answered, the nurse sounded frazzled and distracted. 'Maternity Level Three.'

As Grace outlined the situation, she began to wonder whether the nurse could actually hear her. The noise in the background was like something from a catastrophe movie. 'I've got ladies on trolleys in the corridor here and some poor soul just gave birth in the lift. We are completely swamped. I can't even send out a midwife.' The nurse sounded on the verge of tears herself. 'I have no idea what they were thinking closing down four midwife-led units in the county with no notice, but they had to realise that all these births had to happen somewhere. My advice? If your patient is stable, comfortable and has a doctor on hand, she's already doing better than some of the women here.'

Grace felt sick as she ended the call. Even seeing that Holly and Taffy were now fudging their first dance to Ben's strangled version of 'Edelweiss' on the recorder did nothing to lighten her mood. She grabbed Alice discreetly by the hand and led her away before anyone could question it.

'Are you serious?' exclaimed Alice, turning a deathly shade of pale as they raced up the stairs, Coco in hot pursuit and Grace giving an abbreviated sitrep. 'I'm not sure how much use I'm going to be. Umbilical cords kind of freak me out.'

Grace stared at her in amazement. 'Alice Walker, you are a highly qualified GP and your patient is in distress. Not to mention the fact that, bluntly, your hands are considerably smaller than Dan's, if you get my drift. Now pull yourself together, because there are two very frightened new parents in there.'

Alice nodded, a sickly green colour sweeping over her face. 'I'm on it.'

Pushing open the door, Grace looked sharply to Dan for reassurance but the expression on his face offered none. 'Breathe for me, Mims,' he said gently, 'and whatever you do, don't push.'

Mims let out a strangled scream. 'I was supposed to be in a pool of lovely warm water. This is not how it was supposed to be!' Rupert was holding her hand tightly and looking petrified.

'Is it breach?' he asked Dan, his veterinary knowledge being just enough to worry him.

Dan shook his head. 'I think the cord's wrapped around the baby's neck. Every time she pushes, the baby's heartbeat is dropping, so it could be it's tightening a little.'

Grace knew only too well what that meant. Nuchal cords weren't uncommon, but they did need careful evaluation. If they were at the maternity unit now, there would, in all probability, be that terrifying rush down the corridor at the first sign of foetal distress, where nurses and anaesthetists would appear as if from nowhere, hustling into the operating theatre for an emergency C-section. Her phone bleeped in her pocket. Chris. She read the screen twice and then discreetly showed it to Dan.

Bird 2 still down. Out dealing with a multi-car pile-up on the A40.

They were on their own.

Alice emerged from the en suite, drying her hands and with a sheen of perspiration on her forehead. 'So, Mims, we might need you to change position in a moment,' she said gently, as Dan listened intently to the baby's heartbeat with his stethoscope. Trust Dan to have brought his doctor's bag to a baby shower, thought Grace gratefully.

Alice knelt on the bed beside Dan and they muttered to each other in muted tones. It wasn't the first time that Grace lamented her lack of medical degree and it certainly wouldn't be the last. If she couldn't be useful where it mattered, at least she could help soothe Mims and Rupert as the strain began to take its toll. Mims was clearly flagging now and the energy needed to keep her cries quiet was beyond her. Grace looked sharply across the landing to the windows overlooking the garden, where the party was still in full swing, relaxing only slightly when she saw they were firmly closed and double-glazed.

She watched as Dan talked Alice through what needed to be done and Grace's heart went out to her. If anything went wrong, she knew only too well that Alice would blame herself for evermore. She caught her eye and mouthed 'you can do this' across their patient's belly.

What would it actually take, Grace wondered, for the petty bureaucrats in their comfortable urban world to realise the very real effect of their sweeping decisions on the rural population. How many babies might die, or mothers go through this trauma alone? Grace felt a surge of righteous indignation, not just because right now Chris and his team were having to triage patients at the side of the road, or because Mims's birth plan was no longer even an option – it was a sense of injustice that took her breath away. And she didn't need a medical degree to take action on that front.

As she gently soothed Mims and held her hand through each contraction, Grace felt a solid kernel of determination settle in her chest. Whatever the outcome of today's melodrama, she was steadfast in her resolve – the waiting game was over; it was time to take action. It was time to make themselves heard.

She watched Alice carefully, the fear and trepidation on her face relaxing into wonderment as finally, finally, Mims's baby was freed from its umbilical noose and slithered into the world. Mims gave a relieved and heartfelt sob as its first cries filled the air like a welcome melody.

'It's a boy,' said Alice. 'You've a healthy baby boy.'

She gently handed the baby to Mims, snuggling him neatly onto her mother's chest before quietly and discreetly tiptoeing into the en suite and vomiting loudly.

Grace followed after her, quietly pushing the door closed as she sank down on the floor beside Alice. 'You only bloody did it,' she said. 'I'm so incredibly proud of you.' And they both burst into tears.

Chapter 44

'I know it's not quite a honeymoon in the Seychelles,' said Grace, as she slid the platter of Danish pastries onto the table in the doctors' lounge the next morning. 'But we're all so thrilled for you, we wanted to mark the occasion somehow.' She batted away the bunch of helium balloons that seemed to have acquired a life of their own and kept bobbing towards her head.

'It's just so lovely to have you back, Gracie,' Holly replied, pulling her into a hug. 'We missed you.'

Grace smiled. 'Well, after yesterday, it was an easy decision in the end. Can't hide out for ever when there's all this drama and upheaval going on, now can I?' And she meant it too; some part of her brain had switched from fear to feisty during Jemima's unscheduled delivery and there was no switching it back, it seemed.

'We even got the posh coffee from The Deli,' interrupted Dan with a grin. 'I think we're all feeling a little delicate this morning.' He rubbed a hand across his eyes tiredly and Holly felt a flicker of guilt for not only springing a surprise wedding on their friends, but for doing it on a Sunday. Coming to work this morning felt like a labour of love for all of them.

'How's Mims doing?' Holly asked Dan quietly as the helium balloons took on Taffy, attracted by some kind of static electricity to his hair and making it look as though he were under attack.

'She's doing well. And the baby is a sweetheart. I stayed with them for a few hours and popped into Elsie's again this morning while you lazy buggers were still in bed. Frankly, I think relief is the overriding emotion all round.'

Holly shook her head, frowning. 'I can't believe all of that was going on and you never said a word.'

Dan shrugged. 'We didn't want to spoil your big day. Did you have a lovely time?'

'We really did. It was everything I was hoping for, and more. And some of the photos are just gorgeous – everyone's so chilled out and happy. Nobody stressing about the arrangements or what to wear for weeks in advance. Sort of like a family-friendly elopement.' Holly grinned. 'Sorry you missed out on the speeches.'

'I should be apologising to you. I hardly fulfilled my duties as Best Man – no speech, no Stag Night – not so much as a Bambi-evening.' He looked mildly put out at being deprived of the opportunity for revelry.

'Have the Stag next weekend if you like,' Holly suggested.

Dan stared at her incredulously. 'You do know what goes on at a Stag Night?'

Holly looked over at Taffy and smiled. 'Well, since we live in the real world, not a movie, I'm guessing you could still have a cracking evening out without breaking our marriage vows or any local laws.'

'Maybe,' Dan teased. 'But then – where would be the fun in that?'

'Are you still going on about this Stag Night?' asked Grace, as she wandered over to join them. 'Let it go. They're married already.'

'I hardly held up my end of the Best Man arrangement though, did I?' Dan said grumpily. Grace leaned against his shoulder and he automatically slid his arm around her waist.

For a moment, Holly felt a flicker of concern that these two were more obviously loved-up than the newlyweds in the room. But then, seeing them together, so newly smitten, but so long in the making, it felt churlish to deny them that blissful stage where everything was new and wonderful and shiny. She and Taffy had spent the night in the attic room at Elsie's, where the twins and Eric had joined them at roughly three a.m. when Mims's baby had squawked them all wide awake. It was all very well being spontaneous, but she rather wished she'd thought past 'I do' and on to a wedding night to remember for all the right reasons.

Still, she thought, the night may not have been a runaway success, but her wedding had been Holly-and-Taffy-style perfection, and that was what mattered. A little dose of reality afterwards was actually no bad thing; just part of the tapestry of her life here in Larkford.

'Knock-knock,' said Chris Virtue, poking his head round the door. 'Can I come in?' He didn't wait for an answer but strode into the room and helped himself to a Danish. He looked exhausted, haggard almost, and his usual debonair humour was noticeably missing. As the pastry flaked around his mouth, Holly watched how his gaze always settled on Grace and it was obvious that Dan hadn't missed that either.

'What can we help you with?' Dan said, switching into ultra-polite mode.

Chris sat back against the edge of the table and sighed. 'Look, I'm sorry to interrupt your party, but we need to talk.

We have to ramp things up a notch, guys.' He blew out a breath that ruffled his tousled hair and looked as though he were about to burst into tears. 'Five people died last night. All of them needlessly. Two kids and their dad from that pile-up on the motorway, an older guy with a head injury after a fall, and a cancer patient with an adverse reaction to his chemo.' The tears were choking his voice now and Holly felt the delicious pastry cloy in her mouth. Here they were celebrating, while all of these tragedies had been unfolding in their own back yard.

'Now, I know none of this happened in your patch per se, but your lady last night, with the nuchal cord – it could so easily have been her . . . So I was wondering whether you guys wanted to join me in kicking up a bloody great fuss. The auction is great and everything but I just don't think it's going to be enough – or make things change fast enough.'

'It's all very well pinching pennies,' continued Grace, 'shutting down the local maternity and oncology services, even trying to stretch how far one helicopter can reasonably cover – but people are dying. For want of some understanding about rural roads, people are dying.'

'We need to accelerate this,' said Chris in agreement.

Lucy reached forward and handed him a napkin, as they all uncomfortably took on board what he was saying. It was one thing to understand the theory, but confronting the reality meant that, while they had been celebrating Holly and Taffy's marriage, other families not so far away had been needlessly losing their loved ones.

Taffy clapped a hand on Chris's shoulder, noticeably moved by what they'd heard. 'What's it going to take, do you think, for people in Westminster to sit up and take notice?'

'Remember, this is just one night. One county. How many more deaths were avoidable last night, do you think?' Grace pointed out, choked up by the very notion of how differently things could have ended for Jemima and Rupert, had they been home alone.

'How loudly can we shout this from the rooftops, do you think?' Holly asked, as her brain whirred through a few scenarios. 'Do you think any of the families will actually want to be involved?'

'It feels a little ghoulish to even ask,' Dan said gently. Holly could see what it cost him to say that, as the angry set to his face suggested he too was all for kicking up a bloody great shitstorm.

'If we found out some stats across the South West,' Grace ventured, 'it would give us a clearer picture? Stop thinking quite so local.'

Holly nodded. 'Maybe no names, just photos—'

'Like a slideshow?' queried Taffy. 'With a voiceover? Hope it goes viral?'

Chris turned to stare. 'Well, I was thinking placards outside the Primary Care Trust, but you guys obviously do things a bit differently.'

Grace nodded. 'We've learned the hard way that there's only so much change we can effect with local interest. If we harness the internet and the press, the message reaches a much wider audience. And that's what we want, isn't it? For more people to feel the outrage we do? After all, not everyone *lives* in a rural area, but a lot of them sure come here for their holidays. And if time is of the essence—'

'Maybe we can ask Julia to call Quentin?' offered Lucy, oblivious to how the mention of those two names made all the GPs stiffen. 'He could do a documentary short?'

'And if the grieving families don't want to do an interview, and frankly they shouldn't have to, couldn't we talk to the near-misses? People like Mims who might put a human face on the issue,' suggested Alice quietly.

Holly looked across at Taffy and saw her own emotions reflected in his face. Their sense of responsibility to their patients was so well developed that every loss felt personal to them. She laid her hand on her bump to quieten the fidgeting and kicking match that seemed to be going on in utero. 'We can get together a war chest. We need a fighting fund, if we're going to incur media costs – coverage won't come for nothing.'

'Unless we use the news cycle,' Grace said, her brow furrowed in concentration. 'If we can pull together something for release – a short statement to accompany a video or slideshow – we should be able to kick up quite a lot of dust without spending too much money. I for one would much rather that our fundraising actually covered the Air Ambulance repairs, or some extra midwives, rather than a fancy campaign. Simple, from the heart, no frills. We don't need Quentin for that.'

'I'll ask Mims and Rupert when I see them this morning,' volunteered Dan.

'Can I borrow your camcorder?' asked Lucy.

'And let's think about this auction and how we can boost donations. Maybe Elsie can hit up some of her cronies at Sarandon Hall for a few big-ticket items. If nothing else, maybe we can shame a few bureaucrats into action? After all, this kind of thing shouldn't be necessary just to provide the basics of healthcare,' Taffy said.

'I think that's the point, Taffs,' Holly said gently. 'For someone living in a big town or city, they take it for granted that they can get to a hospital if they need to. It's not the same in the countryside, but they don't necessarily know that.'

'Ignorance,' said Dan, bitterly. 'It always comes down to ignorance.'

'And he who shouts loudest,' Grace reminded him. 'Well, we may not have a fancy London address or a million people in our care, but we can shout loudly with the best of them. Maybe if we stop being an invisible, impersonal line on a balance sheet, the powers-that-be might realise that cutting our coverage actually kills. I wonder how they'd feel about that?'

'If this was America, there'd be wrongful death suits flying around and everybody would be on their toes,' said Chris tiredly.

'Do we really want to go there, though? Surely a litigious approach only ends up with everyone losing but the lawyers?' Grace said, ever the decent and considerate soul.

'We don't have to *do* it though, so much as *threaten* to do it,' suggested Lucy.

'Hint at it, maybe?' Taffy offered.

'I hate this,' burst out Holly suddenly. She hadn't even been aware that the words were in her mind, let alone tumbling out of her mouth. She took deep shuddering breaths to try and calm herself.

Chris looked panicked, obviously feeling responsible for raining on their parade. 'God, Holly, I'm so sorry—' he began.

'Nobody should have to fear for the safety of their baby, or whether their child will get to hospital in time if they get rear-ended on the motorway. This is unacceptable and we shouldn't stand for it,' said Holly.

'Hormones?' queried Chris under his breath to Grace, taken aback by Holly's vociferous eruption.

Holly wheeled to face him. 'Humanity, actually,' she said forcefully.

Taffy put his arm around her shoulder and pulled her face into his chest, attempting to soothe her. 'This is hardly twenty-first-century healthcare, though, is it?'

Chris shrugged uncomfortably. 'I can't tell you how much it means that you all feel this way. I've been up half the night having angry conversations with myself. After all, it's not as though we've been doing nothing, is it? I figured maybe I'd got too close to the problem, was taking it too personally.'

Grace shook her head. 'No such thing, Chris. It *is* personal though, isn't it? I mean, it could be anyone we know and love. Anyone we care about, not getting the help they need.'

Holly looked up, her mascara streaking down her cheeks. 'You know what, I'm not interested in sticking a Band-Aid on this. Something that will peel off in a few months' time and then we're back to square one. Grace is right. We need to make sure our voice is heard in every negotiation. Let's stop thinking local altogether.'

She paused and looked around the room at the expectant faces, some of them tinged with confusion. She took a deep breath to calm her racing heart. Now she'd had the idea, there was no way to put the genie back in the bottle.

'Let's raise some money, and some awareness – the auction can do that obviously – but then let's go for gold: we need a rural consultation on every budget cut. We need someone on the inside, and any future changes need to take both urban and rural needs into account. What works in Brixham and Bristol may not work in Bibury or Broadway,' she proclaimed.

'A Minister for Rural Affairs,' suggested Grace, as though it were the Holy Grail.

'I think there already is one,' ventured Lucy, who clearly

had more time to read the newspaper than anyone else in the room. 'But they cover the environment and farming and food – it's a really wide brief.'

'Jack of all trades and master of none?' suggested Dan.

'Minister for Rural Health then,' countered Grace, unde-terred. 'Or even consultant. Obviously we won't get what we want, but we can raise the level of debate in this country at the very least. It's not just the South West either. Think about the Lake District or Norfolk or Northumberland. This has to directly affect a huge proportion of the population.'

'About twenty per cent,' said Lucy. 'Give or take.'

'How do you know all this stuff?' asked Grace curiously.

'I don't know. The news. The internet. Teddy at The Kingsley Arms,' Lucy replied.

'What are we going to do then?' asked Chris, clearly blown away by the strength of reaction his plea for help had elicited.

'We are going to kick arse,' said Holly with feeling. She swiped the mascara away from her lashes and looked over at Taffy for his support. 'For once, we're going to present a united front for rural England and shout loudest.'

Chapter 45

This wasn't exactly how Holly had foreseen the first day of married life panning out, she thought later that morning. It was hardly romantic to be hiding out in her consulting rooms, breathing deeply and trying to take her own blood pressure so as not to cause alarm unnecessarily. She looked at the reading again: 149/100.

Not horrific, but hardly ideal.

If she were any of her pregnant patients, she'd be giving them a pretty stern lecture about taking things easy about now.

It was the headache that had tipped her off. Sure she was tired and emotional, her feet a bit swollen and puffy, but it was always going to be a difficult balancing act working whilst pregnant, even without the constant spectre of another bout of pre-eclampsia on her radar. It was obviously good news that there was no protein in her wee. Once that happened, all bets were off.

As she knew only too well.

If she wanted to avoid a repeat performance, she was going to have to be fairly ruthless with herself.

Taffy poked his head around the door with unerring timing. 'You okay in here, Mrs J?' The concern was etched on his face and when he saw the blood pressure cuff on her arm, his eyes flashed with alarm. 'And?'

'149 over 100,' Holly said with a shrug. 'No protein. Just a horrid headache and mungo feet.'

'Bed,' he said firmly, with no hint of negotiation or newlywed flirtatiousness. Again, hardly the ideal honeymoon scenario. He picked up her handbag, grimacing with surprise as he realised just how much it weighed. 'Jesus Christ, woman! What have you got in here? You'll give yourself a hernia to boot.'

There was no point explaining to Taffy all the 'just in case' crap that she lugged around on a daily basis. In a few months' time, he'd discover that for himself, once these little muppets made their entrance into the world; travelling light would no longer be an option. She sighed, as the thought occurred to her that, unless she was very careful, there was every chance that her autumn babies might be making an early appearance.

'Can you get my clinic covered?' she asked.

'No problem,' he replied easily. 'We'll get things squared away between the three of us. If you don't mind me coming back here and leaving you to Elsie's ministrations? Maybe Lizzie could pop by and keep you company.' He grinned and kissed her tenderly, clearly unwilling to relinquish her care to anyone else. 'I'll have to have firm words with those two, though. Doctor's orders: no more excitement for you today, my love.'

She attempted a smile, but it never reached her eyes. The disappointment felt like a thump in the ribs – putting aside how she had envisaged her first day as Holly Jones (even if she had every intention of keeping her maiden name), there was so much to be done here.

Thank God Grace had chosen this particular day to come back to work, as the wheels had been due to fall off the wagon

any day now. Thank God her new husband was so understanding and flexible, taking everything in his stride.

Back at Elsie's, Holly felt as though she had stumbled into
the Twilight Zone. Elsie on one sofa, a neat little cashmere
blanket tucked over her legs, and Lizzie on the other, with
Eric draped across her lap. They were nibbling on leftover
goodies from the wedding and appeared to be glued to
Antiques Roadshow.

'Oh, just look at his smug little face,' said Elsie in disgust.
'You just know he's convinced it's worth a fortune.'

'Maybe he'll drop it,' suggested Lizzie, cramming an entire
mini tartlet into her mouth at once. 'I love it when they
drop things.'

'So this is what you two get up to on a Monday morning?' said Holly with a smile. She scooched Eric over a bit
and gratefully sank into the sofa with a groan. The relief of
being off her swollen feet while the weather was so warm
was untold.

'Of course,' said Elsie with a grin. 'It's no fun watching it
on your own, so I record it and we watch it together.'

'It's part of our start-the-week-right routine,' Lizzie
seconded. 'Everybody else is off at work being useful and
sociable.' She frowned for a moment. 'Speaking of which?'
She looked at Holly pointedly. 'Why aren't you off saving
the world today?'

Holly blushed. There'd been no point in ushering Taffy
away before he could tell on her, apparently. 'Blood pressure's
a bit high. Might need to put my feet up for a bit.'

'Well, the more the merrier, I say,' said Elsie, her voice bright
and chirpy, but her gaze sweeping over Holly in concern. 'Tell
me, darling, were your feet always so bloody enormous?'

They all stared at Holly's feet, resting on Elsie's velvet pouffe in her favourite flip-flops. To Holly's eye, they were only marginally swollen.

'Oh, she's always had the most humongous feet,' Lizzie said dismissively. 'At uni, one of her boyfriends actually broke up with her because of them. Said he couldn't sleep with them poking up at the end of the bed like little bald meerkats.'

'Oh my God,' said Holly. 'I'd forgotten about Steve. He was such a wanker. Wonder what he's doing now?'

'Oh you'll love this,' said Lizzie. 'He's a chiropodist. Big ugly feet, all day, every day. Couldn't have happened to a nicer chap.'

Holly snorted with laughter and was immediately shushed by Elsie, who rudely turned up the volume even louder to drown them out. Lizzie leaned over. 'Very strict viewing rules for this. No idle chit-chat. You can talk about antiques, take the piss out of the punters, but no gossiping.'

Elsie shushed them again, rolling her eyes. 'Look, it's that lovely ceramics guy. I wouldn't kick him out of bed,' she said with feeling.

'You definitely shouldn't,' said Holly. 'He'd probably break a hip. Just look at those joints on his hands. Rheumatoid arthritis is a nasty bugger.'

Elsie glared at her. 'Do you find me discussing the physical shortcomings of your TV crushes? No, you do not. Now be quiet and watch.'

They all stared at the screen, mindlessly snacking and cheering when an underdog was occasionally surprised with good news about the value of their tea set, or booing when superior limelight-seekers had their fortune confirmed.

'Six figures for a trinket! A bloody ugly trinket at that!' Lizzie said in amazement.

'I rather like it actually,' countered Elsie. 'It was very in vogue in the Sixties. I think Jackie O used to collect them for her dressing table.'

'I've got Lego and Transformers on mine,' said Holly dolefully, long since having given up on finding any valuable items lurking in her own cupboards.

Elsie just frowned. 'I had no idea these things were still in fashion; there's probably one or two kicking around upstairs,' she said airily. 'Remind me to go and look, won't you, darlings?'

The door to the sitting room swung open abruptly and a flurry of yapping ensued as Noodle and Doodle barged in ahead of a very flustered Grace. 'Well, thank God you're all okay. Didn't you hear me knocking?' she demanded, giving the residents of the room a quick visual once-over and her shoulders dropping in relief at finding them all in relative good health.

Elsie guiltily turned the volume down on the TV, bringing it back from deafening to just plain blaring. Grace reached over and plucked the remote from her fingers. 'Dan sent me over. You're going to want to see this,' she said firmly, as Elsie remonstrated.

The morning news was running on a loop and as the newsreader in question wound up a review of the money markets, Holly, Elsie and Lizzie all turned to her questioningly.

'Just wait,' cautioned Grace, as she adjusted the volume to human level and slid down into one of the winged armchairs.

Suddenly the screen was filled with the distraught face of Connor Danes, his eyes puffy and sore from crying. 'If I can prevent this happening to just one other family,' he croaked, 'then it's worth having the conversation, isn't it?'

'Is that—?' began Holly.

'It's Connor – plays guitar for The Hive,' said Lizzie. 'We know him. What the hell's happened?'

They all sat motionless as the poor guy poured his heart out to the journalist in front of him. Every now and then, his voice would break and he would stifle a sob, but it was clear that he was grimly determined to have his say. The news ribbon streamed across the bottom of the screen: 'Hit guitarist for rock phenomenon The Hive loses wife and unborn daughter.'

'Was it a car crash?' asked Holly, unable to follow his rambling train of thought.

Grace shook her head. 'They live in the middle of nowhere and—'

'They bought that massive country estate on the Dorset border, do you remember?' interrupted Lizzie. 'Just stunning. Worth millions.'

'Well, that just goes to prove that all the money in the world can't buy you happiness,' said Grace sadly. 'It seems she had some complications with a premature labour. They'd been banking on the maternity unit in Shaftesbury nearby, but it closed overnight, no warning. They had no idea. And then, there were no viable alternatives locally and there was no time to get her to the regional hospital.'

'No Air Ambulance?' Elsie frowned.

'Several casualties at a hockey tournament in the next county. So no. It sounds like the perfect storm, everything that could possibly go wrong.'

'What were the complications?' asked Holly, her hands cradling her bump with extra-special care.

'The earlier report cited lots of bleeding. Now they're saying placental abruption, but I guess they won't know for sure until the autopsy.' Grace shook her head in disbelief.

'Connor Danes, you know. You kind of assume that people like that are immune to tragedy.'

Holly swallowed hard. This was horrific news at the best of times. Hearing it whilst pregnant with twins certainly made you think.

Her head shot up in surprise, as Connor went on to echo her earlier sentiment from their strategy meeting, almost word for word: 'What's it going to take,' he pleaded, 'for the authorities to realise that rural lives count too? To stop playing fast and loose with our families, with our loved ones? Can't they see that the decisions they're making in a London office are causing fatalities? My wife, my baby – they didn't need to die. Is it really too much to ask for a maternity service that works or more than one Air Ambulance to be on duty?

'I am *not* going to let this drop. I'm not letting their deaths be in vain. I am coming for you, Westminster, and things are going to change.' He stared straight into the camera lens, his eyes hollow with grief and pain. 'Fame isn't worth a thing when you lose your family, but my God am I going to use it now.'

The news report flicked back to yet another bombing in the Middle East and Holly felt the tears coursing down her cheeks. She looked up to find that she wasn't alone. Even Elsie was sobbing quietly into a lace-edged handkerchief. 'That poor, poor man,' she managed.

Holly swallowed down a wave of nausea and fear. There but for the grace of God. Logically, she knew that unless a severe placental abruption actually happened in hospital, in easy reach of an operating theatre, the chances of mother and child surviving might be slim. But emotionally? To the world he might be Connor Danes, world-famous musician, but to Holly right then, he was a grieving husband and father before all else. 'We should send him a letter of support,' she suggested. 'Some flowers or something.'

'I'll phone him later,' Lizzie said quietly, obviously in shock. 'It looks like he's got his hands full this morning. Poor Con. I just can't believe this has happened. I mean Rachel can only have been mid-thirties – that's not high-risk, is it?'

'So, when you said you knew him?' Holly clarified.

'He went to school with Will. Did I never mention it?' Lizzie looked confused.

'Er, no,' said Holly. 'I think I might have remembered that.'

Lizzie shrugged apologetically. 'He's such a nice guy. Really into bees and honey and stuff. That's why they bought the farm.' She paused. 'You know he has, like, twenty million followers on Twitter? He's Big-Time.' She flicked open her phone and tapped at the screen. 'Oh!' she said in surprise.

Holding up the screen she showed the others his pinned tweet: a beautiful photograph of his pregnant wife and a single line of text:

#RuralLivesCount

Holly blinked hard. It always felt that their issues and struggles in Larkford happened in isolation; that no matter how hard they fought to keep their way of life and their healthcare provision, they were essentially David fighting Goliath.

This time, for the first time, their own battles felt like a part of something bigger than themselves. Connor Danes was the public face of the problems they were dealing with now, whether he liked it or not. But why did it always take such heartbreaking tragedies to act as a wake-up call, Holly wondered.

'That poor man,' she murmured again, as she gently rubbed her pregnant belly and tried to ignore the nibbles of fear in her subconscious.

Chapter 46

Alice stepped through her front door that evening and was struck yet again by the phenomenal changes that she and Grace had wrought together over the last few days. Softly, softly, they had tirelessly worked from room to room, and now the only vestiges of her previously tangled life were the garments on the hanging rail ready to be photographed for her pop-up boutique, Vintage by Alice.

Books were now measured by shelving-mile rather than heaps; the kitchen table was completely clear, bar a stunning jasmine loop; and there was even space on the mantelpiece for any opportune invitations to take pride of place. In short, it had been nothing less than a miracle, and the local charity shop had been thrilled by her donations, not even baulking as their storeroom quickly filled to capacity. It was quite some gesture on their part to agree that all proceeds should go to the Auction Fund, but it certainly had made Alice's keep/lose decisions somewhat easier.

Bumping into Elsie as she'd made yet another donation run last week had been perfect serendipity. Not only had Elsie immediately snapped up two of her Hermès scarves on the spot, but she'd been seemingly thrilled by Alice's resolve to change. Alice could still almost feel Elsie's firm grasp on her shoulders, as she'd looked into her eyes with affection and determination: 'This is only the beginning for you, Alice,' she'd said. 'One of the greatest skills you will ever need is how to edit. You might be starting with your wardrobe, and your bookshelf, but soon it will be your thoughts and your beliefs – master this, my love, won't you? It will honestly change your life for the better. Make it yours – authentically.'

Alice stared at the Post-it on the fridge where she'd hurriedly scribbled this sage advice for future reference. It was so on point, it spoke to her on a deeply personal level. Indeed, it almost echoed Grace's response when they'd talked in the park about relationships. Maybe a little editing of her personal beliefs should be next on her list, she realised.

She looked around, throwing open a window to allow the evening breeze to lift the air in the room. There was only one thing missing, she thought, hesitating, her eyes flicking to the Post-it yet again.

She sank down onto her knees and Coco immediately nuzzled against her, always up for a hug and a tickle. 'What do you think, Coco? Are we ready for this?'

Coco's only reply was the rhythmic thumping of her tail against the floorboards. Alice scruffed her ears adoringly – her relationship with Coco had only deepened through all these months of insecurity. Knowing that they had a plan in place, however tentative, meant that Alice had actually slept this weekend, for the first time in years. Despite all the drama at the wedding, she had come home and slept for eight hours straight.

It was nothing short of revelatory.

And she had Grace and Jamie to thank for that – allowing herself to be vulnerable had been one of the hardest things she had ever asked of herself, and yet look at the rewards. For the first time, she was beginning to feel as though her life was authentically hers, to do with as she pleased—

The chirruping of a Skype call echoed throughout the room – echoed! who knew? – and Alice leapt up to answer. 'Tilly!' she cried. 'You're never going to believe this—' Picking up her iPad, she turned the screen around and gave her friend the full guided tour. Even from the other side of the planet, Tilly's gasps of impressed surprise were voluble and heartfelt.

Alice sank down into the sofa cushions and turned the iPad again, so that her own face, and Coco's as she lay on her chest, filled the tiny square window in the corner. Alice's eyes flickered down to her own image, realising with a jolt what looked so different – well, firstly it was daylight, obviously, but also she looked happy. No, not just happy – content, maybe?

Tilly on the other hand looked utterly drained and bedraggled. 'I am beyond impressed, Walker,' she said with feeling, even as some kind of tropical storm clearly whooped and hollered outside her cabin. 'You actually did it? I was beginning to think I would have to tunnel you out on my next visit!'

'It wasn't that bad!' Alice protested, even as some small part of her brain acknowledged that, in reality, that had been exactly where she had been heading.

'Who knew you could stage an intervention over Skype!' teased Tilly. 'But seriously – does the silly smile on your face mean this is actually just the beginning? Are you in danger of letting people into your life, as well as your wardrobe?'

Her friend's unerring knack to see straight through her was both a blessing and a curse, Alice had long since decided. 'Maybe,' she hedged. 'We have a plan for Coco too – best of both worlds and nobody loses out. It's like a lifeline really.'

'We?' said Tilly casually, focusing in with infallible accuracy on the crux of the issue.

Alice felt her cheeks burn with a sudden intensity. 'We,' she replied with a smile. 'I was actually just working up the courage to call him. Ask him over. Maybe drink some wine—'

'Wow!' said Tilly with feeling, clearly a little blindsided that her teasing was in fact bang on the money. She paused, unusually hesitant. 'So you really are getting your life on track? Kudos, Walker.' She sighed. 'You know, that means I'm all out of excuses.' The wooden door to her cabin swung open and slammed closed again in the storm.

'What do you mean?' Alice asked, squinting at the screen to try and gauge her friend's oddly reticent mood.

'Haven't you noticed?' Tilly asked. 'We're the last men standing, you and I. All our friends from med school are consultants or surgeons in training. You were my justification, Al. I'm not sure how much longer I can flit around the globe and call it a career choice – it somehow feels more like stalling now, don't you think?'

Alice nodded, knowing exactly what she meant. When you didn't know the right choice to make, sometimes making no choice at all felt like the only option. As she'd realised to her cost.

'But how have you been advising me all this time—?' Alice ventured.

Tilly laughed out loud. 'It's always easier to tell other people what to do for the best, or hadn't you noticed?'

'Oh well, in that case—' Alice grinned. 'It has to be my turn, yes?' She rubbed her hands together in mock glee that, after all their years of friendship, the boot was finally on the other foot.

Tilly shook her head. 'You have to pick your moments, Alice. You can't drop a truth bomb on me when I'm in the middle of a tropical storm,' she protested. The signal flickered as though to endorse her message. 'I've got to go. Call Jamie. You know you want to.' Tilly blew her a kiss and the screen went to black.

Jamie, it seemed, had needed little encouragement to hop in the car on the promise of a home-cooked meal. He'd sounded, Alice decided, almost chuffed to hear from her, jumping on her suggestion that they celebrate Coco's future and their cunning plan.

He arrived with a bottle of Prosecco, wearing a clean t-shirt proclaiming that the more people he met, the more he liked his dog. It was almost ironic that Jamie was currently without a dog at home, given his unabashed adoration for the species. He kissed Alice lightly on both cheeks, his eyes widening as he took in her newly streamlined sitting room. Obviously he'd never been upstairs where the true revolution had occurred, but even down here it was a noticeable transformation. 'You've been busy,' he said, ever the master of understatement.

She smiled. 'Well, with all the fundraising going on around here, a few donations seemed like the very least I could do.' She paused, wondering why she continued to hide the reality of the situation. 'Grace helped me through it,' she said, making it very clear that stacking books and boxes had actually been the least of Grace's contribution. 'And you did too, in a way. I could never have even considered it before, while I was still stressing about Coco's future.'

'And do you like it?' Jamie asked, intrigued. 'Or do you keep looking for things you no longer own?'

Alice shrugged. 'I'm – I mean, *it's* a work in progress, I think.' Her Freudian slip made them both smile.

Jamie held up the bottle. 'Have you still got glasses at least? It's already cold.' He followed Alice through to the kitchen and deftly twisted the cork free. 'We have quite a few things to celebrate tonight, then?'

He raised a glass, Alice mirroring his actions. 'Here's to your house, to Coco ticking both boxes and,' he hesitated, 'to my possible promotion.'

They clinked glasses and drank. 'Wow,' said Alice. 'A promotion? Have they finally worked out that you're too skilled to be wasted on mere mortals like me?'

Jamie looked uncomfortable for a moment. 'Something like that. I think, more realistically, Judith is getting her own back for me meddling in Coco's business.'

'By rewarding you with a lovely juicy promotion?' Alice clarified, unable to follow his logic.

'Well therein lies the rub,' said Jamie, watching her reaction carefully. 'It's in Ireland. The new job. So whilst it's a wonderful offer, I'm still not sure I should take it,' he said quietly. 'After all, I have a wonderful life here in the Cotswolds. But this would be a huge promotion. Head of Region over there is basically the same as National Co-ordinator. But then I think about everything I'd be leaving behind . . .'

Alice blinked hard, a wave of nausea hitting the back of her throat with the Prosecco bubbles. Words just wouldn't come; she simply stared at him as her mind swooped and slipped. All the things she'd wanted to say to Jamie this evening now suddenly irrelevant.

'So that's it? You're leaving?' she whispered eventually in disbelief.

'I only said I'd been offered a job in Ireland,' said Jamie uncomfortably. 'The key word being *offered*. I truly haven't decided what to do yet.'

'Well you wouldn't have mentioned it, if it wasn't at least an option,' Alice said, shocked by the petulant tone that had crept into her voice. But at least it proved her right, if that was any consolation.

Men left.

It had ever been thus.

She knew the stats only too well, had witnessed them throughout her extended family. When the going got tough, particularly with incurable illnesses, the men got going. And who could blame them really?

She stared across her kitchen at Jamie, an incredible pressure in her chest. The distance between them had never seemed greater. All his work to help her find a solution? She'd read so much into his actions . . .

She could only be grateful that she hadn't made a complete fool of herself over him. Feeling was one thing; doing was another proposition entirely. Imagine how much worse this would feel then?

At least this way, it was only Coco she need concern herself with.

'I don't know how you can,' she said, with tight control. 'All this talk of supporting Coco. All those promises of working with me to find a middle ground. It was all bullshit then? You're not going to help at all; you're going to leave.'

Jamie had the decency to blush, stammering out his response in the face of her obvious pain and distrust. 'I only told you so you wouldn't hear it from Judith at the centre. And I haven't said yes – could we maybe focus on that part too?' He stepped forward to take Alice's hand as he had a million times before, the hurt and surprise evident on his face as she flinched.

'Look, Alice, let's sit down and talk about this,' he suggested.

She walked through to the sitting room and sank into an armchair and Coco automatically curled in beside her, fitting her silken body into whatever space was available, allowing her to be as close as possible. 'It doesn't sound like there's much to talk about.'

Jamie folded himself onto the end of her tiny, knackered sofa and leaned forward. 'We're not a couple, Al,' he said gently. 'We work together with Coco and you've made it perfectly clear that's where your interest ends. But it's hard, you know. Feeling the way I do and knowing it doesn't make any difference ...'

Alice frowned, her anger deflating by the moment as bewilderment filled the space it vacated. 'What do you mean?'

His eyebrows shot into his hairline. 'You have to be kidding me?'

She shook her head, eyes wide with confusion and mistrust.

He moved over to kneel down beside her armchair, their faces level and inches apart. 'Are you honestly telling me you don't know?' he asked.

Alice simply nodded.

'You don't know that I spend every minute of every day thinking about doing this—?' He leaned forward and kissed her lightly on the lips, pulling away for only a second to gauge her reaction. His fingers laced through the waves of her hair as he held her close and kissed her again.

Alice felt as though the world were shifting around her – all the confusion, the hesitation, was lost in that one perfect moment. It was a kiss like no other and she had never felt this way about anyone before, as though it was hard to say where she ended and he began; their connection in their embrace was absolute.

He was the first to pull away but he stayed, resting his forehead against Alice's as their breathing slowly returned to normal. 'Please,' he murmured, 'tell me you've been dreaming about that too.'

Alice held his gaze, noticing the tiny flecks of yellow in his navy blue eyes, and her own tousled reflection in his dilated pupils. She slid one hand up under his t-shirt, his breath instantly coming faster under her touch. 'Amongst other things,' she said playfully, as she pulled him towards her and kissed him once more, and with feeling.

As they lay tumbled together on the sofa afterwards, Alice realised that she felt none of the customary awkwardness or inhibition. She wasn't counting down the minutes until she, or he, could leave, or pulling on her clothes in a rush of remorse or reserve. She could happily spend the rest of the evening entwined with his semi-naked body, she realised, and still want more.

He poured the last of the Prosecco into her glass. 'I think you'll find there are some notable advantages to dating someone in your home town,' he teased her, dropping his head to kiss her fleetingly on the lips.

'Really?' she smiled. 'You might have to sell me on that one.'

'Give a man a moment,' said Jamie with a grin, as he tugged her cashmere blanket over himself. 'I mean, if I'd known tonight was a booty call, I would've carb-ed up.'

'It was *not* a booty call,' Alice protested, laughing as he tickled her under the blanket. Coco had very wisely made herself scarce ages ago and even Alice's shrieks and giggles didn't bring her running as they normally would.

'Potato, pot-ah-to,' said Jamie, stroking her inner thigh in a most distracting way. 'You just called me over to seduce me, you can tell me—'

Alice shook her head. 'I wanted to thank you, you daft eejit. For helping me see that my choices were *my* choices, if that makes sense?'

Jamie raised one eyebrow. 'Are you telling me that Grace received similar appreciation?'

Alice threw a cushion at him. 'Don't be a pain. You know what I mean. Besides, you were the one on your knees proclaiming your affections, if you recall, Mr Yardley?'

His hand was moving ever higher up her thigh and Alice was finding it increasingly hard to keep a handle on their teasing conversation. 'I still can't believe you didn't know how I felt,' Jamie said incredulously. 'I mean, do you think I spend this much time with *all* my clients?'

Alice shook her head. 'Maybe?' She paused, as the spectre of Jamie's potential promotion intruded into her thoughts. 'Will you take the job?' she asked tentatively.

'Persuade me to stay, Alice,' Jamie whispered, pulling her into his arms, his words warm on her skin. 'You only have to say the word and I'm not going anywhere.'

For a moment, Alice felt a flicker of panic. She hated being put on the spot; the very idea that he would be staying only for her.

But she hated the idea of him leaving even more. The answer came to her quickly - simple and heartfelt.

Her new life was all about authenticity, she realised; allowing herself to be vulnerable and to ask for what she wanted, to aim for her heart's desire.

Back to basics.

Her dog, Jamie and the elusive capsule wardrobe.

The rest would simply have to go.

'Don't leave,' she said with feeling, as she tossed the blanket aside. Never more vulnerable or more honest than in that moment.

'I'm not going anywhere,' he replied.

Chapter 47

'Breakfast in bed?' Taffy suggested, as he rolled over and stretched.

Holly snuggled down deeper under the duvet, refusing to budge, or frankly even admit that it was morning. 'Married two days and already so misguided,' she yawned happily. 'You know the rules – if you want breakfast in bed, sleep in the kitchen.'

He reached under the duvet and tickled her gently. 'I was offering, Mrs Jones, not asking.' He leaned forward and kissed the tousled top of her hair, the only part on show under the pile of bedding.

Her head popped up like a drowsy meerkat. 'Oh well, in that case—' she said with a grin. She cuddled in beside him, tugging his arm around her. 'But don't go anywhere just yet ... I'm calling a micro-honeymoon this morning.'

'Oh really,' said Taffy with delight, 'and what exactly might that involve?'

Holly smiled contentedly. 'You can watch me sleep and think about how lucky you are ...' she offered, waiting for him to protest, but as his hand came round to rest on her bump, there was no protest forthcoming. Instead, Taffy murmured sweet nothings, not to her, but to his children, who kicked and moved at the sound of his voice.

'I rather like being married to you,' Taffy said after a moment. 'Nothing's really changed, yet everything has – if that makes sense?'

Holly nodded. 'We're on the same song sheet. Shared agenda.' She kissed him gently. 'And don't tell Elsie, but she was absolutely right: there is something rather lovely about being married before these babies arrive. I never knew I was quite so old-fashioned.'

'Does that mean you're going to take my name after all?' Taffy asked, having received quite some considerable pressure on this point from his mother.

Holly shrugged. 'I don't know. We can't all have different surnames, now can we?'

'Graham-Jones?' he suggested. 'Although to be fair it's a bit posh and nobby.'

'Is that a technical term, Dr Graham-Jones?' Holly teased him, more fully awake now and savouring these few quiet moments together. Even as her hand slid along the muscles in his back, tiptoeing along the waistband of his pyjama trousers, she knew it was too good to last.

'Morning!' cried the twins, as the bedroom door flew open abruptly. 'We made breakfast!' Ben bit his lip in concentration as he carried two mugs of coffee, which slopped alarmingly with every step. As he got closer, Holly could see the coffee granules floating undissolved on what was clearly cold water. Tom bore two bowls of Rice Krispies with no milk and two spoons in his pyjama top pocket.

Offloading their treasures, Holly and Taffy managed yummy noises for long enough to take one or two cold, disgusting mouthfuls, before admitting defeat and pulling the twins into a duvet cuddle. There was nothing they liked more than an impromptu camping game. Elsie knocked tentatively on the doorframe. 'Sorry to interrupt your feast, but I wondered if I had any takers for pancakes?'

The twins were off the bed and hurtling down the stairs in seconds. Elsie grinned. 'They've been up since five plotting that little surprise.'

'Oh God, Elsie, you must be exhausted,' said Taffy guiltily, pulling on a t-shirt and walking over to relieve her of child-watching duties.

Elsie shook her head. 'It's been heavenly actually, having a little company first thing. I'm up with the lark every day now—' She looked oddly wistful and, as she and Taffy made their way downstairs to ration the volume of syrup feasibly allowed, Holly began to wonder if there was something Elsie wasn't telling her.

That feeling was only compounded by the scene Holly walked into in the kitchen: Elsie at the Aga, her silk dressing gown billowing around her, singing into the spatula as the heart-shaped pancakes cooked on the hotplate and the boys cheered her artistry. Elsie was luminous, her eyes shining and her smile wide. She looked brighter than she had in months.

'There you are, darling. There's some camomile tea in the pot,' said Elsie, waving the spatula towards the beautifully laid breakfast table, where Taffy was already set up with a copy of *The Times* and a fresh espresso.

'Your tea smells like wee,' Tom said in concern, still unused to his caffeine-driven mother turning down a cup of coffee. 'Elsie said so.'

Elsie shrugged. 'It's true though.'

Ben frowned. 'Was it true when you said me and Ben are more fun than old farts?' He looked quite bothered about this particular statement. 'Old farts just disappear, don't they?'

'Right again,' said Elsie with a thoughtful smile. 'They just fade away.'

'Well obviously we're better than that!' said Tom with feeling, rolling his eyes as though Elsie was stating the blindingly obvious.

Holly walked over and wrapped her arms around Elsie, pulling her into a hug. 'Second thoughts?' she asked quietly.

Elsie shook her head, 'Of course not. This is your home and you have babies to grow . . .'

'Takes a village, though, if I recall,' Holly suggested gently, keen for Elsie to have an 'out' if the idea of Sarandon Hall was cooling on her.

Elsie pulled away and expertly flipped the little Scotch pancakes. 'Well, I was thinking that I might just hold out for a garden suite. Celia Price has the prime location and I couldn't help noticing she was looking rather frail the other day . . . So, if you knew anything on that front . . .?' She looked at Holly for a reaction.

Holly just shook her head good-naturedly. 'Elsie Townsend! I am not giving you a heads-up on who is about to die next!'

Elsie shrugged easily and threw her a smile as she slid the pancakes onto the brightly coloured melamine plates that seemed to have appeared overnight. 'Never hurts to ask . . . A nudge and a wink for palliative care, okay?'

Holly was still smiling at Elsie's blatant audacity over breakfast as she flicked on her computer at The Practice and scanned her list of patients. A few frequent flyers, a couple of medication reviews – certainly nothing too taxing. She sensed Grace's hand at work there, as Holly's patient list had lightened considerably in load and intensity. It wasn't something

Holly had asked for – going part-time was inconvenient enough surely – but nevertheless she was grateful.

Amanda Lightly's name caught her eye and she ambled through to the waiting room to collect her; rushing about no longer even an option. Amanda looked positively radiant, her skin glowing with a light tan and her shoulders covered with a light smattering of freckles set off by her mint-green sundress.

'I had a letter about my Well Woman check,' Amanda said as she settled herself into a seat. 'Only feels like five minutes since I had the last one!'

Holly blushed slightly, remembering all too well how she'd offered this summons as a way to placate Amanda's worried husband. Clearly his anxieties about her having depression had been a case of misreading the signs; Amanda's lack of interest in waiting hand and foot on her chauvinistic husband hardly a cause for concern, in Holly's opinion.

'And how are you?' Holly asked, open to any variety of answers. Sometimes she got the family 'newsletter', sometimes a well-rehearsed list of symptoms and, on occasion, a terse 'fine' that told her nothing at all, except that there was probably a problem somewhere.

Amanda just smiled. 'I'm great actually. I've been running a lot and I have a new, er, friend – so that gets me out of the house.' She paused for a moment, obviously debating how much to share. 'I'm leaving Gordon. I know it sounds mad, after all these years together, but he was always at work and we rumbled along okay. But he's retired now. If I stay, I'll be in here begging for Valium in no time, or I'll be locked up for braining him—'

Holly nodded. 'Valium's never the secret to a happy marriage,' she agreed, discreetly jotting an IOU to Dan.

Amanda laughed. 'I'd forgotten what it felt like to be happy, appreciated, sexy – you know? If only you could get *that* on the NHS!'

By the time Amanda had (over)shared her change of circumstances and Holly had been amazed by the improvement in her blood pressure readings, she realised it was enough to make you stop and think. How many of her patients' health problems were actually symptoms of their life problems?

It was certainly the case with her next patient – would wonders never cease – the Major voluntarily walking into her consulting room with a sheepish expression on his face. 'Don't tell Marion I was here,' was his opening greeting.

'Wouldn't dream of it,' said Holly easily, offering him a chair.

The Major tugged at his trousers above the knees and sat down with a tiny exhalation. 'I just wanted to say thank you,' he said. 'I spoke to that lady counsellor you suggested. Have to confess, felt a right plonker doing it, but hey-ho – seems to have helped a little. I'm sleeping a bit better at least. But I wondered, well, if you could, I mean—' He spluttered uncomfortably.

'Major, would you like me to refer you for a few more sessions?' asked Holly gently.

His face bloomed with colour but he nodded his head with feeling. 'Can open, worms everywhere at the moment,' he said. 'I think I need that closed-door they're always talking about on the telly.'

'Closure?' suggested Holly, trying to second-guess him.

'That's the one,' the Major replied. 'But I've been doing my best to move forward. Every little helps, after all. I wrote a note to Jessica, you know – all above board, via her frightful parents – and she even wrote back. That's what I wanted to show you.' He tugged a postcard with a Thelwell pony on the front from his jacket pocket.

Holly scanned the disjointed handwriting, trying to decode Jessica's words. She didn't like to tell the Major that the unnatural breaks between letters and the size distortions were not typical of a child her age, but rather a sign that all was still not completely well after Jessica's traumatic brain injury.

She looked up in surprise. 'She wants to help with the auction?' she queried.

The Major nodded. 'I thought it might make her feel better to know that we weren't just sitting on our hands around here, that we were actually doing something. And now she wants to come along, offer her support.' He sounded a little choked up. 'She sounds like a real trouper. She really enjoyed that little outing to the Flower Festival, apparently. Her friends all persuaded her to come along and join in. That's why she wants to help at the auction, I reckon.'

Holly nodded – brave didn't even come close, to want to be out and about in public so soon after being released from hospital, not to mention when there would undoubtedly be journalists at every turn.

'Have you spoken to Lavinia about this?' Holly asked. 'I can't imagine for a moment that she'd be keen.'

'Ah, well,' the Major dissembled. 'That's rather where I was hoping you might come in.'

'Oh Major,' said Holly in dismay. 'I'm not sure I have the diplomacy skills for that one.'

He nodded understandingly, tucking the postcard carefully back into his pocket. 'I'm not sure anybody does.'

'Well then,' said Holly after a moment's reflection, 'how about a team effort? And a simple task to give Jess a sense of involvement without too much pressure.'

'You read my mind,' said the Major happily.

As he left the room, Holly's mobile bleeped and she slipped outside to take the call. 'Harry!' she said in greeting. 'You keep dropping off the radar and scaring everyone. This is not the time to leave us high and dry.' There was a hint of chastisement in her tone – after all, hadn't Harry volunteered to be their man, only to disappear yet again?

'Understood,' he said, 'but I think you'll be pleased when you hear what I've been up to.' He reeled off the names of three leading medical journalists, big hitters with a huge sphere of influence, and the professional surety not to worry about taking a risk. 'Anyone up for a series of interviews, coverage of the auction, online debate?' he asked casually, knowing that he was basically delivering the Holy Grail of medical media coverage in one fell swoop.

In line with Holly's plan to be the ones shouting loudest, Harry had basically just handed her a proverbial megaphone.

'You star!' Holly exclaimed, swallowing down her guilt at her rather terse greeting.

'I haven't finished yet,' Harry continued. 'I've got Professor Daniel Carlisle and Thomas Ulrahbi on standby to speak out. Both of them are incensed by these cuts and they're leaders in their field – they're both happy to bring a buttload of credibility to our cause.'

Holly laughed at his irreverent turns of phrase, but Harry had a point: a lead consultant in Obstetrics and another from Emergency Medicine on their side? It was a true shot in the arm to their campaign.

'Grace and I have been phoning around other rural trusts,' Holly told him. 'When we're ready to go public, we'll co-ordinate our efforts.'

'I notice that rock star chappy was trending on Twitter,'

Harry said, his tone suddenly more serious. 'It's one hell of a hashtag, but at what price? Poor sod.'

Holly nodded, before realising that Harry couldn't see her. 'The really sad thing is, you know he's not the only one in that situation. He's just the only one that social media know about.'

'Well, we're going to change all that, aren't we, Holly?' said Harry with feeling. 'Never misjudge a pissed-off medic, eh?'

'Or a pregnant woman,' Holly added.

'Well then, you're a double threat right now. I'll see you at the auction.' He hung up decisively and Holly stared across the Market Place, distracted by the enormity of what they were trying to achieve. Had they overreached, she wondered. They were doctors, not PR consultants or political activists, after all. No matter how much it felt as though those three roles ran concurrently these days.

She blinked as the sound of hooves echoed around the square, trying to find the source of the noise. It was a moment or two before she could name the emotions that assailed her.

The sight of Charlotte Lansing back on a horse was all the testament Holly needed to their own particular brand of care. Caring that surpassed the professional and fed out into the community at large. Charlotte, her arm still in a sling and with Rupert on foot with a lead-rope beside her, looked ecstatic nevertheless. Small steps, huge challenges, a world of difference to the rest of her life – simply by feeling supported, understood and by refusing to give up.

It was a timely reminder they would all do well to consider over the next few days, Holly decided, with an emotional sniff.

Chapter 48

The following afternoon, Holly waved the Preggie Pro-testers off with a smile, and a certain amount of relief. Mims hung back for a moment, Baby Hallow – as yet unnamed – in a papoose on her chest. Elsie's kitchen had apparently become the unofficial HQ for the Preggie Protesters, even though both Mims and Emily Arden now had babes in arms.

'Bloody hell, that's a lot of hormones in one room!' exclaimed Mims with feeling. 'Are we sure this is a good idea?'

Holly laughed, the exact same thought having occurred to her an hour earlier when they'd all turned up on her doorstep. 'Well, there's no harm in a bit of solidarity, is there? So long as nobody eats the last Hobnob, I'm good!' Holly's hunger appeared to have ramped up exponentially and it seemed improbable that her bump could actually accommodate two babies growing at this rate for long.

'I quite like that we still get to make a contribution, though,' Holly continued. 'When Cormack said I had to cut back my hours at The Practice, it seemed such a sensible solution, but I'm seriously missing the interaction already.'

Okay, so she was massively playing down her overly emo-tional reaction to this plan. Since Grace had found another gear of determination and Chris had thrown all caution to the winds, there was no shortage of ammunition accruing; if only they knew what to do with it for best effect. Being at home, even for half of each day, felt like the train was leaving the station without her.

But Cormack O'Brien had been firm and no-nonsense with his patient – unless Holly wanted to invite another episode of pre-eclampsia, she was sidelined for this one, at least in theory.

Mims nodded. 'I get that. But it's also good to have a little nesting time. New house; new beginnings. When are you moving in properly?'

It was a simple enough question and one that Holly should have been able to answer, but there was a wealth of confusion behind it. She'd been secretly glad that the paperwork for Sarandon Hall was taking such an age; the prospect of living in Elsie's house without Elsie already felt slightly weird. The fact that Elsie had pinned the legal trans-fer of deeds to Holly's headboard the night before had really brought home the magnitude of Elsie's gift. No matter how often she looked at it, though, Number 42 would for ever be Elsie's in Holly's mind.

It wasn't a conversation she could really have with Jemima Hallow, however.

'Soon,' she dodged with a smile. 'Probably after all this auction business is over and done with.' Mims was a lovely friend, a baby friend, and Holly hoped that their friendship would go from strength to strength, but right now she was a new friend. And what Holly needed was wise counsel from someone in the know.

Baby Hallow kicked it up a gear and Mims regretfully said goodbye.

Holly slipped her phone from her pocket, almost on auto-pilot, unwilling to spend too much time in actual thought. 'Hey, Lizzie? Fancy coming for a cuppa? I feel like a spare tit at a wedding over here.'

Lizzie's guttural laugh echoed down the line. 'Give me five or ten minutes and I'll be there. Get the kettle on. Your pad is much nicer than mine these days.'

Holly looked around her and couldn't help but agree. There was something about Elsie's house that drew people in like a magnet, and it was increasingly becoming the centre of their social circle. She could quite understand how difficult Elsie had found it when her own core alliances had shifted their attentions to Sarandon Hall; her drawing room no longer echoing with laughter, conversation and the inevitable clink of crystal glassware.

She breathed out slowly, trying to follow Cormack's advice to allow some thoughts to simply pass. Just because she thought something, apparently, didn't mean she needed to engage with it and allow herself to get worried – it was almost as though he had never met her before!

Holly duly put on the kettle and made the twins a picnic tea, wrapping their food in greaseproof paper and popping the small parcels into a tiny wicker basket. Ever since watching *Heidi*, they'd been obsessed with acting out scenes in the garden. Picnic time was their all-time favourite. Right now, though, Ben and Tom were lying on their backs as the clouds scudded past in an otherwise azure sky. Their cloud-spotting games were becoming increasingly more anatomical and Holly laughed aloud as she settled down beside them and began doling out crusty bread and slices of ham and cheese, Alpine-style. The babies shifted restlessly in her tummy, as though the sugar hit from the Toblerone she'd virtually inhaled earlier had got them dancing, and she glanced repeatedly at the side gate, poised for Lizzie's arrival.

She untangled her looping bracelet from the handle of the basket, one of the most beautiful wedding gifts she'd received, all the more so as it had been made with such loving care by Alice herself. Holly couldn't help thinking that, with creativity like that, Alice might actually be wasted as a doctor. The question as to whether her young colleague was experienced enough to step up when Holly went on maternity leave was one she didn't dare address right now, for fear of giving her blood pressure an unwelcome boost.

'Coo-ee!' called Lizzie, as she pushed open the garden gate, doing her best impression of a nutty neighbour. 'Anyone for pavlova?' She wore a Pucci-print kaftan, oversized sunglasses and supported a vast confection on the palm of her hand.

Holly burst out laughing. 'Oh you are a card! Have you been at the gin again? *Abigail's Party* eat your heart out!'

Lizzie pushed back the sunglasses and grinned. 'What d'you think? Elsie took me shopping! Too much?'

Definitely too much, but then by default, absolutely perfect, thought Holly, standing up and pulling her friend into an enormous hug.

'Steady there,' said Lizzie. 'Let a girl put down her pavlova before you start taking liberties. Now, what's the matter with you?'

Holly shook her head. 'Nothing. I just wanted to see you.'

Lizzie raised one perfectly pencilled eyebrow. 'Hmm . . .'

Eric had trotted sweetly at Lizzie's side across the garden, sitting down neatly beside her as they said their hellos, with no need for a lead or encouragement.

'Dear God, how did you do that?' Holly asked, intrigued,

as she clocked this unusual display, well used to being dragged around the town by Eric on a mission.

Lizzie grinned. 'Aha! I'm glad you noticed. Jamie took pity on me and gave him one-on-one tuition. He reckons that if I apply the same skills to Will, I'll have him picking up his pants off the floor in no time.'

'Are you high?' Holly asked, genuinely perplexed, as she broke off a chunk of pavlova without ceremony and popped it into her mouth.

Lizzie looked delighted to have found a captive audience. In fact, by the time she'd shared Jamie's pearls of wisdom about how you could train your husband in much the same way as you trained your dog, they were both laughing like drains.

'So, I just ignore any unwanted behaviour and reward him for anything good?' Holly clarified, sitting down heavily on the kitchen sofa and plonking her feet up on the ottoman, a plateful of pavlova now balanced on her bump for easy access.

'So, last night, when Will put the bins out, I offered him a beer. When he left all the plates on the dining table, I ignored it and went to have a bath. I think he might be a work in progress, though, because Eric had, er, prewashed all the plates by the time I came downstairs.'

Holly snorted, knowing only too well Eric's love of a good curry. Strange dog, but oh she did love him. She couldn't help wonder how he was going to adapt to two more pairs of tiny hands pulling at his ears and tail. As if in answer to her private concerns and feeling her gaze upon him, he trotted over and lay beside her on the sofa, resting his head on her bump, ears cocked as though he could hear little noises that were beyond the scope of her own hearing. He jolted up after a moment, shocked and surprised at the hearty boot he'd received to his chin, before curling up tightly beside her, guarding her unborn progeny.

'Well, it looks like we can just hire Eric as the nanny,' Holly joked, stroking the downy fur behind his ears.

'Have you given any thought to what you're going to do about that?' Lizzie asked. 'Nanny or locum? I'm presuming something will have to give?'

Holly nodded. 'I was thinking about it just before you got here. I'd quite like to take some decent maternity leave, actually. Make sure the boys are acclimatised to the babies before I bugger off back to work. In an ideal world I'd take six months off completely and then go back part-time.' She looked uncomfortable. 'To be honest, though, all that seems a bit "First World problems" compared to everything we're dealing with at the moment. Like oh-to-have-the-luxury, you know?'

'I do,' said Lizzie. 'And it's not as though your mum's going to fly in on her broomstick and help out, is it now?' They both snorted with laughter at the very thought.

Holly didn't like to point out to anyone but Lizzie, who had seen her through thick and thin over the years, how jealous she felt, watching the Jemimas and Emilys of her acquaintance as their hands-on and loving mothers swept in to help navigate those first few tricky weeks. Or indeed, in Jemima's case, rented a cottage down the lane for six months for the perfect combination of support and space.

'Taffy's mum has offered—' Holly began, before stopping at Lizzie's open-mouthed expression of surprise.

'You're not really considering it, are you?' Lizzie interrupted.

Holly shrugged. 'They are her grandchildren. And let's face it, I'm not really in a position to turn down a little loving support.' She waved her hand around the room. 'And we've plenty of space now. I keep hoping that maybe this way, my kids might get some grandparents who actually give a damn.'

'They're not short of loving,' scoffed Lizzie. 'They've got me and Will, Elsie has basically made them her own. And I think you gained Dan as family by default when you married the Taffster.'

'I know,' said Holly, swallowing the lump that had nestled in her throat. 'Still—'

'Still?'

'Well, it's not quite the same, is it? Spending all this time with the Preggie Protesters has stirred up a right old hornet's nest in my head. After all, if a girl can't turn to her own mum when she's raising her kids – well, it's a bloody shame, that's all.'

'For her, Holly. She's the one who's missing out. Your kids are wonderful. Honestly. And you know me – I bloody hate kids most of the time. But she's the one who's missing out. And Milo's mum too. Both of them, too selfish to look beyond the end of their own noses. If you want my opinion, you're doing a better job of building your own little family here than you realise. And, yeah, what the hell, let's get Call-me-Patty installed in the guest room for a bit, while we find you the perfect locum to keep your conscience clear.'

'That's what I need,' said Holly. 'A clear conscience. I don't want to feel like I'm letting anyone down.'

'Pshaw,' said Lizzie dismissively. 'This said by the person who spends more time thinking about what other people need than she ever does about what she needs.'

'It's a doctor thing,' Holly protested. 'Alice is exactly the same. Just look at this whole Coco debacle. She's been tearing herself into pieces for months trying to do the right thing by everyone.'

'Does she even know yet that Jamie got offered that job?' Lizzie asked, worry clouding her face. 'Will she even cope if he goes?'

'I have no idea,' said Holly simply, the Larkford rumour mill as always running at warp speed. 'But I can hardly expect her to pick up my slack if she loses Jamie and Coco at once, now can I?'

Lizzie paused, deep in thought. 'Maybe it's just sitting in her kitchen, walking a mile in her shoes so to speak, but did you ever stop to think that Elsie has the right idea, with all her meddling and interfering?'

'I'm not sure she'd call it that,' Holly protested.

'Well hear me out for a minute, yeah? It's not like either of us are in a position to go marching on Westminster, or to tell Alice what to do, but there's no reason we can't still be useful . . . A guiding hand here or there?'

'What did you have in mind?' asked Holly, intrigued.

'Just a few little phone calls,' said Lizzie innocently, her eyes lighting up with impish delight. 'What d'you say?'

Chapter 49

Grace stared at the spreadsheet in front of her later that evening. She never thought she'd be grateful to that bastard Jarley, but even she had to admit that these few weeks away from work had been an unexpected bonus – particularly if you ignored the nightmares and the incipient panic attacks that still had a horrible habit of catching her off guard.

Going back to work this week had been more of a challenge than she'd ever thought possible, and she was almost ashamed to admit that the dramas unfolding around them had been a blessing in disguise, forcing her to focus on the job in hand. Knowing that Jarley had been refused bail and was now awaiting trial on six different theft and assault charges should have made her feel safer.

It didn't.

She still felt hollow on some level she couldn't quite reach, as though she were a sponge to any negative emotion. There had been something about the naked anguish on Connor Danes's face that had touched her deeply, as his story had been picked up by every news outlet imaginable and broadcast to the nation. His willingness to be that vulnerable had stayed with her long after the TV and the internet had been switched off for the night.

She scanned down the list of auction donations, unable to put her finger on the source of disconnect. There was no shortage of treasures: paintings, ceramics, memorabilia aplenty. But it was only when she reached the listing next to Lizzie's name that the penny finally dropped.

One vintage Ralph Lauren trouser suit, limited edition, navy, barely worn.

People weren't donating the tired things they no longer wanted, she realised; they were donating beloved things of value. Each one a significant contribution to the fund financially, but perhaps more importantly an indication of how much this campaign meant to them and their families. Going to bed at night knowing that there were checks and balances in place to keep you safe if the worst should happen was, after all, practically priceless. And she obviously wasn't the only one to think so.

Noodle and Doodle were curled up tightly beside her on the sofa and the comfort from their tiny snuffling snores was immeasurable. She dropped a hand to smooth Doodle's tufty ears away from his face and he moaned and stretched in complaint. How easy it would be, she realised, to become the lady-with-the-dogs. Here she was, still living in the same house in which she had raised her boys and endured her marriage. It would be so easy to just slide into middle age . . .

She glanced at the screen again.

The Major and Marion Waverly: Coronation Waterford decanters – mint condition.

Cassie Holland: Feminist Sculpture number 4 – sculptor unknown.

It was all very well her pushing Alice towards closure on her shopping habits, but was she actually living by her own advice? She was living in a house filled with relics – her sons used their rooms to store childhood trophies, sports kit and instruments, yet rarely came home. Roy's study door was firmly closed and, whilst there was little if anything of value in there, the very idea of going through his things revolted her on some level – not so much because it would upset her to see all the reminders of the man she had so briefly loved, but more so to see how little she had truly known him.

Her own possessions were sparse. She'd never felt the need to buy more than she needed. Her china mugs and her favourite armchair were perhaps her only indulgence. Fashions came and went, and she rarely had the need for many clothes anyway. Nice yoga kit was perhaps her only vice – well that and computer kit, she conceded. Plain white china and a high-spec router, she smiled to herself. God knows, she could probably move out of this house using only her car and want for nothing.

She stopped dead. Why not? Why not take a risk?

Holly and Taffy were moving on. Alice was finally making strides in the right direction. Even her own relationship with Dan was like a breath of fresh air – unless of course they went back to his flat above the Indian restaurant, whereupon a breath of turmeric and cumin was more likely. She checked her watch; he was running late.

Doodle's head shot up and he woofed quietly as Dan pushed open the back door. They were already accustomed to his comings and goings in her life and he no longer warranted the full twenty-one-bark salute.

Grace took a deep breath, skipping hello in favour of a leap of faith. There was no time like the present.

'Let's move in together,' she said breathlessly. 'Ditch all our baggage and make a fresh start.'

He blinked, clearly not the greeting he was anticipating, having turned up half an hour late and without picking up any milk as promised. 'Okay,' he said though, barely missing a beat.

'Not here,' clarified Grace. 'Somewhere new. Somewhere that's ours.'

He walked over to the sofa and deftly scooped Doodle into his arms so there was room to sit down beside her. He grinned. 'This is going to be brilliant,' he said.

Grace laughed, this entire staccato conversation somehow managing to convey a world of emotions. 'Would you think I was mad if I got a house clearance firm in for this place? Most of it isn't worth moving.'

'You're talking to a man whose worldly possessions fit in a Land Rover,' he said easily. 'As long as you bring your amazing coffee machine, I'm good. Oh and your new fluffy towels – I've grown to appreciate a little fluffy in my life.'

Noodle licked his hand in answer, as though misinterpreting his words.

'This weekend?' Grace suggested, fidgeting happily that such a momentous decision could feel so natural and so easy.

'Sure,' Dan said. 'How would you feel about renting Holly and Taffy's old place for a bit while we work out what we're looking for? I know it's not flash, but it has a nice atmosphere, don't you think?'

'I think that has more to do with the people living in it,' Grace replied. 'It certainly didn't feel like that when the Magnificent Milo lived there.'

'True,' agreed Dan. 'But I honestly think that wherever we set up camp, it'll feel like home. Bed, sofa, fridge and we're done.'

'I'm liking your priorities there,' Grace grinned. 'Are we actually going to do this? I mean, so spontaneously. Some might even say recklessly?'

He paused. 'Okay then. Let's think this through. Do you like living here?'

'Nope,' said Grace cheerfully. 'House of horrors. Hate it.'

'So, even if we fell out over something stupid, you wouldn't move back?'

'No, I wouldn't actually,' Grace said, giving the matter proper consideration for a moment. 'I want to sell up. I want to live in a house that's bright and airy and with space to put down a yoga mat.'

'Well, for what it's worth, I travel pretty light since living with Julia. I mean, she cared enough for both of us about rugs and cushions and matching china.'

'Dan,' said Grace, her tone serious for a moment, 'I think you should know that none of my china matches. My bras don't match my knickers and I always forget to go shopping until there are tumbleweeds rolling through an empty fridge. I am not a domestic goddess.' She wobbled for a moment, wondering whether this was news to him.

'Well thank God for that,' he said with feeling. 'Life's too short to worry about that kind of bollocks. We need to focus on the important stuff: Radio 2 or Radio 4? Early bird or night owl? Which side of the bed do you like to sleep on?'

Grace grinned. 'Radio Larkford, permanently exhausted pigeon, wherever there's space beside you.'

'Aw,' teased Dan. 'I didn't know you could be all soppy.'

'Er, hello?' Grace replied, shaking her head and gesticulating towards the two sleeping dachshunds. 'Soppy is my new middle name.'

'And would you like a new surname to go with your new address?' Dan asked quietly, watching her for a reaction. Being widowed was one thing, giving up your name afterwards might be a step too far.

'Wing it?' she replied, leaning in to kiss him and leaving him in no doubt that her lack of haste in accepting his offer, however oblique, had absolutely nothing to do with the depth of her feelings for him.

It felt somewhat adolescent but frankly Grace didn't care. This didn't feel like 'news' until she'd shared her spontaneous leap of faith with someone and, surprisingly, the person who sprang immediately to mind had been Alice.

After years of living at a remove from those around her, Grace couldn't help but feel that the last twelve months had brought her metaphorical riches beyond measure. It was as though, by opening up a little to the possibility of another meaningful relationship in her life, she had inadvertently ended up feeling loved and supported on so many levels.

She certainly didn't feel like a mother to Alice, but there were elements of the 'big sister' about their friendship, not to mention the emotional trials and tribulations of tackling Alice's godawful house, that had thrown them together and strengthened their bond.

She banged on the front door again and fidgeted impatiently. 'Alice!' she called through the letterbox. 'It's me!'

Grace could hear a flurry of activity behind the drawn curtains and worried for a moment that Alice was still cataloguing boxes at this hour of the evening.

Her worries disappeared as soon as Alice – a very tousled and flushed Alice – opened the door a notch. 'Hey,' she said easily. 'How lovely to see you – give me a sec.' And the door closed firmly in her face only to reopen again moments later.

'Hi, Jamie,' said Grace simply, unable to disguise the grin on her face. 'I'm so sorry to interrupt.'

'No, no, it's fine. I mean you're not interrupting. We were just talking about the – you know the . . .' Jamie managed succinctly.

Grace shook her head. 'Oh Jamie. I have two teenage sons. Do you honestly think I'm that naïve?' She grinned. 'So, I take it from all the flustering that I'm not supposed to know about this then?'

Alice blushed deeply. 'We weren't keeping anything a secret. It's all very new—'

It was Grace's turn to look discomfited. 'Oh dear God, throw me out immediately. I can't believe you even answered the door!'

'Well,' said Jamie awkwardly, 'you *were* quite insistent.'

Alice laughed and swatted him with her hand. 'Be nice. Relationships 101 – you have to win over the best friend, remember.'

Grace was a little taken aback. So she wasn't just imagining it. These last few weeks of bonding over bubble wrap had morphed into a genuine friendship. 'I won't stay long,' she promised. 'I just wanted to tell you my news. Although actually I think yours might trump it.'

Alice shrugged. 'It's only taken us a year to become an overnight infatuation.'

'No harm in that. When you know, you know though, right? I mean Dan and I have been working together for ever. Who would have thought we'd go from a first date to moving in together quite so quickly.'

Alice gasped. 'Oh my God! Are you serious? How bloody brilliant is that?'

Grace surrendered to Alice's effusive hug. 'We're going to start over. Together. I'm selling my place, ditching the lot, and we're going to jump in with both feet!' Her words tumbled out over each other excitedly.

Alice's eyes grew large. 'You're ditching everything?'

Grace nodded happily. 'Well, not the essentials – laptop, fluffy towels, coffee maker. Oh and my yoga kit. But yeah. It all comes with bad vibes. So where's the harm?'

Alice shook her head. 'I could never do that,' she said firmly. She turned to Jamie. 'Please don't ask me to do that.'

Jamie wrapped his arms around her shoulders from behind and rested his chin on the crown of her head. 'Never would. Never could. But I still think what you've started here is going to make you so much happier, Al. I know it's been hard and God knows, Grace has been holding your hand every step of the way, but it's worth it, isn't it? Who knows, there might even be room for me one day.'

'Don't tempt me,' said Alice. 'Maybe Dan and Grace have got the right idea and we should just throw caution to the wind!' She stopped and a strange expression flickered across her face. 'But actually I'd be quite sad to miss the dating bit.'

'No problem,' said Jamie, apparently completely relaxed around Alice's about-turns. 'As long as there's plenty of dating—' His eyes twinkled their double-entendre.

Grace took a tiny step back, knowing that her presence was decidedly superfluous. She glanced around the room, at the bottle of wine on the table and the movie flickering on pause. She couldn't help but notice how much bigger the room felt already, even accounting for the six-foot-plus of Jamie Yardley taking up space.

This house might be a work in progress, she decided, but it was on the fast track to becoming a home.

And she hadn't been kidding with Alice when she talked about ditching everything to set up home with Dan. And she already knew the first thing that had to go – she wanted to start this relationship the way she meant to go on, with no expectations and no regrets.

Chapter 50

The whole town of Larkford seemed to have been swept up in auction fever, and by the time the big day rolled around, the excitement was almost palpable. Dan wasn't honestly sure whether to be touched or rattled by this morning's last-minute addition to the auction catalogue. Sure, it was nice to know that Julia was thinking about them, supporting them, even from her new life in Geneva, but watching Grace's face as she'd slipped open the flap and read the handwritten note?

> D Darling - Hoping that this might make all
> the difference
> Jx

It was only too clear that Grace had been wondering: the difference to what?

The vintage cuckoo clock had certainly elicited oohs and aahs from all the auction house staff, until even Dan had begun to wonder why Julia had posted such a valuable piece to him at The Practice, rather than by specialist courier to the auction house.

If only Taffy were here to talk it through, or Holly even.

But he knew perfectly well that they were both focused on keeping Holly hale and hearty as her blood pressure continued to misbehave and the tension mounted. He felt out of his depth and longed for a little male solidarity.

'Let's stop for a drink and a break before the masses arrive?' Dan suggested, gently removing a staple gun from Grace's hand as she attempted to straighten the wonky display boards, only succeeding in making them worse. Grace, who was suddenly looking harried and exhausted by all the little details that seemed to have slipped off everyone else's radar.

'I'm sure there was something else I was supposed to do, though,' she fretted, fishing in her pocket for the omnipresent list that had almost single-handedly brought this evening about. She paused for a moment, taking in her comfy yoga pants and dusty t-shirt. 'I was supposed to go home and get changed!' A flicker of doubt shadowed her face for a moment. 'I know we thought that this auction would make all the difference, but all day I've been wondering whether it will actually be enough. Even if everything goes for its estimated value, it will only cover one Air Ambulance for a year, and maybe if we're lucky an extra midwife to cover house calls and emergencies.' She looked exhausted and near to admitting defeat. 'It just isn't enough, is it?'

Dan pulled her into his arms. 'But it is *something*, Gracie. We're *doing* something, rather than just bewailing our losses. And tonight isn't only about the money; it's about kick-starting the debate, remember? And I for one would rather lead from the front. If we're going to set an example, then let ours be a proactive one, yes?'

He felt her head nod against his chest but she didn't say a word. He glanced at the clock on the wall. Ninety minutes until kick-off. They could afford to take a moment together, just to be, before the flurry of frocks and hairdos took over, couldn't they?

They both looked up, pulling apart at a tentative knock on the door, followed by a familiar but careworn face. 'Hi, I hope I'm not interrupting but Lizzie and Will invited me to come by?' The man's voice trembled with an uncertainty that belied his reputation – of course reputation being nothing, when you'd been through the week from hell that Connor Danes had. 'You must be Grace?' Connor said, stepping forward and tentatively holding out his hand in greeting.

'Mm-hmm,' Grace managed, blushing wildly as Connor leaned forward and kissed her lightly on each cheek as though they were old friends.

'And you must be Dan?'

'Good to meet you, Connor,' said Dan, shaking his hand and trying his hardest not to look as blown away as he felt. He knew Lizzie and Will were friends with the guy, but still? Turning up out of the blue when the paparazzi were clearly on his tail? 'I hope you managed to dodge the local press out front,' Dan offered. 'We've been cajoling them to cover the auction all week, but—'

Connor held up his hand. 'Sorry, I should have said. I have no intention of skulking around in the background tonight. Lizzie called me the other day and, well, I've come to offer my services if you'll have me – I just couldn't stomach another night at home listening to my friends and family leaving awkward messages on the answerphone, or turning up with casseroles – not for even another minute. So when Lizzie phoned – well, look, I hope you don't mind and you won't think I'm hijacking your event, but sod it; there has to be some use to being followed everywhere by photographers, right?' He waved a hand towards the windows and Grace and Dan became aware of the flurry of activity outside, as photographers and journalists bustled for space. A large van bearing the legend 'BBC News' pulled up outside and the large satellite on its roof began rotating as though searching for the mother ship.

'Oh my God,' said Grace weakly.

'I know it's a shock when you see the circus in town for the first time,' said Connor apologetically, the strain written all over his face. 'It's just – well – what you guys are doing here is brilliant. Maybe if we'd all spoken out sooner ...' He swallowed hard and his knuckles turned a stricken white as he gripped the chair-back in front of him. 'Let's just make our voices heard, yeah?'

'Are you sure this is what you want to do?' Grace queried gently, knowing only too well how fresh his tragedy must be and how fragile she herself had been in the days after losing Roy.

'It doesn't feel like a choice.' Connor swallowed hard. 'Please. If you'd just let me help – try and find some meaning in all this? Let me do this?' His plea was heartfelt and vulnerable and Grace felt her eyes fill with tears at his honesty.

'Connor?' said Dan, as the thought occurred to him. 'How would you feel about being our auctioneer for the night?'

'You mean taking the bids and all that?' Connor said, looking to Grace for clarification.

Grace nodded. 'You can't get more front and centre than that. But, in all seriousness, please don't think you have to. That you're here at all is quite something. And really, you mustn't feel that you—'

Connor sighed, interrupting her appeasing words. 'If I'm the auctioneer I can't bid though, can I? And I rather wanted to.' He paused. 'But I suppose this way I could drive the price up a little.'

Dan looked at Grace in concern. This was a small-town auction for charity, not Sotheby's. Their local contingent most likely didn't have pockets as deep as Connor might be used to.

Connor may have been a world-class rock star, but he was Cotswolds born and raised, and the look between them clearly wasn't lost on him. 'Don't worry though, guys, I'm not completely insensitive. I've brought some high-rollers with me too, so I'm not going to mug your patients of their pensions!'

'Okay then,' said Grace, hesitating for just a fraction to give him the chance to change his mind. 'We have ourselves an auctioneer.'

Lizzie barged in without even stopping to knock. 'Come here, you ugly bastard, and give me a hug!' she proclaimed, shocking everyone but Connor.

'Oh, Witchy, you're here and looking almost as shitty as me!' He scooped her into a bear hug as though his life depended on it, pressing his face into her shoulder and refusing to let go. Will followed his wife into the room and barely missed a beat before throwing his arms around the pair of them.

It was an odd little huddle that nobody wanted to disturb.

When they eventually broke apart, it was clear that Connor hadn't been the only one in the hug to have shed a tear or two.

'Rachel's gone,' Connor said, almost uncomprehendingly to Will. 'She's really gone.'

'I know, mate. I can't quite believe it either. She was just so—'

'Vibrant and full of life,' offered Lizzie, squeezing Connor's arm tightly in support.

'Noisy and bolshie, really,' said Connor with a half-hearted attempt at humour. 'But my God is it quiet at home without her.'

'So don't go home,' said Lizzie, wrapping her arms around his waist. 'Stay with us. I mean, there's no space and I'm a truly terrible wife these days. Quite useless really; the place is in chaos and there's never any food but—'

'Yes please,' said Connor with feeling. 'Chaos and starvation sounds so much better than casseroles and silence.'

Will clapped a hand on his shoulder. 'Are you sure you know what you're doing, mate? Standing up in front of everyone whilst you're still so, well, fragile? It's early days.'

'I'm not sure that's a good enough reason not to try and find at least something good to come out of this. It's hideous and miserable and it's not going anywhere. But maybe we can all make sure this doesn't happen to somebody else's family, yeah? So, it's too soon. But I can't ever imagine this feeling any better, so why *not* today? It's not very rock and roll to go all charity but I just don't give a shit.'

'Didn't hurt Bono,' said Grace quietly from the background as all eyes turned to focus on her, still streaked with dust from organising all the various lots to arrive at the last minute.

Connor laughed, the sound so unexpected as to make them all jump. 'The lovely Grace has a valid point.'

'Oh Grace,' said Lizzie, her eyes widening as she realised the implications of Connor's media shadow. 'You weren't planning on going home to change, were you? Have you seen what's going on out there?'

Dan looked at Grace and, behind her bravado that it really, truly, couldn't matter less what she was wearing, he was perhaps the only person to see the moment of disappointment, embarrassment even. 'Isn't Alice popping in to feed the dogs?'

he whispered. 'Maybe she could pick something up and bring it here?'

'I've got some dry shampoo and eyeliner in my bag if that helps?' Lizzie said. 'I keep leaving the house looking a fright and not noticing until I get where I'm going,' she explained, as she rummaged in her handbag.

'What do you think then, Grace?' asked Connor. 'Do you fancy being my right-hand woman for the night?'

Dan stifled a stab of annoyance. For God's sake, the man was newly bereaved, he was hardly hitting on Grace, but the tiny frisson of jealousy still bothered him. What were they like, he thought impatiently. Barely having agreed to throw caution to the winds and move in together, but yet both of them still bothered by petty insecurities. First Julia's bloody cuckoo clock and now a grieving rock star in their midst. Did everybody's relationships have to go through these trials and tribulations, he wondered.

The door from the staging area creaked open and Holly managed to manoeuvre herself into the room, barely missing swiping an ornate tea set with her bump. 'Bloody hell,' she grumbled. 'Which wanker invited half the press in the northern hemisphere?'

'Er, that would be me, I'm afraid,' said Connor apologetically, even as Lizzie inhaled sharply.

'Oh, well, that makes sense,' said Holly reasonably, taking his outstretched hand to shake. 'But you can be the one to explain to Elsie Townsend that they weren't all waiting for her to arrive. She's making them do a photo call with her as we speak.'

Connor cracked a smile. 'I suppose I should do the chivalrous thing and go and join her,' he said.

Holly waved away the suggestion. 'Give her a minute to milk the spotlight or you'll have all hell to pay.' She leaned forward and gently laid a hand on his shoulder. 'I was so sorry to hear of your loss.'

Connor glanced down at her unwieldy bump and nodded, his voice croaky when he spoke. 'It's never what you plan for, is it? The Worst Case Scenario?'

She shook her head. 'Plan for the worst, hope for the best; it doesn't get you even close, does it?' She paused. 'You being here is above and beyond, you do know that, don't you?'

Dan turned away, unable to witness the depth of emotion on both of their faces. It was a silent club of two for that moment – probably the only two people in the room for whom the fear and uncertainty of childbirth were still fresh enough to be so vivid.

'Gracie,' he whispered. 'Come with me a minute.' He took her hand and squeezed through the backstage area, between a globe and a set of vintage Ludwig drums, to where they could find a moment's peace. 'Are you okay with all this? I know it started out as your project, but we've rather lost control, haven't we?'

Grace nodded, seemingly unfazed. 'I know it was my baby to begin with, but trust me, by the time they become noisy, opinionated teenagers, you're quite ready to hand over the reins.' She spoke with feeling and Dan couldn't help but think that she wasn't only talking about the auction project.

'Are the boys coming tonight?' he asked, half hoping that they'd see fit to come and support their mother, as she had supported all of their endeavours over the years.

Grace shrugged. 'It's probably for the best if they don't. There's altogether too much scope for a cock-up, don't you think? Emotions are running pretty high all round – all the pregnant ladies are protesting on the village green, according to Alice.'

'Protesting the auction?' Dan asked in confusion.

'No, you daft apeth. With the hashtag on placards. Rural Lives Count is trending all over the internet, but they wanted some old school photo ops for the news teams.' She dropped her voice to a whisper. 'I just wish all this was happening without such a tragedy driving it forward.'

They looked at each other for a moment, with no need for words. Of course that was both of their wishes, but the media didn't seem to function that way. There was no doubt in both of their minds that their parochial bit of fundraising, their plans to get the second Air Ambulance out of the hangar and into the air, or a community midwife on call, would barely have merited a few column inches in the local paper. What was happening now was nothing short of sensationalising a celebrity bereavement. The only question was: how did they actually feel about that?

In that moment, it certainly seemed to Dan as though their opinion on all this wasn't terribly important and that the genie was well and truly out of the bottle regardless. He took Grace's hand. 'Come on, Cinderella, let's get you sorted for your moment in the spotlight. Stand up there and catch Connor if he falls, though, Gracie, won't you?'

'Of course,' she said simply, and squeezed his hand.

Chapter 51

'For God's sake, stop fidgeting,' said Taffy. 'Here, swap places if you can't see.'

The folding chairs in the hall were hardly the height of comfort for an uncomfortably pregnant lady, but Holly was determined not to miss out. It wasn't exactly that she couldn't see, more that she couldn't see *everything*. She was so used to being in the thick of these barmy events in Larkford that attending as a spectator felt weird and discombobulating.

'Who's that?' she asked, craning her neck. 'Do you think Grace's outfit is okay? Is Dan still back there? Did you see the press outside?'

Taffy blinked hard. 'Er, yes?' he said, hoping to cover all bases. 'You know you sound like the twins at the seaside, don't you? If you start nagging for an ice-cream, then I'll know that the transformation is complete.' He grinned, watching the expression on her face and knowing her only too well. 'Dear God. You're actually thinking about ice-cream now, aren't you?'

Holly flushed guiltily. The very idea of a sundae with sprinkles was suddenly all she could concentrate on. 'No,' she replied. 'Unless of course you wanted one too?'

Taffy shook his head. 'Stay here. I'll go and see what I can rustle up.'

Elsie leaned across Holly's bump. 'Actually, I wouldn't say no to a Strawberry Mivvi, since you're asking.'

'Anybody else?' Taffy said, shaking his head in mock-annoyance, the smile in his eyes softening any irritation.

Alice leaned back in her chair. 'Maybe a choc ice? What about you, Jamie?'

By the time Taffy actually left the room, he was muttering their wish list over and over again, for fear of forgetting it.

'I thought you'd be backstage,' said Holly, secretly pleased not to be the only one consigned to the status of seat filler.

Alice shook her head vehemently. 'Couldn't bear it, actually. Seeing all my lovely things just waiting to be sold—' She pressed a hand to her chest. 'I know it's the right thing to do, and they'll go to loving homes,' she talked about her dresses as though they were much-loved ponies she'd sadly outgrown, 'but it's still going to be awful watching them go.'

Holly nodded. 'But it might also be amazing, seeing how much money they're raising for the Air Ambulance and the Maternity Unit?'

'That too,' agreed Alice.

Holly watched the way Jamie automatically reached for her hand, the way Coco pressed herself tightly against Alice's legs, and couldn't help but think she would be okay. Holly knew how hard the whole process of letting go had been for Alice, but sometimes letting go was the only way to feel free – undoubtedly difficult but incredibly rewarding. Wandering around her little terraced cottage after Taffy's family had finally departed, she'd realised something similar herself.

Even moving into Elsie's temporarily had been like a watershed moment. She was, to all intents and purposes, starting over. A new husband, a new house, two new babies on the way – she could only thank her lucky stars that Ben and Tom seemed to be even more excited about all of these changes than she was. Certainly it felt as though everything was falling into place with an ease and serendipity she was unaccustomed to.

She could only hope that the actual moving day might go so smoothly – after all, there was no going back once the deal was done.

'No sign of Harriet this evening?' she asked Elsie sotto voce, as though the mere mention of her name might actually summon her presence. They'd heard nothing from Harriet at all, since she'd swept off up to London, and the waiting and not knowing was almost worse than her looming presence. Holly had privately assumed that Harriet would turn up here tonight and cause a scene; she was delighted to be proven wrong. Certainly, Elsie's insistence on referring to her as Hurricane Harriet was making a lot more sense: sweeping in, causing devastation and, now it appeared, having swept back to LA to lick her wounds.

Elsie looked guiltily relieved as she confirmed that Hurricane Harriet had, officially, left the country. 'I may have dropped a few heavy hints about reconsidering the property portfolio in California,' Elsie confided. 'Not exactly ethical parenting, but it did prove to be the most efficient catalyst!' She shrugged. 'Sometimes Harriet doesn't leave me with the option to be an adoring mummy like you, Holly.' She waved a hand in the air, as though the topic were now closed for debate.

Holly squeezed her hand supportively, only too happy to change the subject. She looked down to see a little chocolate-coloured nose sniffling at her feet, where Coco had lain down under Alice's chair. The urge to stroke her soft, silky ears was intense, but Holly already knew she could barely reach her feet any more.

'Alice,' she whispered, 'is there a reason that Judith is over there giving me the evil eye?'

Alice didn't even look over. 'It's not you she's glaring at. It's me. We had another meeting to discuss Coco's future, but she's not giving up easily on getting the outcome she wants.'

'And it's hardly helping her case that she's being so melodramatic about it,' Jamie grumbled beside her. 'Even Judith has to see that not everyone has the same single-minded approach to this.'

'Oh God,' gasped Alice. 'Stop looking at her. She's coming over.'

Suddenly there was an intense interest in whatever happened to be lurking in the bottom of Alice's handbag and Holly noticed the back of her neck turn a vivid red. Whether it was her pregnancy hormones, or simply seeing her colleague so flustered, Holly felt an overwhelming surge of protectiveness towards her. Wasn't Alice already 'doing her bit' for their community?

Judith sat primly down in Taffy's empty seat and held out a thin, crêpey hand. 'Dr Graham? I'm Judith Lane, from the Canine Oncology Department.'

COD? thought Holly, trying not to react as Judith's downturned mouth and sulky expression bore a startling resemblance to one. 'Nice to meet you at last,' Holly managed, earning herself a strange look, as she attempted to resist the urge to laugh.

'I gather you support this crazy-hokum scheme that these two have cooked up?' She waved a hand disparagingly at Alice and Jamie. 'I think a little romance has gone to their heads and they can't be relied upon to think clearly, to balance the pros and cons of this decision. Surely the needs of the many outweigh the needs of one individual? Tell me why on earth they have your support?'

Holly's good mood ebbed instantly in the face of this barrage of questions. She began to wish she'd never sent Taffy on his quest for frosty sustenance. She looked over at Alice and Jamie, Coco nestled beneath them, united in their affection for each other and always, always trying to do the right thing. A slow fuse began to burn and Holly fixed Judith firmly in her sights. It didn't matter what 'scheme' Alice and Jamie had put together, she knew full well it would have been considered with the best of intentions and plenty of soul-searching to boot. She had absolute faith in them.

'Of course I support them. And if you heard them out instead of shouting them down, perhaps you would too. It's okay to ask for a little sacrifice, I think, a small stretch out of one's comfort zone to help other people. But is it right to sabotage the life of a valuable, responsible, community-minded person to reach an arbitrary goal? I don't believe so and I'm surprised that you do.'

Judith blanched. 'That's not what I'm—'

'Isn't it though?' Holly interrupted, on a roll. 'If you push Alice to surrender Coco entirely, that's exactly what you're doing. And yes, you may help many patients, but then so does Alice, as their GP. It's a question of perspective really, Judith, with a dash of humanity. I'm concerned that you may have lost sight of what you're trying to achieve. And whilst I appreciate you have your own deadlines and targets, as a doctor, I would ask that you at least *consider* their proposal.' She turned away as Taffy arrived with handfuls of ice-creams, cursing the chill to his fingers and effectively ending the conversation.

As Judith stalked back to her seat, Holly swallowed hard and leaned forward. 'Er, Alice, when you get a mo – can you fill me in on this scheme I'm apparently supporting?'

Alice nodded, swivelling in her seat, her eyes reflecting her gratitude. 'You're going to like it; I know you will. But thank you for supporting me sight unseen.'

Holly smiled. 'I trust you.' She made it sound so easy, but from the expression on Alice's face, that simple statement meant so much more than she could have realised.

Jamie caught the choc ices that Taffy expertly lobbed into his hands. 'We'd love to come and talk to you both about it. Dan too,' he said. 'We want Coco to stay with Alice full-time, but for Alice to volunteer at the Oncology Department in Bath one day each week – in the diagnostic clinic, and with Alice as Coco's handler. Or at The Practice if you'd rather. It's a bit of a compromise, granted, but it's the only way we could come up with, where everybody wins, even if it's only a little bit. We thought maybe a Three Peaks Challenge to kick off some working capital, but we're going to pool our overheads, so it's essentially a cost-free option.'

Holly and Taffy exchanged glances. 'Sounds great,' they both said at the same time and grinned. 'Jinx, padlock, Curly Wurly,' they both said, in unison again, and then fell about laughing.

'We really need to spend more time around grown-ups,' Taffy said. 'I was humming the tune to *Peppa Pig* in the queue just now.' He stretched his arms above his head and Holly quickly pulled them down.

'Don't do that!' she said urgently. 'You might accidentally bid on something!'

He grinned wickedly and flicked through the hastily printed brochure of lots. 'Ooh, now there's an idea,' he said.

A small scuffle broke out at the end of their row. 'Alice? Alice!' called a lanky, slightly dishevelled figure with a small rucksack slung from one shoulder.

Holly watched Alice's face split into wreaths of smiles as she thrust her choc ice into Jamie's hands and clambered between the seats. 'Tilly! Oh my God. What the hell are you doing here?'

Tilly grinned at Alice and threw out her arms in greeting. 'A little bird told me you might be in need of some moral support. And it only took me two flights, one river boat, three trains and a dodgy taxi from Bristol – so I bloody well hope you're pleased to see me.'

Alice nodded, words apparently eluding her at the sight of her dearest friend. 'What about your doctors-without-boundaries plan?' she managed after a moment.

Tilly shrugged. 'Some things are more important.' She swung her rucksack to the ground and pulled Alice into another rib-crushing hug. 'Thought I'd try out the Stepford way of life for a bit.'

Alice automatically glanced down, clocking the minimalist size of her luggage, and her shoulders dropped. 'You're not staying long?'

Tilly looked affronted. 'Don't be daft. I've brought everything I own.' She gave the bag a little kick. 'Besides, rumour has it you've been having a clear-out, so I thought I might scrounge a few hand-me-downs to get me started.'

Tilly plonked herself down in the seat next to Jamie and leaned in to shake him by the hand. 'Good work, by the way. Took you long enough.'

*

Before Connor Danes had even finished his opening remarks, Holly was in pieces. Tilly's arrival had already tipped her dangerously close to the brink, delighted that her first attempt at meddling had proven quite so adept. After all, it was becoming increasingly obvious that they needed another pair of hands at The Practice. Cursing her hormonal state, she peeked over her handkerchief to see who had borne witness to her aquatic response to Connor's frank and vulnerable honesty. She was quietly relieved to see that she wasn't alone.

As though to provide the perfect counterbalance, the entire front row of the audience stood up and turned to face the crowd that packed out the hall.

One by one they introduced themselves.

'Hi, I'm Ellie, I'm fifteen and the Air Ambulance Team saved my life when I was in a car crash.'

'I'm Malcom. Sixty-two. The Air Ambulance Team saved me when I fell off a cliff.'

'Laura. Forty-two. I came off my horse and would have been a quadriplegic if it wasn't for the Air Ambulance Team.'

By the end of the row, the clapping and cheering from the audience was almost drowning out their words and Chris Virtue, as the nominated representative from the Air Ambulance Team, was looking somewhat overwhelmed on the stage beside Connor.

'For every tragedy, there are hundreds of stories of triumph over adversity,' said Connor, holding Chris's hand high in the air – a little more rock and roll than Cotswold stone, but nevertheless heartfelt. 'Let's make sure that everyone who needs their local maternity unit, or an Air Ambulance, or oncology care in their community, can go to sleep at night knowing that's a possibility!' he shouted, now ignoring the microphone beside him. 'And as your auctioneer, I can't bid, so instead I am pledging to match every single pound spent here tonight for a cause that is truly close to my heart!'

The atmosphere in the room was almost electric. Camera flashes spackled the back of the hall and the anticipation for the auction to begin was almost frenzied. Holly noticed that Jessica Hearst had slipped quietly into the back of the room, her face still oddly immobile on one side, but with her mother uncharacteristically holding her hand beside her. As the pair of them handed out envelopes for Gift Aid donations, it seemed that tonight was full of surprises.

'We love you, Connor!' shouted Marion Waverly, startling everyone around her and possibly even herself.

Grace walked out onto the stage, looking stunning in one of Alice's neat little trouser suits, if a little overwhelmed by the rapturous reception.

'We love you, Grace!' shouted Alice, unwilling to let her friend feel outdone, surrounded as she was by pilots and pop stars.

Grace blushed and took to the podium, opening out the auctioneer's folder and whispering into Connor's ear to get him started on the right track.

'Lot Number One,' he said, hesitant now his duties were upon him. He read the entry again and laughed. 'Okay then, let's start as we mean to go on. A rare pair of Degas sketches – ballerinas in repose. Kindly donated by Ms Elsie Townsend.'

'I bet he's regretting offering to match every pound now,' whispered Taffy in Holly's ear.

'Nope,' whispered Holly in reply, 'he's richer than Croesus. We actually had to talk him down from signing away his cut from The Hive's new album. I'm all for charitable giving, but the poor man's got a life to rebuild.'

'Who will start me at six—' He looked up and quailed under Elsie's stern gaze from the audience. 'I mean, ten thousand pounds?'

A flurry of paddles rose in the air like a Mexican wave. 'Er, twenty?' he adjusted.

Still paddles waving furiously and a telephone bidder trying to up the ante. Back and forth, as Connor grew in confidence and disbelief. 'Going once, going twice, at sixty-four thousand pounds to the gentleman in the tweed jacket. I'm sorry, sir, the *other* gentleman in the tweed jacket. Gone!' He wiped his brow and looked around the room. 'Bloody hell!' he said in shock.

Grace gently turned the page in the folder and brought his attention back to the list of lots awaiting his attention.

'Lot Number Two. Ten dog-training sessions from Jamie Yardley – dog trainer and canine problem-solver extraordinaire.' Connor looked up and grinned. 'Quite the variety on tonight's list, ladies and gents – hopefully there's something for every pocket and every taste. Do I hear two hundred pounds?'

Holly barely missed out on a weekend for four in a luxury treehouse, although knowing what they had thought were the consequences of their last treehouse visit, perhaps that was just as well. Although, she reasoned, she couldn't possibly get any *more* pregnant. Taffy and Dan battled it out to the last, outbidding each other on a pair of tickets to the cricket at Lord's, despite knowing they would undoubtedly be each other's plus-one, only to be gazumped at the last moment by a smug-looking Major.

And Elsie, well, Elsie had to be restrained a couple of times from attempting to bid on her own donations, especially the Jackie-O trinkets she'd unearthed, only being allowed free rein with her paddle as she took pity on Alice.

Seeing her vintage Fendi baguette on the plinth, spotlit from above and looking gorgeous, Alice's face had been a picture of remorse and regret. Elsie needed very little persuasion to make the final bid. She leaned forward and tapped Alice on the shoulder. 'You have to promise to share it with me,' she whispered. 'A bag like that should have plenty of outings. No more hiding yourself in the back of the wardrobe.' She stumbled as she realised her Freudian slip. 'And the same goes for your fancy togs,' she corrected herself with an encouraging smile.

By the time two weeks in France, wine-tasting at a vineyard, had surpassed its guide price by one hundred per cent, it was clear to see the pattern evolving, thought Holly. Elsie's chums at Sarandon Hall appeared to have dug deep into their antiques and jewellery collections, and Connor's A-list guests appeared happy to pay over the odds for them. Meanwhile, the residents of Larkford were all happy to donate their services or treasures, to suit those with slightly shallower pockets.

Still, there was no accounting for the element of competition.

A baking lesson with Pru Hartley bid through to four figures once Connor's bandmates had sampled her fudge brownies.

And a meal for two cooked by Teddy Kingsley shot through the roof, once he'd been encouraged to blushingly stand up and take a bow, whereupon the elegant blonde draped across two chairs in the back row and revealing plenty of leg for the cameras insisted on topping any bid if Teddy himself would also be her date for the meal.

Taffy was scribbling busily on the back of his ice-cream receipt. 'We're into six figures,' he breathed. 'So up yours, Derek Landers! You can shove that up your sustainable efficiency regulations. I think this equates to people putting their money where their mouth is, don't you?' He beamed delightedly, throwing his arm around Holly's shoulders and pulling her in close.

'Now then, Holls, any chance of you keeping your blood pressure in the healthy range if I take a bid on the next lot?' he asked cheekily.

Holly's quizzical look didn't last long.

'And the next lot,' called out Connor from the stage, 'is really rather special. 'A Gloucestershire Old Spot piglet. Ten weeks old. Goes by the name of Arthur, apparently.'

Holly raised one eyebrow. 'Please tell me you're taking the piss?' she said laughingly, until he raised his paddle in the air and the smile slid right off her face.

Chapter 52

'I bloody love this place!' cried Tilly with abandon as her jetlag and Pimm's combined to make her shed what was left of her inhibitions. Adjourning straight to The Kingsley Arms after the auction had been a rookie mistake. Tilly pulled Alice into a full-body hug and planted a smacking great kiss on her cheek, before doing the same to Jamie. 'You two are ace together,' she declared.

Alice couldn't stop smiling, it seemed, as she watched her best friend's reaction to the place she called home. 'Didn't I tell you? Not in the slightest bit Stepford.'

'Who are you calling Stepford?' interrupted Taffy, sipping at his pint of local cider, making it seem completely normal that tucked under one arm was Arthur-the-Piglet, or Lot Nineteen, as he would henceforth be known.

Tilly blushed. 'Middle England always seemed a bit parochial looking in.'

'Ah yes, but from the inside looking out, it's not so bad now, is it?' Taffy teased her, waving at the newly printed calendars which adorned every wall. Shirtless, tousled and utterly gorgeous, the Air Ambulance boys had done them proud, and orders were quickly racking up online. 'Sexy pilots and celebrities at every turn.'

He watched as Tilly's eyes followed said local celebrities, including Elsie and Connor, across to the bar of The Kingsley Arms.

Teddy Kingsley, their resident publican and chef extraordinaire, seemed oblivious to their luminary presence, and indeed to the twenty-pound notes they were waving to get his attention and the chance of a round. Teddy Kingsley only had eyes for Tilly, it seemed. It was only when Elsie whistled loudly, as though she were hailing a New York cab, that he managed to bring his focus back to their drink orders.

'Somebody's got an admirer,' commented Taffy, as he allowed Nineteen a sip of his cider.

Tilly glanced over at the bar once more, briefly taking in Teddy's well-honed physique in his Calvin Klein t-shirt and ancient Levi's. She shrugged. 'He's a bit old for me.'

Alice laughed. 'He's the same age as us!'

'Exactly,' replied Tilly firmly.

'And this is *exactly* why it's time to say goodbye to the nomadic, Mrs Robinson thing you've had going on,' Alice said.

Tilly tilted her head appraisingly. 'He is quite dishy, I suppose – don't you think?'

Alice laughed nervously. 'Well, I try not to, actually. He is one of my patients. Totally out of bounds.' Alice frowned for a moment at the sudden flash of interest on Tilly's face: was that all it took to pique her friend's attention, a mention that something was off-limits?

'Maybe I will just go over and say hi,' Tilly said, slipping away from their group with an ease and confidence that was built purely on years of positive validation. Any insecurities were wrapped pretty tightly within the bundle of physical loveliness and professional ability, as Alice well knew.

Taffy scruffed Nineteen under the chin, producing a volley of piglet squeals and snuffles. 'This little chap is going to be brilliant. He'll be a right little porker in no time.'

Holly came over to join them. 'I can't believe you bought a piglet,' she said, aiming for haughty but immediately undone by Nineteen's big brown eyes and endless lashes. 'Well, he can't live in the house,' she said, after a moment, already softening on her no-pigs-not-ever stance of earlier. 'And surely we can come up with a better name than Nineteen?'

Taffy shook his head. 'It's his name. He knows it already.' He proceeded to call the piglet, who appeared to respond to just about any name at all, so long as a slurp of scrumpy was on offer.

Alice laid her head on Jamie's shoulder happily. It had been a bloody long week, but the success of this evening made it all seem worthwhile. Indeed, Grace was still over at the auction house with Dan as they tallied up the final amounts; nobody was going home until they knew whether their target had been reached.

Jamie snaked his arm around her waist and pulled her closer. 'Do you think that will be us one day?' he asked, watching Holly and Taffy fooling around with their new 'baby' and cooing over his slightest accomplishment. As if having two sets of twins and half a labradoodle wasn't enough to keep them busy! They might not be the archetypal picture of newly wedded bliss, but with Holly's burgeoning bump and their obvious adoration for one another, they certainly looked pretty blissful from where Alice was standing.

Alice smiled at the very notion, unable to believe how far she'd come – her customary terse dismissal of any suggestion of relationships, children or livestock in her own future suddenly feeling outdated and ill-informed. 'Maybe,' she said easily instead. 'But perhaps without the multiple births and porcine progeny?'

'No piglets?' teased Jamie.

'Nope,' said Alice. 'There's always the threat of bacon, isn't there?' Spot the girl who'd grown up on a farm, she thought. 'I quite fancy a llama actually,' she confided.

'Oh no,' interrupted Elsie, strolling over with a G&T the size of a fishbowl. 'Grumpy little bastards, llamas. My Monty was an aloof and unrewarding sod. I'm thinking more pygmy goat for my next acquisition.'

'Do they allow pets at Sarandon Hall?' Jamie said, the surprise evident on his face.

Elsie immediately looked shifty. 'Not yet,' she hedged and wandered off to have her photo taken with Connor and his bandmates, never too old to be the consummate groupie.

'I hope I'm not interrupting, Dr Walker?'

Alice turned to see Susan Motherwell, with her five children clustered around her. She looked pale and a little fragile, but one hell of a lot better than she had in Alice's consulting room only a few weeks ago. She fumbled in her handbag and passed Alice a fancy cream envelope. 'We all just wanted to give you a little something, by way of a thank-you,' she said. She pressed her hand to her chest, truly speaking from the heart. 'The doctors at the hospital said we saved so much of my heart muscle because you were so quick with your diagnosis.' She gave a dry cough that immediately told Alice that, post-heart attack, Susan's consultant had her on ACE-inhibitors, no doubt as part of a cocktail of drugs to prevent a recurrence.

Alice smiled. 'You don't need to do that.'

'I know I don't,' said Susan feistily. 'But I want to. These five kids? They owe it you, that I'm still here to boss them around.' She grinned. 'Although I imagine they won't always thank you for that!'

Right now though, fresh from the prospect of a very poorly mummy indeed, they flocked around her tightly like ducklings and Alice had a small flash of insight into how poor Susan Motherwell must have felt as she'd been whisked off to Bath in an ambulance. There was nothing like family to put things into perspective.

She ripped open the envelope at Susan's behest and slid out the gift certificate for a night away with a boutique travel company. Susan looked pleased as punch with herself. 'Well, I'd heard on the grapevine about your new beau and I thought to myself, I bet they need a bit of quality time together! Oh, and I checked, Coco is more than welcome. I've popped it in your Jamie's name – call it a neighbour's gift – just in case your NHS won't let you even have a pressie these days.'

Alice was incredibly moved that her patient had gone to such considerable care and attention to choose not only the perfect gift, but to ensure she could actually use it without compromising her professional integrity. She pulled Susan into a hug and it was hard to say who was more emotional. 'Thank you,' she said with feeling.

'No, Dr Walker, thank *you*,' Susan said as she ushered her brood away with a wobbly smile.

'You don't get *that* in South America,' said Tilly, who had apparently watched the entire scene unfolding with a growing sense of disbelief. 'Although I was offered a husband in Paraguay once—' She left the anecdote hanging.

Jamie grinned. 'Why do I get the feeling that there's more to that story than a simple thank-you?'

Tilly shrugged. 'Plenty of time for all my stories; I want to hear yours. I hope you have honourable intentions towards my Alice?'

Alice snorted attractively at Tilly's blatant interfering. 'I'm quite happy with a few dishonourable ones, to be honest.'

'Although,' Jamie said, his tongue loosened by several pints of cider and only a packet of wasabi peanuts for absorption, 'there's no harm in planning ahead a little.'

'How far ahead?' Alice asked warily, slightly distracted by his hand circling her waist and the look of mischief in his eyes.

'How about tomorrow—?' he asked.

'Oh tomorrow, I can cope with,' Alice interrupted.

Just as he finished his sentence, 'Move in with me tomorrow—'

'Ooh,' said Tilly into the momentary silence, 'things just got interesting.'

Alice hesitated, waiting for the doubts to assail her, the excuses to flood fully formed into her head.

Nothing.

She looked confused for a moment, eyeing up the Pimm's in her hand as though it were personally responsible for her lack of spontaneous acumen.

'The answer's not in there,' said Jamie quietly with a smile. 'Don't think, just go with your gut.'

Alice blinked again. Still nothing. Her gut, it seemed, was strongly in favour of the notion.

'Okay,' she whispered. 'Tomorrow.' He pulled her into a kiss that wasn't entirely PG.

'Get a room!' catcalled Taffy, startling his piglet in the process.

'We are,' said Alice, blushing. 'Or maybe a house? Or a flat?' She looked askance at Jamie as though he must surely have had a plan in mind.

'Or my house,' suggested Grace, having quietly made an unassuming entrance during their discussion. 'After all, I won't be needing it. And you can use the spare room for your jewellery-making, Alice – it's a bit cramped, but wonderfully light.' She gave her friend an affectionate smile, knowing only too well that Alice was finding flow and relaxation in these intricate projects to replace the urge to shop.

'Excellent,' said Tilly, fresh from the airport and with nowhere to live. 'Shotgun Alice's house!' she called out, making everyone laugh at her ridiculous eagerness. She blushed. 'I mean, if it's going begging. I am going to need to live somewhere nearby.'

'Quite right too,' said Holly. 'No point having a new doctor on the team if they can't be on call and on site.'

There was a moment's uncertainty in the pub, as everybody fell silent.

'Oh,' said Holly, 'was I not supposed to announce that just yet?'

Taffy merely shook his head at her daffy indiscretion, Alice noticed, as if his new bride could do no wrong. Instead he simply led the charge to a round of applause to welcome Tilly to the team.

Holly looked over at Alice and smiled. 'You're welcome,' she said pre-emptively. 'Sometimes you just need to have your best friends around you.'

Alice reached out and squeezed her hand, taking a moment to find the right words. She couldn't quite believe that Holly would do something so magnanimous as to hire her best friend, not just for the benefit of the team, it seemed, but to help her too. And having Tilly in Larkford would no doubt help her find her way through this new double role she was creating for herself and Coco.

But then, who was she kidding? This was exactly the kind

of thing that Holly would do, she realised, her Musketeer-complex well and truly developed; perhaps it should be the new Larkford motto, Alice wondered, one for all and all for one . . .

The pub fell silent again as they all belatedly realised the import of Grace's presence and indeed the notepad in her hand. Dan and Harry Grant flanked her on both sides, as though she were delivering one of those oversized Lottery cheques.

Alice held her breath and Jamie's hand just as firmly.

Taffy tinged the side of his glass and Nineteen squealed in reply. 'Well, don't leave us hanging—'

Grace swallowed hard; the attention of every Larkford resident crammed into the bar was focused on her.

'I have good news and excellent news,' she managed, before a storm of relieved applause drowned out her voice, followed by an even louder volley of shushing.

'We have enough to repair the second Air Ambulance and cover its running costs,' she said clearly. 'We have enough to cover a community midwife.' More premature applause; more shushing. 'And,' she paused to make sure she had their undivided attention, 'we have enough to do both for three whole years!' She burst into tears of relief and exhilaration.

'Three?' exclaimed Holly, quickly joining her.

'You guys—' said Taffy, overcome by the emotion thick in the room.

Alice just breathed out, slowly, easily. Her part had been small, after all, but it took any number of these small parts to make the whole she was seeing develop before her. A whole community. A whole medical service – cradle to grave – the way the NHS should be.

She looked up and saw Connor Danes standing at the periphery of the wild and enthusiastic celebrations breaking out in the bar. Their joy in this moment was surely at odds with how he must be feeling. No amount of fundraising was going to bring his beautiful wife and baby back, but his generous and, sod it all, his brave contribution to their cause would save countless lives, and mean countless families would never have to go through his grief.

She walked over to him and wordlessly pulled him into a hug. 'Thank you,' she said, with feeling. 'You know you made this happen?'

Connor just shook his head. '*This* doesn't happen overnight, Alice. This—' He waved his hand expansively around the room at the clusters of friends and neighbours, old and young, embracing each other. 'It takes years and effort and the right stuff. Larkford has the right stuff, you know.'

'I do,' said Alice, her eyes shining. 'And none of it fits in a storage box.'

Connor looked at her weirdly but never questioned her sentiment. 'Maybe one day there'll be a place here for me too,' he said, as Grace and Dan surged towards him, not taking no for an answer in joining their group for a late supper and a chance to recount their glory lot by lot.

Chapter 53

'Tell me again how this is going to work?' said Holly the next morning, as she tried to make sense of the diagram scribbled on the back of a beer mat.

It was the kind of scheme that could only have been cobbled together over a few pints of cider at The Kingsley Arms. Granted, Holly had been stone-cold sober throughout the entire debate, but then she had also been asleep, wedged between Taffy and Jamie in a booth and snoring gently, for at least half of it.

'Well, when I said we'd hired a van—' began Taffy.

'Obviously that was our first mistake,' said Holly, squinting at the beer mat and angling it back and forth in a search for clarity. Their second clearly being to schedule their official moving day to Elsie's on the morning after the night before.

'Look, just follow the arrows. It will work like a dream, and think of all the extra pairs of hands! We move to Elsie's, leaving our house empty. Then Dan and Grace move into ours. Then we whip across town to pick up Jamie's stuff, swing by Alice's and we'll have them both installed at Grace's old place by suppertime. Then Tilly is going to have Alice's place while she works out what to do.'

'And when you say "we"?' Holly clarified.

'Well, obviously you're not going to be lugging boxes around, are you, my little Moomin? Which is why this is so genius. You can be foreman with the clipboard. Lucy's looking after the twins. And if you fancy a snooze, then we have Grace and Alice on hand for sensible female input.' Taffy looked remarkably pleased with himself.

'The lengths you'll go to, not to do this by yourself.' Holly shook her head and smiled.

'Why be mundane? This is going to be SO much fun,' Taffy insisted. 'And I have stickers and labels and marker pens so nothing gets muddled up, plus you get to be Stationery Queen for the day!'

'Stationary Queen is more like it,' Holly grumbled, unable to surrender her role in such a momentous occasion. 'But you'll pack things up room by room, yes? There'll be a system? Because otherwise it will end up as total chaos.'

Taffy nodded. 'We all pack this morning and shuttle boxes this afternoon. We're organised. Relax. What can possibly go wrong?'

Holly's mobile chirruped beside her, Grace's photo lighting up the screen.

'I'm a raging hypocrite!' wailed Grace down the line, her normally unruffled self having clearly left the building. 'All these weeks I've been going on at Alice for holding on to so much stuff. I can't believe it. I've just been in the loft for the first time in a decade . . . Oh, Holly, I'm so sorry – it's going to take weeks to clean this lot out.'

'What have you got stashed up there, Gracie? Do we need to organise another auction?' Holly said, pulling a face at Taffy as their plans teetered on the brink of collapse.

'Nothing fancy enough for an auction,' confessed Grace,

'but there's some nice vintage stuff. And there's the problem –
it's all muddled in with the crap that could go straight in a skip!'

'Okay,' said Holly. Her body might be ungainly, but as
the only one of the team without a hangover, her mind was
decidedly more sprightly than most. 'Hang fire a minute, I
need to make a call.'

She hung up on Grace and dialled Alice. 'Hi, Alice. Oh,
okay, I'll whisper. Or maybe take some paracetamol? Listen,
I have a proposition for you.'

Five minutes later and Holly was three calls down and
looking smug. 'Day saved,' she announced to Taffy, who was
wrangling a reel of parcel tape and pretending not to eaves-
drop. 'Alice is going to take Grace's place even with the loft
full and there's a skip turning up in the morning. Anything
they want to chuck can go straight in there and Alice can
include anything lovely in her pop-up shop. I suggested she
work on commission, but they're going to donate all the
proceeds to the Auction Fund. No such zealot as a convert,
eh? She seems over the moon at the chance to flex her decluttering skills again. Can you believe, out of all of us, Alice is
the only one who's packed and ready to go?'

'I can, actually,' said Taffy with feeling, as he attempted to
wrangle enough Bob the Builder merchandise to entertain
a small island community into yet another box. 'Maybe she
could work her magic on the twins' pack-rat habits while
she's on a roll?'

Holly shrugged. 'Ah, but you're forgetting they've a whole
playroom to fill now. I think they're taking it as a challenge!'
She paused. 'Is it weird that I'm so pleased Elsie isn't moving out
for a while? I know she's got this whole thing about professional
packers and making the Sarandon Hall team jump to, to get her
installed, but part of me keeps hoping she'll change her mind

and stay. Or maybe Celia Price will confound medical science and hang on to the garden suite for a little while longer.'

Taffy sat back on his haunches and said nothing for a moment. 'Who do you think would find it more stressful, though, with Elsie and two sets of twins in the house? Because that's what we're talking about.'

Holly nodded. 'I know. It's just—'

'You still feel like we're kicking her out, don't you?' Taffy said observantly. Even the folder of notarised paperwork had done nothing to dent Holly's discomfort on that front. 'You really need to talk to Elsie, because the way she tells it, we're doing her a favour. She's even bought new clothes to wow the Sarandon Hall set. I think she's excited, Holls, like she's setting out on a new adventure – a chance to rule the roost amongst her peers one last time.'

Holly nodded. 'This whole merry-go-round with the houses makes it all seem so frivolous though, doesn't it? Not to mention worrying whether it's all actually legal and above board?' She fidgeted slightly as another twinge of backache caught her unawares. Moving house and growing two tiny humans at the same time was hardly a winning combination. The fact that Nineteen was clearly having issues acclimatising to Elsie's garden and had spent the whole morning thus far with his little snout pressed against the French windows looking in and squealing was hardly helping her quest for composure.

Taffy stood up and walked over to her, dropping down beside her and massaging her lower back. 'Dan and Grace sublet from us until your lease runs out, or they find their dream wreck to renovate. Alice and Jamie are renting from Grace so they can be love's young dream with no responsibilities and save a bit of money for when Alice goes part-time. Jamie's given notice on his rental. And Tilly's moving into Alice's. They sorted it last night – caught up in the merry-go-round. But all legal. All above board. And we get to move our family into their for ever home while there's four of us, not six. Well six, not eight, if you count the porker and the Muttley.'

'When you put it like that—' said Holly, leaning into his arms and sighing contentedly. 'And I don't have to pack a single box! It does sound kind of perfect.'

'Perfect. Bonkers. Supportive, yet mildly incestuous,' Taffy countered.

'Pretty much perfectly Larkford all over then really,' mused Holly. She couldn't help thinking that her maiden attempts at meddling with Lizzie had gone really rather well; bringing Connor and Tilly into the mix had been a stroke of genius if she did say so herself. 'Speaking of incestuous, do you think Dan will forgive me for hiring Tilly without so much as an interview?'

Seven long hours and several tearful moments later, the entire team were assembled together around Elsie's kitchen table, demolishing mammoth helpings of fish and chips, washed down with Dom Pérignon or Appletiser.

Dan raised his glass. 'You're all bloody wonderful and thank you!'

Taffy guffawed with laughter. This was hardly the senti-ment that Dan had been expressing earlier, when Taffy and Jamie had dropped Alice's sofa on his toe. The entire day had been utterly chaotic and, of course, the romantic notion of having everyone settled in their new homes by bedtime had been a complete fantasy. Instead, they had to settle for the fact that all the furniture and boxes were in the right homes, albeit not necessarily in the right order.

An echoing knock on Elsie's front door had the pack of dogs barking in greeting. Eric, Coco, Noodle and Doodle swarmed into the hall towards the front door, Nineteen scrabbling to keep up, almost drowning out Elsie's magisterial cries of 'Come in, come in!'.

Connor Danes stepped into the hallway and looked utterly disconcerted. 'Are you sure you've got enough dogs in here?' he called. 'And don't any of you *ever* answer your bloody phones?' He pushed the door open wider, submitting to his furry greeting to allow his companions to come in behind him. To be fair, it was hard to know who looked more uncomfortable, Derek Landers with his sweaty, rotund face, or Councillor Malcolm Bodley clutching a briefcase to his chest and shying away from Eric's exuberant attentions and Nineteen's frenzied squeals of delight. Harry Grant walked in with him, completely calm and unfazed.

The four men entered the kitchen and Grace immediately got to her feet to offer them a drink.

'Do you think Malcolm Bodley has any idea how ineffectual he is?' Dan muttered under his breath to Taffy. 'He's about as useful as a chocolate teapot when it comes to representing the residents' wishes, don't you think?'

'It's a pretty thankless task, though, isn't it?' Taffy replied. 'The poor bloke obviously had no idea this would all fall into his lap when he stood for councillor. Besides, he's up for re-election soon and we're hardly going to find anyone else around here with the chops to stand up to the man on a voluntary basis.'

'Hmm,' said Dan thoughtfully.

Taffy gave him a hard stare. 'I mean, it's not like you're going to throw your hat into the ring, now, is it?'

When Dan didn't answer, Taffy simply gaped. 'Council-man Dan?'

Dan grinned. 'Challenge accepted.' He clinked his glass against Taffy's. 'But keep it under your hat for now. I need to see how Gracie feels about being First Lady of Lark-ford first.'

'If I could have your attention for a moment—' said Malcolm, clearing his throat ineffectually and making barely any difference to the hubbub in the kitchen.

'Oi! Guys! Shut up and listen!' said Connor, projecting his voice as if controlling a rowdy rock and roll crowd.

Instant silence and Connor grinned. 'We've been trying to get hold of you all afternoon. We have news!'

Derek Landers stepped forward, every molecule of his corpulent frame screaming with silent antagonism. 'I have been in constant liaison with my superiors over the last few days. And of course, they in turn have consulted the decision-makers in Westminster. I'm sure you realise that the little publicity stunt you pulled last night is hardly the most profes-sional way to influence policy.' His tone was pretentious and patronising and he certainly did not respond well to Connor elbowing him in the ribs.

'Bloody effective, though,' Connor said, with no regard for his authority whatsoever.

Derek glowered. 'As I was saying, there appears to be a consensus that the budgetary changes did not receive suffi-cient consultation in our more rural constituencies.'

'We did try to tell you that—' Malcolm cut in weakly, perspiration beading his forehead.

'Pompous arse,' muttered Dan, eliciting a small smile on Harry's otherwise poker face.

Derek simply ignored them both and carried on talking.

'Now obviously, your efforts last night were appreciated, but please don't make the mistake of thinking that they were in any way responsible for the adjustments that are now on the table.'

Connor snorted, and for a moment Holly wondered whether he was actually a little bit drunk. Certainly there was a fierce wildness in his eyes that had only been muted before. 'What the wanker in the suit is trying to say,' Connor blurted loudly, 'is that now that people are dying as a direct result of his department's ignorance and arrogance, they might be prepared to give the situation another look. Not that they did anything wrong or negligent the first time around, of course, when they toyed with people's lives without getting their facts straight first. Obviously.' He leaned into Derek's face, until Malcolm wasn't the only one breaking out in a sweat. 'And don't worry. I have no intention of suing your sorry arse – I don't think Rachel would have liked that very much. But I have every intention of watching you very closely. One step, one tiny fucking step off message here, Derek, and I can promise you I will see it. Who knows how you might respond to a little press attention of your own?'

Holly was stunned. She wasn't used to witnessing such overt power plays, let alone over fish and chips. Of course, there was one person in the room who didn't bat an eyelid. Elsie stood up and quietly walked over to Connor, slipping her arm through his, and resting her head against his shoulder fleetingly. He glanced down at her and nodded, message received and understood.

'You'll find we all pull together around here,' Elsie said, her voice like crystal and her determination equally clear. 'Not just in times of trouble, but always. You might want to remember that next time you're looking at one of your woefully misleading spreadsheets. Never make the mistake of reducing us to mere statistics.'

Dan stood up too. 'I think you'd be surprised how many people outside the M25 feel that way.'

Derek spluttered at the vehemence of his words. 'Well, perhaps you'll be happy with what I'm here to offer? There's to be a discretionary fund offered to each Primary Care Trust, allocated according to rural population. A committee of local GPs and consultants in key areas will decide on its distribution – whether the Air Ambulance, the midwife-led maternity units, or indeed the oncology support teams.' He cleared his throat. 'I am assuming you'd like to be represented on the committee?'

Holly, Dan and Taffy exchanged glances – too bloody right they would.

'I'm in,' volunteered Dan.

'And me.' Grace stood up. 'I gather that my skillset within the practice management community is somewhat unique.'

'Unique and indispensable,' said Harry Grant, the professional voice of reason, carrying composed authority in a roomful of emotion. 'Mr Landers has kindly appointed me to head up the committee, reporting straight to the Department of Health. And I, for one, would be keen to have as much input from your team as possible. After all, there's no point finally having an official inside man if your wishes are not being represented by the best talent I can assemble.' He gave Grace a wink and she blushed prettily.

Holly smiled at her across the table, their gaze locked for a moment at the enormity of what they were hearing; it was everything they'd hoped for and more. Money, yes, but also a chair at the table. A voice with direct access to the decision-makers.

Connor leaned in towards Derek Landers, as though a thought had just occurred to him. 'And just to clarify, who funds the committee? I know you said they were volunteers, but is this where the budget gets creamed off?'

Derek didn't even get a chance to answer. 'Well, let's nip that one in the bud straight away,' said Connor. 'I'll cover the running costs of this region's committee. Well, The Hive will. That way every single penny goes to where it's needed. Deal?'

Holly sat back in her chair and let the discussions ebb and flow around her. Even as Derek and Malcolm were being herded towards the door, she kept thinking that nobody had actually said thank you. Obviously mistakes had been made, and nobody believed that the publicity from the auction had played no part, but at least change was on the horizon. Change for the better, she could only hope. After all, it wouldn't be long before she was welcoming two new additions to the Larkford family and she longed for them to enter a world of security and comfort.

Taffy pulled up a chair beside her. 'How you doing there, my little Moomin? This is hardly the peace and quiet that the doctor ordered.'

Holly nodded. 'Peace and quiet are overrated,' she said simply, as she watched Dan sweep Elsie off her feet in an attempt to waltz her around the kitchen in celebration. The music was cranked up and champagne corks flew.

'To moving day!' cried Alice in exuberant spirits, sloshing fizz from the bottle as she attempted to fill Jamie's glass and kiss him at the same time.

'To our inside man!' called out Taffy, nodding his thanks towards Harry Grant.

'To making a difference! And to my Rachel!' added

Connor quietly, by no means raining on their parade, but with his eyes shining with unshed tears, barely finishing his toast before Dan could pause mid-fleckle to clap him on the back and pull him into a manly hug.

'We'll be okay, won't we?' Holly whispered to Taffy, in a moment of vulnerability.

'I think every single person in this room will make sure of it,' he said with absolute conviction, resting his hand on her bump and kissing her lightly on the end of her nose.

As the summer evening sunlight faded into pink and rose, and the laughter and conversation in the kitchen spilled out into the garden and across the treetops of Larkford, Holly breathed in the scent of sweet peas and jasmine.

She knew they still had a few hurdles to jump on their way to happy-ever-after. But for the first time in a long time, it felt as though she was finally on the right path to get there. And she was most certainly starting in the right place; there really was no place like home.

Chapter 54

FOUR MONTHS LATER . . .

Holly gazed down at the pair of swaddled bundles in her arms in awe and amazement. No matter how many babies you delivered, or indeed gave birth to yourself, the arrival of these tiny humans still seemed like some kind of mystical magic.

Taffy dozed fitfully beside her. It had been a long night; their beautifully planned arrangements for her scheduled Caesarean the following week thrown into complete disarray by two babies intent on making an appearance sooner rather than later. Thank goodness Cormack had been on call to facilitate their arrival and Lizzie had swept in, ever supportive, to take care of the boys.

Holly smiled as the smaller of the two babies startled in her sleep, throwing out her tiny hands like a starfish and her deep navy-blue eyes flying open. The heavy dark lashes that framed them were almost Disneyesque in proportion.

'Hello, you,' whispered Holly quietly. 'What was that all about? You're safe, quite safe, with me, my darling.' She offered a finger and the baby grasped hold of it immediately, tightly, and without once breaking eye contact. It was a moment of intimacy and wonder. 'We need a name for you, don't we, poppet?' Holly said, watching the absolute determination of the baby as she tried to pull Holly's finger into her mouth.

'Mmmhhhmmwah,' yawned Taffy abruptly, startling all three of them.

For all that the smaller baby was calm and serene, the larger of the two was noisy and demanding. It was like a slice of history repeating itself, for it had been the exact same dynamic with Ben and Tom from the very beginning.

Holly managed to juggle both babies until their cries subsided and they were feeding happily, even as Taffy hovered, as though with a catcher's mitt, just in case. 'It doesn't seem quite real, does it?' he said after a moment, so fixated had they been on their allocated date that the entire night had thrown both of them completely. For Holly, post-op and sore, with two babies feeding simultaneously, it felt very real indeed, momentous even.

Taffy couldn't resist stroking their hair, marvelling all over again at the miniature size of all four little feet. 'We did it,' he said in wonder.

'We did,' said Holly with a laugh, trying incredibly hard not to mention that Taffy's contribution had very much been of the standing-there-fidgeting variety. 'How are you feeling, Daddy?'

Taffy looked up, his eyes welling with emotion. 'I'm good.'

'You know you're going to be amazing at this, don't you?' she said, glancing down to check that all was well, as the twins settled into a dream feed.

'*We're* going to be amazing at this,' he corrected her. 'Team Taffy all the way.'

Holly shook her head; it had been one thing when he started calling them that, quite another when the printed t-shirts began to arrive. One for him, one each for the boys, Eric and Nineteen, babygrows in anticipation, and two for Holly, in 'before' and 'after' sizing.

She glanced over at the photo stuck up haphazardly beside the bed by Taffy when the emotion of the night had overcome her earlier and she'd been missing her boys with a startling intensity. Ben and Tom, in their team t-shirts, cradling a most amenable piglet, who seemed to have quite the knack when it came to 'working' the camera.

'You know we need to come up with their names before the boys come to visit,' Holly said. 'God knows what they'll end up as, if we leave it up to them.'

Taffy stroked the babies' heads gently, making sure that his attention was equally divided between the two. All the names on their shortlist somehow felt hackneyed and uninspired, compared to the fresh and innocent beauty of these two baby girls. The fact that their wristbands held the unfortunate monikers of 'Big Baby Girl Jones (1 of 2)' and 'Small Baby Girl Jones (2 of 2)' was something that needed their urgent attention before the troops arrived and either of these nick-names followed them for their entire childhood!

'And we're still dead set against something Welsh and tradi-tional, are we?' Taffy checked, more in hope than expectation of a reversal on that position.

Holly shook her head. 'It's not a blanket ban, Taffs. I just want to be able to pronounce them.'

'Fair point,' he conceded, having spent most of his time at medical school in England correcting the pronunciation of Meirion. Hence the change to Taffy upon graduation; some-times it was just easier to admit defeat. On the other hand, they both knew how happy it would make Patty to have a Dilwen or an Angharad in the family.

Holly shifted slightly, the weight of the babies pressing on her scar. She'd quietly joked with Cormack as they'd wheeled her at alarming speed down the corridors towards the operating room about whether he could give her a nice tummy tuck 'while he was there'.

'Don't worry, Holls,' he'd replied. 'I've been practising my embroidery all summer. You won't be disappointed. You'll have an interesting few months, with four kids and Taffy in the house while you recuperate, but I'll take care of my part with precision.' Good as his word, he'd spent an age putting her back together; eventually Taffy had been ushered next door with their two babies to have a little quality time.

Apparently that quality time had resulted in one very emotional, somewhat tearful husband, with a whole new list of names to run past his ever tolerant wife.

'What about Luna?' he suggested, as the light of said moon emerged from behind a cloud and lit up the city skyline of Bath. 'Or Jane, you know, like Jane Austen?'

Holly shook her head. These two girls were virtually identical in every way but size, their features still delicate and their hair downy and brunette. 'What about Katie?'

'Or Tabitha?' Taffy countered.

Just as they spoke, both girls stopped feeding and stretched languorously, their tiny fingers reaching out and tangling in Holly's hair.

'They do look like happy little cats,' Holly said. 'Katie? Tabby?'

The girls slept on in disinterest.

'Bert? Ernie?' Taffy tried, just to test. Nothing.

Holly laughed, wincing for a moment as she did so. 'You silly arse, what would you have done if they'd responded?'

'I can think of worse names. Meirion, anybody?'

'Lottie?' Holly tried, and to her absolute amazement, the larger baby opened her eyes in an instant. 'Lottie? Is that who you are, gorgeous? Are you my Lottie?' The small hand that suddenly clasped hers made it perfectly clear that she was.

Holly looked up at Taffy. 'Well, she certainly seems to know her own mind.' She smiled down at the baby, whose lashes were fluttering sleepily again. 'Night-night, Lottie,' she whispered and the tiny mewling noise in response made it official in her mind.

'Livia?' tried Taffy, following her lead. 'O–livia?'

In an uncanny mirroring of her older sister, the second baby opened her eyes. It couldn't be a true smile, Holly knew that, but nevertheless the response was there.

'Olivia,' cooed Holly and the baby snuggled into her more deeply, utterly sated and serene.

'Lottie and Olivia,' said Taffy after a moment. 'Well then, I think you're nearly ready to meet your big brothers.'

As the clock ticked around to nine a.m. Holly jolted awake. Some sixth sense had alerted her, because only moments later she heard her sons' voices and the sound of their pattering feet as they ran down the corridor. 'Mummy? Mummy? We're here!'

Pausing only for a second in the doorway, they were both on the bed in moments, throwing their little arms around Holly's neck and covering her face in butterfly kisses. 'I missed you,' said Ben solemnly. 'So did Nineteen, so he slept on my bed.'

Lizzie appeared behind them with Dan on her heels, both of them out of breath. 'Crikey, they've got a turn of speed. Sorry about the pig in the bed thing.'

'Pigs in blankets?' snorted Dan. 'Oh come on . . . we were all thinking it!'

The room fell silent for a moment, as they all turned to watch Ben and Tom being introduced to their sisters. 'This one's Olivia,' said Holly. Ben reached into the basinet gently, managing only a breathy 'wow' as Olivia opened her eyes and grasped his finger.

'Can I call dibs on this one, Mummy?' Ben said after a second. 'I think she likes me.'

'What's mine called?' asked Tom, automatically assuming that the other, larger, baby was to be his.

'This is Lottie,' said Taffy. 'And Lottie and Olivia are joining our family. We'll all have to share a little, okay?'

'Okay,' said Tom easily. 'You can have her when she poops.' He shot a look over at Holly to see if she'd heard, nervously laughing at his brave use of a 'swear word'.

'Coo-ee! Is it alright if we all come in?' Elsie said, giving Dan no choice but to step aside.

Suddenly their tiny side room was filled with their nearest and dearest. Elsie, Lizzie, Alice and Grace all clustered around the babies and the boys, oohing and aahing their delight. Dan held back a little, shaking Taffy's hand repeatedly and occasionally slapping him on the shoulder for good measure. Jamie was the absolute surprise, though, as he sat down on the bed beside Holly and asked her how she was feeling.

Obviously that prompted everyone else in the room to remember they had a new mother amongst them and to ply her with enquiries as to her health and recovery. It was some measure of the excitement in the room, though, that nobody really listened to the answers, all too busy waiting their turn to cradle these beautiful babies in their arms.

It was so wonderfully, typically Larkford that Holly could

only sit back against her wall of pillows and smile – no boundaries, no pretence, just one large family for her children to join.

Holly looked down as a small chocolate-coloured nose nudged her hand and Coco curled in tightly beside her on the bed, the little dog's empathy and compassion growing daily as she took on each and every new challenge she was presented with. She yawned widely and rested her head on Holly's legs, her eyes full of affection.

'Tilly sends her love,' said Alice. 'We've left her holding the fort until we get back.'

And no doubt she would do a formidable job of it, thought Holly. Hiring Tilly had been the best hormonally-driven choice she could possibly have made. At a time when personal relationships meant so much more than professional posturing, Tilly had proven to be exactly the kind of team player they needed, especially as the new Rural Affairs Committee was taking up more and more of the partners' time with success after success at the negotiating table. The *Panorama* special had been the icing on the cake, bringing their message to millions of viewers and yet more weight to their cause.

They certainly had a lot to feel proud of this year, Holly thought. On every level. And all these successes gave her permission to take this time now, to enjoy her maternity leave with a clear conscience and a full heart.

'Have you considered any middle names?' asked Elsie. 'I'm sure you could borrow mine if you asked nicely.'

'Lottie Elsie Graham-Jones,' experimented Holly.

'Olivia Ava Graham-Jones,' said Elsie, offering her own middle name for good measure.

'Fine by me,' said Taffy easily. He glanced up to find Holly watching him.

'I love you,' she mouthed across the crowded room, across their four children and their very best friends. She honestly had never dreamed she could feel this contentedly happy.

'I love *you*,' he said in reply, loudly, unapologetically and with absolutely no hesitation, despite his audience.

'Aw, mate,' said Dan, deliberately misunderstanding. 'It's a mutual thing, Taffs. I love you too.' He took Taffy's face in both hands and kissed him loudly on the forehead. 'Now, which one of these gorgeous girls is going to be my goddaughter?'

Acknowledgements

I am quietly convinced that the feeling of belonging to a team, of being part of something bigger than oneself, can build confidence like nothing else – and so it has proven to be. The learning curve on my path to publication has always been exponential and, at every point, the Books and the City Team at Simon & Schuster have been there with insightful advice, encouragement, excitement and even (on occasion) cocktails and cupcakes ... To work with such wonderfully passionate and like-minded people is a true privilege – Jo Dickinson, Sara-Jade Virtue, Emma Capron, Laura Hough, Dominic Brendon, Jess Barratt, Hayley McMullan, Rich Vlietstra, Claire Bennett and Joe Roche – a huge and heartfelt thank-you for all your hard work and your fabulous support. Never before has 'going to work' been such a joy.

A special thank-you is required for Sian Wilson who continues to produce such beautiful artwork in bringing the town of Larkford to life and humouring my aversion to all things pink.

Cathryn Summerhayes – you rock. Thank you for your boundless enthusiasm and, of course, for making sure I get to spend even more time in Larkford with my imaginary friends!

Thank-yous must also go to those lovely friends – authors and otherwise – who somehow manage to keep me (vaguely) sane, as I lurch between realities:

Thank you to the Cotswold Posse – Katie Fforde, Caroline Sanderson and Nikki Owen, true radiators one and all (also tops for spot-on advice and gin); AJ Pearce – it's your turn next!; Milly Johnson – seeing your cover quote for PMP was a fabulous moment – you're a star; Julie Cohen for taking me to Reading and for your pearls of wisdom; Emma Gill for prosecco, treehouses and hot tubs and always being there – here's to another three decades of fun; Emma Horan for the laughs, the compassion and generally being a legend in your own lunchtime; Ali Turtle for keeping me on track when the odds seemed stacked against it and for (finally) making it back to Bath; not to mention the wonderful mums with whom I share the juggling, sharing, wondrous (daunting) task of keeping our children entertained and deadlines met during the long school breaks – we all deserve a medal (and gin).

And no acknowledgements could ever be complete without the most enormous hugs, kisses and general embarrassment of thanks to my two gorgeous children, my ever-tolerant (and thankfully resourceful) husband and to The Ginger Ninja, who had very large paw-prints to fill, but who has nevertheless filled my writing day with unconditional love and companionship. Larkford wouldn't be the same without her.

Turn the page for an exciting extract from
the next book in the series . . .

Private Practice

Chapter 1

Dr Holly Graham swirled the pancake batter onto the Aga hotplate with almost surgical precision; just another one of the imperceptible ways she was subconsciously keeping her eye in whilst on maternity leave. Taffy wrapped his arms around her waist and rested his chin on her shoulder lovingly, 'Can I just have one really huge one—' He paused, weighing up the likelihood of success, 'With lots of chocolate chips?'

Holly arranged a stack of perfect circles on to his plate and shook her head with a smile, 'Keep dreaming, Taffs. We're leading from the front, remember?'

They both glanced over at the huge oak kitchen table, round and stocky, their four children marking out the four points of the wooden compass that had dictated virtually every moment of Holly's universe for the last six months. Typically, Elsie had stationed herself between Lottie and Olivia, seemingly oblivious to the mangled rusks that now adorned her silk dressing gown, perfectly happy to spoon dollops of apple-sauce-swirled yoghurt into their willing mouths. Ben and Tom, on the other hand, their appetites growing as quickly as their gangly five-year-old legs, wanted none of it. They were holding out for pancakes, gazillions of pancakes to be precise, with lashings of maple syrup.

'Well, at least the maple syrup's organic,' offered Taffy, his own tendency towards mainlining junk food having been brutally curtailed in his quest to become a decent role model, and to stand a chance of fitting into his morning suit for the wedding.

'Do top up my coffee, there's a darling,' said Elsie, having recently decided that life was just too short to drink camomile tea, whatever her consultant may say. As a result, the entire household had been cunningly and covertly switched to decaf and Holly's mood was suffering a little as a result.

'Anything good on the cards today?' Holly asked Taffy, as she flipped another batch of Scotch pancakes to top up the rapidly diminishing supply on the table. Her tone was almost wistful with enquiry; she was missing her patients and the cut and thrust of practice life far more than she was willing to concede. Of course, it didn't help that they seemed to be coping so indecently well in her absence. All her offers to step in, help out, lend a hand, had been politely but pointedly declined by the team at The Practice.

'Don't worry about it,' Dan said. 'Enjoy your babies,' Alice said. 'Make the most of your time off,' they all repeated ad nauseam. Her grip tightened on the spatula at the very thought.

Time off!

Who were they kidding? Being at home with new-born twins had hardly been a picnic in the South of France.

Throw in another set of twins, five years ahead, and

bouncing with all the energy of Duracell bunnies, a time-share Labradoodle and an increasingly needy (and enormous) piglet and Holly's slate was full. Speaking of which, Nineteen grunted at the French windows for his breakfast, still seemingly disgusted at no longer being allowed into the kitchen, on the sofas, basically wherever he pleased – but at nearly 70lbs, Nineteen was no longer an adorable, snuffling piglet, he was a hog in all senses of the word. Every attempt to give him more room in the meadows nearby had resulted in him making a break for home. It was yet another thing on Holly's mental To Do list that needed attention.

Taffy swallowed his mouthful of pancakes and took a slug of coffee for good measure, looking at his mug in confusion when it failed to deliver that morning boost he had come to rely on. 'Not much on today, really. Same old, same old.'

Holly sighed, realising he had no idea how appealing the notion of 'same old' was to her right now. Not that she hadn't adored this special time with her babies – and they were an absolute delight – she just sometimes felt as though her brain was turning to Play-Doh and her conversation to mindless jibber-jabber. Thank heavens for Elsie's ongoing vacillation about her living arrangements. Although duly installed at Sarandon Hall – the retirement destination for the blue of blood and heavy of wallet – she still seemed to spend most of her days, and quite a few of her nights, here at Number 42 being generally eccentric and inspiring. Although once Elsie's own family home, ensuring that Holly's growing brood could now call it *their* home, had been one of the greatest acts of generosity that Holly had ever witnessed. Spending the first few weeks of Olivia and Lottie's lives quite literally holding Holly's hand, as Taffy had been subsumed gradually back into work, had been another. From where Holly was standing, Elsie's presence was a reassuring constant she'd be lost without.

'Tell me,' Holly said. 'How's the Major doing? Is Alice coping with her new clinic hours with Coco? What happened about Pru's mammogram in the end?' She wasn't so much firing questions at him, as machine-gunning them into the room, the way Ben and Tom did when they were on a mission for information, snackage or attention.

Taffy just nodded, 'It's all good. Hey, haven't the boys got a May Day rehearsal this afternoon?'

Holly swallowed her frustration, along with a bite of pancake. At this rate, she'd be the size of a house before she found her balance. She nodded. 'Dress rehearsal today, boys,' she reminded them.

Ben and Tom looked at each other and scowled, perfect mirror images of disgruntlement. 'I hate May Day,' Tom said firmly, always the more outspoken of the twins.

'I hate my costume and Tarquin is a big meanie,' Ben continued. 'He keeps messing up my ribbons so I trip over.'

Holly frowned. She'd initially been quite on board with the new head teacher's plan to celebrate the holiday with a performance by the primary school pupils, until she'd realised the commitment required to persuade twenty-eight children, each seemingly with two left feet, into their white jangly costumes and around the May pole without anyone being strangled, garrotted or embarrassed to death. Even accounting for the little sod that was Tarquin Holland and his painfully right-on mother, Cassie, these May Day preparations had been a labour of love for all the parents of Larkford Primary. Of course, for some, the love had been somewhat enhanced by the very presence of said new head teacher. Mr Alec French had certainly swayed the pyjamas-to-mascara ratio on the school run in the opposite direction since his arrival.

The front door swung open and Alice and Coco barrelled through the parquet hallway and into the kitchen. Since her boyfriend Jamie had taken a temporary work placement in Ireland, it had become Alice's custom en route to The Practice, to call in at Holly's for the first coffee of the day – Elsie's kitchen providing the central focus for most of their socialising these days. At times, Alice seemed quite lost without him, and Holly was only too delighted to provide company, coffee and distraction, in exchange for a little update now and then.

'Morning! I hope you haven't eaten already – I picked up Danish pastries!' said Alice chirpily, her assistance dog Coco at her feet, as she carefully hung up her beautiful velvet coat. No longer one to keep things for best, she was a close contender with Elsie for the role of Larkford's style icon these days. Not that Elsie seemed to mind.

'I hope one of those pastries has my name on it!' Elsie said, deliberately ignoring the look that passed between Holly and Taffy. 'I'm in need of decadence today. All this puréed fruit is giving me a glimpse into my future and I'm not sure I like it.'

Holly noticed that Taffy, Ben and Tom had quickly squirrelled away all evidence of their pancake extravaganza and were holding out their plates expectantly. Seriously, thought Holly, it was like feeding an army in this kitchen most days.

Needless to say, Alice had thoughtfully picked out a

dairy-free offering for Ben and soon contented yummy noises filled the room, to the accompaniment of Olivia banging her fists on her high chair in excitement at the slivers of buttery goodness heading her way.

'Stick the radio on,' said Alice, as she poured coffee for everyone, and Holly handed out orange juice in a tried and tested manoeuvre of choreography. 'Lizzie had me in stitches just now. She's on cracking form, have you noticed?'

Holly had in fact noticed that giving her best friend, Lizzie, ready access to a microphone and a Nespresso machine had been a masterstroke in her recovery from anxiety, not to mention with all three of her children now being at school, Lizzie was indeed generally on the up. It was fair to say that, in their small community, the 'anonymous' part of Lizzie's Agony Aunt phone-in show on Radio Larkford was really anything but. Nevertheless, Lizzie's advice was often on message, despite being off the cuff, and generally hilarious in its bluntness.

'All I'm saying,' came the emotional tones of today's unwitting caller across the airwaves, 'is that I'd just like a small break from my children climbing all over me, before my husband starts, you know?'

Holly and Alice both snorted their coffee across the table as they burst out laughing, recognising only too clearly the voice of Hattie from The Deli in town. Taffy merely looked perplexed.

'But, surely it's nice that he still fancies her—' began Taffy, unwittingly stepping into a barrage of abuse from the women at the table.

Lizzie clearly had no scruples when it came to telling it like it is, even when on the airwaves, 'You're not a cappuccino machine,' she said with feeling. 'He can hardly expect you to be on the go with kids and The D—, I mean, with work all day and then get hot and steamy at the flick of switch.'

Taffy swallowed his laughter in a moment, when he saw how intently his beloved was listening to the answer. Holly offered him a watery smile in reassurance, but Lizzie was on a roll.

'Seriously, any new dads out there feeling all hard done by because they're not getting much duvet action need to take a long hard look at themselves. You can't be Mary Poppins one minute and Jessica Rabbit the next. Your wives may be mothers now, but that doesn't mean you should stop wooing them. When's the last time you ran them a bath, or cooked them supper? Maybe looked after your kids for a bit so they could regroup. Hat— I mean, our caller has a point – there needs to be a transition from mother to partner and you guys need to make that happen!' She spoke with feeling and gusto and Holly laid odds that there were women all over Larkford cheering her on, not to mention husbands curling their toes. 'Ask them what they want! And now here's Journey with a little reminder—' As the lyrics of 'Anyway You Want It' blasted out around the kitchen, there was uncomfortable silence for a moment.

Ben looked around the table in consternation. 'Aunty Lizzie gives weird advice on the radio. If they like climbing so much, she should just tell them to buy a climbing frame—'

Alice excused herself from the table as orange juice spurted from her nose and Holly held her sides laughing.

'Out of the mouths of babes,' said Elsie drily, as her magpie attention was caught by Alice's vintage necklace, as she handed over handfuls of napkins to deal with the problem.

Taffy took Holly's hand as she went to stand up and clear the table. 'Tell me what you want—' he whispered with a smile, taking Lizzie's advice to heart.

Holly's eyes flashed at the possibilities, 'Anything?'

Taffy smiled wolfishly, 'Anything at all.'

She sat back down beside him and kissed him, 'Can I take your diabetes clinic today? You could stay with the girls?'

Taffy laughed, 'Oh Holls, you're so funny.' He stood up and dropped a kiss on the top of her head. 'Think about it though, I'm serious. Dinner? A spa day with Lizzie maybe? Whatever you need, just say.' He kissed Olivia and Lottie, somehow escaping their outstretched sticky grasp and chivvied the boys to get their school shoes on.

Holly mutely watched as he turned away, momentarily speechless, 'But I just *did* say,' she managed, only for her words to be drowned out by the chaos of locating last minute school clobber and May Day paraphernalia.

She bent down to kiss both the boys as they swung their arms around her thighs and to check their faces were free of maple syrup. She couldn't quite face a 'friendly chat' on the tiny chairs from the glorious Mr French just yet. It would surely be better to meet him properly before her first official dressing-down.

'I'd best be off too,' said Alice, as everyone realised the time and hustled together. Even Elsie wandered through into the hall to prepare for her morning ahead. Another class with the Silver Swans, no doubt, reliving her misspent youth at the barre and brushing up her pliés.

In fact, in less than three minutes, Holly's kitchen went

from being a hive of sociable activity to the front door swinging quietly shut behind them with a dull whumpf.

She turned to the girls, their hands outstretched and their faces smothered with sticky pastry crumbs. 'Well,' she said after a moment, mustering a cheery smile, 'as I'm obviously not playing doctor today, you two are going to be my partners in crime, okay?' She dropped kisses on their foreheads adoringly. 'Now, what do you two little poppets want to do today?'

FIND OUT MORE ABOUT

Penny Parkes

Penny Parkes is the author of three novels and the winner
of the Romantic Novelist Association's Romantic Comedy
of the Year Award 2017.

To find out more about her writing, visit
www.SimonandSchuster.co.uk
or follow Penny on twitter:
@CotswoldPenny

All of Penny's books are available in print and eBook,
and are available to download in eAudio

OUT OF PRACTICE

Penny Parkes

Come and visit Larkford, a hotbed of rivalry, rule-breaking and romance ... and that's just the doctors!

Meet successful GP Holly Graham as she relocates her family to join the team at The Practice in Larkford, hoping to revive her marriage in the process. But can she keep her private and professional lives separate in such a tight-knit community?

Her colleagues have their own issues to contend with. Dr Dan Carter is struggling to focus on work; having his ambitious ex-girlfriend Dr Julia Channing working alongside him isn't really helping. Thankfully, the rather delectable Dr Taffy Jones is on hand to distract Holly from the escalating troubles at home.

Feisty octogenarian and resident celebrity, Elsie Townsend, is Holly's favourite patient and saving grace. Elsie's inspirational Life Lessons come at the perfect moment, as The Practice is under threat of imminent closure and Holly rediscovers her voice and her priorities just in time ...

'A pure delight from start to finish' Julie Cohen

OUT NOW IN PAPERBACK, eBOOK AND eAUDIO

PRACTICE MAKES PERFECT

Penny Parkes

'If dishy doctors, cute dogs, hilarious OAPs and idyllic country settings are your thing, you're in for a treat. Funny, moving, romantic and full of characters you'll love – it's perfect in every way' *Heat*

The Practice at Larkford has suddenly been thrust under the spotlight – and its nomination as an 'NHS Model Surgery' is causing the team major headaches. Dr Holly Graham should be basking in the glow of her new romance with fellow doctor, Taffy – but she is worried that the team is prioritising plaudits over patients, and her favourite resident, the irreverent and entertaining Elsie, is facing a difficult diagnosis. Add to that the chaos of family life and the strain is starting to show . . .

Dr Dan Carter's obsession with work is masking unhappiness elsewhere – he can't persuade girlfriend Julia to settle down. It's only as Julia's mother comes to stay that he realizes what she has been hiding for so long. Alice Walker joins the team like a breath of fresh air and her assistance dog Coco quickly wins everyone round – which is just as well, because Coco and Alice will soon need some help of their own. Can they pull together and become the Dream Team that the NHS obviously thinks they are?

'This book has everything: warmth, humour, drama, laughter and a few tears. I wolfed it down'
MILLY JOHNSON

OUT NOW IN PAPERBACK, eBOOK AND eAUDIO